**Praise for The Fatal Series
by *New York Times* bestselling author
Marie Force**

"This book starts out strong and keeps
getting better. Marie Force is one of those authors
that will be on my must-read list in the future."
—*The Romance Studio* on *Fatal Affair*

"This is a suspense that never stops.
Add it to your book list today."
NightOwlRomance.com (Top pick)

"Marie Force's second novel
in The Fatal Series is an outstanding romantic suspense
in its own right; that it follows the fantastic first installment
only sweetens the read."
—*RT Book Reviews* on *Fatal Justice* (4.5 stars)

"The author makes the reader part of the action,
effortlessly weaving the world of politics and murder
in which the characters come alive on the pages.
The plot was addictive and scandalous with so many
family secrets…. Drama, passion, suspense—
Fatal Affair has it all!"
—*Book Junkie*

"Force's skill is also evident in the way that she develops
the characters, from the murdered and mutilated senator
to the detective and chief of staff who are trying to solve
the case. The heroine, Sam, is especially complex
and her secrets add depth to this mystery."
—*RT Book Reviews* on *Fatal Affair* (4.5 stars)

Also available from Marie Force
and Carina Press

FATAL AFFAIR
FATAL CONSEQUENCES
FATAL DESTINY
FATAL FLAW
FATAL DECEPTION
FATAL MISTAKE
FATAL JEOPARDY

**And look for the next book in the Fatal series
coming in January 2015**

FATAL JUSTICE

MARIE FORCE

carina press®

ISBN-13: 978-0-373-00222-1

FATAL JUSTICE

Copyright © 2011 by Marie Sullivan Force

Recycling programs
for this product may
not exist in your area.

FATAL JUSTICE

Acknowledgments

Thank you to my husband, Dan, and our terrific kids, Emily and Jake, for supporting my writing career every day. To my readers, thank you for being the best part of this crazy ride. To my editor, Jessica Schulte, and the amazing, dynamic team behind Carina Press, thank you for your support and encouragement. It's a pleasure to work with each and every one of you. And finally, to my darling puppy, Brandy, thank you for helping me build my presence on Facebook. Your mischievous antics have provided entertainment for people neither of us will ever meet but who now call both of us "friend."

For Cindy, Cheryl, Kendra and Linda—my writing BFFs.
How did we ever survive before the Lair?
And for all the readers who've written to say
they LOVE the idea of a romance series featuring
the same couple in every book, thank you, thank you,
THANK YOU! I knew you were out there!

ONE

As Sam raised her right hand to take the oath that would make her a lieutenant, every cell phone and pager in the room began to vibrate.

Tearing her eyes off the city clerk, she ventured a glance at her partner, Detective Freddie Cruz, and noted the grim expression on his handsome face as he checked his pager.

The moment Sam said the final words of the oath, several of the other officers in the room bolted for the doors, calling out that they'd see her later at the party. She heard one of them say, "DD, mass cas."

Ugh, Sam thought, *domestic disturbance, multiple casualties—the worst kind of hell for cops.*

"…I have tremendous confidence that she'll continue to serve with honor and distinction in her new role," concluded Chief Farnsworth, a man she'd called Uncle Joe when she was a child. "It's my great personal and professional honor to introduce for the first time, Lieutenant Sam Holland."

Contending with a huge lump in her throat, Sam received the thundering applause from the colleagues who remained in the room. Her sisters, Tracy and Angela, stepped forward, followed by their father in his motorized wheelchair.

As her sisters pinned on the gold bars, Sam marveled at the surreal sensation. Thanks to the dyslexia she'd battled all her life, she hadn't allowed herself to imagine this moment. Tears wet her father's cheeks as he watched from his chair. He loved his three girls passionately, but the special bond he shared with Sam was obvious to everyone who knew them.

Once the bars were in place Tracy and Angela stepped back.

Sam leaned forward to rest her head on her father's shoulder, which was a poor substitute for the hug she'd have given anything to receive from him right then. Two long years had passed since he'd last been able to hug her.

"Congratulations, Lieutenant," he said in a gruff tone.

"Thank you, Chief."

He kissed her cheek.

She turned to shake hands with Chief Farnsworth.

Watching the remaining cops leave the room, Sam had to hold herself back.

"It's okay if you want to go with them," Nick said from behind her.

"No way," she said as she turned to him. "I'm off today."

"Sam."

"Nick."

He leaned in and kissed her square on the lips in front of her father, her sisters, the chief and the mayor. The *mayor,* for God's sake!

"Congratulations, Lieutenant," Nick whispered.

"Thank you," she muttered. She planned to speak to him once again about his inappropriate PDA habit once they were back in that stupid limo he'd insisted on to transport them around the famously congested District of Columbia on their big day.

"The uniform is *h-o-t,*" he whispered in her ear. "I'll need a private viewing later."

"Stop." She pushed at his chest. Even through the

suit she could make out the pronounced contours of his muscular pectorals.

His full, sexy mouth lifted into the smile that promised carnal delights, and Sam's panties went damp. That was all it took, and he knew it.

As they partook in the coffee and pastry reception, Sam felt twitchy with anxiety as she waited to hear something—*anything*—from the scene of the domestic disturbance. Sipping her second diet cola of the day, she watched Nick share a laugh with her father and was grateful that the two of them had bonded over their shared concern for her safety. She wished they were a little *less* concerned, but hey, at least her father had stopped trying to intimidate Nick every chance he got—something Skip was still quite good at, even from his wheelchair.

Angela and Tracy materialized out of the crowd and linked their arms through Sam's.

"Ready to move on to part two?" Tracy asked.

"Do I have to?" Sam asked, a shaft of pain through her midsection reminding her of her many worries about Nick's new job. It also reminded her that she'd promised him she would have this annoying stomach situation checked by his doctor once the O'Connor case was closed. She hoped he would forget but knew he wouldn't. "I need to get changed."

"We'll go with you," Angela said.

Sam signaled to Nick that she'd be right back and headed for her new corner office in the detectives' pit where she had stashed a change of clothes earlier. The suit she'd paid way too much for hung on a hook behind the door.

"Come in here and help me, you guys," Sam called to her sisters. "I'm all thumbs."

Angela and Tracy marched through the door and took

over, changing Sam out of her uniform and into the black suit with a subtle silver pinstripe. The three-button jacket revealed just a hint of her substantial cleavage, but she worried it was too much. They capped off the outfit with Sam's prized black Jimmy Choo heels and their grandmother's pearls, which Sam hoped lent her an aura of respectability.

Angela helped Sam with the shoes, straightened and then wobbled. "Whoa," she said, reaching for the wall to steady herself.

"What's the matter?" Sam asked.

"Nothing. Just got dizzy for a minute there."

"Did you skip breakfast again?" Tracy asked.

"Maybe," Angela said sheepishly. "I'll grab something on the way to the Capitol." Turning her attention on Sam, she added, "You look fabulous, Sam. Absolutely gorgeous."

Sam tugged at the top button of the suit, willing it up another half inch. But the moment she let it go, it slid back down over breasts she thought were far too big. "It's not conservative enough."

"Well, since Nick is a flaming liberal, that shouldn't be a problem," Ang joked.

"Very funny," Sam said. "The chief justice of the Supreme Court is swearing him in. He isn't going to want to see my boobs."

"Wanna bet?" Tracy said with a smirk.

Sam fought to swallow the lump of panic forming in her throat. "I can't do this, you guys. I'm not cut out to be a senator's whatever I am."

"Love of his life?" Angela said.

The poignant simplicity of her sister's statement nearly undid Sam.

"You look beautiful, classy and elegant." Tracy

smoothed her hands over Sam's lapels. "Nick should be honored to have you by his side today."

"He is," Nick said from the doorway.

Startled, they turned, and the love Sam saw in his gaze chased away all her fears.

Tracy cleared her throat. "We'll, ah, go get Dad and Celia and see you at the Capitol." Grabbing Angela's arm, she steered her younger sister out of the office.

Sam continued to fiddle with the low-cut jacket.

Nick retrieved her hand and brought it to his lips. "You're stunning."

"This suit is all wrong," she said, unaccustomed to wardrobe malfunctions of this magnitude. Fashion was the one area of her life where she was usually one hundred percent confident. "I don't know what I was thinking. It shows too much—"

He put his arms around her. "It's beautiful, you're beautiful and I love you. I was so proud of you in there, watching your sisters pin those gold bars on your collar."

Touched, she worked up a smile for him. "You understand why I asked them and not you, don't you?"

"Of course I do. They stood in your dad's place. It was perfect."

"Thanks," she said, relieved that he understood—that he always seemed to understand. Tall herself, she had to tip her head back to meet his hazel eyes. At six-four, he was one of the few people in her life who towered over her. "Are you ready?"

The slight hitch in the deep breath he released was the only sign of nerves she could detect in his otherwise cool demeanor. "As ready as I'll ever be." He offered her his arm. "Shall we?"

Sam hesitated but only for a second. He was everything. To deny that would not only be foolish, it would be pointless. She hooked her hand through his arm. "Absolutely."

AN HOUR LATER, as Sam stood under the Capitol dome and held the O'Connor family Bible while Nick swore to preserve and protect the Constitution of the United States against all enemies foreign and domestic, it occurred to her that his big day trumped hers by a mile. The president of the United States, a close friend of the O'Connor family, surprised Nick by showing up with the first lady.

It was the second time in a week Sam had seen President and Mrs. Nelson. The first time had been at John O'Connor's funeral, where she'd also met Nick's father, Leo. Today, Leo had brought his pretty young wife and adorable three-year-old twin sons, and Sam was once again struck by Leo's youthfulness. Since he was only fifteen years older than Nick, it made sense that he looked more like Nick's brother than his father.

The entire O'Connor family had come. Sam could only imagine how difficult it must be for them to watch their murdered son and brother's best friend replace him in the Senate. John's father, retired Senator Graham O'Connor, had handpicked Nick for the job. And while Graham and his wife Laine's eyes shone with pride as they watched the man they thought of as a son take the oath of office, Sam could also see the heartbreak. Their loss was so recent and raw, and was made worse by the fact that John had been taken from them by his own son.

Before Sam knew it, Nick was declared a United States senator, and he had committed the next year to the people of Virginia. As Nick shook hands with the president, Sam hoped her crazy job wouldn't somehow ruin it for him.

TWO

NICK RECEIVED HUGS from his father, the O'Connors and the first lady. Amazing. The son of high school-age parents, he'd been raised by his grandmother in a one-bedroom apartment in Lowell, Massachusetts. He'd landed an academic scholarship to Harvard, where he'd met John O'Connor and later, John's family. Over the years, the O'Connors had become Nick's family, too, which was the only reason he was now a United States senator.

From the setting under the Capitol rotunda to the chief justice to the governor of Virginia, this whole thing felt like it was happening in a movie rather than to him. As the president of the United States extended his hand and said, "Congratulations, Senator," it finally became real. He was Senator Nicholas Cappuano, Democrat of Virginia. But when he remembered how he'd gotten here, that his best friend had been murdered, and that he had been tapped to take his place, Nick's heart ached. As if anyone could take John's place.

The crowd moved toward his suite of offices in the Hart Building for the reception the Virginia Democrats were throwing in his honor. Nick went against the flow to find Sam as he continued to accept congratulations. He saw her at the end of the line, tagging along behind her father and his fiancée, Celia, as they headed to the elevator. Reaching for Sam's hand, Nick held her back.

"We'll be right there," he said to Skip and Celia.

"Take your time, Senator," Skip said, the half of his face that wasn't paralyzed lifting into a grin.

"That sounds so weird," Nick said to Sam when they were alone.

She reached up to brush a stray lock of hair off his forehead. "You'd better get used to it."

Moved by her loving gesture, he still wanted to pinch himself when he realized he could touch her, be with her, sleep with her and love her every day after six years of dreaming about her. The one who'd gotten away was back in his life, and there was nothing he wouldn't do to keep her there. "Are you all right?"

"Sure," she said. "Why wouldn't I be?"

"You're a little pale."

"Am I?"

"Uh-huh. Are you still worried about all this?"

She looked up at him with those light blue eyes that betrayed her every emotion. "No."

"Liar," he said, smiling as he leaned in to kiss her.

She tried to pull back from him, but he resisted. "You can't do that here," she said. "You're a senator now."

He glanced around at the deserted rotunda. "Who's looking?" Tipping his head, he brushed his lips over hers and was gratified to feel some of the resistance leave her shoulders.

"Do I have to call you Senator now?" she asked with a glint in her eye.

"Only in bed."

Her cheeks flamed with color. "Why do you have to say that stuff?"

"Because it flusters you."

"It does not."

"Liar."

She poked his ribs, making him laugh.

A throat was cleared behind them. They turned to find Nick's communications director, Trevor Donnelly, waiting for him. Nick had retained all of John O'Connor's staff, including the perpetually frazzled, mop-topped Donnelly.

"Um, excuse me, Senator, but the media is waiting to have a word with you, and the president and first lady were looking for you in the office. They have to get going."

"I'll be right there."

"Should I, ah, wait?" Trevor asked.

"No, go on ahead."

With an awkward nod, Trevor left them.

"It has to be weird to them," Nick said, watching him go. "Two weeks ago, I was a staffer, too. Now they have to call me Senator."

"There'll be some adjustments, but you'll make it work."

"Thanks for the vote of confidence. I hope you're right."

"You'd better go. The president's waiting for you."

"Before I do," he said, reaching for her hands and bringing them to his lips, "I have to do something about that anticipating-disaster look on your face." When he had her full attention, he said, "I love you, Samantha, and you're the most important thing in my life. More important than my job, my new title and all the perks that'll come with it."

"That's sweet of you to say." She finally cracked a grin as they walked toward the elevator. "Do you know how many police lieutenants there are in this country?"

"Maybe a couple thousand plus one more today?" he said, perplexed by the question.

"That's about right. Guess how many U.S. senators there are?"

"That one I know—exactly one hundred. What's your point?"

"No point. I was just doing the math."

In the elevator, he backed her up against the wall. "Your big day was every bit as big as mine."

"No, it *wasn't,*" she said, her hands resting on his chest. "I got the mayor. You got the *president.*"

"Big whoop. He came out of respect for John and because he's an old friend of Graham's."

"He came because he wants to court the newest Democratic senator."

Nick shrugged. "None of this is going to change me, Sam. I swear. I'm the same guy you woke up with this morning. I'm the same guy you're going to sleep with tonight. I promise."

"Making a lot of assumptions, aren't you?" She tossed a saucy grin over her shoulder as she stepped off the elevator ahead of him.

"No assumptions." He took her hand and fought her efforts to break free of him as they stepped into his crowded office. "Just stating the facts, Lieutenant."

"You'd better go talk to the president."

"Come with me."

"You go ahead. I'll be right over there." She pointed to where her father, Celia, Tracy, Angela and their families had congregated, outside of what used to be Nick's office.

Ignoring that, he tightened his grip on her hand and moved toward the president. As she reluctantly followed him he could feel her tension, but he refused to allow her to put distance between them. That was *not* going to happen.

"Mr. President," Nick said, extending his free hand. "I can't thank you enough for being here."

"My pleasure, Senator," President Nelson said. Turning his attention to Sam, he added, "And it's nice to see you again, Sergeant."

"Actually," Nick said, sliding an arm around Sam's waist, "it's Lieutenant. As of about two hours ago."

"Well, congratulations to both of you."

"Thank you," Sam said.

"We have to be going," President Nelson said, "but I look forward to working with you. If I can do anything for you, my door's always open."

"Likewise, sir," Nick said.

"We'll be hosting a state dinner for the prime minister of Canada in a couple of weeks," the president added. "I hope you both can make it."

Nick felt Sam stiffen. "We'd be honored," he said.

President and Mrs. Nelson left a few minutes later. While Nick and Sam visited with his father's family, Trevor approached them again.

"I'm sorry to interrupt, Senator, but several reporters are waiting for you in the conference room."

"Would you please excuse me?" Nick said. "I'll be back in a few minutes."

He left Sam with his family and followed Trevor. Over the next thirty minutes, he made it clear to the press that his top priority was ensuring passage of the immigration bill that had been scheduled for a vote by the full Senate on the day John was found murdered.

"Will you be a cosponsor?" a reporter from *The Hill* asked.

"Senator O'Connor's name will remain on the bill as a cosponsor with Senator Martin. My office will work with Senator Martin's staff to get the bill on the floor for a vote."

"Have you been apprised of your committee assignments yet?" asked a reporter from the *Richmond Times-Dispatch*.

"No, but I imagine I'll take Senator O'Connor's assignments since I'm only here for a year."

"Your relationship with Lieutenant Holland has gotten a lot of attention lately—"

"I'm not going to discuss that."

"The public is interested."

"My personal life is of no consequence to my duties as a United States senator. Let's keep the focus on that."

"Do you plan to get married?"

Frustrated, Nick stood up. "I have an office full of guests, so if you'll please excuse me, I'd like to get back to them." He left the conference room and bumped into Christina Billings, whom he had promoted from deputy chief of staff into the job that used to be his—chief of staff.

"What's wrong, Senator?" she asked. "You look pissed."

He ran a hand through his hair, noting the odd sound of his new title coming from his longtime friend and colleague. "The country's at war, the economy's in shambles and all they want to talk about is my love life."

"People are curious. It's to be expected."

"It's annoying."

Nick watched her glance across the room to where Sam was in the midst of an animated conversation with her father and sisters.

"Are you going to be able to get past it, Chris? She matters to me."

"She was a total bitch to me. Treating me like a murderer. As if I could've killed John."

"She was just doing her job."

"Her job sucks."

"On many days, she'd agree with you, but I need you to get over it. She's not going anywhere."

Her eyes clouded as she tucked a strand of short hair behind her ear. "It's only been a couple of weeks."

"I know." Nick's heart went out to Christina, knowing she'd suffered from unrequited love for John O'Connor and had been heartbroken by his death as well as the murder investigation that briefly focused on her. Nick spotted John's brother Terry in the crowd and realized he was heading for the door. "I'll catch up to you," he said to Christina as he set out to stop Terry.

"Hey, Terry!"

At forty-two, John's older brother had settled into middle age after a string of problems added ten extra years to his once-handsome face. With dark hair gone to salt-and-pepper and dark, dead-looking eyes, he bore no resemblance to his late blond-haired, blue-eyed younger brother. Broken capillaries in Terry's face were a testament to his long-running battle with alcohol.

After Terry was caught driving drunk three weeks before he'd been scheduled to announce his candidacy for his father's Senate seat, Graham O'Connor had turned to his younger son John, who reluctantly buckled under enormous pressure to run for the seat that had been in their family for nearly forty years.

"Hey, Nick, er, I mean Senator," Terry said.

Even more than five years later, Nick could still sense the bitterness in Terry. It had kept Terry on Sam's short list of suspects in his brother's murder, especially when Terry had been unable to produce the woman he'd had a drunken encounter with on the night John was killed. "May I have a minute?" Nick gestured to Christina's office since it was closest.

"Sure," Terry said with a shrug.

Nick ushered Terry into the room and closed the door behind them.

"What's up?" Terry asked.

"How've you been?"

"Fine. You know, it's tough."

The brothers hadn't been close, but Nick had no doubt Terry's grief was real. "Yeah. I keep waiting to feel better, but I'm not quite there yet."

"Mother says these things take time."

They shared a smile over their mutual love for Laine O'Connor, a pillar of strength and gentle wisdom, even during the darkest days of her life.

"Listen, the reason I wanted to talk to you is I'm sure you heard I promoted Christina to chief of staff."

"That's a good move," Terry said. "She'll be great."

"I agree. But her promotion leaves me in need of a deputy. I wondered if you might be interested."

If Nick had said Martians were landing on the south lawn of the Capitol, Terry probably wouldn't have looked more surprised. "What?" he whispered.

"Would you like to be my deputy chief of staff?"

Terry stared at him.

"Terry?"

"Why me?" he stammered. "Surely you can find someone who's not dragging a shitload of baggage behind him."

"I want you."

"Why?" he asked again, his face still slack with shock. He had a bullshit job at a lobby firm that his father had gotten for him, but otherwise his prospects had been slim since his once-promising political career flamed out following the DUI.

Nick took a step closer to the other man. "John was my best friend, my brother as much as he was yours."

"No question about that."

"I think he'd approve of you helping to ensure that all his hard work wasn't in vain, that what he started here continues. And I could use someone with your political acumen on my team."

"You mean it?" Terry asked, his expression wary.

"Yes, I mean it, but I have a condition."

"I should've known there'd be strings."

"No strings, just a condition—thirty days in-patient alcohol rehab, followed by daily AA meetings. This is a one-shot deal, Terry. One screwup, and you're out. I may not have any illusions of a career in politics, but I won't stand for anyone disgracing me, John or this office."

Terry jammed his hands into his pockets and appeared to think it over.

"So what do you say?"

"Don't you need someone now?"

"Christina can handle it for a month. We'll hold the job for you if you want it."

Terry was silent for another long moment, during which Nick wondered if he'd asked too much.

"Yes," Terry finally said. "I'd be honored."

"Great. I'm sure your doctor can refer you to some treatment facilities. If that doesn't pan out, let me know, and I'll have someone here look into it for you."

"That won't be necessary. I'll work it out." He extended his hand to Nick. "Thank you."

Nick nodded. "I hope this'll be a whole new start for you, Terry." He paused. "There's one other thing."

"What's that?"

"Sam."

Terry's expression hardened. "What about her?"

"She's in my life to stay. You'll be running into her."

"Yeah, so?"

Nick didn't care for his tone but let it slide. "Can you handle that?"

The woman Terry had been with the night John was murdered eventually come forward to cement Terry's alibi, but not before Sam reduced him to a shell of a man in the interrogation room.

"If I have to."

"I'm going to need better than that," Nick said. "Either you assure me you'll treat her with courtesy and respect, or the deal is off."

"I'll do my best," Terry said.

Nick extended his hand to the other man. "Then I'll see you in a month or so."

"I'll be here." He shook Nick's hand.

Terry opened the door to find his father approaching.

"There you both are!" Graham said, smiling. "You have a special guest, Senator." Graham stepped aside to usher Julian Sinclair into the room.

Nick let out a surprised gasp. "Julian! What're you doing here?" He was shocked to see Graham's close friend. Nick had known Julian since his years on the Harvard hockey team when Julian, a Harvard Law professor, had been one of the team's most ardent supporters.

Grinning, Julian returned Nick's embrace before greeting Terry just as warmly. "I have a meeting in town tomorrow," Julian said, "and I wanted to be among the first to congratulate the newest United States senator."

Nick took a good long look at his friend, noting that his hair had gone entirely to silver since the last time Nick had seen him. The hint of sadness in Julian's brown eyes was also new. John's sudden death had hit them all hard.

"Listen to him being modest," Graham said. He looked happier than Nick had seen him since John died, which made Nick feel lighter, too. "Tell them who the meeting is *with*."

"Nelson," Julian said with a sheepish grin.

"Oh!" Nick said, understanding dawning on him all of a sudden. "The court." Longtime Justice William Jeremiah had recently announced his retirement, giving President Nelson his first opportunity to make a nomination to the Supreme Court.

Graham clapped his hands together. "You said it, Senator. You boys are looking at the next Supreme Court Justice!"

"Wow," Terry said. "Congratulations."

"Thank you, but it's all up to the Senate, of course," Julian said. "I'm told I should prepare for one hell of a dogfight."

Nick couldn't disagree with him. Julian's liberal views on abortion and other hot-button issues made him a polarizing choice on Nelson's part.

"You've got at least one vote sewn up, right, Senator?" Graham said.

"Of course," Nick said. "I'll do anything I can to help. This is one of those times when I'm glad I only have a year in the Senate and can piss off anyone and everyone without a worry."

Julian laughed. "Don't expend all your political capital on me, my friend."

"I can't think of anyone better to spend it on," Nick said sincerely. Julian was one of his favorite people. "How long are you in town?"

Julian shrugged. "For the duration, come what may."

"We'll have dinner at my new place next week," Nick said. "I want you to meet Sam."

"I can't wait to meet this woman who's got our boy's head all turned around—and a cop, no less," Julian said, grinning at Graham.

"When you meet her, you'll see why his head is turned," Graham added with a wink.

"All right, you two. That's enough." Nick was thrilled to see Graham's playful side reemerging after the grim days that followed John's murder. "She's here somewhere."

"I have to take a rain check. I don't have any time right now, and I'd like to be able to really get to know her." Julian checked his watch. "I'm due to meet with Hanigan," he said, referring to the White House chief of staff. "I just wanted to pop in and say congratulations." He extended his hand to Nick. "I'm so very, very proud, and John would be, too. He always said you were the brains behind the entire operation."

"Thank you," Nick said softly. "That means so much coming from you."

"Make us proud."

"I'll do my best."

THREE

NICK SPENT THE next half hour working the room, visiting with Judson Knott and Richard Manning, the chair and vice chair of the Virginia Democratic Committee, as well as Virginia Governor Mike Zorn and his wife, Judy. While Nick made polite small talk and sipped a glass of wine someone had pressed into his hand, he scanned the room in search of Sam.

"Would you all excuse me?" Nick asked the others. As he made his escape, he realized he didn't see Sam's family, either. After circling the big room, he finally ducked into John's office. Of course, it was his office now, but Nick would probably always think of it as John's. He found Sam staring out the window at the Washington Monument off in the distance.

"Hey, babe," he said, closing the door. "I was looking for you."

She turned to him with a small smile. "Here I am."

"Everything all right?"

"Uh-huh. You?"

"Yep. Did your dad leave?"

She nodded. "They all said to tell you congratulations and they'll see you later at the party. Celia wanted my dad to rest up before tonight."

"What're you thinking about?" he asked, as he massaged her shoulders.

She turned to him. "Just about everything that happened to put you in this office."

"We need to put that behind us," Nick said. Touching his lips to hers, he was startled by the charge of desire even though he knew he should be used to it by now. He wondered if it would always be like that between them and suspected it would. Their connection had spanned six years and survived her manipulative ex-husband Peter's efforts to keep them apart. "Everything's new today. It's a new beginning for both of us." His hands shifted from her waist up to cup her face as she ran her tongue over his bottom lip. He gasped. "I wish we could fly away right now, today, to somewhere tropical, where I could do nothing but make love to you for a whole week."

"You'd get tired of me before the week was up."

"No," he whispered, sliding one hand down her back to align her with his erection. "Never."

"Doesn't Congress take a recess around Easter?"

"Yes," he said, nibbling her earlobe.

She trembled. "Let's go then."

"Really? Can you get away?"

"To spend a whole week in bed with you? I think it can be arranged."

He rested his forehead against hers. "But that's months from now."

"We'll both be so busy, the time will fly."

"Once we move into the new place, things will calm down a bit." He'd bought a townhouse three doors from her dad's on Ninth Street so she could be close to her father and to work. "The Realtor is putting my place in Arlington on the market right after the New Year, but we can move into Ninth Street next week."

She shifted out of his embrace and turned back toward the window. "That's good."

He rested his hands on her shoulders. "What's going on inside that head of yours?"

"Nothing."

"Samantha. I know you better than that. What gives?"

"Everything's moving so fast. I'm having trouble catching my breath."

"It's been crazy, I won't deny that, but once we get settled in our place in the city, it'll calm down. And just think, we'll be able to sleep later when we don't have to drive in from Arlington."

"True."

"So then what's the problem?"

With a deep sigh, she turned to face him. "I'm not ready to move in with you yet."

He tried to hide his disappointment from her. "I wanted us to do this together. Set up the house and stuff."

"It'd probably be better if you set things up your way. You're the one who's particular that way."

"How long are we talking? A week? A month?"

"I'm not sure. I just know I'm not ready yet."

A jolt of anger took him by surprise. "Because of Peter." He'd love to get five minutes alone with her asshole ex-husband, but since the guy was in jail for strapping crude bombs to both their cars and nearly killing Sam, that wasn't going to happen.

"Not entirely. More because of me." She rubbed her hand over her belly, a sign that the conversation was stirring up her nervous stomach. "After everything that happened, I'm more cautious than I used to be."

Anxious to stop the stomach thing before it became a full-blown incident, Nick said, "We can talk about it later, babe. Don't let your stomach get going. And by the way, you promised you'd get that checked after you closed the O'Connor case."

"I will. Soon."

He hugged her, loving the way they fit together so perfectly, like two halves of a whole. "I'll hold you to that."

Her cell phone rang, and she pulled back from him to retrieve it from the inside pocket of her suit jacket. "Holland."

Since the phone was on speaker, he heard Freddie Cruz say, "Lieutenant."

"What's going on?"

"Four vics."

Sam winced. "Kids?"

"Three, one a baby."

"Damn."

"Yeah," Freddie said with a weary sigh. "It's bad. The father was seen running from the house covered in blood. But, um, you might want to get over here."

"Why's that?"

"We found a bunch of stuff about your dad's case in the house, newspaper clippings and other stuff about the shooting. I thought you might want to take a look." He rattled off the address.

"I'll be right there." Her eyes became hard and dispassionate, the way they got when she worked a case. She returned the phone to her pocket and looked up at Nick. "You don't mind, do you?"

"Of course not." Nick could see that she had already slipped into her zone. "Do you want me to come with you?"

She shook her head. "You have guests. I'll call you."

Leaning in to kiss her, he said, "Be careful."

"I always am."

SAM DID HER best to stay calm as a taxi ferried her to the southeast corner of the city. They had waited so long for a break in her father's case. Could this be it? After many disappointments, she refused to allow herself to hope.

Just over two years ago, Deputy Chief Skip Holland had been on his way home from work when he pulled over an erratic driver on G Street. The last thing he remembered was reporting in to dispatch and then approaching the car. A bullet lodged between the C3 and C4 vertebrae had left him a quadriplegic with just one slightly functioning finger on his right hand. A week after the shooting, a mild stroke rendered the left side of his face paralyzed.

They hadn't a single clue—no witnesses, no ballistics since the doctors decided removing the bullet could kill him, the car hadn't had a license plate, and they had no description of the driver since Skip was shot before he saw the driver's face. A long time ago Sam and her colleagues concluded that the only way the case would be solved now was if someone bragged about shooting a cop and one of their snitches passed it along. As the case went cold, Sam had learned not to get her hopes up.

If her newfound media notoriety had any upside it was the opportunity to remind the press that her father's case remained unsolved. Someone knew something. If only they'd come forward. They just needed a thread. One thread to pull and the whole thing would unravel. Her sisters and even her father, to some extent, were resigned to the fact that they might never catch the shooter. Sam would neither rest nor retire as long as the case was unsolved.

Skip had been just ninety days shy of retirement at the time of the shooting. The months that followed were filled with fear and frustration as his family and friends did what they could to help him adjust to his new reality—confined to a wheelchair by day, hooked to a respirator by night and reliant upon the specially outfitted van the union bought for him.

When the taxi pulled up to a dilapidated row house on First Avenue in the violent, poverty-stricken neighborhood of Washington Highlands, Sam retrieved her 9 millimeter handgun from her purse, tucked it into the back of her skirt, and clipped her badge to the lapel of her coat.

Ignoring the crowd of onlookers gathered outside the yellow police tape, she tossed a twenty to the driver and wove her way between cop cars, an ambulance and the medical examiner's van on her way to the chain-link front gate. Pushing the rusty gate open, she hurried up the sagging stairs and almost bumped into Freddie as he emerged from the house looking pale and drawn.

Sam ached for her kindhearted, compassionate partner who would suffer more than most over a scene like this. She rested a hand on his trench coat–clad shoulder. "Take a few breaths."

He did what he was told, but his complexion was ashen, and his brown eyes were flat with grief and anger. "I just can't imagine how anyone does that to helpless kids. A dad is supposed to *protect* his kids."

"It's always harder when it's kids." A memory of the child who was killed when she ordered a shootout at a crack house resurfaced suddenly, sending a shudder rippling through her.

"He shot the mother in the kitchen," Freddie said. "Seems like he took her by surprise. No defensive wounds. Point of entry on the back of her left shoulder. McNamara said the bullet probably hit her heart. We found a gun thrown into a box in the back of the bedroom closet. There was another box in the closet that had the clippings about your dad."

Sam watched him struggle with his composure as he proceeded with the rote recitation of the facts.

"The kids were beaten. We found a baseball bat with brain matter on it."

Sam winced. "Do we know him?"

"Clarence Reese, thirty-nine, long list of priors, mostly B&E and drug stuff. Juvie record, too, but nothing violent."

Sam wished she could say she recognized the name. "Next of kin?"

"Gonzo and Arnold found an address for Reese's mother. They left about twenty minutes ago. We've got an APB out for Reese."

The front door opened and Chief Medical Examiner Dr. Lindsey McNamara emerged behind paramedics wheeling a tiny body in a bag out of the house. Known for her stoicism, Lindsey's green eyes were bright with tears. "Unreal," she whispered on her way by.

Sam squeezed the other woman's arm.

"That's the last one," Freddie said, sounding relieved.

Tearing her eyes off the black bag being loaded into the M.E.'s vehicle, Sam returned her attention to Freddie. "Have you found any connection to my dad in any of Reese's priors?"

"After we came across the stuff about the shooting, Captain Malone ordered a more detailed run of Reese's record. He went back to HQ to move that along."

"Show me what you've got."

As if to fortify himself, Freddie took another deep breath of the cold air before he led Sam into hell.

The smell hit her like a fist to the face. Death. Blood. Bodily waste.

Old toys covered the floor of a Spartanly furnished living room dominated by a big-screen TV. Spattered blood coated the screen and the walls behind it. A tan sofa had clearly been ground zero for one of the murders as the cushions were soaked with drying blood.

Crime scene officers sifting through the carnage nodded to her as she entered the room.

"Jesus," Sam whispered, and for once Freddie didn't object to her use of the Lord's name.

He led her past the kitchen where Clarence Reese had shot his wife in the back. They went up a flight of stairs to a second floor with three small bedrooms and a tiny bathroom.

Sam noted disarray throughout the house—dishes piled in the kitchen sink, toys everywhere, scuffed walls, pictures hanging at crooked angles, towels and dirty clothes scattered about the floor of the bathroom and a filthy stained rug lining the hallway. Things had been difficult in this household long before today, long before Clarence Reese lost his mind and butchered his family.

In the master bedroom, a king-size bed took up almost every inch of the room. Freddie pulled a box from the closet floor, set it on the bed and then moved aside so Sam could take a closer look.

She slipped on the latex gloves he handed her before she touched yellowing newspaper articles from the aftermath of her father's shooting, carefully clipped from all the local newspapers, as well as coverage taken from the department's website. Under the clippings were photos, and various other news stories about her father's thirty years on the force that ran after the shooting.

"Was it him?" Sam asked in a small voice, glancing up at the family photo that hung over the bed. Nothing about Clarence Reese was familiar to her. He had the stocky build of a former high school football player, coffee-colored skin, brown eyes and a thick shock of dark hair. He was handsome in a quirky sort of way. His wife was white with a plain face, stringy brown hair, dull eyes and a world-weary expression. "Do you think he shot my dad?"

"We don't know, but we're going to find out. You're not the only one who wants to know, believe me. Farnsworth and Conklin were both here," Freddie said of the chief and deputy chief, both of whom were old friends of her father's. "Farnsworth had fire in his eyes when Malone showed him this stuff."

"Let's bag it all and have the lab work it up. Not that the gun will tell us anything about my dad." How she wished they could get at that bullet lodged inside him.

"Malone said the same thing. I was just waiting for you to see it."

With a nod she stepped out of the room so he could tend to the evidence. Drawing a deep breath in through her nose, she blew it out her mouth, a process she had discovered helped to short-circuit the stomach pains before they could spiral out of control. She made the mistake of glancing into what had been the baby's room and quickly looked away from the gruesome scene.

"I don't want my dad to know we found this stuff until we have more," she said.

"I'll put out the word."

"I'd hate to get his hopes up."

"I understand, and so will everyone else."

"If we can't find a connection from Reese's arrest record, we'll have no choice but to ask my dad."

"We can cross that bridge if we come to it, but you're right—there's no need to tell him until we have something solid. Hopefully, we'll find Reese fast and get him into interrogation."

"What was the wife's name?" she asked.

"Tiffany. Kids were Jorge, Ramon and the baby was Maria."

Sam studied the family photo, zeroing in on the plain-looking mother. "She doesn't look like a Tiffany."

"No." Freddie zipped the plastic evidence bag closed and pulled off his gloves. "Let's get out of here. If there's anything else, crime scene will let us know."

She took another long look at the photo of the shattered family before she followed Freddie out of the house.

FOUR

HOURS LATER, SAM stood in front of the mirror in her bedroom at her father's house and adjusted the cowl neck of the plum-colored cashmere sweater he'd given her for Christmas. Of course Celia had picked it out, but that didn't matter. It was the thought that counted, and her father had always been a thoughtful gift-giver. A tough, don't-fuck-with-me cop with a soft spot a mile wide for his family, Skip had loved to shop, to find the perfect gift, to hide it away, and then present it with a flourish for a birthday or Christmas or just because it was Tuesday.

Bitterness threatened to consume her as she added another item to the long list of things a nameless, faceless shooter had taken from her father, from all of them. But now when she imagined the person who shot her father, she pictured Clarence Reese. She just wished they could find him. They'd scoured the city all day but had turned up no sign of him either with family members or at any of his usual haunts.

Hands braced against the dresser, Sam let her head hang between her shoulders, rolling off the tension— or attempting to. Hours of sifting and digging had also found no connection between Skip Holland and Clarence Reese. Not an arrest, a traffic stop, a verbal warning, nothing—unless Skip had had some sort of undocumented altercation with Clarence. To find that out, she'd have to ask her father, but she wasn't prepared to do that until they had more. She refused to set him up for yet another disappointment.

Taking a deep breath, she attempted to shut down her mind, to leave the investigation for tomorrow. Tonight was for celebration—at least that was the plan. Sam didn't feel much like celebrating and was almost resentful that her new personal obligations were pulling her away from what she really wanted to be doing right now.

She ran a brush through her long toffee-colored curls and applied a light touch of eye shadow. Maybe she wasn't in the mood to party, but she'd be damned if she'd go out looking like crap.

As she bent to zip high-heeled black boots, Nick stepped into the room and closed the door behind him. From between her legs she saw that he wore a black sweater over well-faded jeans that hugged him in all the right places.

"Mmm, mmm, *mmm,* that's one hell of a view," he said, taking a good long look at her ass.

She shot him an upside-down scowl.

"Uh-oh. What's wrong?"

Righting, she ran her fingers through her hair. "Nothing."

"Something."

"Stop acting like you know me so well," she snapped.

With a slow, sexy smile that she watched unfold in the mirror, he came up behind her and rested his hands on her shoulders. "I do know you so well." He punctuated his words with a brush of his lips over her neck that made her tremble. "See?"

Sam tried—and failed—to shake him off.

"I know you're frustrated, babe—"

"You don't know anything."

"I know I love you, and I hate to see you hurting."

Damn if he didn't always know just how to get to her! The starch left her spine, and she sagged into his embrace.

His chin settled on the top of her head, his arms tightened around her waist. In the mirror, he found her eyes. "Talk to me."

"It makes me so mad!"

"What does?"

"That my dad is stuck forever in that chair, and the person who shot him is walking around, living his life, like nothing ever happened. He took my dad's freedom! He took *everything!* He should have to pay for that." A lump of emotion in her throat reduced her voice to a whisper. "He should have to pay."

"Yes, he should. And I have no doubt that he will, because you won't give up. You'll never give up until you find him." He turned her so they were face-to-face. "And guess what? *He* knows that, too. He *worries* about you. The best detective in this city is on his trail, and he *knows* it, Sam. I'll bet it keeps him awake at night."

She rested her cheek against the hard muscle of Nick's chest. "It makes me mad."

"Mad is good." He held her tight against him. "Mad is motivating."

"Mad is debilitating."

"Only if you let it be. Your dad was so proud of you earlier." Nick's lips brushed through her hair as he spoke softly to her. "He all but radiated with it, Sam. Watching your sisters pin those bars on your collar, he had tears rolling down his face. That was enough for him today. So maybe it can be enough for us, too. Why don't we put Clarence Reese on the back burner until tomorrow so you can enjoy tonight? Every cop on duty in this city is out there looking for him, so why don't you let it go for tonight? You've worked so hard to get to this day. Don't allow anyone to make it less, especially someone who could do what that guy did to his family."

Begrudgingly, Sam looked up at him. "You're good."

His face lifted into the sexy grin that made her bones go weak. "I try."

"You're good for me."

"I want to be." He pressed his lips to hers and sucked the oxygen right out of her lungs with a soul-stirring, mind-altering kiss that cleared her brain of every thought except the urge to tear the clothes off his body.

"I know you're bummed about what I told you earlier, about moving in," she said when they came up for air.

Pressing another kiss to her lips, he said, "I'll be there whenever you're ready to join me."

"It's not you. I hope you know that. It's just that I lived with a man, for four years I *slept* with a man who was capable of trying to blow up both of us, but I never saw that in him. I'm a cop, for Christ's sake, and not once did I imagine he had that in him."

"Sam—"

"I know you're going to say that has nothing to do with you and me, with us."

"It doesn't."

"It *does,* Nick. My ex-husband tried to *murder* us. How do I just put that behind me like it never happened and move in with you? There must be something wrong with me that I didn't see—"

Again, he kissed the words right off her lips. "There's *nothing* wrong with you. You were a victim. We both were. He's headed for prison, Sam. There's no sense in you going with him."

"I need some time to process it all. I need to be sure

I've put the pieces back where they belong before I take the next step with you."

"That's fair enough."

Feeling madly vulnerable, she glanced up to find his hazel eyes hot with emotion and desire. She still had trouble believing that was all for her. "You don't mind waiting?"

"I'd wait forever for you. And in the meantime, I'll be three doors up the street anytime you want to make a late-night booty call."

She laughed. "That'll probably be most nights."

"So you just want me for my body. I see how it is."

She slid her hands under his sweater and up to cup well-defined pectorals. "What are you doing right now, Senator?" she asked with a coy smile.

His jaw tightened with tension as he removed her hands from under his sweater. "Taking you to our party."

"Damn."

He leaned in to catch her earlobe between his teeth. "But later we'll be having our own *private* New Year's party."

Sam shivered with anticipation and marveled at how he had managed to put her in the mood to celebrate. This love stuff definitely came with some major benefits.

"*THIS* IS YOUR idea of a *small* party?" Sam asked an hour later as she took in the mobbed K Street lounge Nick had reserved for the occasion. When she suggested a beer and pizza party at O'Leary's—her favorite cop bar— he'd turned up his senatorial nose, so she'd left it to him to orchestrate this joint celebration.

"I can't help it if you have a hundred cop friends."

"I don't even know most of these people."

"Like who?"

"Her." She pointed to a voluptuous brunette flirting shamelessly with Freddie. "An old girlfriend of yours?"

"Hardly. That's Ginger, one of the legislative aides in my office."

"*Ginger* needs to get her filthy hands off my partner," Sam said, even though she was relieved to see Freddie smiling again after the gruesome day he'd put in.

"I think we've got a bigger problem over there."

Sam's head whipped around. "Where?"

Nick pointed to one of the cozy booths where his chief of staff, Christina Billings, was having an intimate conversation with Detective Tommy "Gonzo" Gonzales.

"Get her off him!"

"Why?" Nick asked, amused. "They're both consenting adults."

"She doesn't like me."

"So she can't talk to your friend?"

"He's not just my friend. He's my subordinate now. She'll turn him against me."

"Honestly, Samantha." Nick led her to the dance floor. "The twists and turns of your mind are a constant source of fascination to me."

"Glad I'm available to entertain you," she grumbled.

"You do." He brought his lips down on hers. "Endlessly."

"Get a room, you two," Sam's sister Tracy said as she danced up next to them with her husband, Mike.

Sam tried to put some space between herself and Nick, but he just tightened his hold on her.

"Great party," Mike said.

"Thanks," Nick replied. "Did your dad get something to eat?"

"Celia's on it," Tracy said. "He's having a great time visiting with all his cop buddies."

They glanced over to find Skip with Celia, Chief Farnsworth, Deputy Chief Conklin and their spouses, as well as Detective Captain Malone and some of the other department captains.

"He's in his glory," Sam said to her sister.

"It's been a good day for him," Tracy said.

"Yes." Sam thought of Clarence Reese and wished she could share the possibility with her sister, but didn't want to disappoint her, either.

"The O'Connors just got here," Nick said, his eyes on the door. "We need to go say hello." To Mike and Tracy, he added, "You guys have a good time."

"We're kid-free," Tracy said, beaming at her husband. "We're already having a good time, and it's only going to get better."

"I like her," Mike said with a lascivious grin. "I like her *so* much."

Laughing, Nick and Sam left the happy couple on the dance floor.

"They're awfully cute together," Nick said.

"They always have been. I've been envious of how easy they make it look."

He squeezed her shoulder and leaned in to kiss her cheek. "No need to be envious anymore. We'll show them easy."

Heartened by Nick's words, Sam tried not to feel awkward as Senator and Mrs. O'Connor greeted her with warm hugs. Nick thought of them as his adopted family, and Sam knew she needed to get over the resentment she harbored from when they'd lied to her during the investigation into their son's murder. Sam had uncovered John's illegitimate twenty-year-old son who'd been kept hidden from the public in deference to the senior Senator O'Connor's political career and reputation. That son, his mother and that secret turned out to be a motive for murder.

"What a lovely party," Laine O'Connor said to Nick.

"I'm glad you could come," Nick said.

"Oh, we wouldn't miss it. Royce and Lizbeth are right behind us," she said, referring to her son-in-law and daughter. Laine reached for Nick's hand. "And what you're doing for Terry. I just can't thank you enough. *We* can't thank you enough."

"It was a generous move, Senator," Graham added gruffly. "He won't let you down."

"Of course he won't."

"Julian sends his regrets," Graham said. "He'd hoped to be here, but his meeting at the White House ran late."

"I'm sure they've got a *lot* to talk about."

"Gonna be a battle royal," Graham said with a gleeful grin. "The Republicans will flip their lids—especially Stenhouse." Graham O'Connor's bitter relationship with Senate Minority Leader William Stenhouse went back decades, and for a brief time, he, too, had been on Sam's short list of suspects in John's murder.

"Good thing we don't need 'em," Nick said with a grin of his own.

Graham rubbed his hands together. "I love being in the majority."

Sam found his use of the present tense interesting. You could take the man out of the Senate...

"Hopefully, he can find a free night for dinner next week," Nick said. "I want to show you all my new place in the city."

Sam wondered if he had lost his mind. A dinner party for a potential Supreme Court justice at the place he hadn't even moved into yet? Next week? Right. But even as she thought it, she knew he would pull it off the same way he had pulled off their party—effortlessly.

"Sounds like a plan," Graham said.

"I can't wait to see your new house, Nick," Laine said. "I'm sorry. I should call you Senator now."

"You should call me Nick." He kissed her cheek. "Why don't you grab a drink, have something to eat and we'll catch up to you in a bit?"

"Excellent," Graham said, putting his arm around his wife to lead her to the bar.

"They seem better," Nick said to Sam when they were alone.

"What did you do for Terry?"

Nick had his eyes—and obviously his mind—on the O'Connors. "What?"

"Terry. What did you do?"

"I offered him the deputy chief of staff job."

"*What?* Why?"

"Because he knows his stuff, and he's wasting away in that bullshit lobby job. He's also John's brother. It felt like the right thing to do."

"But he hates me, too! Your two most senior staffers hate me!"

"I've made it very clear to both of them that if they can't treat you with courtesy and respect they'll be looking for new jobs."

"You did?" Sam squeaked, her heart pounding in her chest. The emotion could hit hard when she least expected it.

"They can be replaced. You can't."

"You have a way with words, Senator," she said with a sigh. "You really do."

FIVE

AT TWO MINUTES to midnight, Nick couldn't find Sam and panic was setting in. A heartbeat away from asking the DJ to page her, he spotted her tucked into a corner, checking text messages on her phone.

Pushing his way through the crowd, he took the phone, stuffed it into his back pocket, reached for her hand and tugged her up.

She resisted. "Hey! What're you doing?"

"Come," he said, leading her out of the room to a stairway.

"Where are we going? Isn't it almost midnight?"

"Yep." Nick charged up the stairs, almost dragging her along with him. At the top of the darkened stairwell, he pushed open the door to the roof. Their city stretched out before them. Above, the clear sky twinkled with stars.

"Oh, *wow,* Nick," she said breathlessly. "Oh, look at this!" She spun on her heel to get the full view of the Capitol, White House and monuments at the far end of the Mall.

Nick drew her into his arms. "You like?"

"Totally. This is amazing!"

"Are you cold?"

"No," she said, gazing up at the stars.

From the sidewalk below, they heard revelers counting down the final ten seconds of the year.

He brought his hands up to frame her face. "I love you. This year, next year, every year."

She reached for him, and as fireworks burst into the sky above them, she kissed him softly, thoroughly, deeply. "I love you, too. Thank you for the best New Year's ever."

"The first of many." He kissed both her cheeks. "I promise."

"Can we do this every year?" Her eyes brimmed with excitement, the way he liked them best. "Can we come back to this very spot to ring in every New Year?"

"It's a date," he said, his throat tight with emotion. He'd had no idea, no idea at all, that it was possible to love someone this much. "Next time, I'll remember the champagne."

"We don't need it."

Even though it was cold, even though their breath came out in puffy clouds, they stayed on the roof to watch the entire fireworks display. Nick kept his arms tight around her from behind, immersed in the jasmine and vanilla fragrance he would recognize anywhere as hers.

"I love the way the colors in the fireworks reflect on the monuments," she said, her hands covering his at her waist.

"Mmm, me, too."

The fireworks ended with a booming finale of color and sound.

Sam sighed. "That was fabulous." She turned to him. "Thank you so much."

"I have a theory."

Her mouth quirked with amusement. "And what's that?"

Unable to resist, he touched his lips to hers. "That how you spend the first minutes of the New Year is how you'll spend the year itself." Adding a light brush of his tongue over her bottom lip, he leaned into the kiss when her arms curled around his neck. The tangle of teeth and tongues took his breath away. Reaching down, he cupped her ass and lifted her right off her feet. She surprised him when she wrapped her long legs around his waist.

"I take it you like my theory," he said when he had no choice but to come up for air. He wanted her desperately, as if he had gone without for years rather than hours.

"It's a great theory—and a great way to spend a year." Grinning, she pressed against his erection. "But I'd hate for my favorite new senator to be caught in such a *compromising* position on his first day in office."

Reluctantly, he let her slide back down. "Let's get the hell out of here."

"We can't leave our own party."

"No one will notice. I guarantee it."

NICK SURPRISED HER when he directed the cab to her father's Capitol Hill neighborhood. After the way he'd sprinted her out of the party, she assumed he wanted to be alone with her at his place in Arlington.

"We're going to my dad's?" she asked.

"Nope."

"Then where?"

"You'll see."

She eyed him suspiciously. "What are you up to?"

"Nothing," he said with a smile that said her hunch was dead on.

"Tell me!"

"Patience, Samantha."

"Not my best quality."

"*No,* really?"

She tried pouting, cajoling and even a few dirty tricks, but nothing worked. Except for a couple of heated make-out sessions, he kept his mouth shut until they pulled up to the house he had bought on Ninth Street. "What're we doing here?"

He paid the cabbie and reached for her hand. "Come on, I'll show you."

Puzzled, Sam followed him to the house three doors up the street from her dad's. "Do you even own this place yet?" she asked as he used a key in the lock.

"Not yet, but the owners didn't mind me moving in a few things early."

"What things?"

"God, you're such a pain in the ass!"

"Thank you."

He turned, kissed her nose and took her coat. "You're the only woman I know who would take that as a compliment."

"That's why you love me."

Laughing, he led her into the kitchen. "What do you think?"

"Oh," she said, taking in the large, stylish kitchen where everything was brand-new. "I knew they were renovating this place, but I never imagined this." She ran a hand over the stone countertop. The cabinets were dark wood, the appliances sleek stainless steel. Above the bar that piggybacked the kitchen and living room, teardrop lights hung from the ceiling. "I love it."

"I hoped you would."

She stepped into the living room and gasped at the size of it. At the far end, a marble mantel framed a large fireplace. "What the heck?"

"I take it you didn't know he bought the place next door and knocked out the walls."

"I had no idea! This place is huge! What're you going to do with all this space?"

He shrugged. "Maybe raise a bunch of kids with you?"

Her heart stopped at the mention of kids. He knew she couldn't have them but had made it clear he didn't care and that they'd adopt if and when the time came.

"Sam? Are you all right?"

"Sure," she said, shaking it off. "Show me the rest."

Besides the kitchen and living room, the first floor of the double-sized townhouse boasted an enormous dining room as well as a full bathroom. The floors were a light wood and recently refinished. The second floor had four bedrooms and two more bathrooms.

"I thought for now we could use that one for a guest room, that one for an office and maybe a gym in there," he said of the extra bedrooms.

"You've got it all figured out."

"When I first looked at it, I could see us here together. That's why I bought it."

"It's a really nice place," she conceded. "I've certainly never lived anywhere nicer."

"Neither have I. Come check this out." He led her to the master bedroom where a new king-size bed with an elaborate wrought-iron head- and footboard was the only furniture in the room.

Startled, Sam said, "You bought a bed already?"

"Yep." He sat on the bed and kicked off his shoes. "I wanted to stay here tonight."

"And they just let you truck a bed in here?"

"They, um, they think it's cool that they're selling to a senator."

Seeing him flustered made Sam laugh. "Already taking full advantage, are you?"

"I wouldn't say that—exactly. Take a look at the closet. I figured you'd like that."

"Nice way to change the subject." Sam stepped into the walk-in closet and took a good look at the decent-sized space, deciding that about half her clothes would fit in there.

"Isn't it great?" he asked with a smile.

"Where would you keep your stuff?"

His smile faded. "I figured we'd share it."

"Um, sure. Okay."

"You don't have *that* many shoes."

"What I have at my dad's is about one-tenth of the total. The rest are in storage."

His mouth dropped open in shock. "Are you *serious?*"

"I never joke about shoes."

Scratching at the stubble on his chin, he studied her. "Well, I guess we can put the gym on the third floor and build you a big old closet in one of the extra bedrooms."

She sat down next to him on the bed. "You'd do that for me?"

"Sure, I would. Besides, it's probably better if we don't share a closet. You're not quite as, um, neat as I am."

"Anal you mean."

"I prefer neat."

Laughing, she said, "I'm sure you do." She kissed him and rested her head on his shoulder. "It's a great place."

"I'm glad—and relieved—that you think so. As I was buying it without telling you, I told myself I was probably making a huge mistake."

"It wasn't a mistake. A place like this wouldn't have lasted long on the market."

"That's what the Realtor said, too." He rubbed her back and nuzzled her neck. "I want you here with me, Sam." With his other hand, he produced a key.

Touched, she took it from him and slid it into her back pocket. "I promise I'll be here so much you'll feel like I live here."

"That's not the same."

"Can it be enough for now?"

"I guess I'll have to settle for what I can get," he said with a dramatic sigh that was offset by the twinkle in his eye.

"I hate to disappoint you."

He brought her hand to his lips. "You're not." Standing up, he tugged her along with him. "There're two more things I want to show you." In the master bathroom, he pointed out the huge Jacuzzi tub.

"Oh, man, *seriously?*"

"Have you got something against Jacuzzis?"

"I *love* them. I've always wanted one in my house." Stomping her foot, she added, "This is so not fair!"

"All this could be yours."

She scowled. "What's the other thing?"

He pointed back the way they'd come. In the bedroom, he went to the fireplace and flipped a switch under the mantel to start the gas fire.

Sam sighed. "So not fair."

"Let me guess—you've always wanted a fireplace in your bedroom, too?"

She nodded, reached for the pillows and throw blanket on the bed and brought them over to the carpet in front of the fire.

"What're we doing?" he asked as he let her draw him down next to her.

"Camping."

"So I could've skipped the bed?"

Tugging the sweater up and over his head, she tossed it aside. "Uh-huh." She urged him onto his back and dropped kisses on his chest in a trail to his belly.

Nick sucked in a sharp deep breath and combed his fingers through her hair. "Am I getting this special treatment because I have a Jacuzzi?"

"No," she said, adding her tongue to the mix.

"Then why?" He gasped when she unzipped his jeans and dragged a finger over his straining erection.

She looked up at him with a mischievous expression on her face. "I've always wanted to screw a senator." Taking him into her mouth, she kept her movements slow and precise.

His laughter faded into a groan. *"Sam."*

"What?" She swirled her tongue, lapping at him like a hungry cat.

Sighing, he sank back into the pillow. "God, you're good at that."

She cracked up. "Can I put it on my resume?"

Shaking his head, he said, "That's only for me." He reached for her and brought her up to rest on top of him. "Kiss me."

Her lips fused to his, she broke the connection only to let him remove her sweater. Helping him get rid of the rest of their clothes, she moved quickly, craving the feel of his skin against hers, the soft brush of his chest hair, the firm muscles, his scent. Everything about him appealed to her—and scared her. To love like this was to risk so much, things she'd sworn to never risk again after her disastrous marriage.

"What?" he asked, his lips coasting over hers.

"I was just thinking that if this is how we're going to spend it, I'm going to like this year."

"That's not what you were thinking," he said, reversing their positions so he was on top. He kissed her softly, his eyes intent on hers, letting her know she could hide nothing from him.

"I was thinking how much I love you and how sad I'd be if—"

"Don't say it." He slid into her. "Don't think it. It's not going to happen."

Sam arched her back to take him in. *"Nick."*

"What, babe?" he asked, his lips soft against her jaw.

"Faster."

"Not tonight."

"Why?"

"I read in the paper today," he said close to her ear, his hips moving with aching slowness, "that sex therapists say intercourse should last between three and thirteen minutes."

How can he talk right now? she wondered. *I'm having trouble breathing!*

"Since we usually work the lower end of the spectrum," he continued, "I thought we'd see what the other side is like."

Burning up from the inside out, she gripped a fistful of his silky brown hair and wrapped her legs around him. Thirteen minutes? She'd be dead in five. But nothing she did, nothing she tried, got him to move any faster.

His mouth descended on hers, his tongue sweeping into her mouth as he cupped her breast. Suddenly, he withdrew from her and kissed a path to her nipple.

Sam could have wept from the loss and the sweet torture of his kisses even as she felt the now-familiar signs of impending climax. It happened so easily with him that she'd almost forgotten how unattainable it had been in past relationships.

His lips were on her belly, his tongue laying a trail to her burning center.

The rosy glow of the fire burnished his skin. Just looking at him took her breath away, but watching him watch her as he made slow love to her was about the sexiest thing she'd ever seen. She reached for him.

He shook his head. "Not yet." His broad shoulders forced her legs farther apart as he settled between them. Touching his tongue to her, he stayed with the slow theme, teasing her until her legs quivered and her heart raced. Leaving her clinging to the precipice, he kissed his way back up to her lips, pushed into her and sent her over the edge with a sharp cry of release that took him with her.

With his lips pressed to her neck, he whispered, "Happy New Year."

SIX

WHILE NICK SPENT New Year's Day packing up his Arlington house, Sam sat hunched over her laptop scrolling through every scrap of information she could find on Clarence Reese. In the meantime, Gonzo and Arnold were leading the manhunt for him on the streets. Through her research, Sam learned he'd grown up blocks away from her Ninth Street childhood home and wondered if perhaps he'd had a neighborhood altercation with her father. A call to Tracy, who was just a year older than Clarence, yielded nothing useful since she had no recollection of being in school with anyone with that name.

By noon, Sam was ready to tear her hair out. The connection had to be there. It *had* to be. Her stomach rumbled, and she decided to venture downstairs on a fishing expedition. She found her father sitting at the kitchen table scanning the reading device propped in front of his wheelchair. Bending to kiss his cheek, she said, "How's it going?"

"All right. What've you been up to all morning?"

"Just catching up on some paperwork."

"Nice party last night."

"That was all Nick."

"No kidding, really?"

His sarcastic eye roll amused her. "Would've been beer at O'Leary's if I'd gotten my way."

"Gives you a run for your money, that boy. I like that about him."

Anxious to change the subject, she nodded to the reader. "What's that?"

"The *Post*."

"What're they saying about the DD yesterday?" she asked in what she hoped was a nonchalant tone as she opened a diet cola and joined him at the table.

"Most of what you already know. They interviewed some neighbors and friends who're shocked. Never would've suspected he'd be capable. The usual. The kids and the wife were well liked, but he kept to himself. Apparently, he just got laid off."

"Something about his name is familiar to me." Sam watched her father intently. "Ring any bells with you?"

"Nope."

She hoped the disappointment didn't show on her face. "I read that he grew up on Seventh."

"I saw that. Who's running the investigation?"

Nothing, Sam thought with dejection. If Skip Holland had ever met Clarence Reese, he didn't remember it. "Gonzo and Arnold."

"Losing his job could've triggered something."

"Maybe. Judging by the condition of the house, things had been rough for some time. But the job thing might've been the final straw."

"Nice article about Nick's swearing in if you want to check it out. The *Post* did a poll in Virginia yesterday, and more than eighty percent of those surveyed approved of the governor choosing him to finish out O'Connor's term. That's a hell of an approval rating to start with."

Sam reached for the front page and almost choked on her soda when she saw the huge picture of her holding the Bible as Nick took the oath of office. "Oh, my *God!* You could've warned me!"

"And miss that reaction? No way."

The caption read, "Metro Police Lieutenant Sam Holland holds the Bible as Chief Justice Byron Riley administers the oath of office to Nicholas Cappuano. A Democrat from Virginia, Cappuano will complete the last year of recently murdered Senator John O'Connor's term. The romance between Cappuano and Holland has captured the attention of the entire capitol region over the last few weeks."

Skip laughed. "It's quite a picture. You look petrified."

Sam dropped her head to the table. "*Why* do they care about us so much? *Why?*"

"You're young and attractive, you have important jobs and people love a good romance."

"Why can't they just mind their own business?"

"Not gonna happen, honey. It's probably going to get worse before they lose interest—*if* they lose interest."

"Great."

Skip's nurse and fiancée Celia emerged from the basement carrying a laundry basket. "Hey, Sam, did you see the paper? What a wonderful picture of you and Nick!"

Skip smiled as Sam scowled.

"Yes, it's *wonderful,*" Sam said.

"Sam's not loving her moment in the spotlight," Skip said.

"I think it's so sweet," Celia said with a dreamy expression. "You two are just *adorable* together."

As Skip chortled with laughter, Sam banged her forehead against the table.

DETECTIVE FREDDIE CRUZ paced the sidewalk in front of Total Fitness on Sixteenth Street. On this first day of the New Year, he was all about resolutions and none of them involved spending more time at the gym. No, this was the year he was finally going to get laid. No matter what it took, no matter what he had to do, no matter what personal ideals he had to sacrifice, he was going to have sex.

Raised a devout Christian by a single mother, he'd done his best for twenty-nine long years to make his mother proud by saving himself for marriage. But since he didn't even have a girlfriend, let alone a potential wife, and with rampaging hormones making his life a living hell, he had decided to give in.

Nick's aide Ginger had practically thrown herself at him at the party last night, but Freddie wasn't interested in her.

Since he and Sam interviewed personal trainer Elin Svendsen during the O'Connor investigation, he found himself fantasizing about her day and night. The way she'd been so free about her sexuality and talked so openly about the kinky sex she'd had with the dead senator. She was all Freddie could think about. She was the one he wanted.

That was why he was lurking outside Total Fitness, wearing one of his trademark trench coats while trying to work up the nerve to step inside to inquire about personal training. She didn't need to know he was interested in personal training of a different sort. At least not right away.

"Detective Cruz?"

Startled, he looked up, and there she was. Tall, blonde—so blonde her eyebrows were almost white—she had dark blue eyes and a smile right out of a toothpaste commercial. Carrying a tray containing four coffees and wearing a light blue down vest and black yoga pants, it was all Freddie could do to keep from drooling. She was even sexier than he remembered—and he remembered every excruciating detail of the night he'd spent protecting her in a hotel room while Thomas O'Connor hunted down his father's ex-girlfriends.

"I thought that was you," she said. "How are you?"

"I'm, um, fine. And you?"

"Crazy today. It's the busiest day of the year for us—all the resolutions."

"Right," Freddie said, remembering his own resolutions.

"Are you working on a case?"

"Me?" *No, idiot,* Freddie thought, *that other guy she's talking to.* "Not today. I was just in the neighborhood and thinking about resolutions."

She smiled.

He went hard as a stone and was thankful for the long coat.

"Do you want to come in? I could show you around and tell you about our program."

"Um, sure, that sounds good." He wondered if she'd think it strange if he kept his coat on inside.

AFTER SPENDING SUNDAY helping Nick finish packing up his place in Arlington, Sam woke up Monday morning with a stomachache. She lay still in Nick's big new bed and tried to breathe her way through pain that had become predictable. Anytime she was nervous or stressed out, she could count on her stomach to let her know. And judging by the particularly sharp pain, she was some kind of nervous.

Today she would officially take command of the HQ detectives. She had wanted the job for as long as she'd been a detective, but was nervous about all the responsibility that would come with overseeing forty detectives, hundreds of cases each year and all the accompanying personnel matters.

Another stabbing pain made her whimper.

Nick looped an arm around her. "What?"

"Stomach."

"That's it. I'm making you an appointment."

"I'll do it. Today."

"Promise?"

Sam bit her lip and nodded as another sharp pain took her breath away.

"Come here." Arranging her head on his shoulder, he rubbed her back and spoke softly to her.

Sam couldn't help but relax into his embrace. Surrounded by the fragrance of soap and sporty deodorant, the scent of Nick, she focused on breathing her way through it. "Are you nervous?" she asked. "About today?"

"Nah. We're both going to work in the same place with the same people."

"Except we're the bosses now."

"Is that going to change you?"

"I'm not planning to let it," she said.

"Neither am I. So everything will be just fine. Be yourself, be fair and you can't lose. The other detectives love you. They'd do anything for you, and they know you'd do anything for them."

"Some people in the department think I got this promotion because of my father and his connections."

"Which you know isn't true."

Sam swallowed hard and glanced up at him. "It kind of is."

His eyebrows narrowed with confusion. "What do you mean?"

"I had trouble with the exam. I flunked it the first two times—because of the dyslexia. I just barely passed this time."

"But you *did* pass."

"My dad told Farnsworth about the dyslexia. He used his discretion as chief to authorize my promotion. If that ever gets out, people will scream favoritism."

"Is the exam the only qualifying factor?"

"No, there's more to it than that—experience, training, interviews, the graduate degree I worked my ass off to get. It all counts."

"Then it sounds to me as if Farnsworth promoted the most worthy candidate."

Sam smiled and realized her stomach no longer hurt. "And you're not the slightest bit biased."

"Not one bit," he said, tipping her chin up to receive his kiss. "You're going to be the best lieutenant that department has ever had. I have no doubt."

She needed to get up and get moving but couldn't seem to bring herself to leave the warmth of his embrace. "Thanks."

"Anytime." He shifted so he was on top of her.

"What's this?" she asked with a coy smile.

"Just making sure you get a good breakfast on your first day," he said, entering her.

Sam laughed even as she gasped from the impact. "We don't have time…"

"Then we'd better be quick."

"Mmm," she said as she sighed. "I love quick."

SEVEN

EMERGING FROM NICK'S house forty-five minutes later, they were blinded by camera flashes.

"What the hell?" Sam muttered, covering her eyes.

With his hand on her elbow, Nick guided her down the stairs. "Let us through," he said in a tone full of controlled fury as he pushed his way through the half-dozen photographers. "Goddamn it," he whispered.

Not wanting to give the photographers any more fodder, Sam tried to shake off his hand, but he just held on tighter.

They reached her car, and Nick took her keys to unlock it. As more flashes exploded around them, she looked up at him with a forced smile. "This is fun."

His face was set in an unreadable expression. "I'll call you. Good luck today."

"You, too." Without the kiss she would've liked to have had, Sam got into the car, and he closed the door. She watched him until he was safely inside his black BMW. Her cell phone rang. "Holland," she said without checking the caller ID.

"Are you okay?" Nick asked.

"Fabulous. You?"

"Terrific," he said with a laugh. "I'm sorry."

"For what?"

"All this attention. It'll die down. Eventually."

"I don't think it's going to."

"You sound pissed," he said.

"I'm more resigned than pissed."

"When are you going to mention that you told me so?"

"I'm saving that for when I *really* need it," she joked. The combination of his sexy voice and their teasing banter helped to restore her good mood.

"I'll look forward to that," he said. "See you later?"

"Yes, you will. Love you."

"Love you, too, babe. Be careful today."

"I always am."

Sam navigated her way through rush-hour traffic and arrived at the public safety building fifteen minutes later. Her good mood once again dissipated when she found Lieutenant Stahl waiting for her in the office that used to be his.

"I need to call maintenance." She flipped on the lights and hung her coat on a hook behind the door. "The rat traps they set in here clearly aren't working."

"You think you're so funny, don't you?"

The revolting wiggle of his double chin made her want to puke.

"Things not working out for you in the rat squad?" she asked, referring to his new post in the department's Internal Affairs Bureau.

"Actually, I'm settling right in." He bit a chunk of skin off his cuticle and spit it onto the floor.

Sam made a mental note to stay away from that corner of the office until it was fumigated.

"And you're my first order of business."

"I'm flattered."

His beady eyes narrowed. "You won't be so mouthy when your sordid affair with a witness gets you busted down to patrol."

She leaned on her desk to look him in the eye. "Three words, Lieutenant—Bring. It. On."

Fuming, he hauled his portly ass out of the chair. "Your wish is my command." He slapped a piece of paper on her desk. "Administrative hearing next week. Be there, and be ready to explain yourself."

"I'll look forward to it," she said, taking a shallow breath to short-circuit the pain grinding in her belly.

"Don't think your precious daddy can get you out of this one, Lieutenant." He stopped at the door and turned to leave her with a greasy smile. "And you'd better enjoy that title while you can. By the time I'm through with you, you'll be thankful for a night security job at a parking garage."

Sam let him have the last word because she couldn't have spoken if she had to. The moment she was alone she lowered herself into her chair and fought to breathe through the pain. This was *not* how she wanted to start her first day.

Freddie came to the door. "Getting settled, Lieutenant?" He took a closer look at her. "What's wrong?"

Sam made a huge effort to shake off the pain and anger. "Nothing. How are you? Good holiday?"

He stepped into the room and closed the door behind him. "You're pale as a ghost. What gives?"

She handed him the paper Stahl had left with her.

As Freddie glanced at it, his brows furrowed. "A summons to an IAB hearing? What the hell?"

"Nick."

"What about him?"

"Stahl's got Internal Affairs investigating me for hooking up with him in the middle of the O'Connor investigation."

"Are you serious? Without Nick's help we'd *still* be looking for O'Connor's killer."

"He was the one who found O'Connor dead, so technically I shagged a witness. Stahl's going to find a way to screw *me* for that."

"You don't have anything to worry about. Farnsworth and Malone will back you."

"They'll be forced to confirm that I became involved with Nick during the investigation." She ran her fingers over the hair she'd corralled into a clip for work. "God-damned Peter." Just the thought of her ex-husband made her stomach turn, but with disgust rather than pain. In a jealous rage, he'd planted crude bombs on her car and Nick's. When her car had exploded and injured them both, it also blew the lid off their secret relationship. "This is all his fault. Without him dicking with me, no one would've known about me and Nick until Thomas O'Connor was locked up and we were ready for them to know."

"It'll be fine, Sam. Stahl's got a beef with them giving you his command. That's all this is, and everyone will see right through it."

"I hope you're right," she said with zero confidence that he was. "Do me a favor and don't say anything about this to Nick or my dad."

"You aren't going to tell Nick?" Freddie asked, incredulous.

"Not if I can avoid it. He's got enough on his plate right now, and this'll just upset him."

"Won't he be more upset when he finds out you kept it from him?"

Sam's scowl answered for her. She'd handle this her way, and if Nick didn't like it, that was too damned bad. She wasn't about to start telling him how to run his career. "Are Gonzo and Arnold here yet?"

"They caught a sexual assault first thing. They're at

the George Washington E.R. taking a statement from the victim."

"Send them in the minute they get here. I want to know what they've got on Clarence Reese so far. I worked his name into conversation with my dad and got zilch. If he had contact with Reese, he doesn't remember it."

"Frustrating."

"To say the least. I just keep asking myself—why would Reese have all that stuff about the shooting if he wasn't involved somehow? Let's see what Gonzo and Arnold found out, and then we'll hit it ourselves this afternoon. I want to talk to Reese's mother and brother."

"You're the boss, L.T."

"It's going to be kind of weird around here until I figure things out. I'd understand if you wanted to partner with someone else—"

He held up his hand to stop her. "I'm all set with the partner I have."

"I'm planning to work some second and third shifts in the next few weeks to touch base with everyone. You don't want to do that."

"I'll work when my partner works."

She eyed him suspiciously. "Are you sucking up?"

"Always."

Taking another long look at him, she sized him up. "What's with you? You're all spiffed up today."

"Nothing," he said, but he blushed.

Sam stood up and walked around the desk for a closer look. Standing almost eye to eye with him, she turned on her most intimidating expression. "Tell me the truth—did you hook up with that Ginger chick from Nick's office?"

"No!"

Sniffing, she realized he was wearing cologne. "Something's up."

"I don't know what you're talking about." He stepped back from her. "Just because you're Little Miss Romance these days doesn't mean the rest of us are, too."

She raised an eyebrow. "Who said anything about romance?"

"I've got work to do," he huffed, his *GQ*-handsome face turning red again.

Oh, yes, something was *definitely* up.

"Let me know when you're ready to head out," he said as he beat feet to the safety of his cubicle in the detectives' pit.

"You'll be the first to know."

She watched him go, noting the pressed khakis and the untucked striped dress shirt that were wildly out of character for her denim-wearing, T-shirt–clad partner. *Does my little boy have a girlfriend?* Scratching at her chin, she decided to keep a very close eye on young Freddie.

Returning to her desk, she read and re-read the IAB summons. With a sigh, she put her aching head down on folded arms.

"I guess that answers my question about how your first day is going."

Jerking her head up, she found Captain Malone standing in her doorway. Her mentor was almost as tall as Nick with broad shoulders and gray hair. His warm brown eyes crinkled with mirth. Today he wore a crisp white uniform shirt and dark pants. His gold shield was pinned to his chest, his service weapon holstered to his hip.

"Is it time to go home yet?"

"Not even lunchtime, I'm afraid."

She rested her head against the back of the desk chair. "I've never understood the expression 'be careful what you wish for' until today."

He laughed.

"I may not be cut out for this," she confessed. "Not even an hour in the office and I'm already jonesing for the streets."

"No reason you can't do both."

She shot him a skeptical look.

"You're the *boss,* Lieutenant. Set things up the way they best suit you. Delegate, delegate, delegate."

Sam pondered that advice. "I'll go out of my mind if I can't work some cases."

He shrugged. "So pick and choose what you want."

For the first time since she arrived, Sam had reason to smile.

"It's called *command,* Lieutenant. Take command."

"Stahl did all his own admin," she reminded him.

"Stahl sucked, his people hated him and his commanders did, too. Don't take your cues from him. Pave your own path. Just don't let your shit roll uphill to me, and we'll be fine."

She reached for the paper Stahl had left, handed it to the captain and watched his mouth tighten with displeasure.

"Since I'm sure you won't forget what this says, do you mind if I take it to show the chief?"

"Be my guest."

"Try not to worry. Stuff like this tends to blow over more often than not."

"He's got a beef with how I ended up here," she said, gesturing to the office. "He can't prove the promotion was bogus, so he's going after me with the gift-wrapped package I handed him during O'Connor."

"Nick was never a suspect," Malone reminded her. "Worst possible outcome is a disciplinary letter in your jacket."

"It's still a slap."

"Put it out of your mind for now. I'll do what I can on my end."

"Thanks."

"Hope your day improves," Malone said with an encouraging smile as he left her to the piles of paper Stahl had bequeathed to her.

NICK'S FIRST ORDER of business was a meeting with Christina and Trevor.

"We need to talk about a deputy," Christina said, pulling a sheet of paper from her binder. "Here're a few people to consider."

Nick scanned the list of staffers. "I've already taken care of that."

Startled, Christina looked up at him. "Who?"

"Terry O'Connor."

She stared at him. "You're kidding, right?"

"Nope."

Her face went slack with shock. "But, I don't understand. Why?"

"Because he was groomed his whole life to hold this office, and I guarantee he'll bring more to the table than anyone on that impressive list of yours."

"This is you being loyal to the O'Connors, isn't it?"

Nick suppressed the burst of anger that shot through him. "This is me doing what I want to do, Christina."

"He's got a lot of baggage," Trevor observed.

"Luckily we're not running for anything," Nick said. "What's next?"

They exchanged glances.

"What?"

Trevor tugged a paper from his pile and held it up for Nick to see.

"Son of a bitch," Nick muttered as he got a look at

a printout of the photos taken that morning outside his house. "They're already online?"

"On the *Post* site and the *Star*'s."

"Great," he said, imagining Sam's reaction to the suggestive photos.

"We've got some new polling data in, too," Trevor said with a nervous look at Christina. "Your approval rating in the Commonwealth is hovering right around seventy-eight percent. Unfortunately, the other twenty-two percent tend to be in the conservative, family-values column, and they don't approve of this." He referred to the picture.

"Well, that's too bad." Nick's jaw felt tight with tension. "Again, I'll remind you that I'm not running for anything."

"No, but that moral minority can make the next year awfully unpleasant for us," Trevor said.

"It'll be a distraction, Nick, er, I mean, Senator," Christina said. "Sorry."

"This subject is off-limits, people," Nick said.

"You could take care of the whole thing," Trevor said hesitantly, "if you, you know, married her."

"I can't even get her to officially move in with me. She's not ready for that, and she's certainly not ready for the *M* word. Not after what she just went through with her ex-husband."

"I know you don't want to hear this, Senator," Trevor said, "but your relationship with her is going to pull the focus off the issues. All I'm saying is if you could convince her to marry you, it'd take the wind out of the media's sails. Even an engagement would make things a lot easier."

"He's right," Christina added. "Once the relationship is legitimate, it loses its appeal."

"Are you guys finished analyzing my personal life?" Nick asked.

They had the good grace to at least squirm a little.

He leaned forward to make sure he had their full attention. "The relationship is *already* legitimate, and I couldn't care less what anyone thinks of it. Is that clear?"

"We get it," Christina said. "All we're asking is that you think about what Trevor said. If you're heading toward marriage, sooner would be better than later."

"You've met Sam," Nick said, amused by the ridiculous conversation. "How do you think she'd take the idea of marriage for political expediency?"

"If I were to guess," Christina said, "I'd say not well."

"Precisely. So can we please drop this and move on to what we're here for?"

Clearing her throat, Christina consulted her notes. "You're set to meet with Senator Martin on the phone at ten to discuss getting O'Connor-Martin back on the floor after the recess. Also, Senator Cook's office called, and he'd like to have lunch with you today if you're free."

"That's fine," Nick said, anxious to meet with the senior senator from Virginia, a fellow Democrat, as soon as possible.

"Finally, we have studio time booked this evening so you can record the welcome message they play in the Virginia airports."

"I remember John doing that years ago," Nick said, smiling at the memory of John fumbling through about fifty takes to get the one-minute message nailed. The pain of his loss resurfaced with surprising ferocity, reminding Nick of how he had gotten there. He took a deep breath and forced himself to focus. "Anything else?"

"You've had a slew of interview requests," Trevor said, handing him a two-page list of reporters.

"I'll take a look," Nick said.

"Trevor, would you give us a minute, please?" Christina asked.

"Sure." Trevor got up and left the room, closing the door behind him.

Nick eyed his aide warily. "If you're going to start in on me about Sam again—"

"No," she said, twisting her hands in a rare show of nerves. "I was going to ask you if you'd mind, or if it would be weird at all or, um…"

Laughing, Nick said, "Spit it out, will you?"

"Sam's friend, Tommy Gonzales, asked me out. I just wondered if you'd have any problem with that."

As he tried to decide whether or not he was in the mood to mess with her, Nick sat back in his chair and studied her. "Why would I mind?"

"Two reasons—one, I'm not exactly Sam's favorite person."

"She has no beef with you, Chris. Yes, she hassled you during the investigation, but nothing about that was personal."

"Felt kind of personal to me."

Since he couldn't argue with that, he didn't try. "What's the second reason?"

"John," she said softly. "It's only been a few weeks. It's too soon for me to be thinking about going out with someone else."

Nick stood up and came around the desk. "You were a loyal and faithful friend to him. I know you had strong feelings for him, but you weren't a couple as much as you might've wished otherwise. I can't see how going out on a date would be inappropriate."

She brightened. "Thanks." With a wicked smile, she

added, "Sam's going to flip her lid when she hears I'm going out with Tommy."

"Probably."

"Why does that make it even *more* exciting?"

"You're being nice to her," he reminded her.

"Absolutely," she said, smiling over her shoulder as she left the room. "Always."

EIGHT

At noon, Senator Robert Cook escorted Nick into the Senate dining room. "So glad you could join me today, Nick."

He was nervous in the company of Cook, a senatorial institution. Sure, he had worked closely with Cook's staff for many years but he'd had limited contact with the man himself. Dining alone with him was certainly unprecedented. "Thanks for asking me."

"It's a good chance for us to get better acquainted while we're out of session," Cook said in a deep southern Virginian drawl.

They were shown to a table in the ornate room where only one other table was occupied.

"Southern Comfort, neat, darlin'," Cook said to the waitress.

She smiled. "Sweet tea, Senator?"

"Oh, all right," Cook said with a hangdog expression that made Nick grin.

"Same for me," Nick said.

"Millie's told everyone about my damned blood pressure," Cook grumbled about his wife. "Can't get a decent drink anywhere in this town."

Nick smiled at his dismay.

"You've gotta try the Senate bean soup," Cook said.

Nick ached when he remembered how much John had enjoyed the traditional soup. "I've had it before. Senator O'Connor loved it."

"Yes," Cook said. "He did."

When the waitress reappeared with their drinks, they ordered two bowls of the soup along with turkey clubs.

When he shook his head with dismay, Cook's mane of snow-white hair barely moved. "Such a terrible shame what happened to him. I know I don't have to tell you."

"No, sir."

Cook squeezed a lemon into his tea and stirred, his every movement and gesture signaling his utter comfort in his own skin. Nick couldn't help but be a little intimidated. "What's that saying?" Cook asked. "When life gives you lemons, make lemonade?"

"Where I grew up in Massachusetts we say you squeeze them on a lobster."

Cook's lined face lifted into a smile. "I like that. Very good." He took a long drink from his glass. "Life has handed you some lemons lately, Nick. It's time to squeeze them on a lobster."

"That's my plan. In fact, I talked to Senator Martin earlier, and between the two of us, we're going to call every member and try to get O'Connor-Martin back on the floor as the Senate's first order of business after the recess."

Cook nodded his approval. "I hate to say it, but we need to play the grief card and get it done before people move on and forget about O'Connor's untimely death."

Nick was quite certain he would never forget John O'Connor's untimely death but chose not to say so, knowing the older man was speaking from decades of political experience—and that he was right. It wouldn't take long for official Washington to forget that John had once graced the halls of power. The time to act on the landmark immigration legislation he had cosponsored was right now.

Leaning in, Cook lowered his voice and seemed to choose his words carefully. "You've only got a year, Nick. I'd like to help you make it count."

"I'd appreciate that, Senator."

"Call me Bob. But as I was saying, the time will go quickly, and I'm sure you're interested in making as big an impact as possible."

Nick ate the flavorful soup and nodded in agreement. "Of course."

"I think it would be best if you just followed my lead, son. Let me blaze the path, make it easier for you."

Nick rested his spoon in the bowl and wiped his mouth with the white cloth napkin. He might be younger and he might be green, but he recognized condescension when he heard it and wondered if Cook had tried to pull the same thing on John. If so, Nick hadn't heard about it. "I'm afraid I don't follow you, Bob," he said, deciding to play dumb in case he was reading it wrong.

"Well, let's face it, you don't have time to strike out on some independent path all your own. We're both serving the same constituency. If you let me call the shots, you come out looking good, the people are taken care of and the party gets what it needs from both of us."

Nope. Not reading it wrong. Swallowing his anger, Nick forced himself to stay quiet and let the other man continue to dig the hole.

"Take this nomination of Julian Sinclair, for instance."

"What about it?"

"He's a poor choice for the high court. Way too far out to the left. I don't know what Nelson was thinking." Cook scowled. "He's put us in a terrible spot—what choice do we have but to confirm him? After all, we can't hand the Republicans that kind of easy victory."

"Sinclair's a respected jurist. I think it's a wise choice."

"He's a divisive and inflammatory son of a bitch," Cook snapped, his amiable expression hardening as it seemed to dawn on him all of a sudden that Nick had a mind of his own and fully intended to use it. "Surely you can't tell me you support this nomination."

"I more than support it. In addition to being a good friend of mine, Julian is a respected attorney, and I have nothing but the utmost regard for him."

Cook scowled. "Wait 'til the protestors get ahold of him. I hope he's watching 'his back. Someone might take a shot at him."

"Is that a threat?" Nick asked, appalled by the implication.

"Don't be ridiculous. Of course it isn't a threat." Cook took a long drink of his tea before turning hard eyes on Nick. "Son, you haven't been around long enough to know how much damage a nomination like this can do to the Senate. It'll split us right down the middle, and the ill will could infect the entire session."

Nick could tell he startled the older man when he stood up and dropped his napkin on the table next to his half-eaten bowl of soup. "I appreciate you laying out the ground rules for me, Senator, but I'm fairly certain I've been around just long enough to know how to get the most out of my year in office." He took a step away from the table before he turned back. "Oh, and you can feel free to call me Nick or Senator, but I'm not your son. You have a good day now."

SAM STOOD IN Clarence Reese's bedroom, staring at the photo of him with his wife and children. They had scoured the city and found no sign of the man who'd slaughtered his family. If Reese's mother or brother knew where he was hiding out, they weren't talking. Until they located him, Sam could only wonder what involvement Reese had in her father's shooting.

"Are we done here?" Freddie asked from the doorway. "This place gives me the creeps."

Taking another long last look at the man in the picture, Sam turned to her partner. "We're missing something."

"Crime scene took this place apart." The disheveled condition of the house backed up the statement. "There's nothing else here."

She rested her hand over her gut, her most trusted ally when it came to situations like this. "There's something. I know it."

"What do you want me to do? Where should I look?"

"That I *don't* know," she said, feeling defeated. "I wish I did."

"Sam, listen, maybe it's just a coincidence that Reese had those clippings—"

"You don't believe that any more than I do."

The clatter of metal in the alley behind the house caught their attention.

"What was that?" Freddie whispered.

Sam drew her weapon and gestured for him to do the same. She pointed him toward the front door and headed for the back of the house.

Moving slowly, her gun leading the way, Sam crept toward the back door. Another clatter rang through the alley, announcing the presence of a cat, a raccoon or a foolish perp returning to the scene of a crime. Sam hoped and prayed it was the latter. The door swung open.

"Freeze!" Sam caught a brief glimpse of Reese's startled face before he turned and bolted. "Freeze, police!" She took off after him, down the back steps and through a fetid alley stacked three feet deep on both sides with trash. Normally, she might've taken a shot at him, but he was no good to her dead. He had information she desperately needed. Hoping Freddie would cut Reese off at the other end of the alley, Sam chased after him, her thighs burning from the exertion, her lungs tight from the cold air pumping in and out.

Reese looked back, saw she was gaining on him and fired an erratic shot over his shoulder. The bullet whizzed past Sam's right ear, fueling her rage and her desire to catch him. *That might've worked on my dad, you son of a bitch, but it's going to take more than a cheap shot to take me down.* Running on adrenaline, she jumped over the bag of trash he threw in her path, came down on a patch of black ice and went flying.

Her chin took the full brunt of the fall. Sam howled with pain and tried to get her unarmed hand down to break the second half of the fall. Elbows and knees connected with hard pavement. She looked up in time to see Reese round the corner at the end of the alley. Freddie was nowhere in sight.

For a long moment, Sam lay there assessing her injuries and trying to catch her breath. The cold air made breathing painful, but that pain was nothing compared to the burn in her chin, knees and elbows. Forcing herself to move, she got up and called for backup to start a canvas of the neighborhood. Clearly, Reese hadn't gone far after butchering his family.

With each step more agonizing than the last, she made her way slowly to the end of the alley. Not seeing Freddie, she moved around to the front of the house to find him slapping cuffs on the arms of a stocky, dark-haired man. Her heart began to race. Had he gotten Reese after all? But when he turned the cuffed man around, Sam could see that it wasn't Reese but his brother, Hector, whom they'd interviewed the day before.

"What've you got?" Sam asked Freddie as she limped up to them.

"What happened to you? You're hurt."

"I'm okay. I fell on some ice chasing Reese. No biggie. What's up with him?"

"You have blood pouring from your chin, and you say no biggie?"

Sam wiped away the blood with an impatient sweep of her hand and gave him a look that said he'd better start spilling on Reese's brother.

"Caught this guy coming in the front. He said he needed to get a few things, and he has every right to go into his brother's house."

"It's a crime scene," Sam reminded Hector Reese. "You were told to stay out of there."

"My mama wanted some of the kids' things," he said in a surly tone, glaring at her. "This is hard on her."

"If that's so, why'd you bring your brother with you? The same brother you told us earlier today you couldn't find? The same brother who killed those kids your mama is grieving over."

"I didn't bring him here," Hector retorted. "And he didn't kill no one."

"Oh, so we're supposed to believe it's a coincidence that you and your brother were sneaking into the house at the same time?" Glancing at Freddie, Sam added, "You buying that, Cruz?"

"Not for one second, Lieutenant."

"Got anything you want to tell us, Reese?"

Hector looked down at the ground, his posture tight with hostility.

"I'll take that as a no." Sam gestured to one of the newly arrived officers. "Take Mr. Reese to HQ and book him."

"On what?" Hector cried. "This is my brother's house!"

"Tampering with a crime scene, aiding and abetting a fugitive from justice."

"I told you! I *don't know* where he is!"

Sam got right up in his face. *"I told you.* I don't believe you."

"Cunt cop," he muttered under his breath.

"What's that, Hector? I didn't hear you."

He glared at her.

"Add a disorderly conduct charge to that list," Sam said to the officer leading Hector to a cruiser. "Oh, and if you want to tell us where your brother's hiding out, I'd be happy to talk to the U.S. Attorney about lesser charges for you."

"Fuck you."

"I try to be nice and it just gets thrown back in my face," Sam said to Freddie. "That hurts my feelings."

"If you had feelings, I'd be sorry for you."

Sam snorted. "Good one, Cruz. You're getting better."

"I work on it in my spare time." He glanced at Sam. "We should hit the E.R. and get that looked at."

"I've got bandages at home." Or at least she hoped Nick did. She took a long look around. "Reese is hiding out close by."

"Wonder what he left behind in the house that was important enough for him to risk coming back."

"I want twenty-four-hour surveillance. Tomorrow, we're getting crime scene back here to find out what he was after. And then we'll take down the tape and set a trap. He came back once. Whatever he's after, he'll be back for it again. Next time, we'll be ready."

MUCH LATER THAT night, after what seemed like at *least* sixty takes to nail the recording that welcomed visitors to Virginia airports, Nick let himself into the Capitol Hill house he was due to close on the next day. He was greeted by throbbing music coming from the second floor. Smiling, he leaned back against the front door. He had learned in the past few weeks that Sam had a passion for all things Bon Jovi, and volume was key to her relationship with the band.

Tilting his head, he listened intently and recognized the song "Make a Memory," a particular favorite of hers. Even though Nick was anxious to see her, he took a moment to look around at the vast emptiness of the first floor, realizing he felt more at home in this house he didn't even officially own yet than he ever had anywhere else.

Doesn't take a rocket scientist to figure out why, he thought, as he dumped his coat, work bag and keys in the kitchen and headed upstairs to her. The music grew louder the closer he got to the bedroom. Jon Bon Jovi's distinctive voice soared through the melodic chorus. In the doorway, Nick stopped to study the scene. Sam was asleep in bed, a book folded over her chest, every light in the room on and the music set to ear-splitting.

Shaking his head with amusement and the ongoing delight at finding her in his bed each night, he bent to turn off the combination alarm clock and iPod docking station she had shown up with a few days ago. He'd been encouraged by her moving something of hers into the new house until it dawned on him that, other than a toothbrush, it was the only thing she had brought.

He took a closer look at her and noticed the bandage on her chin and the bruises surrounding it. Hurt again. His heart ached and his mind raced when he allowed himself to think about the many ways she risked herself every day. The idea that she could one day be taken from him without any warning chilled him to his bones, and suddenly he needed to be close to her.

Draping his suit over the footboard, he shut off every light but one, hit the bathroom and crawled into bed. When he saw what she'd been reading, he laughed softly: *Congress for Dummies*. Gently, he attempted to lift the book off her chest.

She stirred and studied him with sleepy eyes.

He leaned over to kiss her. "Sorry, babe," he said, brushing the hair off her forehead.

"You're late," she said, her voice hoarse and sexy from sleep.

"I tried to call, but I guess you couldn't hear the phone over Bon Jovi."

She flashed him a sheepish grin. "Sorry."

Trailing a finger lightly over the bandage on her chin, he studied her face. "What happened?"

"Me versus black ice. The ice won."

He winced.

She tugged two badly bruised and scraped elbows out from underneath the comforter.

"Ouch." Dropping soft kisses on each elbow, he said, "Did you have X-rays?"

"Nah. Nothing broken." She made a brave attempt to bend each arm to prove her point.

"Stop. That's making me hurt just watching it. Anything else?"

"Knees. Same as the elbows."

"Samantha, my poor baby." He brushed a soft kiss over her lips. "Did you put something on the road rash?"

"Celia fixed me up."

"So this was really just you and some ice?"

"Uh-huh," she said, looking away.

"You can either tell me the truth or I'll tickle it out

of you, which, in light of your injuries, might not be as fun as usual."

"You wouldn't do that to an officer wounded in the line of duty."

He raised his fingers in a menacing claw over her ribs. "Try me."

"Fine! I was chasing Reese. He came back to his house when Freddie and I were doing another walk-through."

"Without backup?" Nick asked, alarmed.

"I had Freddie. Do you want to hear this or not?"

He gestured for her to go ahead, and she told him the rest.

"He *fired* at you?"

"It was a wild shot. Missed by a mile."

Nick put his head down face-first into his pillow and groaned.

"I heard that, and you made me tell you."

Turning on his side, he faced her. "You wouldn't have, though, would you?"

Her eyebrows knitted with confusion. "What?"

"You wouldn't have told me if I hadn't forced it out of you."

"I don't like to upset you, and my job can be upsetting. I'm fine, so what's the point in dumping it on you and getting you all wound up?"

Reaching for her hand, he laced his fingers through hers. "The point is I want to know. If you get shot at or hurt in any way, I want to know. Deal?"

"You promise not to freak? That was kind of an issue with Peter. I never told him anything because he always freaked out. But then he would find out from someone else, and that was always worse."

"I can't promise not to be upset, but I won't freak. At least not at you."

"Or anyone else from the MPD."

He hesitated.

"Nick…"

"Or anyone else from the MPD, unless—"

She silenced him with a kiss. "No unless. We have a deal."

"Where'd you get this?" He held up the book she'd been reading and couldn't believe it when his brave, competent cop blushed.

"You weren't supposed to see that." She took the book from him and dropped it to the floor.

Careful to avoid her injured chin, he gently turned her face to force her to look at him and raised an eyebrow in question.

Sighing in defeat, she said, "I've lived in this city all my life, just a mile from the Capitol, but I don't really know what goes on there."

"I could tell you."

"I wanted to be able to talk to you about it," she said with a shy glance that staggered him. "I wanted to know what your day would be like."

His heart galloped in his chest as he brushed his lips over hers. "I love you," he whispered and was thrilled when her mouth opened under his to welcome him in. Her injured arms encircled his neck, and Nick sank into the kiss. "So what did you learn?" he asked many minutes later as he sprinkled kisses over her face.

"That a filibuster is a technique used to prolong debate in order to stop or postpone a vote," she said with a proud smile. "I've always wondered what that was." Her smile transformed into the coy grin he loved so much. "Do you think you'll ever get to filibuster?"

"I don't know," he said, laughing. "I suppose if desperate times call for desperate measures…"

With an exaggerated shudder, she said, "Oh, that's *so* sexy, imagining my man hijacking the Senate floor with his eloquent rhetoric. But you know what's *not* sexy?"

Reveling in being referred to as her man, he nuzzled her neck. "What's that?"

Shifting onto her side to face him, she rested her hand on his chest. "Seersucker Thursday," she said, wrinkling her nose.

"What?" He feigned offense. "You don't think I'll look hot in my seersucker suit?"

The hand caressing his chest stilled. "You aren't serious."

"I want the full experience, babe. Besides, it's a tradition, a harbinger of spring."

"Seersucker is seriously *not* sexy."

"It will be on me."

"A little full of yourself, aren't you?"

"I'm just saying." He hooked his leg over her hip to tug her in close to him.

"I won't be seen with you."

Cupping her breast, he rolled her nipple between his fingers. "Yes, you will."

"No way."

"Other than getting shot at, how was your first day, Lieutenant?"

As he toyed with her nipple, her eyes fluttered closed. "Fine. Nothing special. And don't try to change the subject."

"You want to talk about Congress some more?"

"Just one more thing." She rolled onto her back and brought him with her.

"What?" he asked, breathless with wanting her as he hovered over her, mindful of her injuries.

With a big grin, she raised her hips and pressed against his erection. "Fill her, buster."

Laughing, he did as she asked.

NINE

Late on Friday night, Freddie brought his battered Mustang to a stop at the curb in front of Elin's apartment building and cut the engine. His heart beat fast with nerves and desire. All he had to do was send the signal and he could spend the night in her bed. But now that "the moment" had arrived, he was filled with uncertainty. The decision that had seemed so clear a few days ago was back in play. Twenty-nine years of celibacy had come down to this.

She turned to him and rested her hand on his arm. "Do you want to come in?"

Studying her, thoughts and images of all kinds spiraled through his mind and landed in his lap in a surge of lust.

"Freddie?"

"Can I take a rain check?" He couldn't believe the words were coming out of his mouth. "Sam's got us working funky shifts so she can touch base with everyone. I'm wiped, and I have to work again at seven."

"I've been reading about her and the senator in the paper."

"She *loves* all the attention they're getting," he said, rolling his eyes.

"I can imagine."

Freddie hadn't expected to enjoy being with Elin as much as he did. He found her easy to talk to, engaging and funny. She had caught on right away that he had come around the gym looking for more than personal training, and when he suggested dinner, she enthusiastically agreed. He'd spent most of the night trying to rein in his raging hormones. He hadn't even kissed her yet despite the signals that she'd be receptive.

He knew if he touched her he wouldn't stop until he had all of her.

"Freddie?"

"Hmm?" He glanced at her and found her watching him. In that moment, he remembered learning during the O'Connor investigation that she had a heart with a Cupid's arrow tattooed on her left breast and her nipples were pierced. His cock twitched, and he shifted to ease the ache.

She reached for him and crushed her lips to his.

Startled, his eyes flew open to find hers closed as she ran her tongue over his bottom lip. He sank his hand into her hair to tug her closer. Her fingers danced over his chest, unbuttoning his shirt and tunneling in until skin reached skin. When she scraped her fingernail over his nipple, he almost came in his pants.

Tearing his lips free of hers, he caught her hand. "Elin."

"Yes?" she asked with a sexy grin as she ran her free hand up over his thigh to cup his straining erection.

Freddie swallowed hard and fought to keep his mind off the fire burning in his lap. He had never been with a woman who was so brazen, but that was what had attracted him to her in the first place.

She stroked him through his jeans.

He let his head fall back against the seat in surrender.

"Are you *sure* you can't come in?" she asked, sliding her tongue along his neck.

"Got to work," he said through clenched teeth. Locked in a haze of desire and temptation, he was unaware of her freeing him from his pants until the cold air hitting his fevered skin jolted him out of his reverie. "Whoa."

The words died on his lips when she bent to take him into her mouth. Oh, *God*. He figured he should at least try to stop her, but couldn't seem to get the neurons in his brain to form the words he needed. This was going to be fast. And *damn* if the woman didn't know exactly where to squeeze, to lick, to suck.

"Elin, honey," he said, his voice full of warning.

As if he hadn't spoken, she took him even deeper, and he climaxed with a roar that surprised him. His breath came out in puffy white clouds as he fought to recover from the intense orgasm.

She sat up and licked her lips, looking quite pleased with herself. "Too bad you have to work so early," she said with a playful pout.

"Yeah," he gasped. "Too bad."

"Next time?"

"Sure," he said, still having trouble catching his breath. He glanced at her and rested his hand on her leg. "What about you?"

She smiled. "I can take care of myself. Don't worry."

Something about the way she said that stirred his recently satisfied libido back to life as he imagined her "taking care of herself." He released a ragged deep breath, feeling like he was in *way* over his head here. "I should go."

Leaning over, she touched her lips to his. "I had fun tonight. Thanks for dinner."

He caressed her baby-soft cheek. "My pleasure."

"Call me?"

Freddie nodded, knowing he should walk her in but not sure his legs would follow his directions. He watched her until she was safely inside and then zipped up his pants and started the car. For a long time, he sat there trying to collect himself before he shifted the car into gear and drove home.

WITH THE MEDIA clamoring for justice for the murdered family and Sam pursuing her own personal agenda, they tore apart the Reese home the next day. Hours later, the house lay in tatters, and the only interesting thing they'd found was ten thousand dollars in a metal box in the basement.

"At least we know now what he was after," Freddie said, referring to the fat wad of hundred-dollar bills.

"He's desperate and on the run," Sam said. "He needs money to get out of the city, and this is probably all he has. I'd bet my badge that he'll be back for it."

"I talked to Gonzo. They've scoured the neighborhood, but no one's seen him."

"Or they're protecting him."

"Why would they protect a guy who did what he did to his family?"

"Who knows? Neighborhood dynamics and loyalties run deep."

Freddie's handsome face shifted into a scowl. "I guess no one was loyal to Tiffany and her kids."

"She didn't grow up here. I read that she moved here from Pennsylvania seven years ago."

"Then she had the good fortune to meet Reese."

"Yeah."

"There's not much more we can do here, Lieutenant."

Sam took a hard look around the messy living room. "I know."

"You want to split?"

"I'm going to hang for a while. See if he comes back."

"You can't stay here by yourself," he protested.

She rested her hand on the weapon holstered to her hip. "I won't be by myself."

"I'm not leaving until you do." He plopped down in a chair and crossed his arms defiantly.

"Suit yourself." She took another chair and put her feet up on the dilapidated coffee table. After a long period of silence, she fixed her eyes on her partner, noticing once again his above-average attire. "Since we have some time to kill, why don't you tell me about your girlfriend?"

"What girlfriend?" he sputtered, his blush giving him away. "I don't know what you're talking about."

"Uh-huh." Sam settled into the chair, warming up to bust his chops. "How about we examine the evidence?"

"Here's a big idea—let's not."

NICK RUSHED THROUGH a quick shower and shave while reviewing his mental checklist for the dinner party one final time. The past week had been beyond chaotic. He'd closed on the new place, moved in and focused all his energy on getting the downstairs portion of the house ready for tonight's gathering—on top of contacting half the senate to rally support for John's immigration bill.

The second floor was a maze of boxes and unassembled furniture. He expected Laine would want to see the upstairs, but she'd understand about the mess.

Nick hated disorder. He hated chaos, and more than anything, he hated that Sam seemed to be avoiding him. While pursuing Clarence Reese with relentless determination, she'd also been working crazy shifts as she attempted to connect with all the HQ detectives who now answered to her. Other than a few rushed phone calls, Nick hadn't had any time with her since the night he discovered her reading *Congress for Dummies* in his bed a week ago. She had been sleeping at her dad's house because, as she said, she didn't want to disturb him with her middle-of-the-night comings and goings. He hadn't succeeded in convincing her that he *wanted* to be disturbed by her.

"Maybe I'm the dummy," he muttered to his reflection.

He knew she was uncomfortable about acting as his cohost at the dinner party for Julian, which was why he'd limited the guest list to Julian, Graham and Laine, and refrained from discussing it with her during their brief conversations. Caterers had handled the food, a florist had taken care of the flowers and he had set what he considered to be a rather elegant table for the five of them. All she had to do was show up. He glanced at his watch, dismayed by how close she was cutting it.

That he had to wonder if she was going to show up at all flat out pissed him off. It wasn't like he asked so much of her. *No, you've only asked just about everything of her, and you're unhappy because she's not ready to give it to you.*

As he tugged a burgundy cashmere V-neck sweater over his head, Sam came flying into the room, her cheeks red from cold and exertion. "Sorry, sorry, sorry."

"For what?" he asked, working to keep the frustration out of his tone.

"I'm running late. Today was the funeral for Reese's family, and the day got away from me."

He turned to her and was wowed by the beaded top she wore over formfitting black dress pants. "How was the funeral?"

"A total horror show," she said with a sigh as she used the mirror on his dresser to fix her hair, which she had left down the way he liked it best. "We interviewed brothers, sisters, friends, cousins. No one ever heard Reese talk about my dad. And no sign of him, either."

"I'm sorry, Sam."

She shrugged. "Another dead end." Rolling her head on her shoulders, she added, "The longer he's in the wind the less likely we are to find him."

"You should talk to your dad about what you found at Reese's house. He's stronger than you think, and he might be able to shed some light."

"You're right. I was thinking the same thing earlier." She turned from the mirror to face him. "The house looks great. I can't believe how fast you got it done. You've even got pictures on the walls!"

"Any of it can be changed if you don't like it."

"What's not to like?"

He bit his tongue to keep from telling her he didn't like the way she was avoiding him. Instead, he said, "You look gorgeous."

"Thank you." She reached up to adjust the collar of his shirt. "You're not looking too bad yourself." Going up on tiptoes, she planted a kiss on him. "I've missed you."

Because he couldn't help himself, he looped his arms around her waist and brought her in close to him. "Me, too."

"What's wrong?"

"Nothing."

"Something," she said, stealing his usual line.

He shook his head. "Thanks for coming tonight."

She looked up at him, studying him. "Of course I came tonight. It's important to you, but I wish you'd tell me what's wrong. Are you mad because we haven't seen much of each other—"

Bending his head, he captured her mouth in a deep, passionate kiss.

"—the last few days," she muttered against his lips,

her eyes closed, her cheeks flushed anew with color that had nothing to do with cold or exertion.

"If you lived here with me, we'd see more of each other."

"Nick."

He rested his forehead on hers. "I know. You don't want to talk about that." Releasing her, he went to find his shoes.

"You're pissed. I knew it."

"I'm not pissed." He shoved his feet into loafers. "I'm frustrated."

Sam nibbled on her bottom lip. "I'm sorry."

"Stop apologizing to me," he snapped, his tone sharper than he'd intended.

She came to him and slid her hands up over his chest. "Why? It's my fault. You've offered me so much, and I'm holding back. I know that bothers you."

"I want this to work so damned bad," he said, surprised by the urgency he heard in his own voice. "I want it more than anything."

"I do, too." Her eyes implored him to believe her. "We knew it was going to be crazy."

"I don't want to go days without seeing you. I can't stand that. I need you, Samantha."

"Do you think it's *not* working?" She massaged his shoulders. "Is that why you're so tense?"

"It's working," he said but hardly managed to convince himself.

Her hands fell from his shoulders. She wrapped her arms around herself protectively, a gesture that tugged at his heart. "Wow. You're really wound up. I'm sorry I had to work so much this week."

"You're apologizing again."

Her eyes flashed with anger and what might've been

panic. "Then tell me what I'm supposed to say, Nick! What do you need to hear? That I love you? You know I do. If you're doubting that—"

"I'm not."

"Ugh!" She threw her hands into the air. "This is exactly why I haven't gotten involved with anyone since I split with Peter. I can't deal with this!"

A blast of fear charged through Nick, leaving him staggered in its wake. "I'm the one who should be sorry. I've been burning the candle this week, and I'm fried." He ran a hand through hair still damp from the shower. "I don't know why I'm taking it out on you."

"Do I need to be worried?" she asked, her face a study in vulnerability, which was in sharp contrast to her usual confident, cocky demeanor. He hated that he had given her reason to question him—to question *them*.

He went to her and hugged her fiercely. "No, babe. No worries. I just need some time with you."

She clung to him. "I'm off until tomorrow night at eleven. I'm all yours."

"Good," he said, his voice husky with emotion and relief as he held her close to him. How had this even happened? How had he managed to give them both reason to doubt the only thing in his life that truly mattered?

The doorbell rang downstairs.

He released her reluctantly. "Ready?"

"As ready as I'll ever be."

"I love you," he said, kissing her hand, "and I'm really glad you're here."

"So am I."

TEN

RATTLED BY THE odd conversation with Nick, Sam did her best to put on her party face as they greeted the O'Connors and Julian Sinclair, who arrived at the same time. She was still getting used to the warmth the O'Connors directed her way simply because she was with Nick.

He slipped a possessive arm around her and introduced her to Julian, who held her hand between both of his. "It's such a pleasure to meet you, Sam. I've read all about you in the paper."

She rolled her eyes. "Oh, joy."

"What did today's article say? 'Not since Jack and Jackie has Washington been so riveted by a political couple'?"

"Thanks, Julian." Nick shook hands with him. "She really needed to hear that again."

Julian laughed. "You're looking good, Senator. Power becomes you."

Sam was amused by Nick's befuddled reaction to the compliment. Julian was shorter than he appeared on television, his forehead barely reaching Nick's shoulder. He had smooth skin, silver hair and a warm smile. *Erudite* was the word that came to mind as she watched him interact with the others. Classy, elegant and right at home with Nick and the O'Connors—so at home, in fact, that Sam felt like an outsider looking in at a family reunion.

In the kitchen, Graham opened a bottle of merlot. "It's so great to have you in town for a while, Julian."

"I was so sorry I couldn't be here for John's service," Julian said. "I was in Sacramento for a wedding the day before the funeral. If I hadn't been the best man, I'd have been on the first plane."

"We got your lovely note." Laine patted his arm. "And the flowers, too. You were there in spirit."

"What's the latest with Thomas's case?" Julian asked as he accepted a glass of wine from Graham and followed the others into the living room.

Sam opened a bottle of pinot grigio and poured herself a glass before she joined them.

"They're exploring an insanity plea," Graham said.

"Not a bad idea," Julian said.

Graham's face tightened with grief. "It was my fault for keeping Patricia and Thomas hidden away for all those years. I forced John to live a double life and to lie to them. When Thomas found out there'd been other women in his father's life, he just snapped."

"You did what you thought was right, Graham," Julian said. "Those were different times. You would've taken a hard political hit if people found out that your teenage son had fathered a child—not to mention what it would've done to John's future."

"Did you know?" Nick asked Julian. "About Thomas?"

Julian glanced at Graham. "I did."

Expelling a long deep breath, Nick sat back against the sofa.

Sam knew Nick was still dealing with leftover shock and disbelief that John had kept his son hidden from even his closest friend and most trusted aide.

"He was one of the few," Graham said quickly, tuning

in to Nick's dismay. "I didn't know what to do, so I asked a couple of close friends for their advice."

"I agreed with what you did, so that makes me partly culpable, I suppose," Julian said, swirling the wine around in his glass, a rueful expression on his face.

"There's no point in second-guessing," Laine said, sending the message to the others that she had heard enough about the circumstances of her youngest child's death.

"You're absolutely right, Laine," Julian said, turning his attention to Sam. "So you're a detective."

"And a recently promoted lieutenant," Nick added with a proud smile.

"Congratulations," Julian said. "A wonderful accomplishment."

"Thank you."

"How's the new job, Sam?" Laine asked with what appeared to be genuine interest.

"Chaotic."

"She did a first-class job on John's case," Graham said. "First-class."

With a small smile to acknowledge the compliment, she said, "Thanks."

"So your sister-in-law is getting as many headlines as you are lately," Laine said to Julian.

"Indeed," Julian replied with a chagrined expression. "She does have her opinions."

"I never knew she was so hateful," Graham said. "To say what she does about homosexuals, Jews and African-Americans, and on television, no less. I heard they're giving her a prime-time show. A whole hour of hate and venom."

"It's shameful," Julian said. "I never have understood

what my brother sees in her. From the day he met her, he's been completely besotted. Did you hear the latest?"

"About her book?" Graham asked.

Julian nodded. "It'll be out in two weeks. An update on a book her minister father did years ago on how homosexuals will be the downfall of the republic."

Nick released a low whistle. "Wow."

"She's on a roll, lately," Julian said.

"Do you ever hear from them?" Laine asked.

Julian shook his head. "I haven't spoken to either of them in years."

"Were you surprised to be nominated to the Court?" Sam asked, sensing they were all anxious to change the subject.

"Well, since David warned me I'd be at the top of his list the first chance he got, I can't say I was all that surprised to get the call."

"David did, did he?" Sam wasn't sure where this edge to her voice was coming from. She chalked it up to the mood Nick had put her in with his odd behavior earlier.

Nick directed a raised eyebrow her way.

"I'm sorry," she said in a more conciliatory tone. "I'm still getting used to being around people who call the president of the United States by his first name."

"I call him Mr. President when I'm with him," Julian clarified.

"I've seen your face on the front page as much as I've seen my own lately," Sam said.

"We knew the nomination would generate some controversy," Julian acknowledged.

"Protestors will be descending on this town in the next few days," Graham added.

"We had a meeting yesterday about crowd control," Sam said. "They're expecting up to a million people."

"That many?" Julian said, seeming taken aback.

"You're surprised?" Sam asked.

Nick's face was set in a stony, unreadable expression Sam hadn't seen before.

"I knew there'd be some protests," Julian said quietly. "But a million. Wow."

"People feel very strongly about this," Sam said. "After all, your confirmation would tip the court firmly to the left."

"Are you opposed to that, Sam?" Laine asked. Her question seemed to contain only interest and not judgment.

"I'm a cop."

"With no beliefs?" Graham asked, arching a white eyebrow with what might have been delight at her sauciness.

A quick glance at Nick told her he was anything but delighted.

"I have a few. Usually, I keep them to myself."

"Please," Nick said. "Enlighten us."

Something in his tightly spoken words sent a trickle of discomfort through her. "I'm sure you all have other things you'd rather talk about."

"Actually, you've got us riveted," Nick replied, his eyes boring a hole in her.

Her stomach churned with anxiety. "I'd like to see the abortion issue resolved definitively," she ventured.

"And you don't think it was with Roe v. Wade?" Julian asked.

"If it had been, we wouldn't still be talking about it more than thirty years later."

"That's a good point," Laine said.

"So if you were Julian," Nick said, "and a case came

before the court that would overturn Roe, how would you vote?"

Sam squirmed under the heat of his gaze. "I don't know. Don't ask me that."

Clearly flabbergasted, Nick stared at her. "You don't believe in a woman's right to choose?"

"I never said that."

"You don't know if you'd vote to overturn Roe? That doesn't make you much of a supporter of women's rights."

"No," Sam shot back, "it makes me a supporter of those who can't speak for themselves."

"I never would've guessed," Nick said, incredulous.

After a long period of uncomfortable silence during which Nick stared at her, Sam cleared her throat. "I think I smell something burning. I'll go check." Getting up quickly, she went into the kitchen and leaned against the counter, trying to stop the pounding in her chest. How had she let the conversation get so heated and out of control?

"What the hell was that?" Nick fumed as he followed her into the kitchen.

"What?" Sam asked, opening the oven and peering inside—more for something to do than anything.

"Were you baiting him?" he asked in an exaggerated whisper.

"*You* were baiting *me!*"

Ignoring that, he said, "Have you forgotten he's our guest?"

"*Your* guest."

"Right." He stormed around the kitchen, adding dressing to a tossed salad and retrieving dishes warming in the oven. "It's not like we're a couple who'd do something so *committed* as entertain together or anything."

Sam folded her arms, her back rigid with tension. "Maybe I should just go."

"Fine. Run away. That's what you do, isn't it?"

"No," she said softly, "usually I stay, which is how I ended up unhappily married for four long years to a man who tried to control my every thought and action."

Nick's expression shifted from anger to regret.

The anger, she decided, was easier to handle.

"Sam—"

She held up a hand to stop him from approaching her. "I'm going to go so you can visit with your friends in peace. I don't belong here."

"That's not true. You know it isn't."

"Tell them I got called in to work," she said, desperate to get out of there before she embarrassed herself by getting emotional. "I'm sorry." With a last glance at his unreadable face, she darted from the kitchen, grabbed her coat and headed out the door while contending with a huge knot in her throat.

ELEVEN

THE LOBSTER HAD been flown in from Maine, but to Nick, it might as well have been cardboard. The meal he had planned down to the garnish received rave reviews from his guests. He couldn't have cared less. Oblivious to his dismay, the other three laughed and talked and told old stories. Even though he participated in the conversation, Nick wished they would leave so he could go after Sam and nip this thing growing between them before it couldn't be fixed.

They lingered over dessert and coffee and then asked to see the rest of the house.

He took them through the three floors, answered their questions about his plans for the place, and withstood their good-natured ribbing about his oh-so-public romance with the pretty lieutenant.

By the time they finally left at eleven, Nick was on the verge of a nervous breakdown. He grabbed his coat, rushed down the street and up the ramp to Skip's house. After a month of being in and out of there, it didn't occur to him to knock. Bursting into the darkened living room, he found Skip and Celia on the sofa locked in a passionate embrace.

"Oh, shit," Nick muttered through his mortification. "Sorry."

Like a teenager who'd just been caught in a clutch with her boyfriend, Celia scrambled off Skip's lap and pressed her hand to her swollen lips. Skip's empty wheelchair sat next to the sofa where he was propped into the corner with pillows under his arms. Clearly, they had given this arrangement some serious thought, and Nick was horrified to have interrupted them.

"I'll, ah, just go up to see Sam."

"She's not here," Celia said. "We thought she was with you. At your dinner party for the justice."

"She was. Earlier. But we had an, um, a thing."

"A fight," Skip said, his sharp eyes trained on Nick.

"Sort of." Nick pushed a frustrated hand through his hair. "Where do you think she'd be?"

"How upset was she?" Skip asked.

"Pretty upset."

"Lincoln."

"Excuse me?"

"She goes to see Lincoln when she's upset or needs to think."

"As in the *monument?*"

"One and the same."

"At eleven at night?" Nick asked, incredulous.

"She carries a gun. The dark doesn't faze her."

"All right. I'll check there. Thanks for the info."

"What did you do to her?"

"Nothing!"

"It wasn't nothing if she's gone to see Mr. Lincoln."

"It's nothing we can't work out," he said with more confidence than he felt.

"Go find her, Nick," Celia said, sending a pointed glance at Skip.

"Sorry again for the interruption," Nick said on his way out the door. He jogged down Ninth Street, cut through Eastern Market and hailed a cab on East Capitol.

"Lincoln Memorial," he told the cabbie.

"Not much happening there this time of night," the

driver said, no doubt thinking he'd picked up a misguided tourist.

"I know," Nick replied in a clipped tone that discouraged further conversation. They arrived ten minutes later. Nick paid the driver, emerged from the car and took off jogging toward the lighted memorial.

"Help you, sir?" a park ranger said as Nick headed for the marble stairs.

He could've said no. The monument, like all the others, was open twenty-four hours a day, and he didn't need permission to be there. But for the first time in the two weeks since he was sworn in, Nick decided to take advantage of his newfound rank. "I'm Senator Nick Cappuano. I'm meeting someone here."

"Pleased to make your acquaintance, Senator." The ranger shook Nick's hand. "I believe your friend is on that side," he said, pointing, "under the Gettysburg Address."

Nick still found it hard to believe that he was half of a couple everyone in the capital region recognized. "Thank you." Over his shoulder, he caught the ranger's grin as he watched Nick take the stairs two at a time. He found Sam right where the ranger had told him she'd be. Sitting on the floor, she had her knees pulled up to her chest, her arms tight around them and her face tucked into the valley formed by her knees.

"Samantha."

Her head shot up, a shocked expression on her tear-streaked face. "What're you doing here?"

"Your dad told me I might find you here." Undone by her ravaged expression and wondering if he was responsible for it, he glanced at Lincoln. "Is it a coincidence that you flee to the first Republican president when you want to be alone?"

"I don't come because he was a Republican."

Nick sat down next to her on the cold floor. "Then why?"

She shrugged. "It's so peaceful here. I've always loved it."

"I'm drawn to Jefferson myself."

"Naturally. The original Democrat."

"One of them." He studied her for a long moment before he said, "Are you a Republican, Samantha Holland?"

"Will you love me less if I say I am?"

He shook his head and reached for her hand. "Nothing could make me love you less."

Her face tightened with strain that confused and scared him as he rubbed some warmth into her chilled hand. "Don't be so sure."

"That doesn't answer my question."

"Like I told Graham before—I'm a cop. I'm not affiliated with either party."

"But if you *could* be, which one would it be?"

She glanced up at Lincoln. "Neither, really. I'm more of an issues kind of gal."

Nick released a long deep breath.

"Are you disappointed I didn't say I'm a Democrat?"

"Of course not."

"I may not always agree with your position on issues that really matter to you."

"I don't expect you to."

"Are you sure of that? Politics is such a big part of who you are, Nick. Now more than ever. I'd understand if some differences were too big for you to deal with. After all, we rushed into this. We didn't really know each other—"

He stopped her with two fingers over her lips. "I know you. Do I know everything there is to know? Nope. Do I want to? Absolutely. Will there be other surprises? I sure as hell hope so. But don't tell me I don't know you. I know your heart, Samantha. I know what matters." He didn't expect her to break down into gulping sobs. Sliding his arm around her, he brought her head to rest on his chest. "What's going on, babe?"

"I'm sorry for the way I acted with Julian," she said when she could speak again. "I was way out of line. You were right. He was our guest, and I *was* baiting him."

"He's used to people with strong opinions. You can't have beliefs like his without generating some controversy."

"But you weren't expecting that from me, and I embarrassed you."

"No, you surprised me."

"I surprised myself. I had no plans to get into that with him."

"So why did you?" he asked, more curious than anything.

"All the coverage about him coming to town, about his nomination, knowing I was going to meet him. It's stirred up some stuff for me."

"What kind of stuff?"

"It's kind of a long story," she said with a wary glance at him.

He sat back against the marble wall and brought her in close to him to keep them warm. "Mr. Lincoln and I aren't going anywhere."

She was quiet for a long time—so long that he wondered if she was going to tell him what was causing her such dismay. "I've never told anyone this," she finally said. "Other than my sisters, that is."

Bracing himself for whatever he was about to hear, Nick linked their fingers and held her hand between both of his.

With a deep sigh, she said, "When I was a junior in college, I dated a French exchange student named Jean Paul for a couple of months toward the end of the school year. You probably don't want to hear this, but it was one of those relationships that was long on sex and short on relating, if you know what I mean."

He knew exactly what she meant and hated the idea of her with anyone else, but he kept his mouth shut so she'd continue.

"Jean Paul had already gone home to France when I discovered I was pregnant."

Sensing where this was going, Nick fought to retain his composure.

"Tracy had just had Brooke," she said of her fifteen-year-old niece. "I told you about Brooke's father leaving Tracy to raise her alone, right?"

Nick nodded, recalling how Tracy's husband, Mike, was raising Brooke as his own child.

"After watching what Tracy was going through, I totally panicked. I had one more year of school to finish and had my sights set on the police academy. With the dyslexia, school was a huge struggle, but I was determined to get that degree because I knew it would help me get promoted. How in the world was I going to fit a baby into that picture? And I had no one who could help me. My mother had run off to Florida with that guy she'd hooked up with, my dad was a mess over what my mother had put him through, Angela had a new job and was dating Spencer. Tracy was struggling to take care of Brooke. I can honestly say it was the only time in my life when I had no idea what to do."

Nick wiped the tears from her cheeks. "You couldn't have put the baby up for adoption?"

"My dad was so upset and disappointed with Tracy.

Not that he ever expressed that to her, but he talked to me about it. No one even thinks about that anymore because we love Brooke so much, but at the time, it was a big deal."

"You didn't want to disappoint him, too."

"No," she said, sounding so utterly defeated. "I couldn't have taken that on top of everything else I was dealing with."

"So what did you do?"

After a long pause, she said, "I made an appointment at a clinic," in a voice so soft it was almost a whisper. "I couldn't see any other way out. I was awake the entire night before with what I thought were stomach pains, but when they examined me before the procedure, they discovered I was miscarrying."

"You didn't do anything wrong, Sam."

"I was going to *kill* my baby!" The hysteria he heard in her voice alarmed him. "How can you say I didn't do anything wrong? My periods were never the same afterward, and then the endometriosis set in a year or so later. It was like my body was punishing me for this awful thing I almost did." Her voice caught on a sob. "I'm so ashamed, Nick. Even all these years later, I'm still so ashamed."

Because he didn't know what else to do, he held her tight against him and let her get it out.

"I cried for two weeks afterward. My sisters took care of me, saw me through the worst of it, but I've never told another living soul about that day until right now. I know it's why I miscarried twice more, and it's why I can't have others."

"How do you figure?"

"I'm being punished for being so willing to toss away the one I didn't want."

"Sam, honey, how can you think that?"

"Because! Look at what's happened! When I *wanted* to get pregnant, I couldn't, and then when I finally did, I couldn't *stay* pregnant. How else am I supposed to see it?"

"As an awful coincidence. How would you have supported that child as a twenty-year-old college dropout?"

"I would've found a way."

"But you never would've been a cop. Think of the lives you've saved and the murders you've prevented by getting all those killers off the streets. Doesn't that in any way compensate?"

She shook her head. "Nothing can compensate for not wanting my own child."

"You were a kid yourself. You felt trapped and alone. It wasn't about *wanting* your child. It was about knowing you couldn't care for him properly."

"Sometimes I wonder if he knew I didn't want him, and that's why I miscarried."

"I'm sorry this happened to you. That you were put in this position and had to make such an awful choice."

"I know you must think less of me."

"I don't, Sam. I swear I don't. I support a woman's right to choose—any woman. Even you."

As if he hadn't spoken, she said, "Your own mother was only fifteen when she had you, and you turned out fine."

"No thanks to her."

"But still." Sam took a deep shuddering breath. "At the crowd-control meeting we had at work the other day, they showed us some of the propaganda so we'd be prepared for what to expect from the protestors. They had pictures of aborted fetuses. I hit the recall button on my pager to get myself out of there. I got so sick in the bathroom. I thought it would never stop."

"I'm sorry, babe," he whispered. "I'm so sorry you had to see those pictures. I'm sorry you had to go through this whole ordeal and that you carry such a heavy burden."

"In some twisted way, I think maybe I baited Julian because I wanted to tell you. I just couldn't figure out how. But I wanted you to know."

"I'm glad you told me."

Resting her head on her knees, she turned her face so she could see him. "This is why we won't have kids."

"You can't know that for sure. You may have ended up with endometriosis anyway, even if you hadn't had that miscarriage. Maybe you already had it, didn't know it, and that caused the miscarriage."

Startled, she looked up at him. "You really think that's possible?"

"Anything is possible. The point is you'll never really know so why assume the worst? Have you tried to have kids with anyone other than Peter?"

"Of course not."

"How much you wanna bet he was the problem, not you?" Nick waggled his eyebrows at her. "We've already proven *he* was the problem in another important area, right? You've never tried to have *my* kids. And remember what I told you—when we're ready, we'll have them. If we can't have them the usual way, we'll adopt, we'll hire a surrogate, whatever it takes. We'll have them."

"I don't know if I deserve them—or you."

He got up and reached out a hand to her. "Sure you do."

She took his hand and let him help her up.

Because he needed it as much as she did, he hugged her close to him.

Under his coat, her fingers clutched his back. "I love you," she whispered. "I love you so much."

"And I love you even more than I did earlier, if that's possible." With his arm around her shoulders, he led her to the stairs. "Let's go home. I saved you a lobster."

She glanced up at him, a hint of a smile on her face. "Thanks."

He knew she wasn't talking about lobster. "Anytime, babe."

TWELVE

THIS WAS IT, Freddie decided, as he let Elin drag him through her dark apartment. He wasn't going to back out, he wasn't going to think of his mother, his faith or the promises he made to himself years ago before he'd become a man with man-sized urges. In his right mind, he would've preferred some romance, some candles maybe. Love would've been nice, too.

But that hadn't happened, and this was going to. And it was going to be over before it started unless he could find a way to slow things down.

He reached for her hands, which were at work on his shirt buttons. "Hey."

She nuzzled his chest hair. "What?"

"How about we take our time?"

Rolling his nipple between her teeth, she said, "We *have* taken our time. We've been out three times, Freddie."

"Three whole times," he said more to himself than to her.

"What's wrong with you? Don't you want this?"

Did he? Did he really want it this way? Then he remembered his resolution. This was the year. He had chosen this woman, knowing she would be easy and uncomplicated. It wasn't her fault that uncomplicated had turned out to be empty and unsatisfying. "Yeah," he said, pulling off his coat.

She took it from him and with a saucy glance over her shoulder, she said, "Get comfortable. I'll be right back."

Freddie sat on the bed and looked around at the surprisingly feminine room. He wasn't sure what he'd been expecting, but pink and frilly wasn't it. Maybe she'd surprise him in other ways, too.

"Freddie."

He looked up and almost swallowed his tongue. Stark naked, she stood in the doorway. Zeroing in on the cupid tattoo on her left breast, he watched in stunned fascination as her pierced nipples sprang to life.

"See anything you like?"

"Uh-huh," he managed to say. "Come here."

She sashayed over to him and stepped between his parted legs. With her hands on his shoulders, she offered her breasts to him.

Flipping his tongue back and forth over one of her nipples, he cupped her firm ass and brought her in closer to him. Every toned inch of her was proof of the hours she spent at the gym. "Did it hurt?"

"What?" she asked breathlessly.

"Having them pierced."

"Like a sonofabitch."

"Then why do it?"

"Because it makes what you're doing right now even more intense, and they make me feel sexy."

"I can't believe you need any help feeling sexy."

She glanced down at him, a vulnerable expression on her usually confident face, and shrugged. Pushing the shirt off his shoulders, she tossed it to the floor and urged him to lie back.

He watched her as she divested him of his pants and underwear. And with that, with both of them naked and needy, he had already gone further than ever before.

Elin kissed her way down the front of him, and Freddie let her, knowing he needed to take the edge off if he was going to get through the main event without embarrassing himself. No doubt a woman like her had some pretty significant expectations. Over and done with in under thirty seconds probably wasn't one of them.

Wrapping her hand around his erection, she stroked him until he was harder than he could ever recall being.

"Mmm," she said as she wrapped her lips around him.

He had heard his friends and coworkers talk about women who actually liked giving blow jobs versus those who did it just to please their partner. If the enthusiastic way in which she stroked, licked and sucked was any indication, he had found one who seemed to like it as much as he did. Clutching her hair, Freddie discovered that watching her make love to him with her mouth was every bit as hot as the act itself.

When she cupped his balls and took him deep into her throat, Freddie cried out as a powerful orgasm gripped him. On the way back down to earth, he realized he still had a firm grip on her hair and loosened his hold.

She lapped at him, cleaning him up. "How can you come like that and still be so hard?" she asked, stroking him.

He reached for her, bringing her up to rest on top of him. "Stamina." And lack of use, he wanted to say but didn't.

"We need a condom," she said.

"In a minute." He captured her mouth in a hot, penetrating kiss, and suddenly it didn't matter that he didn't love her or that he'd been taught this was wrong outside of marriage. It didn't feel wrong. It felt good, and he wanted more. He wanted everything. "Let me grab that condom."

"Oh, no, let me," she said with a sexy glint in her eye.

Just as he was about to tell her about the condoms he'd been carrying around in his back pocket—just in case—she reached for her bedside table and produced a black foil packet.

"Ribbed, to enhance *my* pleasure." With her eyes fixed on his, she used her teeth to tear off the wrapper and rolled it on.

Freddie bit his lip to keep from losing it as she moved her hand slowly over his straining length.

When she was finished, she straddled him and leaned forward to touch her lips to his.

He filled his hands with her breasts and had to remind himself to breathe. This was really happening. Finally.

"How do you like it?" she whispered.

"Any way you like it."

"In that case, it's a good thing we have all night."

Using her hand, she led him to her slick channel and sank down on him.

Buried to the hilt in her heat, Freddie gasped.

"Does that hurt?" she asked, looking down at him with concern.

Unable to breathe let alone speak, he shook his head and gripped her hips.

She leaned back and took him even deeper.

Freddie wasn't sure if he should move or let her ride him, but his hips seemed to have a mind of their own as they surged up to meet her thrusts. *Oh, God, why had he waited so long to do this? Why?*

As if a wild beast had been unleashed inside him, he sat up, wrapped his arms around her and turned them over so he was on top. Bringing her to the edge of the bed, he kept his feet on the floor to gain maximum leverage and pounded into her. Sweat pooled at the base of his spine, burned his eyes and wet his forehead, but he felt nothing beyond the velvet heat surrounding his cock.

She sank her fingers into his ass, holding him deep inside her when she came with a sharp cry.

Somehow, Freddie managed to hold on to his control long enough to take her up and over once more. When he finally gave himself permission to join her, the relief that he'd managed to get through this without embarrassing himself tempered the mind-blowing release. Panting on top of her, still joined with her, he wondered how long he had to wait before he'd be able to do it again.

SAM RESTED HER head on Nick's chest and listened to the soft cadence of his breathing. They had shared the left-over lobster and a bottle of wine, inaugurated the new Ja-cuzzi and done some serious power snuggling. He hadn't tried to make love to her, and she had been relieved that he seemed to know she needed something else tonight: a shoulder to lean on. His shoulder.

Touching her lips to his chest, she sighed with con-tentment. An odd sense of peace had come over her after she shared her deepest, darkest secret with him. That he knew the worst of her and loved her anyway was such a special gift in the midst of everything else he had brought to her life.

"Why are you awake at four a.m.?" he whispered, startling her.

"Why are *you?*"

"Insomnia."

"How come I don't know that after a month of sleep-ing with you?"

"Because you're usually sawing logs when I'm awake."

"I do not 'saw logs,'" she said indignantly.

"Um, yeah, you do."

"Want me to rub your back?" she asked.

"Really?"

"Turn over."

They shifted into position so she could caress his back. He released a long deep breath. "Feels good."

"What's the deal with the insomnia?"

"It comes and goes, usually depending on the stress level at the moment."

"And you thought being a senator would be good for that?"

He laughed into his pillow. "It was a concern. One of many."

"You should see a doctor about it."

"As soon as you see Harry about your stomach." He referred to his friend, the internist, who'd agreed to sneak her in.

"I have an appointment on Friday."

"Good. Want me to go with you?"

"You'll be knee-deep in nomination hearings on Friday."

"I can be there if you need me."

"I'll be fine." She kissed his shoulder. "Go to sleep."

He put his arm around her and drew her in close to him. "Only if you do."

"Deal."

They were both on their way when the phone rang.

"It's mine." She reached for her cell on the bedside table. "Holland."

"I'm sorry to disturb you, Lieutenant," Detective Jeannie McBride said. "We've got a homicide, and you asked us to let you know."

"Where?"

"Lincoln Park."

"I'm on my way." She got up and reached for the

clothes she'd worn the night before and realized they were inappropriate for a middle-of-the-night winter crime scene. "Crap. I'll have to go to my dad's to change."

"You know, if you lived here, your clothes would, too," Nick muttered.

"Ha-ha."

He got out of bed.

"What're you doing?" she asked.

"Saving you some time." He stepped into his closet and emerged with a sweater of his that he tossed to her. In his other hand, he held up a pair of running shoes. "You left these here last week."

"Excellent," she said, as she pushed her arms into the sweater. "Mmm, smells like you."

"Do you need socks?"

Pulling on her black dress pants, she flashed him a sheepish grin. "Um, yeah."

He handed her a pair.

"Thanks." Wrapping her arms around his warm, naked body, she went up on tiptoes to kiss him. "Try to get some sleep."

"Be careful out there, babe."

"I always am."

SAM RAISED THE yellow crime scene tape and stepped into Lincoln Park. The blustery winter wind smacked at her face as she worked to shake off the stupor of a sleepless night. She shivered, yearning for Nick and the warmth of his bed.

The first hint of sunrise graced the horizon. Across the park, under the glare of lights that had been brought in, two patrol officers stood watch over the victim.

"What've we got?" she asked Detective Jeannie Mc-Bride.

McBride consulted her notebook. "Victim is male, Caucasian, late sixties. Killed with a single gunshot wound to the back of the head. His hands and feet were bound."

"Execution style?"

"Yes, ma'am."

"ID?"

"None on him, but he's well dressed."

"Start a log of everyone who's here now or comes in later."

"Got it."

"Where's Cruz?"

"Not answering his phone or pager."

Startled, Sam glanced at Jeannie. "That's odd."

"Yes, Lieutenant."

Wondering where in the hell her partner was, she jammed her hands into her coat pockets. "Try him again." Sam's long-legged stride ate up the distance to where the victim lay crumpled on the ground.

Nodding to the patrol officers, she tugged on latex gloves and squatted down to examine the twine that had been used to bind his hands and feet. His shoes, she noted, were missing. Blood pooled at the site of the gunshot wound. With her hand on his shoulder, she turned him and gasped as she looked down at the dead face of the man they'd dined with the night before.

"Oh, God," she whispered. "Oh, poor Nick." Standing over the lifeless body of Supreme Court nominee Julian Sinclair, all Sam could think about was the day she and Nick had gone to Leesburg to tell the O'Connors their son had been murdered. And now their longtime friend was dead, too. She couldn't imagine how any of them would withstand this new blow on top of the one they'd so recently sustained.

"Lieutenant?" Detective McBride said from behind her. "It's Julian Sinclair."

McBride gasped. "The Supreme Court nominee?"

Sam nodded. "Contact Malone and Farnsworth. Let them know that Senator Cappuano, Senator and Mrs. Graham O'Connor, and myself were among the last people to see him alive."

McBride stared at her for a long moment.

"Make the calls, Jeannie."

"Yes, ma'am."

Jeannie walked away, and Sam returned her attention to the victim. "What happened, Julian?" she whispered, feeling horrible about the odd confrontation she'd had with him the night before. She checked his hands and found no defensive wounds. Whoever grabbed him had caught him off guard. "What happened after you left Nick's house?"

"Lieutenant," McBride said a few minutes later, "the medical examiner is here. The chief and the captain are on their way. No luck reaching Cruz."

"Thank you." She took another long last look at Sinclair before she stood up and tugged off the gloves. "Who found him?"

"A drunk tripped over him. The guy is freaking out." She pointed to an ambulance parked at the curb. "Paramedics are with him now."

"Let me brief the brass, and then I want to talk to him. Canvass?"

"Tyrone and a couple of uniforms are on it," she said, referring to her partner.

"Good job, McBride. Thanks."

"So, um, you met him? The vic?"

"He had dinner with us at Nick's new place on Capitol Hill. They were friends."

"Jeez, and he just lost his other friend."

Her lips tight with tension, Sam said, "Yes."

Captain Malone and Chief Farnsworth arrived minutes apart, and Sam filled them in. "I left before dinner, so I need to talk to Nick about what time it ended and how Sinclair got back to the hotel."

"Get to it," the chief said, his expression grim as he studied the gunshot wound to Sinclair's head.

"I'm waiting on crime scene to get here," Sam said.

"I'll wait for them," Malone replied. "You go on ahead."

"Gonna be another hot one, Lieutenant," Farnsworth said.

"And the spotlight will once again be on me and my personal life," she grumbled.

"Will it be too much of a distraction?" Farnsworth asked.

"No, sir. McBride, you're with me." She gestured for the other woman to follow her.

Jeannie trotted along behind Sam as she stalked across the park to talk to the wino who'd found Sinclair. He was all but incoherent, adding nothing to the investigation.

Furious, she took off for her car, again with Jeannie in hot pursuit.

"Do you want me to try Cruz again for you?"

"No." Sam struggled to find the words she would need to break the devastating news to Nick. The very thought of it broke her heart, but there was no room for her emotions in the midst of what needed to be done in the next few hours. "He'll have to catch up when he resurfaces."

THIRTEEN

SAM PARALLEL PARKED on Ninth Street and stared at the front door to Nick's house.

"How do you want to do this?" Jeannie asked.

"He's still asleep," Sam said, glancing up at the dark window on the second floor. "I'll wake him up and have him come down. I want you to witness the conversation."

"Right." McBride twisted her fingers in her lap.

"I know this'll be uncomfortable for you, Detective, but I need you there to record and witness the conversation. Everything about this has to be by the book. He's a potential witness."

"I understand."

Sam concentrated on breathing her way through the pain that circulated in her gut.

"Are you all right, Lieutenant?"

"Yeah." In a cold sweat brought on by the pain, she reached for the door handle. "Let's get this over with."

Jeannie followed Sam up the stairs and waited while she used her key in the door.

Inside, Sam flipped on a light.

Jeannie released a low whistle. "Wow, nice place."

"Uh-huh. Have a seat. I'll be right back." With a deep breath to calm her nerves and her stomach, Sam started up the stairs. Turning on a light in the hallway, she went to the bedroom doorway and stood there for a long moment watching him sleep and wishing with all her heart

that she could spare him from what she was about to do
to him.

Moving to the bedside, she leaned down to kiss his
cheek. "Nick." She shook his shoulder. *"Nick."*

"Mmm, hey, babe. Back already?"

"I need to talk to you."

"'K." He gave her hand a tug to bring her into bed
with him.

Sam resisted. "Nick."

His eyes fluttered open.

"I *need* to talk to you."

"What's wrong?"

"Can you come downstairs?"

Running his fingers through his hair, he looked up at
her. "Why not right here?"

She swallowed hard. "I need it on the record."

"What the hell, Sam?" he asked, sitting up.

"Please."

"Fine." He tossed back the covers and reached for his
sweats. "Am I allowed to take a leak first?"

"Yes, but hurry. Detective McBride is downstairs waiting for us."

He shot her a furious scowl but thankfully didn't ask
any more questions as he headed into the bathroom and
closed the door.

Sam went downstairs to find Jeannie wandering
around. "He'll be right down."

"This place is huge!"

"The guy who lived here before bought the place next
door and knocked out walls."

"Are you living here, too?"

"No. I'm still at my dad's three doors down."

"Why?"

"Because—"

"Because she's not ready," Nick said, now wearing a T-shirt with his sweats, as he came down the stairs to join them. He slipped an arm around Sam and kissed the top of her head.

She shook him off.

Startled and possibly hurt, Nick stared at her.

"This is Detective Jeannie McBride."

Nick extended his hand. "Yes, I remember from the party."

"Nice to see you again, Senator."

"Please, call me Nick." He turned to Sam. "Are you going to tell me what's going on?"

"Sit," Sam said, gesturing toward the sofa.

"I'd rather stand. Thanks."

Hands on her hips, Sam said, "Detective McBride, please record this conversation."

Nick stared at her. "Sam—"

Sam nodded to Jeannie, who set the pocket-sized recorder on the coffee table. "I'm sorry to have to inform you that Julian Sinclair was found murdered early this morning in Lincoln Park."

Nick took a step back, shook his head and whispered, "No." He shook his head again and then dropped into a chair when his legs seemed to give out beneath him.

"I'm very sorry," Jeannie said.

"But he was just here." Nick looked up at Sam, his eyes shiny with tears. "How?"

"He was shot," Sam said, deciding quick and dirty was the best strategy. "His hands and feet were bound."

Nick buried his face in his hands and wept, all the while continuing to shake his head.

Jeannie shot a nervous glance at Sam and tipped her head, silently imploring Sam to go to him.

Desperate to maintain her professional edge but aching for him, she moved over to perch on the arm of the chair. She put her arm around his shoulders.

He turned into her embrace and shook with sobs. "How could this have happened? First John, and now this. Oh, God, Graham and Laine. This'll kill them."

"I know it's a terrible shock for you, but I need to ask you a few things."

Wiping his face, he nodded. "Whatever I can do."

"What time did Julian leave here last night?"

"It was just after eleven," he said, quickly adding, "I was watching the clock, because I wanted them to leave so I could go find you."

Sam glanced at Jeannie, who hung on their every word. "Did he say or do anything to indicate he was worried about something or had been threatened by anyone?"

"No, nothing like that. He was anxious about the confirmation hearings, but he didn't mention anything else."

"Would he have? If he was anxious or worried, would he have said something?"

"I think so. Especially after you left and it was just the four of us. He and Graham are the best of friends, and he knew he could trust me, too."

"How did he get back to the hotel?"

"Since he had taken a cab over here, Graham and Laine dropped him off."

She glanced at Jeannie. "I need to talk to them."

"I'll go with you," Nick said, standing up.

"You don't have to," Sam said. "We can take care of it."

His eyes narrowed. "Don't ask me to sit here while you're in Leesburg crushing them—again. Don't ask that of me, Sam."

They stared each other down in a fierce battle of wills.

"I could have Tyrone pick me up here," Jeannie interjected. "We can go to Sinclair's hotel, interview the door-man, get the security tapes and go through his room."

When Sam realized it wasn't necessary to win this standoff, she glanced at Jeannie. "Do it." She turned back to Nick. "Why don't you go get dressed?"

With a long, hard look at her, he turned and went back upstairs.

THE STONY SILENCE in the car worked on Sam's nerves. She had no idea what she should say or if she should reach out to him. Something told her he wouldn't welcome anything from her just then. What she didn't know was why. Was he blaming her for this latest wave of devastating news? She'd just been doing her job.

She glanced over and found him staring out the window, lost in his own thoughts, far, far away from her. The distance frightened her.

"Nick."

He didn't answer, didn't blink, didn't seem to even know or care she was there.

Reaching over, she curled her hand around his. "Talk to me."

"Nothing to say."

"I'm sorry this has happened to your friend. And to you."

"Thank you."

"Are you mad at me?"

His eyes finally shifted from the window to focus on her. "Why didn't you tell me when we were upstairs? When we were alone?"

"Because I couldn't."

"Right."

"I did it that way to protect you! So your statement and your reaction would be witnessed and on the record.

You were one of the last people to see him alive. I was trying to ensure that you'd be cleared of any suspicion."

Sagging into his seat, he said, "I didn't think of it that way."

"I hated having to tell you that, and I hate that we're once again on our way to deliver devastating news to two people who don't deserve it."

"No," he said softly. "They really don't."

"Neither do you."

"I don't have a lot of close friends," he said, once again looking straight ahead. "There're not a lot of people I feel completely comfortable with. Julian was one of them."

Her heart aching for him, she tightened her grip on his hand. "You have me now," she said. "I'm right here with you."

He replied with a small nod.

As Sam drove, she kept one eye on him. The combination of the two murders had plunged him into such deep despair that she had no idea how to reach him.

At the O'Connors' country home in Leesburg, Laine greeted them with a warm smile and hugs.

"Nick! Sam! How nice to see you again so soon." She ushered them into the foyer. "What brings you out this way?"

Nick fell into Laine's embrace and broke down.

Alarmed, Laine held him close. "Sweetheart, what is it?"

Sam had never seen Nick quite this undone, even after John died, and was unnerved by it. She was also struck by the odd sensation of once again being on the outside looking in. That he'd waited to get here, to his adopted mother, before he gave into the full depths of his devastation hurt Sam.

"You're frightening me, Nick," Laine said, reaching up

to brush the tears from his face. "Will one of you please tell me what's wrong?"

"It's Julian," Nick said softly.

Laine gasped and took a step back from him. With her hand over her heart, she stared at him. "No."

"Is Senator O'Connor at home?" Sam asked.

"He's in his study."

"I'll get him," Nick said, wiping his face as he left the room.

"How?" Laine asked with the steely, patrician strength Sam had grown to admire in the weeks she had known her.

Sam told her what she knew.

"This'll demolish Graham," Laine whispered.

"I said the same thing about Nick."

Their eyes met and held, two women united in their worries about the men they loved.

A ravaged howl came from a room off the living room. Laine rushed off in the direction of the study.

Sam followed her. They found the two men sitting on the sofa, Nick's arm around Graham's shoulders.

Laine went to her husband.

"I just can't believe this," Graham said through his tears. He reached for his wife's hand. "He was fine. We just saw him."

Sam stepped into a room made cozy by the heat coming from the fireplace. "I'm sorry for your loss," she said.

Laine gestured her over to join them.

Sam took the seat next to Nick.

Graham turned his grief-stricken eyes on Sam. "Will you find out who did this? I need to know who could've done this."

Grateful for the opening, she said, "I know this is a terrible shock, but you were among the last people to see him alive. Can you tell me about taking him back to the hotel?"

Graham wiped his face with the back of his hand. "He was staying at the Willard, so we said we'd drop him off."

"What time was that?"

He glanced at his wife. "About eleven-fifteen or so?" She nodded.

"Did you watch him enter the hotel?"

Laine thought about that. "I can't say that I did."

"I didn't, either," Graham said.

"Were there any other people around?"

Laine paused for a moment. "I believe one of the hotel staff was working the door."

"Yes," Graham said. "I saw someone in a uniform."

"How about other cars?" Nick asked.

"We were the only ones in front of the hotel," Graham said. "I remember commenting to Laine that the middle of the night was the only time Washington isn't gridlocked."

"During your visit with him," Sam said, now addressing the three of them, "did he talk about anything or anyone he was having a problem with? A friend, girlfriend, acquaintance?"

They exchanged glances.

"What?" Sam asked.

"Julian was gay," Nick said.

Processing the information, Sam sagged into the leather chair. "Did people know?"

"Those closest to him, but he was discreet," Nick said. "The media hadn't zeroed in on his orientation yet."

"But he knew they would," Laine said. "He suspected it would come up during the confirmation hearings."

"Was he concerned about that?"

"Not particularly," Graham replied in a soft voice. The

devastation wrought by the double-whammy of losing his son and now his close friend seemed to have diminished him. "His mother died several years ago without ever knowing he was gay. Her death liberated him in many ways. He didn't care quite as much if people found out."

"Was he in a relationship?"

"Not anymore," Laine said, looking to Nick when she added, "How long ago did he and Duncan break up?"

"More than a year."

Graham nodded in agreement.

"Were they together a long time?" Sam asked.

"Had to be twenty years," Graham said.

"Was Duncan out of the closet?"

"Only to the people closest to him. Duncan wanted to retire and move to Florida," Nick said. "Julian wasn't ready to stop working, which is what broke them up. Julian loved teaching at Harvard, and when Nelson was elected, he knew the Supreme Court nomination was likely." His voice faltered. "I just can't believe he's gone."

"Is it possible," Sam ventured, "that Duncan was worried about unwanted attention during the nomination hearings?"

"Worried enough to tie Julian up and shoot him in the back of the head?" Nick asked.

Laine gasped. "Oh, God. *God.*"

"I'm sorry," Nick said. "I didn't mean to just blurt that out."

"Duncan loved Julian," Graham said. "I've never really understood how two guys, you know… But seeing them together…"

Laine dabbed at tears. "They were a lovely couple. We adored them both."

"I'll need to talk to Duncan," Sam said. "Do you know where I can find him?"

"He lives in South Beach." Laine rose and crossed the room to the smaller of the two desks. Returning, she handed Sam a piece of paper. "Here's his address."

Sam tucked the address into her back pocket and checked her watch. Almost nine o'clock. "I need to get back to the city," she said to Nick. "Do you want to stay here?"

He glanced at Graham.

"You need to be at the Capitol for the start of the new session," Graham said.

"Are you sure?" Nick asked. "I don't mind staying."

"Go to work, Senator. Get John's bill passed."

Nick clutched the older man's hand and leaned into his embrace.

"We'll get through this," Graham said gruffly. "Somehow, we'll get through it."

Nick nodded and stood to hug Laine.

Sam followed suit.

"You'll be gentle when you tell Duncan?" Laine said.

"I promise."

Laine reached up to caress Sam's face. "I don't envy you your job, but I have full confidence that you'll find the person who did this to Julian."

Taken aback by the loving gesture, Sam said, "I'll do my best."

FOURTEEN

AFTER ANOTHER QUIET ride, Sam was even more alarmed by Nick's withdrawal. Her attempts to lure him into conversation failed, and he passed most of the ride staring out the passenger window. As she pulled into a parking space on Ninth Street, her stomach began to ache. She desperately needed to get to HQ, but how could she leave him like this?

"Nick?"

He stared unseeing out the window.

Reaching out to him, she rested her hand on his arm. "Nick, honey, come on. We're home."

All at once, he seemed to snap out of the stupor he had sunk into. "You must need to get to work."

"I'll walk you in." She got out of the car and went around to open his door. Following him up the stairs and into the house, Sam watched him lower himself into the first chair he encountered and drop his head into his hands.

In her pocket, her pager vibrated for the sixth time in the past ten minutes. Her cell phone rang, but as much as it pained her to let it ring, she ignored it—again. She went into the kitchen to make him some coffee and found his cell phone on the counter. Debating for a moment, she reached for it and scrolled through his list of contacts. Second to her on his speed dial list was Christina. Sam pressed send.

"Senator," Christina said. "I just heard about Julian Sinclair. I'm so sorry."

"Um, it's Sam."

"Oh. Hi. Is he—"

"He's a mess. I need to go to work, but I can't leave him like this."

"I'll be right there."

"Do you mind?" Sam asked, cringing at how foolish she sounded.

"Of course not. I care about him, too, you know."

"I know you do."

"I'm sorry. I just can't believe this has happened."

"No one can."

"I'll be there as soon as I can."

"Thank you."

SAM WAS ASTOUNDED when she opened the front door twenty minutes later to find Christina *and* Gonzo.

"What're you doing here?" she asked Gonzo as she stepped aside to let them in.

Right before Sam's eyes, the formidable Tommy "Gonzo" Gonzales blushed. "I was, uh, with her when she got the call about Sinclair. I thought maybe I could help."

Sam looked from Gonzo to Christina, who had gone straight to Nick on the sofa, back to Gonzo. "Define *with* her."

He squirmed. "You know, *with* her." Nodding to Nick, he added, "The way you're *with* him."

"Are you freaking kidding me?"

"What? We're both consenting adults."

Before she could reply, Sam's cell phone and pager rang simultaneously. She checked both LCDs and took the call from Captain Malone.

"Lieutenant. I've been trying to reach you for an hour."

"I was interviewing Senator and Mrs. O'Connor, probably the last people to see Sinclair alive."

"What've you got?"

She recited the O'Connors' version of the routine drop off at the hotel. "I sent McBride and Tyrone to the Willard to get the security tapes and interview the staff."

"She's back with the tapes. They're viewing them now. The bellman who was working the door is coming in at noon."

"Good, tell her to let me know what he has to say. I need you to authorize travel to Miami for myself and Detective Gonzales."

"Where's Cruz?"

"Good question."

"What's in Miami?"

Sam checked the sofa and saw Nick speaking softly to Christina. She tried not to be bothered by the fact that he had been unable to talk to her but was having no problem unloading on his chief of staff.

"Lieutenant?" Malone said.

Tearing her eyes off the scene on the sofa, Sam said, "Sinclair's longtime lover. Duncan Quick."

"He was gay?"

"Yes. He ended a twenty-year relationship with Quick a year ago, and apparently, Quick is still partially in the closet."

"The confirmation hearings would've blown the lid off that."

"Your thinking parallels mine. I want to see Quick's reaction to the news that Sinclair's dead."

"Approved."

"We'll be back tonight."

"Do we need to be worried about Cruz?"

"Hang on a sec." She did a quick scroll through her

missed calls and pages, but found nothing from Freddie. "No word from him at all this morning. That's not like him."

"I'll send patrol by his apartment."

"Let me know." She ended the call and turned to Gonzo. "I'll meet you outside."

"Got it."

Sam approached the duo on the sofa. "Ah, would you mind giving us a minute?" she said to Christina.

"Sure." She released Nick's hand and got up.

Sam sat next to him and lifted her hand to brush the hair from his forehead. "I'm going to Florida to talk to Duncan."

"Okay."

"I don't feel right about going. About leaving you." She rested her forehead on his shoulder.

"I want you to find out who did this."

"Are you going to work?"

"Yeah. Christina told me the Senate is going to take up John's bill as its first order of business in the new session."

"Oh, Nick. That's great news."

That he seemed to barely care only added to her growing list of worries.

She pressed a kiss to his cheek. "I'll be back. As soon as I can."

"I know."

Reluctantly, she got up and went into the kitchen where Christina was pouring coffee. "You'll be with him?" Sam asked.

"Every minute."

Sam glanced at Nick staring off into space in the next room. "This is worse than after John."

"Yes."

Running her fingers over hair that she'd corralled into a clip, Sam considered taking a pass on the case. It was up to her, after all. She could put Gonzo in charge, send him to Florida and stay in D.C. with Nick. But he'd rebuffed all her efforts to comfort him.

"Sam."

She turned to find Christina studying her intently. "He'll understand if you go. He knows it's your job, and he has to go do his today. We need his vote."

Sam nodded. "Don't leave him alone." And then she remembered Christina wasn't one of her detectives. "Please."

"You have my word."

"Thank you." She went into the living room and bent to kiss Nick's forehead. "I'll see you tonight."

If he heard her, he gave no indication.

Only when she was outside did she realize he hadn't told her to be careful.

SAM APPROACHED THE car where Gonzo waited for her. With every step she took away from Nick, she became more conflicted. Pacing the sidewalk, she tried to figure out what to do. Unused to being paralyzed by indecision, she examined every angle and kept coming back to the same conclusion. Before this, before Nick, there'd never been a decision. The job came first. Always. Now it wasn't quite so simple.

Gonzo waited patiently, watching her as she moved back and forth.

Finally, Sam stopped and turned to him. "Go to Florida." From her pocket, she withdrew the slip of paper Laine had given her, handed it to him and filled him in on what she knew about Duncan Quick. "He was with Sinclair for twenty years, so be gentle in how you deliver the news. I want to know where Quick has been for the last twenty-four hours. I want confirmation from anyone he names as an alibi."

"You aren't coming?"

Sam glanced at the front door to Nick's house. "No."

Gonzo's eyes widened with surprise.

"Don't say it," she growled.

His expression one of total innocence, he said, "Say what?"

"Call me the minute you have anything."

"I'm on it."

She watched him walk to his car and drive away, and then she kicked the living shit out of one of the tires on her own car.

"Sam?"

Looking up, she found her father and Celia watching her.

"What's wrong?" her father asked, directing his chair around a patch of ice on the sidewalk as he came toward her.

"Did you hear about Sinclair?"

"The chief called your father," Celia said. "We're stunned. How's Nick?"

"Horrible."

"Is that why you're abusing your car?" Skip asked.

"I need to go to Florida to interview Sinclair's ex-lover, but how do I do that when he's practically catatonic?" Sam asked, gesturing to Nick's house.

"Is anyone with him?" Celia asked.

"Christina, his chief of staff," Sam said. She should be the one offering comfort to Nick, but for some reason he didn't want it from her.

Nick's front door swung open, and they watched as Christina held the storm door open, urging him out ahead of her. He had changed into a suit, but hadn't bothered to shave.

Sam, Skip and Celia watched them come down the stone stairs.

"What are you still doing here?" Nick asked Sam in a dull, flat tone.

"I sent Gonzo to Florida."

"Oh."

"We're going to the Capitol so he can be there for the opening of the new session and to vote on O'Connor-Martin," Christina said.

"I'll catch up to you after," Sam said.

"Talk to Senator Cook," Nick said, still wearing a faraway expression on his face.

"Why?" Sam asked.

"He made a comment to me about Julian," Nick said. "That he should watch his back because someone might take a shot at him."

"I'll talk to Cook." Sam went up on tiptoes to kiss his cheek. "That helps. Thank you."

Christina ushered Nick into her car, and they drove off.

"Wow," Skip said. "You weren't kidding."

"What do I do?" Sam said. "I don't know how to help him through this."

"You love him," Celia said. "You just love him. That's all you can do."

FREDDIE AWAKENED FROM a deep sleep, his body languid and replete after an all-night sex fest. With his hand tucked into the soft lushness of Elin's breasts, he wondered if there was any special morning-after stuff he should say or do.

As he pondered that question, she stirred, her muscular ass brushing against his groin.

His dick actually ached from what he'd put it through during the night. It was a good thing he had to work this morning. Otherwise, he might be expected to perform again, and he wasn't sure he could.

Stretching his stiff muscles he raised his arm to check his watch to see how much time he had before his cell phone alarm would tell him it was time to get up. "Shit!" He sat up so fast that Elin almost fell off her side of the bed.

"What?"

Freddie bolted from the bed and ran for his coat, which Elin had put in the living room the night before. Rifling through the pocket, he found his cell phone and stared at it in stunned disbelief. It was off. He never shut off that phone. Ever. "Did you shut my phone off?" Returning to the bedroom, he powered up the phone.

Still half-asleep, she muttered, "Hmm?"

"Elin! *Did you shut off my phone?*" It went crazy beeping with messages. *"Sonofabitch."*

"You were off duty," she said without opening her eyes. "I wanted you to relax."

"Are you *serious?* I'm a homicide detective! I'm never off duty!" Multiple calls from Jeannie McBride, Sam and Captain Malone popped up on the list of missed calls. "Shit, shit, *shit*," he whispered, tugging on his clothes as fast as he could, his heart racing with anxiety and dread. What had he missed?

Elin watched him from the bed, the sheet pulled up snug against her ample breasts. "Are you mad?" she asked in a small voice.

He was so far beyond mad he was afraid to say anything for fear he'd totally lose it with her. Pushing his feet into the hiking boots he favored in the winter, he headed for the door without tying them.

She got up, donned a robe and followed him into the living room. "I'm sorry, Freddie. I wasn't thinking about your work."

Without a single look back, he stalked out the door and let it slam behind him.

On his way to HQ, Freddie fought back surge after surge of nausea. He had no one to blame but himself. This was his punishment for abandoning his morals for a night of mindless sex. If he hadn't given into his base urges, he'd be at work right now where he belonged rather than desperately trying to come up with an excuse that Sam would buy.

"PLAY THAT BACK again." Sam watched the screen with intense focus. "There. Freeze that." She pointed. "Is that him talking to the doorman? The height is about right."

Jeannie consulted her notes. "The doorman said he didn't remember Sinclair talking to him."

"It's kind of fuzzy, Lieutenant," Malone said from behind her. "Could be anyone."

"No one recalled talking to him," Jeannie said. "We interviewed the entire shift."

"Take it to the lab," Sam said. "See if they can enhance that frame for us."

Freddie came bursting into the room.

"Cruz," Sam said. "Nice of you to join us."

"I'm sorry, Lieutenant," he said, breathing hard. "I overslept. My phone died."

"Which is it, Detective?" Sam said, studying his disheveled appearance.

Freddie took a deep breath. "My phone died and the

alarm didn't go off so I overslept. I apologize. It won't happen again. What did I miss?"

"A homicide," Sam said, filling him in on the details.

"Isn't that Nick's friend?"

"Yes."

"Oh, man," Freddie said.

He turned his head, and Sam zeroed in on the hickey on his neck.

"What can I do?" he asked. "Give me something to do."

Still eyeing him suspiciously, Sam handed him the tape and repeated the instructions to have the lab zero in on the frame in question. "I'll be partnering with Detective McBride on this one."

"Why?" Freddie cried. "Because I was late *one* time?"

"No." Sam leveled him with a cold stare. "Because you lied to me."

"I told you what happened! I've never been late before. Ever."

"Take the tape to the lab, Detective, and then go relieve the officers watching Reese's house."

Freddie's mouth fell open. "For real?"

"You heard me."

He stalked out of the conference room, slamming the door behind him.

"I'm, um, going to check on the canvas," McBride said, scooting out after him.

Malone studied Sam.

"What?" she snapped.

"Being kind of hard on Cruz, aren't you?"

"You told me to run my command any way I see fit. That's what I'm doing."

"How do you know he lied?"

"I know him."

"Very well," Malone said. "I'll leave you to it. You know where I am if you need me."

When she was alone, Sam paced the small room. The frustration threatened to boil over. Where was Clarence Reese? Who had killed Julian Sinclair? How would she deal with Nick and his devastation in the midst of two homicide investigations? And last, who had been chewing on her partner's neck?

FIFTEEN

GONZO SAT ON the floor outside Duncan Quick's apartment for more than an hour. A window at one end of the hall looked out over South Beach, eleven stories below. The boredom gave him far too much time to think about the incredible night he had spent with Christina Billings.

She had surprised him with her willingness to sleep with him after just two dates. He'd expected to have to work harder to win over a sharp, successful woman like her. Not that he was complaining. No way. The woman was h-o-t. It was just that not too many people surprised him anymore after ten years as a cop.

Not only did she surprise him, she intrigued him. He wasn't used to being intrigued by women. Entertained, yes. Intrigued? Not so much. He'd expected her to be like most of the women who passed through his life as transients. They were on their way to something more lasting, something they knew they wouldn't find with him. So he had a reputation for being a bit of a player. So what?

"I think I might keep this one around for a while," he muttered to himself. "See what transpires." Of course the fact that Sam had freaked when she saw them together only added to Christina's appeal. "A smart man wouldn't antagonize his boss." Laughing to himself, Gonzo combed his fingers through jet-black hair. "I guess I'm not that smart."

He checked his watch again. Where the hell was Quick? The neighbors hadn't been able to shed any light on his whereabouts. In fact, no one had seen him since the previous morning. Gonzo had already checked all the neighborhood haunts he'd been told Quick frequented to no avail.

His cell phone rang. "Gonzales."

"What've you got?" Sam asked.

"Nothing yet. No sign of Quick anywhere."

"Interesting."

"How long do you want me to wait?"

"As long as it takes. He has to come home eventually."

"I was afraid you'd say that. What's happening there?"

"We've got jack. No one at the hotel remembers seeing Sinclair after the O'Connors dropped him off. We've got some grainy film that seems to show him talking to someone, but the image isn't clear enough to be of any help."

"Is it possible he was meeting someone?"

"We're looking at that. His estranged brother lives here in town. McBride and I are on our way to talk to him now."

"Keep me posted. Any sign of Cruz?"

"He rolled in about an hour ago with a hickey on his neck and a boatload of excuses about his phone dying."

Gonzo howled with laughter. "Aw, our little boy is finally growing up."

"He needs to grow up on his own time."

"It's the first time he's ever been late. Lighten up, Lieutenant."

"I wish everyone would stop saying that to me!"

"Would you ride anyone else this hard?" Gonzo asked, bracing himself for her retort.

"What're you saying? That I favor him?"

"He's your partner. Of course you favor him. But

maybe you expect more of him, too." Again he braced himself. "Because you trained him."

"Hmm. I hadn't thought of it that way."

"So he had a big night out. It's high time, don't you think?"

"Maybe," she conceded. "I should probably partner up with you or someone more experienced so I don't have to deal with this crap."

"You'd break his heart, Sam. He's totally devoted to you."

"Christ," she muttered. "All these entanglements. When did I get so *entangled?*"

Gonzo laughed. "It's such a bitch having people care about you, isn't it?"

"Seriously! Call me when you find Quick."

"Will do." Gonzo stashed the phone in his pocket and got up to wander to the window again. Looking out at the palm trees, sugar-white sand and crystal-blue water, he wished he were here on vacation. *When was the last time I had a vacation?* he wondered. His grandparents had lived here when they first came from Cuba, but the family later moved north. Maybe after they closed this case, he'd bring Christina here for a week on the beach.

"Whoa," he said. "Where'd that come from?" He wasn't the kind of guy who took a woman on a vacation. Hell, he rarely saw them again after he slept with them. The ding of the elevator arriving at the other end of the hallway jarred him out of his disturbing thoughts. Turning, he found an older man coming down the hallway at a determined clip. Only when he drew closer did Gonzo spot the bruises on the man's face and the drying blood on his lip. He carried a small duffel bag and was dressed in khakis and an untucked button-down shirt.

"Mr. Quick?"

The other man jolted, clearly startled by Gonzo's unexpected appearance.

"I'm sorry to scare you. Are you Duncan Quick?"

"Who wants to know?"

Gonzo flashed his badge. "Detective Tommy Gonzales, Metro Washington, D.C. Police."

Quick ran a trembling hand through thinning gray hair. "I'm Duncan Quick. What can I do for you?"

"What happened to your face?"

"I had an accident."

Gonzo didn't believe him but decided not to push it—yet. "Do you mind if we go inside?"

"What's this about?"

"Let's go in, and I'll tell you."

Warily, Quick opened his apartment door and gestured Gonzo into a stylish, contemporary space.

"Nice place."

"Thank you. Now what can I do for you, Detective?"

"I'm sorry to have to tell you that Julian Sinclair has been murdered in Washington." Gonzo had learned to cut to the chase in these instances.

Quick gasped and took a step back, his face ashen with shock. The bruises stood out against the sudden pallor. "That's not possible," Quick stammered. "He's going to be on the Supreme Court. I saw the news."

"He was murdered last night."

"How?" he whispered.

"He was shot. His body was found early this morning in a Washington, D.C., park."

"That just can't be," Quick said, sinking to the sofa as if his bones had liquefied. He dissolved into deep gulping sobs.

Gonzo found himself looking out at the water view,

anything to avoid watching the raw display of grief. "Can I get you something?" he asked a few minutes later.

Without looking up, Quick shook his head.

Gonzo gave him another couple of minutes. "Mr. Quick, I'm sorry to have to do this, but I need to know where you've been for the last twenty-four hours."

Quick released a harsh laugh. "Where have I been? I was getting the shit beat out of me by a guy I met in a bar." His voice caught on a sob, and he buried his face in his hands. "Julian, oh, God, this is all my fault."

Gonzo sat down across from Quick. "What do you mean?"

"I forced the issue." He wiped tears from his face. "I wanted him to retire and move down here with me, but he wasn't ready. If I had stayed with him, if I had been with him, maybe..."

"I'm going to need the name of the man you were with last night."

Quick raised his anguished face, his eyes connecting with Gonzo's. "You suspect *me?*"

"I need to rule you out." Gonzo nodded toward the duffel Quick had dropped inside the door. "What's in the bag?"

"Gym clothes."

"Mind if I have a look?"

With the weary wave of his hand, Quick granted permission.

Gonzo went over to squat down next to the bag. Unzipping it, he pulled out a bloody T-shirt and turned to Quick.

"What I was wearing when this happened," he said, pointing to his lip.

Studying the older man's battered face, Gonzo believed him. According to Sam's report, Sinclair's body had shown no sign of a struggle the likes of which Quick had obviously endured. "Who were you with, Duncan?"

Quick ran a weary hand though his hair. "You really have to talk to him?"

"I really do."

"I'd appreciate it if you didn't mention all of this," he said, gesturing to his face.

"Why would you want him to get away with that?"

"I've been so lost without Julian, Detective." The statement and the grief behind it touched Gonzo. "I took a risk and paid the price." He shrugged. "Not the first time, probably won't be the last."

"When did you last speak to Julian?"

"A couple of months ago. He called to tell me the nomination was imminent and to assure me he would do his best to keep my name out of the proceedings."

"And that was important to you?"

"There are people in my life who aren't aware."

"What was at stake for you if they found out?"

"Plain old bigotry." He paused, gathering his thoughts. "Julian has a brother who stopped speaking to him after he found out about us. They hadn't spoken in thirteen years." Sadness radiated from him. "Can you imagine? Not speaking to your brother simply because of who he loves?"

"No, sir. I can't."

"That's how it is for people of our generation." He got up, went to a bar set up by the windows overlooking the beach, and poured himself a shot. "We often have to hide who we are from even those closest to us."

Gonzo shook his head at the offer of a drink.

"We were very discreet. Always. For the first seven years we were together, only a small circle of close friends knew that we were more than the best of friends. We even maintained separate residences, at least on paper. Then his sister-in-law found out about us and went ballistic. We were much more careful after that." Duncan poured another drink. "But I reached a point where I couldn't live a lie for one more day. Twenty years is a long time, you know?"

Gonzo nodded.

"Julian's mother died. His brother was out of the picture. My family hardly would've been surprised if I officially came out. I couldn't understand what was standing in our way."

"So what was?"

Duncan smiled, but it didn't reach his eyes. "Ambition." He returned to the sofa and sat down hard. "Julian wanted the court more than he wanted me."

"That must've angered you."

"It hurt me. I'd planned to grow old with him." His voice hitched on a sob. "I loved him. More than anyone else in this world. I *loved* him. After he was nominated, I kept hoping the press would find out."

Gonzo waited for him to continue.

"I figured if it got out, it might derail the nomination. As far as we've come, I don't know if America is ready for a gay Supreme Court justice. I'm ashamed to say I even considered leaking it. But I discovered I couldn't do that to him. That's how much I loved him. So when I heard he was in Washington for the hearings, I went out, got drunk, met a thug named Ron and went home with him. You know the rest."

"Ron's last name and address?"

Grimacing, Duncan rattled off the information.

THIRTY MINUTES LATER, Gonzo stood at the door to Ron Spaulding's apartment, accompanied by two South Beach police officers. Obviously, they had gotten Ron out of bed, and Gonzo was gratified to note that his bottom lip was split and swollen. Duncan had gotten off at least one good shot in self-defense.

"Waddya want?" Ron mumbled. He was blond and handsome in a cocky sort of way with a pierced ear and perfect pecs. Gonzo wanted to smack him around for roughing up Duncan, a man thirty years older.

"Ron Spaulding?"

"What's it to you?" he grumbled, scratching his belly above the waistband of gym shorts.

Gonzo flashed his badge. "Detective Tommy Gonzales, Metro Washington, D.C. Police. Did you spend last night with a man named Duncan?"

"Yeah, so?"

"What time did you two hook up?"

"I don't know. Nine maybe?"

Sinclair was still alive at eleven-fifteen when the O'Connors dropped him off at the hotel. "Were you with him all night?"

"Uh-huh."

Whereas Duncan had seemed ashamed of hooking up with a stranger, this guy was so matter-of-fact about it that Gonzo suspected it was a regular occurrence in his life. He turned to the cops he'd brought with him. "He's all yours."

"You're under arrest for the assault of Duncan Quick," one of them said.

"What the *fuck?*" Spaulding said. "Get your fucking hands off me!"

Gonzo left them to fight it out. He had what he needed.

SIXTEEN

"WHAT DO WE know about Preston Sinclair?" Sam asked Jeannie McBride as she drove to Sinclair's place in Georgetown.

Reading from her notes, Jeannie recited what she'd uncovered when she ran his name. "History professor at Catholic University. Grew up in Massachusetts, one of two sons. Went to Princeton for undergrad, Harvard for graduate school. Has a Ph.D. in American history. He's lived in the District for twenty-three years. Estranged from his brother, Julian, for the last thirteen years. Married with two grown sons, one an accountant, the other an attorney. His wife, Diandra, is a conservative commentator on the Capital News Network."

"Yes, the hatemonger. We talked about her the other night at dinner. Julian was horrified by her."

"I can see why, but she has a huge following."

"Good work, McBride." Pulling onto Sinclair's street, she found a parking space and turned to Jeannie. "I appreciate your help with this one."

"No problem. Have you spoken with the senator? Since we saw him earlier?"

"No."

"I feel sorry for him."

"I do, too." Sam was trying her best not to think about how crushed Nick had been earlier. Lately, she had grown so accustomed to leaning on his quiet strength that she had no idea how to help him. "I'm sure he'll be fine. He's strong." But even as she said it, Sam wasn't entirely sure that he'd be okay. "Let's see what Mr. Sinclair has to say about the murder of his brother."

Located in one of Washington's more affluent neighborhoods, Sinclair's brick-front townhouse was well tended. His wife, a striking blonde, answered the door.

"Mrs. Sinclair?" Sam showed her badge. "Lieutenant Holland, Metro Police. My partner, Detective McBride. May we have a moment of your time?"

"What's this about?"

Nonplussed by the other woman's curtness, Sam said, "We need to speak to you and your husband. May we come in?"

Resigned, Diandra Sinclair stepped aside to allow them in. No doubt decorated by a high-price interior designer, the house was furnished with an eclectic mix of antiques and contemporary pieces.

"Is your husband at home?"

"He's very busy. It'd be better if you came back at another time."

"We need to see him now." Sam held the other woman's furious gaze until Diandra turned away.

"I'll get him."

"Chilly," Jeannie whispered.

"Seriously."

She returned five minutes later with a man who bore a resemblance to his late brother but was several inches taller and a couple of years older.

Sam introduced herself and Jeannie to him.

"I've seen you in the paper," Preston said.

"Mr. Sinclair, I'm very sorry to have to tell you your brother was murdered early this morning."

Preston gasped. "What?"

Diandra reached out to her husband.

Sam gave them the few details she knew.

He moved to a sofa. His wife followed, sitting next to him and taking his hand.

"I'm sorry for your loss," Sam said.

"Thank you," he said, his voice little more than a whisper.

"I understand you and your brother were estranged."

"That's right," he said, looking pained. "Thirteen years."

"And why was that?"

"A difference of opinion that got out of hand. You know how these things happen."

"Actually, I don't. It wouldn't occur to me to not speak to my sisters for thirteen years."

"You have no right to judge him," Diandra snapped.

"No judgment," Sam said. "Just stating the facts, ma'am." Turning back to Preston, she said, "You've had no contact with him since he was nominated for the Supreme Court?"

Preston glanced at his wife and then back at Sam. "No." He cleared his throat. "Well, except for an email I sent to congratulate him."

Diandra stared at her husband, shocked. "When?"

"The other day." He seemed chagrined. "I wanted him to know I was happy for him."

"Did you get a reply?" Sam asked.

Preston shook his head. "I know he must've been so busy. He would've written back when he could."

"Have you communicated with him by email before this?" Diandra asked, stealing Sam's next question.

"Once or twice."

Diandra's eyes flashed with anger. "I can't believe this!"

"He was my *brother,* Di. My only sibling."

"He was a liar and a fraud."

"He was my brother," Preston whispered, wiping a tear from his face.

"Stop it," she snapped, seeming appalled that he was crying over Julian's death.

As Preston obediently mopped up his tears, Sam and Jeannie exchanged glances. This was one twisted relationship.

"Did you expect to see him while he was in town?" Sam asked.

"I'd hoped to. In the email, I offered to meet him, but like I said, I never heard back from him."

"Unbelievable," Diandra muttered, glaring at her husband.

Preston looked down at the floor like a chastened child whose mother was angry with him.

"Mrs. Sinclair, can you tell me how your husband and his brother came to be estranged?" Sam said.

"Why don't you ask him?"

"Because I'm asking you."

"Fine. I saw them—Julian and that fag he referred to as his 'friend.' They were kissing! Right out in public! And I'd allowed my children—my *sons*—to sleep at his home. He'd exposed them to his immoral lifestyle, and God knows what else." She shuddered.

"He adored those boys," Preston snapped. "You know he did! And they adored him." To Sam he said, "They'll be crushed by his death. They'd reestablished contact with him and saw him regularly."

"They did not!" Diandra said, her face flat with shock.

"Yes, they did," Preston retorted defiantly. "Once they were out of your house, they made their own decisions."

Diandra sent him a venomous glare, and once again he wilted.

"Where were the two of you last night?" Sam asked, imagining the chewing out Preston was in for after they left.

Taken aback by the question, Preston said, "We had dinner out and went to bed early. Around ten or so, I guess."

Her lips tight with fury, Diandra nodded in agreement.

"And neither of you left the house again after you returned from dinner?"

"No," he said.

"Of course not," she said.

"Do either of you require medication in order to sleep?"

"What kind of question is that?" Diandra asked.

"It's a simple yes or no kind of question. Do you require medication to sleep?"

"I take a sleeping pill every now and then," Preston said.

"Did you take one last night?"

He nodded. "I've been having trouble sleeping since Julian was nominated."

"Why's that?" Sam asked.

"I've had some concerns," Preston said haltingly, "about his nomination stirring up old hurts. Things that are better left in the past."

Sam turned to Diandra. "Do you take sleeping medication?"

"I do not."

"Tell me, Mrs. Sinclair, what does it do to a 'career' like yours if your brother-in-law comes out as a gay man to all of America during his confirmation hearings?"

"I have no idea," she said, spitting the words at Sam. "I guess we'll never know."

Sam stared her down for several long seconds. "I'd like to speak to your sons. Are they local?"

"What for?" Diandra asked.

"This is a homicide investigation. I can talk to anyone I want."

"I'll write down their information," Preston said with a pointed look at his wife. "They're both here in the city."

Sam and Jeannie left after requesting that the Sinclairs stay local until the investigation was completed.

"Wow," Jeannie said when they were in the car. "That woman was tightly wound, huh?"

"And a total homophobe. You don't see that kind of hatred very often these days."

"No question she's the reason the brothers were estranged."

"She didn't approve of Julian," Sam said. "I want to know what kind of problems it would've caused her 'career' if Julian's orientation became public."

"Definitely worth looking into."

"Yeah, she knew damned well that it would be a disaster for her if he came out just as her book was released. I also want to talk to their sons. I'm willing to bet they were his heirs."

"Probably. Why'd you ask about the sleeping medicine?"

"A hunch," Sam said. "They're each other's alibi, but if one of them was drugged up, the other could've snuck out."

"I never would've thought to ask that," Jeannie said, her voice tinged with admiration.

"Shit," Sam muttered. "Now you're starting to sound like Cruz." A pang of guilt struck her as she thought of him sitting in the cold watching Reese's place. Then she got over it. One shift spent on surveillance wouldn't kill him, and it was the least of what he deserved for lying to her.

"Let's go have a chat with Senator Robert Cook," Sam said.

AT THE CAPITOL, Sam and Jeannie were told that Senator Cook was in a meeting and couldn't be disturbed.

Sam narrowed her eyes into her most intimidating stare and watched the administrative assistant shrivel before her. Excellent. "Either you can go in there and get him, or I'm going to. Your choice."

"Please wait right here," the admin said, scurrying away.

"Can you teach me that look?" Jeannie asked.

"It's a gift. You have to be born with it."

Jeannie laughed. "I should've known you'd say something like that."

The admin returned. "Right this way, please."

"See that?" Sam said to Jeannie, loud enough for the admin to hear her. "I love when the citizenry cooperates with their law enforcement professionals."

"It's critical to maintaining law and order," Jeannie replied, playing along.

The admin probably would've scowled at them if she had dared.

Cook's spacious office, Sam noted, was easily four times the size of Nick's. Seniority had its perks.

"What can I do for you?" Cook growled. "I'm very busy."

"Then we won't take much of your time," Sam said. "You told Senator Cappuano that Supreme Court nominee Julian Sinclair should watch his back. That someone might take a shot at him. Can you tell me what you meant by that?"

"It was a figure of speech," Cook said, visibly ruffled by the question. "What does he do—run home and tell the little woman everything that transpires around here?"

"No, just comments that factor into murder investigations."

"Murder investigation? What're you talking about?"

"Julian Sinclair was murdered last night."

Cook's portly face turned an unbecoming shade of purple. "You aren't *possibly* insinuating that I had anything to do with it."

"Do you know of anyone who might've had something to do with it?"

"Of course I don't. I hardly associate with murderers."

Sam consulted her notebook. "Weren't you once associated with Robert 'Junior' Despositio, who's doing time in federal prison for attempted murder and racketeering?"

Cook's face twisted with rage. "He was a high school classmate of mine who made poor choices. I haven't been 'associated' with him in thirty years."

"Had you ever met Mr. Sinclair?"

"I had not. I believe we had a meeting on the schedule for sometime in the next week. Meeting with the senators who'll be voting for them is part of the routine for Supreme Court nominees."

"Where were you last night after eleven?"

"Home in bed."

"Can anyone confirm that?"

"My wife."

Sam held out her notebook to the senator. "A number where I can reach her?"

Cook stared at her for a long moment. "I'm a United States senator. My word should be more than good enough."

"It isn't," Sam said. "The number please?"

He snatched the notebook from her hand. "Your superiors will be hearing about this."

"They enjoy getting complaints about me doing my job. Should I give you the best number to reach them?"

Cook thrust the notebook back at her. "Tell your *boyfriend* he needs to learn to keep his mouth shut if he plans to make any friends around here."

"You aren't threatening him, are you, Senator?"

"Of course not," Cook huffed. "I'm just pointing out that blabbing to cops is no way to make friends."

"I'm sure that making friends around here is of far less concern to him than finding the person who killed his *real* friend. Detective?"

Jeannie followed Sam from the room. "That was *ill*."

"Is that good or bad?" Sam asked, baffled.

"Good," Jeannie said. "Very *good*."

"Ill. I like that." Sam filed it away for future use.

FREDDIE SHIVERED IN the icy cold, his eyes fixed on Reese's house. He'd turned on the car and heater half an hour before, but the warm air had made him too sleepy. Even though he was freezing, he burned with anger directed at Sam, Elin and mostly himself. This was his own fault. If he had remained true to his faith and his beliefs, he'd be working a homicide with his partner right now rather than sitting in a frigid time-out. The day grew dark early as heavy clouds hung over the city, and Freddie fought to stay awake.

He should've known Sam would zero in on the lie. "Stupid," he muttered, his breath coming out in puffy clouds. Shrinking deeper into his coat, he wanted to smack the crap out of Elin. Except, of course, he never would. But it sure was nice to fantasize about spanking that perfect ass. When his body reacted with infuriating predictability to that image, Freddie roared with frustration, aggravation and shame.

Since he hadn't gotten to take a shower, her essence clung to his skin. Images from their erotic night together tortured him like a movie he couldn't seem to escape. As much as he wanted to throttle her, he feared that if she appeared beside the car right now, throttling wouldn't be the first thing he'd do to her.

Freddie checked the clock on the dashboard. "Three more hours. I'll die before then." He wanted a shower, a warm bed and eight uninterrupted hours of sleep so bad he was tempted to sell his well-protected soul to the devil to get them. With a mighty yawn, he reached for his cell phone wishing he could call Sam to find out what was going on with the Sinclair case.

He hated that he'd let her down. After his mother, Sam was the most important woman in his life—not that he'd ever admit that to her. Tomorrow, he would find a way to fix this. They worked too well together and meant too much to each other to let this fester.

He stared intently at Reese's house. He'd give everything he had to be the one to snag the guy who shot Skip Holland. Freddie loved the hell out of Skip and wanted to close his case almost as much as Sam did.

Another hour passed in frigid silence, until Freddie thought he'd lose his mind if he had to stare at the dark house for one more minute. Suddenly, he saw a narrow beam of light moving through the house. Were his tired eyes playing tricks on him? No, someone was definitely walking through the house with a flashlight.

Reaching for his radio, he started to call for backup but stopped himself. How much would it mean to Sam if he arrested Reese? It would certainly go a long way toward repairing the rift between them. But going in without backup went against all his training. Regardless, Freddie kept his eyes on the beam of light as he got out of the car and crossed the deserted street.

Cutting through the alley behind the house, he drew his weapon and approached the back door, his heart pounding with adrenaline and excitement. An arrest like this would make him a hero at HQ, and even though his better judgment urged him once again to call for backup before he went in, he didn't.

His heart beat like a bass drum in his ears. The back door was unlocked. He eased it open and stepped into the kitchen. Down the hallway, he could see the flashlight moving around and headed in that direction, his gun leading the way. Just as he was about to take the intruder by surprise, Freddie's cell phone rang, alerting the other man to his presence. Cursing himself for being so stupid, he grabbed the phone and flipped it open to stop the ringing.

The man, dressed all in black, spun around and fired.

The bullet hit Freddie in the shoulder, the force propelling him back against the wall. As he sank to the floor, his gun and phone fell from his hands. The last thing he saw before he lost consciousness was a gun pointed at his chest.

SEVENTEEN

In the HQ conference room, Sam labored over the murder board. Starting to the left with grainy images retrieved from the hotel security to photos of Julian Sinclair dead in Lincoln Park to autopsy photos, Sam laid it out in chronological order. Each piece to the puzzle would eventually add up to the whole. So many threads to this one—the secret sexual orientation, the family rift, the extreme views on hot-button issues—his and his sister-in-law's—and the connection to the O'Connors.

Sam thought about the man she'd dined with two nights prior and was surprised by a wave of sadness over his loss. He'd come to town, to *her* town, expecting to be confirmed as a Supreme Court justice and would leave in a body bag. As someone charged with ensuring the safety of visitors and residents alike, the loss of his life offended her on a deep, personal level.

"I'll get him, Julian," she promised the deceased face in the photo. "I promise you, I'll get him."

The conference room door flew open.

"Shots fired at Reese's house," Jeannie McBride said, her eyes wide with dismay.

Sam's heart contracted. "Cruz?"

"Not answering his radio, and his cell just rings."

Sam ran from the room, grabbed her coat and headed for the door. "Tyrone, McBride." Sam's throat contracted, robbing her of air and speech.

The two detectives scurried after her and sprinted with her to the parking lot.

"He's fine," McBride said. "He's got Reese, and he'll be calling it in any minute."

"Make sure rescue is on the way," Sam ordered, feeling considerably less optimistic.

"His mother called dispatch," Tyrone said. "She had reached his cell and heard gunfire. She's freaking out."

"And there's no word from Cruz?" Sam asked.

His face grim, Tyrone shook his head as the radio crackled with reports of a possible officer down.

Sam couldn't seem to get oxygen to her lungs. Flying across the city with sirens and flashing lights, she tried to take a deep breath but couldn't get air past the huge knot of fear in her throat. She sent him there as punishment and now... *Please don't let him be dead.*

"Lieutenant," Jeannie said.

Startled out of her thoughts, Sam glanced over at her.

"Patrol is on the scene. They want to know if they should go in ahead of us."

Sam's mind raced. If the shooter was still in the house, she'd be risking additional people by sending them in. But if Freddie was in there and wounded, time could be critical. "Do they have vests?"

Jeannie conveyed the question. "They do."

"With vests, two in the back, two in the front. Go in together."

Jeannie relayed Sam's order.

They waited in tense silence as they wove through traffic on their way to the scene.

When the code for an officer down came over the airwaves a few minutes later, Sam wanted to wail. *"Shit,"* she whispered, pressing the accelerator to the floor.

They arrived just as paramedics wheeled Freddie out of the house.

"Oh," Jeannie gasped, taking a step back.

Freddie's face was sheet-white, and the paramedics running alongside the gurney were working frantically to stop the blood streaming from his shoulder.

"Jesus," Tyrone muttered, slipping a supporting arm around Jeannie's shoulders.

"What've we got?" Sam asked one of the officers in an effort to keep from shrieking at the sight of Freddie's lifeless form.

The rattled officer took a deep breath. "Gunshot wound to the shoulder. Significant blood loss. We found a flashlight, still lit, in the hallway. It's possible Cruz took the shooter by surprise."

"No sign of the shooter?"

"No, ma'am."

"Where're they taking him?"

"GW Trauma." He reached into his pocket. "Cruz's cell phone has been ringing like crazy."

Sam took the phone from him and checked the missed calls. "His mother," she said, watching the ambulance pull away. "I'll take care of it." She gestured for Jeannie and Tyrone to follow her inside. They assessed the first floor and found the still-lit flashlight as well as the large pool of Cruz's blood. Fixated on the blood, Sam said, "You two are in charge here. I want a full sweep of this entire neighborhood. First shift is retained. Recall third shift. Let's find this scumbag."

"Yes, Lieutenant," Tyrone said, his eyes hot with fury. "Will you let us know about Cruz?"

She bit her lip and nodded.

Jeannie squeezed her arm. "He's going to be fine. He's young and strong."

"Yeah." Before she could embarrass herself by breaking down in front of her detectives, she left them and headed back to HQ. Her heart beat fast from the rage that overtook her, and her fingers were so tight around the steering wheel that her knuckles turned white.

Freddie's cell phone rang again, and bracing herself, Sam answered it. "Mrs. Cruz, this is Lieutenant Holland."

"Sam! Tell me what's happening! I heard a gunshot! *Freddie.*"

"He was shot in the shoulder."

"Oh, no. Oh, *God.*"

"They're taking him to GW Trauma. Do you want me to send a car to take you there?"

"Is he going to live, Lieutenant? Please. Tell me the truth."

"I don't know, ma'am. He lost a lot of blood."

The other woman's wretched wails rattled Sam's already frayed nerves. "I'll send a car. Sit tight. They'll be there in a few minutes, and I'll meet you at GW, okay?"

"Thank you."

Sam called in the order for Mrs. Cruz's ride as she tore into the HQ parking lot, slammed the car into Park and took off running. At the city jail, she ordered the flustered officer at the desk to put Hector Reese in an interrogation room.

Reese smirked when he saw her coming five minutes later. "They told me the cunt cop—"

She ripped him out of his chair and hurled him back into the wall.

"What the fuck?"

Sam slapped his face as hard as she could. "Shut the fuck up."

"You can't hit me—"

Her fist slammed into his midsection. "Your word

against mine, you useless piece of shit. Who's going to believe you?"

Gasping for air, Hector winced when she tightened her grip on his shirt collar. "What'd you want?" he choked out.

"Where's your scumbag brother? And do *not* tell me you don't know."

"I don't—"

Sam gut punched him again.

He sank to his knees. "I swear to God. I don't know."

"He shot my partner."

Startled, Hector looked up at her.

"Every cop in this city is looking for him. They won't hesitate to shoot if they find him. He's already suspected in the shooting of one cop—"

"What cop did he shoot? He didn't shoot no cop."

"My father, you asshole." She hauled him back up. "So don't fuck with me. Tell me where he's hiding out."

"I'm not telling you shit," he said. "You want him, you find him."

"He's gonna wind up dead. You could stop that."

"He can take care of himself, and so can I."

Sam jammed her knee into his groin, dropping him once again to his knees.

He howled in pain. *"You fucking bitch!"*

Gripping a fistful of his hair, she forced him to look at her. "You can sit in here and rot for all I care. But if you decide to cooperate, I might be willing to deal. You think about that." She released him and headed for the door.

"Cunt cop," he muttered from the floor.

Sweating, frustrated and infuriated, Sam left the room and found Captain Malone waiting for her.

"Anything?" he asked, his face tight with stress.

Sam wiped the moisture from her forehead with a hand

that was sore from repeatedly connecting with Hector's ribs. "No." She signaled to the officers guarding the door to return Hector to his cell and looked up at the captain. "I roughed him up pretty good."

"Okay," he said, even though they both knew it wasn't. When one of their own went down, many of the usual rules were overlooked.

"Any word on Cruz?"

"He's in surgery. The blood loss is a big concern."

"I need to get over there."

"I'll go with you."

Sam used the lights and siren to expedite their trip to the hospital.

"President Nelson called the chief earlier," Malone said. "He wants to know what's being done to find Sinclair's killer. They were good friends. He's beside himself."

"We're working the case," Sam said. "But I've directed all available resources toward the search for Reese. For the time being anyway."

Malone nodded his approval. "We'll give that everything for a couple of hours, and then we've got to get back to Sinclair."

They encountered a media circus outside the hospital entrance.

"Lieutenant, who was shot?"

"Is the shooter Reese?"

"What's being done to find him?"

"How close are you to an arrest in the Sinclair case?"

Malone gestured for her to go ahead into the hospital while he dealt with the media.

Thankful for his assistance, Sam entered the hospital and was directed to the surgical waiting room where she found Freddie's mother and extended family engaged in a prayer circle. With her hands jammed into her coat pockets, Sam waited for them to finish. Thinking about her handsome, sensitive, energetic, junk-food-loving partner, Sam's throat closed and she feared tears might be next. She fought back the rush of emotion to focus on Freddie's mother.

Juliette Cruz wiped her face and turned to Sam. "Oh, Lieutenant."

"It's Sam." She hugged the attractive, youthful woman she had met a few times. "What've you heard?"

"Nothing more since they took him into surgery."

Sam led Freddie's mother to a chair and encouraged her to sit.

"It's good of you to be here," Juliette said.

"I wouldn't be anywhere else."

"He's all I have," Juliette whispered. "I don't know what I'll do if—"

Sam's stomach clenched with pain as she gripped Juliette's hand. "He's going to be just fine."

The alternative was unimaginable.

NICK SAT IN his office, staring out the window. John's bill had passed by ten votes—nine more than they would've gotten before he was killed. The O'Connor name was now forever linked to sweeping immigration reform. After more than a year of hard work on that bill, Nick knew he should be euphoric, but all he felt was numb.

In its opening session, the Senate paid glowing tribute to John and held a moment of silence for Julian—two of Nick's closest friends, both murdered in the scope of a month.

Christina rushed into the room. "Trevor just got word that a cop was shot in the house where that guy killed his family last week."

Her words cut straight through the numbness, the panic snapping him out of the stupor he'd sunk into after learning of Julian's death. Nick was out of his chair before she finished the sentence. "Who?" He resisted the urge to grab her shoulders and shake the information out of her. *"Who is it?"*

"They haven't released a name. Trevor said they took the injured officer to GW."

Running, Nick skipped the elevator and took the stairs on his way to the car, aware that numbness had been replaced by bone-crushing fear. Sam was obsessed with finding Reese. It had to be her. If he lost her, too… He stopped running when his legs threatened to buckle under him.

Christina caught up to him and guided him into her car.

On the way, Nick focused on breathing. His chest ached under the weight of the dread. No one could have this much bad luck. He kept telling himself that, over and over. Breathe in. Breathe out.

"You don't know it's her," Christina said tentatively. "It could be Tommy or someone else."

Nick shook his head. "Sam's been after Reese. She thinks he had something to do with her father's shooting."

"Try not to think the worst."

"Why would I do that?"

They drove the rest of the way in uncomfortable silence, every minute feeling like a year.

At the hospital, Nick once again made use of his new-found clout to learn that the injured officer was in surgery on the seventh floor. With Christina trailing behind him, Nick emerged from the seventh floor elevator and ran down the hallway to the waiting room at the end. He came to a stop when he saw Sam talking to a pretty dark-haired woman. Taking a step back, all the stress of the last palf hour came out as an anguished moan that caught Sam's attention.

She got up and rushed over to him. "I'm so glad to see you."

Christina was right behind him.

"What happened?" he managed to ask, still trying to catch his breath and slow his racing heart.

"It's Freddie," Sam said in a small voice, her arms curling around him, her head resting on his chest. In a rush of words, she continued, "I sent him to watch the house because I was mad at him. He went in there alone, and Reese shot him. It's bad, Nick. He lost a lot of blood."

Christina stepped around them into the waiting room.

Nick knew he should comfort Sam but couldn't seem to move his arms. All at once, fear became anger. "I can't." He shook her off.

"What?" she asked, startled.

"I can't be here. I'm sorry." Spinning around, he started back down the long corridor to the elevator.

She followed him. "Where're you going?"

He walked faster, needing to get out of there. Immediately. "I don't know. Home. I can't do this, Sam. I thought I could, but I can't."

"What can't you do?" She grabbed his arm, forcing him to look at her. "What're you saying?"

"I thought it was you." His heart breaking, he studied her one-in-a-million face. "I thought you'd been shot."

"But I wasn't, Nick." She rested her hands on his chest, beseeching him with her eyes. "I'm right here. I'm fine."

"This time."

"You're upset about Julian. Let's talk about this later. When I get home."

He shook his head. "I can't spend my whole life waiting for it to be you. I'm sorry, Sam."

The elevator doors opened and Skip and Celia emerged.

"Sam!" Celia cried. "How's Freddie?"

Nick got into the elevator and punched the button for the lobby. As the doors closed, he caught a last glance of Sam's stunned expression.

EIGHTEEN

"Sam?" her father said. "What is it? Is Freddie worse?"

Fixated on the elevator doors, she shook her head. "I think Nick just broke up with me." She couldn't believe how much it hurt to say those words.

"No, honey." Celia slipped an arm around Sam's shoulders. "He'd never break up with you. He's upset."

"This was more than that."

"Once things calm down, he'll come around," Skip said.

In that moment, Sam realized things would never calm down, not with two all-consuming jobs sitting at the center of their relationship. "I don't know, Dad. He sounded pretty sure."

"Look at me."

Startled by his sharp tone, Sam let her eyes drop down to meet his. "He's upset about Sinclair. You can't take anything he says or does right now to heart. Give him some space. He'll come around."

"Sam," Captain Malone called from the waiting room, waving at her to come.

With her father and Celia in tow, Sam headed down the hall. She couldn't think about what'd just happened with Nick. Right now she needed to stay focused on Freddie, the search for Reese and the Sinclair case. She'd do what she always did when life became too much for her— she'd work until she dropped from exhaustion. Nick loved her. Of that she had no doubt and in that she would have faith until she could be with him again.

An O.R. nurse had been sent to inform them that Freddie was out of surgery and in recovery. The surgeon would be down to speak with them shortly.

Upon hearing that news, Sam sagged into a chair and closed her eyes to say a silent prayer of thanks. She reached for her cell to call Gonzo, who had texted her to let her know he was back in town and at Reese's house. "He's out of surgery," she said when he answered.

"And?"

"That's all I know right now. What's up out there?"

"No sign of Reese anywhere," Gonzo said, his voice tight with strain. "That bastard had better hope I'm not the one to find him."

"I want him alive," Sam said. "Put out the word. I know he had something to do with my dad's shooting. He's no good to us dead."

"You got it, L.T."

She checked her watch. Ten after midnight. She'd been up almost twenty-four hours and was starting to feel muzzy around the edges. "Release first shift now. Let second shift go at four. Get everyone back to HQ by eight to regroup. We'll divide the resources—half on Reese, the other half on Sinclair. Everything else is back burner for now. Any sign of Reese, I want a call."

"I'll put out the word, and I'll be over there as soon as I can. Everyone wants to come."

"I'd rather you went home and got some sleep." She glanced at Christina across the waiting room and wondered why she was still there since Nick had left. And then it dawned on her—Christina was hoping Gonzo would show up. Sam wasn't about to tell him his "girlfriend" was waiting for him.

"I'm not sleeping until Cruz is out of the woods."

Knowing there was no point in arguing since she agreed with him, she said, "I'll see you when you get here."

She closed the phone and found her father watching her.

"What does Reese have to do with my case?"

Her stomach clenched with pain. "Let's go out in the hallway."

Leaving Celia to comfort Freddie's mother, Skip followed her out of the room.

Sam willed herself to stay calm, to take deep breaths, and to keep her stomach out of the equation.

Skip looked up at her expectantly. "Tell me."

"We found stuff in his house. Newspaper articles, pictures—"

"About the shooting?"

She nodded.

"And when were you planning to tell me this?"

"When I knew more. I didn't want to get your hopes up until I was sure."

"It's a good thing I can't throttle you right now."

"*For what?* Wanting to protect you from more disappointment?"

"I want him caught, Sam. I really do. But once he's behind bars, I'll still be in this chair. Nothing's going to change for me."

"How can you stand knowing he's out there living his life when you're trapped in hell? How can you *stand* it?"

"What choice do I have? I've got the best detective in this city looking for the guy. I know she's going to get him one of these days. Beyond that, I don't give it much thought, to be honest with you."

She stared at him. What was *with* the men in her life

tonight? "You don't give it much thought?" Tossing up her hands, she said, "It's *all* I think about."

"That's because you have the ability to actually *do* something about it. I don't."

Fixating on the wall behind him, she recalled all the near misses and dead ends she'd pursued over the past two years. "Every time I think we're getting close, it turns into nothing. I constantly feel like I'm letting you down. I hate that."

"Sam, you've never let me down. Not once in your whole life. I know you'll get him. And when you do, we'll have the biggest party to celebrate. The biggest party ever."

Back in the day, Skip Holland's parties had been the stuff of legend.

Sam bent to rest her head on his shoulder. "I'll look forward to that. Might be sooner than we think if we can just find that bastard Reese. He's got two cops to account for now, not to mention his family."

"You'll keep me posted?"

"Yeah." She raised her head to meet his eyes. "I'm sorry I kept it from you."

"And you won't do it again?"

"No."

"No matter what happens?"

She squeezed the finger that retained sensation. "I promise." The elevator at the far end of the hall opened, and Sam blinked, certain her eyes had to be deceiving her. "No way," she muttered. "No fucking way."

"What?" Skip asked.

A woman with light hair and eyes red from crying approached them.

"I'm not sure if you remember me, Lieutenant—"

"I do. What're you doing here?"

"I heard about Freddie," she stammered. "On the radio. He's… We're friends."

At least Sam now knew who'd been chewing on her partner's neck.

"Are you the reason his phone was off last night?"

"He was tired—"

"He's a *homicide detective!* He's in here because I punished him for being late! I sent him over there, and he got shot!"

Elin broke down into sobs. "I'm so sorry. It's my fault."

Suddenly, a lot of Freddie's recent behavior made sense—the snappier clothes, the cologne, the befuddlement. The minute he was out of the hospital, Sam was going to beat the hell out of him for this.

"I just wanted to know if he's going to be okay," Elin said between sobs.

"We don't know yet. He got through the surgery."

"I don't want to upset you any more than you already are, so I'll go."

"Wait." Later, Sam would blame exhaustion for the weak moment. "Would he want you here?"

"I don't know." Elin wiped her face. "He was so mad this morning. About the phone. I've never seen him like that before."

Sam smiled to herself. She could only imagine. If someone turned off her phone, they wouldn't still be walking around. "Have you met his mother?"

Elin blanched, which made Sam want to laugh for the first time in hours. "No."

"Allow me to do the honors," she said, sending her father a shit-eating grin.

Skip rolled his eyes, but she could tell he was enjoying the show.

Thirty minutes later, the waiting room was overrun with HQ detectives who had left the search for Reese in the hands of second and third shift so they could check on Cruz. In the hallway, Gonzo huddled with Christina, speaking quietly to her while keeping a firm grip on her hand. Sam couldn't say why the idea of the two of them together bugged her so much. It just did. She didn't like her worlds overlapping. And then she remembered that Nick had stepped out of her world earlier.

Her stomach clenched with dread. This was exactly what she'd been so afraid of—that the moment she allowed him to become essential to her, something would happen to drive them apart. Well, she couldn't let that happen. She *wouldn't* let that happen.

An hour later, Freddie was delivered to a room in ICU. His mother rushed in to see him the moment he was settled. She emerged fifteen minutes later, visibly rattled. "He's asking for you, Lieutenant."

Sam swallowed the huge lump in her throat and went into the darkened room where the beep of machines was the only sound. Venturing a glance at Freddie, she bit back a gasp at how pale and sick he looked. *God.* She rested her hand over his.

His eyes fluttered open. "Hey," he croaked, fighting to keep his eyes open. "I almost had him. If my phone hadn't rang—"

"*That's* what happened?" She struggled to keep her voice down. "How many times have we talked about that?"

He closed his eyes and swallowed. "Too many for me to forget so easily."

"And to go in without backup? What the *hell* were you thinking?"

"I wasn't thinking." He kept his eyes closed. "I wanted to get him. For you."

Sam's own eyes burned. "Stupid. Totally and completely insane. You're lucky he only hit you in the shoulder."

"I know. I'm sorry."

"You're sure it was him?"

"Yeah."

"Has Elin Svendsen been chewing on your neck?"

His eyes flew open. "What're you talking about?"

"Don't screw with me, Cruz," she said, glaring at him.

He released a resigned sigh. "How do you know?"

"I'm the best detective in this city. I know everything."

"Whatever," he said with a grimace that had nothing to do with his injuries.

"She's here."

"She is? Really?"

Thrilled and relieved to have her partner back, she said, "Would I lie to you?"

"Ah, *yeah.*"

"I would not! She's in the waiting room with your mother."

He swallowed hard at that news. "You let her stay? You didn't make her feel like shit and chase her out?"

"I started to," Sam said, a bit disturbed to realize he knew her so well. "But I was too tired to chase."

"I'm sorry I lied to you. I figured you'd freak."

"You figured right, and I plan to beat the crap out of you as soon as you're out of here."

He laughed and then winced. "Thanks for the warning."

"You have a right to a life outside the job," she said begrudgingly. "But don't ever let anyone shut off your phone again, do you hear me?"

"Don't worry. Lesson learned the hard way."

"So, you want to see her or what?"

"Yeah," he said. "I really do."

"Oy vey," Sam muttered on her way out the door to get Elin.

SAM PULLED ONTO Ninth Street at three-thirty in the morning, nearly twenty-four hours after she'd received the call about Sinclair. Parking between her father's house and Nick's she debated as to whether she should wait until the morning to confront Nick. Then she looked up and saw the light on in his bedroom.

"Now," she whispered, her breath a cloudy puff in the cold air. "I won't sleep if I don't."

She used her key in his door and dropped her coat on the sofa on the way to the stairs. In his bedroom, she found him sitting up in bed asleep, a whiskey bottle on the bedside table, his hair a tousled mess and his jaw sprinkled with whiskers. She'd never been so happy to see him.

She contemplated whether she should wake him and hated not knowing if she'd be welcome. She decided to let him sleep. After a quick shower, she shut the light off and slipped into bed.

Lying there next to him, Sam felt lonely for the first time since they'd been together. More than anything, she wanted his strong arms around her. She wanted him to tell her that everything was going to be all right the way he always did. It was unsettling to realize how much she had come to depend on his steady presence. How would she ever go back to living without that? Without him?

She snuggled up to him, dropping soft kisses on his chest.

He came to slowly, and his whole body stiffened. "What're you doing?" he asked, trying to get away.

She held him tighter, knowing if she let him escape now he might never come back. "I need you, Nick."

"I told you. This isn't going to work."

"Yes, it is. It works on every possible level." She caressed his chest. "I know you were scared earlier, and I'm sorry about that." His silence grated on her already frazzled nerves. "Talk to me," she said, punctuating her words with kisses. "Tell me what you're thinking about."

He was silent for a long time, so long that Sam wondered if he was going to say anything. "Every time I hear that something's happened to a cop in this city," he said in a halting staccato, "I'm going to think it's you. I don't want to live like that. I *can't* live like that."

"You'd rather live without me?" Her lips left a trail from his collarbone to his jaw. "Without what we have?" When he trembled, she began to feel hopeful that she was getting through to him. "I love you so much, Nick. So, so much. If you take that away from me, I'll never get over it." She sprinkled kisses on his face and encountered dampness on his cheek. "I know you're sad about Julian. I am, too. I only met him once, but I could see what a special person he was. Let me help you, Nick. Let me love you."

His lips found hers in a hungry, desperate kiss as he rolled her under him.

Sam clung to him, meeting the thrusts of his tongue with her own, tasting whiskey and Nick.

He tore his lips free. "Things happen in threes. My grandmother always said that."

"You thought I was the third thing."

Nodding, he rested his forehead against hers. "I knew you were chasing Reese. I was so sure it was you."

"Freddie getting shot was the third thing."

"How is he?"

"He'll be fine in a few weeks."

"Did they get Reese?"

"Not yet. But we will."

"What if he shoots you next time?"

"He might," she said, knowing this was a time for honesty. "Every time I step foot out the door, it can happen. It's a risk we all take, but I don't spend even one minute of my day worrying about it."

"I can't bear it, Sam," he said, his voice hoarse with emotion. "I thought I could, but I found out today that I can't."

"Do you know," she said, tilting her hips against his erection, "that my dad and now Freddie are the only cops I know personally who've been shot on the job? And I've known a lot of cops in my life."

"Don't try to tell me it can't happen to you. Just since we've been together, you've been nearly blown up, shot at—twice—you scraped the skin off your chin, arms and knees, took an elbow to the face, got your throat squeezed by your ex-husband, who wanted you dead, and your partner got shot. Have I forgotten anything?"

Running her hands over his ribs, she fought the urge to giggle at the ridiculous inventory. "That about covers it."

Exasperated, he flopped onto his back. "And that's only our first month."

Sam straddled him and bent to kiss him. "At least it'll never be boring." She teased him by sliding her slick heat over his erection before taking him deep.

He reached for her hips to stop her from moving. "I'm trying to talk to you, Sam."

"And I'm listening," she said as she rode him slowly.

"I can't when you're doing that."

She took his hands and moved them from her hips to her breasts. "What am I doing?"

"Samantha."

"Were you really going to break up with me?"

"Yes."

Filled with overwhelming sadness, she stopped moving. "You told me there was nothing that would make you not want to be with me. You said that." When he didn't answer, she ran her hands over his chest. "More than once."

"That's what I thought, but then, what happened today..."

"Can I ask you something?"

His hands traveled from her breasts to encircle her. "Yeah."

"Isn't it better to have this, for how ever long it lasts, than to let fear drive us apart?"

He turned them over and withdrew from her. "That's not fair. You don't have to worry every day that I'm going to get shot or blown up or run over."

"No one's tried to run me over. Yet."

"You're not taking me seriously."

"You don't think so? I haven't been able to take a deep breath since you walked away from me at the hospital. Just when I was finally starting to have some faith in this, in *us,* you went and changed the rules on me."

"I didn't take a deep breath myself from the second I heard a cop had been shot in Reese's house until I saw you in the waiting room."

"So then we're even. Can we get back to normal?"

He caressed her face. "I don't know what I'd do if something happened to you. If I lost you that way."

"Then don't lose me. Keep me. Take a chance that maybe it'll all be fine."

"I don't ever again want to feel the way I did today."

"I can't promise that you won't."

He ran his fingers through her long hair, a gesture so familiar, so totally his, that her heart fluttered in her chest. "I know."

"So where does that leave us?" she asked.

"I need some time."

A prickle of fear worked its way down her spine. "To do what?"

"Losing Julian has messed me up, Sam. I don't want to say or do anything right now that I'll regret later."

"Okay," she said, suddenly finding it hard to swallow.

"I was unprepared for how it would feel to be certain you were injured or worse."

"Take all the time you need." As she said the words, she wondered where this new, evolved Sam Holland was coming from. With any other guy she would've shown him the door. However, *this* guy, this one was different. "But I do have one condition."

"What's that?"

"If you decide to give us a chance, you can't do this to me again. I can't be worried every time something goes wrong at work that I'm going to have to come home and fight for us, too. Either we're going to do this or we're not."

"Fair enough."

"How much time are we talking?"

He reached for her, brought her in close to him and kissed her forehead. "I don't know. The only thing I know for sure is that I love you. I found out today just how much."

Closing her eyes tight against the rush of emotion, she slipped her arm around him and burrowed into his embrace, painfully aware that sometimes love—even this kind of love—wasn't enough. "I'm sorry you were so scared. If anything like that ever happens again, I'll call you as soon as I possibly can so you'll know it's not me."

He replied by tightening his hold on her.

She nibbled on his neck. "You want to finish what we started?" she asked, forcing a lighter tone.

"Do you?"

She curled her hand around his arousal. "Mmm."

His lips found hers for a soft, sensual kiss that was all about gentle seduction. The usual fire simmered just below the surface as he worked his way from her lips to her neck.

Sam buried her fingers in his hair and closed her eyes, floating on a cloud of sensation despite the nagging worry that this could be their last time. If he walked away. No. He wouldn't. Hadn't he just said how much he loved her?

He cupped her breasts and tended to each nipple, his tongue darting in teasing circles.

Sam arched her back seeking him, wanting him desperately. "Nick."

"What, baby?" he whispered against her breast.

"Now."

He moved up to capture her mouth in a deep, carnal kiss and entered her in one smooth thrust.

Steeped in sensation, Sam rode the wave, knowing deep in her soul that no one else would ever make her feel this way. She wrapped her arms around him, holding him close and slowing the pace to make it last as long as possible.

Their eyes met in the inky darkness.

"I love you," she whispered. "Only you. Always."

"Samantha."

She could tell by the tight set of his jaw that he was

close. Her body tingled and surged, trying to meet him at the top.

Breaking free of her embrace, he gave it to her hard and fast, the way she liked it best, but nothing he did could melt the cold knot of fear that remained in her belly.

"Sam," he said, begging her to join him.

For the first time since they'd been together, she closed her eyes and faked an explosive finish.

NINETEEN

SHE'D FAKED IT! Did she think he wouldn't be able to tell the difference? After all the times they'd made love, did she think he wouldn't know? Curled up to him, she snored softly while he lay awake churning.

The insomnia that plagued him during times of stress had kicked into high gear lately, and he had almost no hope of going back to sleep that night. He would've gotten up, gone downstairs and attempted to review the files Christina had sent home with him if he didn't so love having Sam sleeping all over him. Plus, he didn't want to disturb her when she had so little time to sleep.

He hated that she'd felt the need to fake it with him. He knew she'd had trouble in that regard with her ex-husband, but never once with him. Of course it was because he'd scared her with their conversation, and he hated that his worries had that effect on her. But he couldn't help the way he felt. If he let his mind wander back to the sheer terror, the absolute certainty that she'd been shot… No, he couldn't go there again. He'd already relived it a thousand times.

He stewed for what seemed like hours. A week ago he would've been unable to imagine a scenario whereby he would walk away from her. And now he had good reason to wonder if he had the stomach to be the significant other of a homicide detective. Turning on his side, he brought her in closer to him and breathed in the scent he'd come to crave. His tired eyes burned shut, but he had no expectation that sleep would come.

However, it must have because he startled awake in the gray predawn and reached for Sam. He encountered cold sheets where hot woman should've been and realized she was long gone. Wide awake, he knew it was pointless to try to go back to sleep so he got up to get ready for work. In the shower, he thought of John and Julian and relived the horrible fear that followed Freddie's shooting. Nick's nerves and emotions were raw and close to the surface, an unsettling state for a man used to being in control at all times.

As he was drinking a cup of coffee in the kitchen, he noticed a pile of mail on the counter that Sam must've brought in. Nick flipped through the stack of mostly junk before finding a registered mail envelope Sam had signed for bearing the name of an insurance company. He opened it and sucked in a sharp deep breath when it registered that he was looking at a check for two million dollars. Made out to him. John's life insurance payout. After staring at the check for several long minutes, he tossed it on the counter with the rest of the mail and reached for his suit coat, not wanting to think about the money just now. He had enough on his mind.

SAM RUSHED DOWN the ramp from her father's house, attempting to juggle her cell phone, half a bagel and the bottle of diet cola tucked under her arm. "So we're no closer than we were last night?" she asked Gonzo.

"We're scouring this city. Every square inch." His voice was full of frustration. "No sign of the bastard anywhere."

"I've got that meeting at eight, and then I'll be out there with you."

"You don't need me at the meeting do you? I'd rather stay out here. I'm working a couple of angles on Sinclair, too."

She slid into the car without dropping the bagel and secured her soda in the cup holder. "No, don't bother coming in. I'll call to see where you need me when I'm leaving HQ."

"Any word on Cruz?"

"I called the hospital an hour ago, and he had a good night. They're thinking he can go home tomorrow or the next day."

"That's good. I'll see you soon."

As Sam slid the key into the ignition, the back door to her car slammed shut. She spun around to find Clarence Reese pointing a gun at her.

"Give me the phone," he growled, "and drive."

Scanning the empty street, Sam swallowed hard, handed him the phone and reached for her own weapon.

"Don't even think about it." The cold metal of Reese's gun pressed against her neck. "Hand it over."

Sam gave him the gun.

"Clutch, too."

Reaching under the cuff of the jeans she had worn to work the streets, she released the second smaller gun strapped to her leg and passed it back to him.

"Now drive. And no funny business."

Sam cleared the panic from her throat. "Where are we going?"

"Head north. Out of the city."

She glanced at the clock. Seven forty-five. In fifteen minutes, they'd be looking for her. On the way past Nick's house, she fixed her eyes on his door, willing him to hear her silent cries for help.

"Is that your senator's place?" Reese asked.

"Yes," Sam mumbled.

"Maybe we should pick him up and take him on our little ride, too."

Sam hit the gas to get out of there before Reese could make good on his threat to drag Nick into whatever nightmare he had planned for her. "What do you want?"

"I want the money you took from my house."

"I don't have it. It's been seized as evidence."

"I want it. Until I get it, I'll be keeping you."

Her cell phone rang. "If I don't answer that, they'll know something's up."

"Don't try to pull no shit."

Sam held out her hand, and Reese gave her the phone. "Holland."

"Lieutenant," Captain Malone said. "Everyone's here for the meeting you called. Where're you?"

"Hi, honey," she said, her heart pounding. She checked the rearview mirror to find Reese's cold eyes monitoring her every move. "No, I'm sorry. I didn't get a chance to pick up the dry cleaning."

"Holland, what the hell are you talking about?"

"You don't have *any* shirts?"

"Is something, wrong?" Malone asked, his voice suddenly tense.

"Yes, honey. I know I promised. I just left the house, otherwise I'd come back to find something for you to wear."

"You're still on Capitol Hill?"

"That's right. You might have to break out the iron."

"Is it Reese?"

"Uh-huh. You can do it."

"Stay calm," Malone said. "We're coming."

"I love you, too. Have a good day."

"Barf," Reese said from the backseat as he reached

out to snatch the phone from her hand. "He's already got you picking up his dry cleaning? I didn't figure you for the domestic type. You disappoint me."

Relieved that he had bought her side of the phone call, Sam looked at him in the mirror. "I take care of him. He takes care of me."

"I'll bet he does." Reese reached forward to run his finger down the slope of her neck, left bare by her clipped-up hair. "I'll bet he takes *good* care of you."

Sam worked at not flinching.

"A woman like you needs a real man. Not one who treats you like his little wife."

"Is that how you treated your wife?" she asked him in the mirror.

His eyes narrowed. "She was a nag. Nothing was ever enough for her. She always had to have more."

"So she deserved to be killed?"

"She needed to shut up."

"What about your kids? What did they do to deserve what they got?"

"None of your business! Just shut the fuck up and drive."

Sam did as she was told while keeping a watchful eye out for backup. She took Massachusetts Avenue, a main artery that headed northeast. Another five minutes passed in tense silence before Sam became aware of an unmarked Metro Police car behind them.

A bead of sweat slid down her back. All she could think about was Reese being killed before she could ask him the most important question. Her mouth felt pasty and dry so she reached for her soda and took a long swig. Of course her stomach reacted with annoying predictability. Taking a couple of deep, calming breaths, she said, "Did you shoot my father?"

"*What?* What the hell are you talking about?"

"My father, Metro Police Deputy Chief Skip Holland." She watched him in the mirror, waiting for any indication that he recognized the name and got none. "He was shot on G Street two years ago."

Baffled, Reese said, "I didn't shoot no cop on G Street."

Sam gritted her teeth against the urge to scream. "There were newspaper clippings and reports in your house."

"That stuff in the closet? It ain't mine. Belongs to the guy who lived there before me. He was supposed to come get it, but he never did."

"You lived there for more than a year and never got rid of the crap the previous people left behind?"

He shrugged. "We were busy."

For whatever reason, Sam believed him and her heart sank with disappointment. Another dead end. "Who lived there before you?"

"How the hell am I supposed to know? I ain't the freaking landlord."

"Why'd you shoot my partner?"

"Who's your partner?"

Keep him talking, Sam. Get as much as you can out of him before this goes bad. "Yesterday? In your house?"

"He was a cop?"

Gratified to see Reese's complexion go pale at that news, she said, "Yeah."

"I didn't mean to shoot no cop. He snuck up on me. I thought he was trying to rob the place. Man's got a right to be in his own house, to protect his property."

Thrilled to have at least gotten his confession on Freddie's shooting, she released a long deep breath, satisfied with the partial victory. "Not after he kills his family in that house he doesn't."

The gun pressed hard into her neck. "Shut the fuck up and drive."

NICK ARRIVED AT his office to find the staff huddled around the television in the conference room. "What's up?"

"That guy Reese who killed his family and shot the Lieutenant's partner?" Trevor said.

His heart slowing to a crawl, Nick nodded. "What about him?"

Trevor swallowed hard. "He's taken a Metro cop hostage. They're showing it live. A helicopter is following them on Mass Ave."

Nick moved closer for a better look. At the sight of the dark blue sedan, he gasped. And then he told himself the department had hundreds of those cars assigned to their detectives and high-ranking officers. It could be anyone. "They haven't said who it is?"

Trevor shook his head.

Nick reminded himself of Sam's promise to call him the minute she could to let him know it wasn't her. He retrieved his cell phone from his coat pocket and checked for missed calls. None. Staring at the phone, he willed it to ring.

"WHAT'S THAT?" REESE asked, bending to look out the back window.

"Sounds like a chopper."

"What the fuck? Are they *following* us? How do they even know?"

As he grew more agitated, Sam could think only of Nick and the conversation they'd had the night before.

If he knew what was going on—and he probably did by now—he was waiting to hear from her. She ached when she remembered how upset he'd been after the shooting, and now this. Two days in a row, and this time she was actually in danger. No way would he stick around after this. The thought made her unbearably sad.

"They're following us!" He threw the phone at her. "Call them. Tell them to back off."

Her hands shaking, Sam reached for the phone and flipped it open. With only a moment's hesitation, she called Nick.

"Sam!" He sounded as if he had pounced on the phone. "Are you okay?"

Gauging Reese through the mirror, she worked at keeping the hysteria out of her voice. "He wants you to call off the chopper."

"I'll tell Malone. I came over to HQ as soon as I heard the news. He's right here. Do you want to talk to him?"

"Yes." Then, realizing she might never get to talk to Nick again, she said, "Wait. No. You."

"Babe," he said, the single word full of agony. "I love you. I love you so much."

"Me, too."

Reese grabbed the phone from her hand and closed it.

Sam wanted to weep. She had so many other things she needed to say to Nick. If she had a lifetime, she'd never get to say them all.

"What the hell is taking so long?" Reese roared, his eyes fixed on the chopper.

Sam startled at his loud tone. "It could be the press."

"Motherfucker," he muttered.

In the mirror, Sam watched his eyes dart from one side of Massachusetts Avenue to the other.

"There." He pointed with the gun. "Pull in there."

Using the signal to alert the unmarked car behind them, she turned into the parking lot in front of a diner.

"Nice and slow," Reese growled. "Get out and come to the back door." He gripped the clip holding her hair.

Sam winced as he pulled her close enough to whisper in her ear.

"One wrong move and you're dead. You got me?"

"Yeah."

"Hurry up."

Sam hoped her legs would hold up under her as she got out of the car and moved to the back door. Out of the corner of her eye, she watched her colleagues move into position. If she could somehow give them enough room, if they could get off a shot…

But Reese had thought of that. When she opened the back door, he grabbed her and brought her down close to him. Hooking his arm around her neck and pressing the gun to her temple, he whispered, "Get out. Slowly."

Sam took her time standing up.

He half walked, half dragged her into the diner. "Listen up," Reese yelled, keeping the gun pressed to her head. "I want everyone out of here in one minute or this bitch cop is dead and so is anyone left."

Eyeing the gun, customers scrambled for the doors.

"You." Reese nodded to a paunchy middle-aged man who appeared to be in charge of the diner. "Over here."

The man's eyes almost popped out of his doughy face.

Now that they were out of the car, Sam waited for her opportunity to call upon her years of training to immobilize Reese. But not while there were still civilians in the diner.

One of the waitresses escorted the last elderly customer to the door, casting a panic-stricken glance at her boss on her way out.

"Go out there and tell them I want my money." Reese pointed the gun at the petrified manager. "I want every cent of the tcn grand they took from my house. They got one hour. *She's* got one hour. Go."

The manager didn't have to be told twice.

Sam checked the clock on the wall. Eight twenty, only thirty-five minutes since Reese grabbed her. It felt like hours. Maybe if he kept her long enough, she'd get out of appearing at Lieutenant Stahl's internal affairs hearing this afternoon. That thought almost made her giggle. As if. Stahl would probably write her up for missing the hearing. Would he care that she'd been taken hostage by a man who'd killed his entire family and had nothing to lose by killing her, too? Probably not.

"Sit," Reese said, ordering her into a booth at the far end of the diner.

Pissed that she'd missed her chance to overtake him, she did as she was told and watched him move from one end of the long, narrow restaurant to the other, closing the blinds as he went.

Sam felt claustrophobic as she imagined what was no doubt happening outside. Her cell phone rang.

Reese groped for it in his pocket.

"They'll want to establish contact with you," she said.

He handed her the phone. "Answer it. Put it on speaker."

She kept her eyes fixed on Reese. "Holland."

"Lieutenant," Malone said. "You're all right?"

"I'm fine."

"Mr. Reese, this is Detective Captain Malone. We want to help you."

"Sure you do. I want my money."

"We're working on getting it for you."

"You'll bring it here?"

"As soon as we recover it from the evidence locker."

"I don't want no games. You give me my money, I'll let her go."

"If Lieutenant Holland is hurt in any way, there's no money. Do you understand?"

Reese ended the call and put the phone back in his pocket.

TWENTY

Sam FIGURED SWAT probably had the place surrounded by now. She wondered if Nick was outside, too. Her mind wandered back to what he'd said the night before. *No, I can't go there. I'll go crazy if I think about that.*

She noticed Reese talking to himself and strained to hear him.

"It's her fault I had to do the babies, too," he muttered. "I never wanted to hurt them."

Sam swallowed hard. "So then why did you?"

He stared at her. "What did you say?"

"Why did you hurt the babies?"

"I didn't mean to. She was screaming at me again. We had no money for groceries."

"Where'd you get the ten grand?"

Reese seemed almost ashamed. "I got a second job, and it still wasn't enough. So I started selling drugs. Didn't mean to get into that, but no matter how much I brought home, it wasn't enough for her. She said she hated me and was going to take the babies and leave me. I didn't want her to know I had the money. If she got her hands on it, she would've left me."

Sam hung on his every word, forcing herself to stay still and let him get it out before she made her move.

"I couldn't let her take my kids. That wasn't going to happen." He didn't seem to notice the tears that tumbled down his face. "I went to get my gun. Just to scare her into shutting up, but she didn't care. She just kept spewing shit at me."

"Why'd you shoot her?"

Clarence's eyes met hers. "She called me a loser. Said she never should've married me." He shook his head. "After everything I'd done for her."

"What happened with the kids?"

"Jorge started screaming. I told him to shut up so I could think. He wouldn't shut up." Clarence's voice caught on a sob. "I didn't mean to hit him. I loved him. I loved all of them, but nothing I did was enough."

Sam wanted to go to him, but was mindful of the gun in his hand. "I can help you," she said. "We can walk out of here with no one getting hurt. If you let me help, this doesn't have to end badly for you."

"It already has," he said in a tone devoid of hope.

"Your life isn't over. I'll talk to the U.S. Attorney. I'll tell them your wife emotionally abused you. I'll make sure you get a good attorney who'll enter a temporary insanity plea. You'll do some time, but in a hospital not a prison. Let me help you."

Reese shook his head. "You can't bring my family back."

Sam stood up. "But I can—"

"Stop!" He aimed the gun at her. "Just stop talking. I want my money. If I get the money, I won't need your help. I won't need anyone."

Moving past the fear, Sam took a step toward him. "They've got this place surrounded by now. SWAT is making a plan. They'll come in and take you out. They won't care about you." She took another step, reaching outside herself for the fortitude. "All they care about right now is saving me. I'm the only one who cares about you, Clarence."

"You don't care about me. I shot your partner."

"He startled you. You thought he was robbing your house."

"I never meant to shoot him."

"I know." She took another step. Three feet to go. "Give me the gun. I'll call them. I'll tell them you're unarmed. No one has to get hurt."

He eyed her warily. "Why do you want to help me? I took you hostage."

"You were desperate. I understand that." She thought of Nick, of what he'd said the night before, and forced herself to concentrate. "I don't want you to get hurt. Think of your mother. She just lost Tiffany and the children. She doesn't want to lose you, too."

His shoulders sagged, a sob hiccupping through him. "Why couldn't Tiffany be happy with me?"

"I don't know, Clarence, but maybe you'll have a chance to make someone else happy. I can help you. I promise I'll help you." She had him. She could see it in his eyes as she took yet another step toward him.

The door to the diner burst open, startling them both. "Freeze, police!" Two SWAT officers dressed in black riot gear aimed their weapons at Reese.

He spun toward them, waving the gun.

"No!" Sam screamed to the officers. "Hold your fire." She held out her hand to Reese. "Give me the gun. I can still get you out of here alive."

He shook his head, his eyes focused on the two officers at the door.

"Drop the gun, Reese," one of them ordered.

"Clarence, I can help," Sam pleaded.

"No, you can't." His eyes shifted to her. "No one can."
He put the gun to his temple and pulled the trigger.

THE GUNSHOT RANG through the diner's parking lot.

"Oh, my God!" one of the reporters cried.

Nick couldn't have said it better himself. Four people
were inside—three cops and Reese. Nick's money was
on the cops. "Come on," he whispered, watching the
door so intently his eyes watered from the need to blink.

Christina squeezed his arm.

Five long minutes passed before one of the SWAT officers escorted Sam out of the building.

A cheer erupted from the crowd gathered in the parking lot.

Nick's legs went weak with relief as he watched her
talk to Captain Malone. A few minutes later, Malone gestured behind him to point Nick out in the crowd.

"Thanks for waiting with me," Nick said to Christina. "I'll check in later." He moved toward Sam. The
crowd between them parted, their eyes met, and nothing mattered more to Nick than getting to her as fast as
he could—not the worries he'd expressed the night before, not the media watching their every move. Nothing
mattered but her.

He put his arms around her and brought her in close
to him, attempting to shield her from the blinding blur
of camera flashes.

"We'll be on every front page in the city tomorrow,"
she said.

"That's okay."

He held her for a long time before he pulled back to
study her pale face.

"I had him," she said. "I just needed one more minute…"

"All that matters is that you're safe."

"I called you. The minute I could. Just like I said I would."

"I know, babe. I know." He noticed there was something gray all over her. "Let me drive you home so you can change."

She brushed at the lapels of his coat. "You'll need to have this cleaned."

"What is that?"

"Clarence Reese's brain."

Nick shuddered. "Jesus, Sam." Ignoring the media clamoring for a word from her, he ushered her to her car and held the passenger door for her. He took off his overcoat, rolled it into a ball and tossed it into the backseat.

"I had him," she said again as they pulled out of the diner.

"I'm sure you did everything you could."

Looking over at him, she said, "He didn't shoot my dad."

"But the stuff in his place…"

"Previous tenant."

"Shit."

"Yeah. Back to square one—again. But at least I have a lead to work with."

"I hope Malone gave you the rest of the day off."

"He tried to, but as soon as I get a shower, I'm back on Sinclair."

"You should take the day, Sam. This was a traumatic thing."

"I'm fine. I need to work."

Nick knew it was pointless to argue with her.

"I was surprised to see you when I came out," she said after a long period of silence. "I wasn't sure if you'd be there."

"Of course I was there."

"I thought you were 'taking some time.'"

Nick's jaw tightened with tension. "I needed to know you were all right."

"Will you still need to know I'm all right if we break up?"

"Sam…"

"I'm just wondering."

"I'll always worry about you, no matter what."

"If that's the case, then it seems kind of stupid to break up. What if I'm with someone else and I get taken hostage? You won't be able to show up like you did today. It won't be your place."

The idea of her with someone else tore at him, which of course was her goal. "I know what you're trying to do."

"I'm trying to show you how dumb you're being."

"Gee, thanks." He was so damned glad to be arguing with her that the barb didn't bother him in the least. On Ninth Street, he parallel parked between his house and her dad's.

"Thanks for driving me," she said. "You must need to get back to work."

"I've got some time. Let's go in. I'm sure your dad is anxious to see you."

He followed her up the ramp to her father's house where Skip, Celia, Angela and Tracy waited for them.

When her sisters started to rush over to Sam, Nick held up a hand to stop them. He shook his head, and they seemed to get the message that Sam needed someone else just then.

She went straight to her dad and rested her forehead on his shoulder. "It wasn't him," she said. "He didn't shoot you."

"That's the least of my concerns right now. How are you?"

"I'm fine," she said, straightening. "I need a shower, though. Reese offed himself right next to me."

Angela winced. "God, that must've been horrible."

Sam shrugged off her sister's sympathy. "I'd almost talked him out of the gun."

Nick's heart ached as he watched her attempt at stoicism. He could see the truth in her eyes. No doubt her family could, too.

"I'm sure you did everything you could," Tracy said. "Just like you always do."

"That's right," Celia said.

"Go on up to the shower," Skip said. "You'll feel better once you get cleaned up."

After Sam went upstairs, Sam's sisters followed Celia into the kitchen.

Skip turned his gaze on Nick. "Takes a special kind."

"Sir?"

"It's not easy loving a cop. You get to do all the worrying."

Hands on his hips, Nick struggled to contain the surge of emotion that hovered just below the surface. "Yeah."

"She needs you," Skip said. "She'd die before she admitted it, but she does."

Nick marveled at how Skip saw right through him.

"I'm, ah, going up to check on her."

"You do that."

SAM SCRUBBED HER skin until it burned. She washed her hair and then washed it again. The horror was harder to get rid of than Reese's brain matter. Standing under the hot water, she relived the whole thing, from the moment he got into her car until the fatal shot. She'd done all she could to bring about a positive conclusion. Of that she was confident. But that didn't change the fact that a man had died a foot from her. All her training and time on the job only went so far on days like this.

She leaned against the shower wall and closed her eyes. All she could see was Clarence's face in the moment she knew she had gotten through to him. And then she saw the gun at his temple. Sometimes the waste, the sheer destruction she witnessed on the job was too much to bear.

The shower door opened, and Nick stepped in.

He reached for her, but she shook him off. "Don't."

He lifted her into his embrace anyway.

Sam fought him. "You can't come in here and do this. Not after what you said last night. You don't have any right."

"I have every right."

"I can't allow myself to rely on you if you're not going to be here next time."

"I'll be here next time. Every time."

"Because you want to be?"

"Because I wouldn't know how not to be." He left a trail of hot kisses from her neck to her shoulder. "I'm not sure why, but for some reason I wasn't as afraid today as I was yesterday. You were in real danger this time, but I knew you'd find a way out of it." Brushing his lips over hers, he added, "You're so smart and resourceful. I had faith, Sam. I *have* faith. In you."

"So what happens the next time someone takes a shot at me? Or if I actually get shot? Will I have to worry about you freaking out and hitting the road?"

He shook his head. "We have a deal, remember? I can't ever do this again."

"I need there to be *one thing,* Nick. I need one thing in my life I can be sure of."

"You can be sure of me, babe. I'm here, and I'm not going anywhere."

"Promise?"

"I promise."

"So this is a forever kind of thing?"

"Absolutely." His lips came down hard on hers for a deep, devouring kiss.

When she came up for air, Sam said, "I need to get to work, and so do you."

"Another couple of minutes won't matter." He pressed her back against the wall, hooked her legs over his hips and thrust into her.

"Only a couple of minutes?" she asked with a coy smile.

"However long it takes." He tipped her chin up so he could see her eyes. "But there'll be no more faking."

Her heart skipped a beat. "How did you know?"

"After experiencing the real thing, there's no mistaking a fake."

"I'm sorry."

"I'm sorry I filled your head with doubts." Cupping her breast, he said, "The way I see it, I owe you two."

Eyes fluttering shut, Sam floated on a cloud of sensation. "Must. Go. To. Work."

He kissed his way down her neck. "You'll get there. Eventually."

TWENTY-ONE

SAM AND JEANNIE pulled up in front of Devon Sinclair's swanky Dupont Circle townhouse just after one o'clock. She had two hours before the Internal Affairs hearing and intended to put the time to good use. Through a call to Devon's law firm, she had learned that he was on bereavement leave.

"Nice digs for an associate," she said.

"You're sure you're up for this, Lieutenant?" Jeannie asked as they climbed the stone stairs. "Tyrone and I could take the lead on this one." She referred to her usual partner.

"I keep telling everyone I'm fine," Sam said, exasperated.

"Just asking."

She turned to Jeannie. "What would you do? If it'd happened to you, would you go home and take to your bed?"

"I'd probably do what you're doing."

"Good, so maybe we can drop it now?" She missed Cruz, who was a lot more fun to abuse than McBride.

"You're the boss."

"Lieutenant Holland!"

Sam spun around and groaned when she saw Darren Tabor, her least favorite reporter from the *Washington Star,* and several other reporters chasing after her. "Not now, Darren."

"Just a couple of questions about what happened with Reese."

"Not now." She pushed past them and went up the stairs to Devon Sinclair's townhouse.

"You're so popular," Jeannie muttered under her breath.

Sam made a face at her and rang the bell.

Devon Sinclair came to the door. An interesting mix of his parents, he was tall and handsome with close-cropped brown hair and devastated, red-rimmed eyes.

"Mr. Sinclair?"

"Yes."

"Lieutenant Holland and Detective McBride." Sam held out her badge for his inspection. "May we have a few minutes of your time?"

He ushered them into a stylish, contemporary living room where another young man was stretched out on the sofa. "My brother, Austin," Devon said, introducing them. "I assume this is about Julian."

"Yes," Sam replied. "Would you mind if we tape our conversation?"

With a weary gesture, Devon granted permission.

"We're sorry for your loss," Sam said.

"Thank you." Devon took a seat next to his brother, who sat up to make room. Austin was blond and favored their mother.

"You were close to your uncle?"

"Very. This is just the most horrible thing." Devon's eyes filled. "I'm sorry. We're still in shock."

"I'm sure you are. Had you seen him recently?"

"We had lunch with him the day he got to town. He was so excited about the nomination—nervous about the hearings, of course, but mostly excited. We said later that he seemed truly happy for the first time in a long time."

"Did either of your parents know you had seen him?"

"We told our dad," Austin said.

"Did you know Julian's friend, Duncan Quick?" Sam asked.

"Yes, we knew him quite well. Julian had been really down since they broke up, but the nomination seemed to have lifted his spirits."

"I understand from talking to your parents that your father and uncle had been estranged for a number of years," Sam said.

"Since we were young," Austin said. "We'd always been very close with him, spent a lot of time at his house, went on trips. But that all ended after my mother saw him with Duncan."

"She totally freaked," Devon added. "We didn't see him again for years—until we were adults and could make our own decisions."

"Did you know the reason for the estrangement?" Jeannie asked.

Austin glanced at his brother. "We had our suspicions. We knew Julian was gay and that our mother didn't approve. It's not that she's a bad person."

"She has strong views," Devon said. "She's worked really hard for the career she has."

"And an openly gay brother-in-law on the Supreme Court might not help her ambitions," Sam said.

"While we don't necessarily agree with her, we admire her tenacity," Devon said, sounding more like a sound bite than a son.

"Was your mother ambitious enough to kill your uncle to keep the family's dirty little secret in the closet?" she asked.

Both men blanched.

"*Kill* him?" Austin asked, his eyes wide. "She's a deeply spiritual person. She could never harm anyone."

"Were her ambitions more important than the two of you or your father?"

"Of course not," Devon said, but Sam detected a note of hesitation. "She's very devoted to her family."

"How would you describe your parents' marriage?" Sam asked.

"Loving," Austin said. "They're the best of friends."

"Would you say that your mother is in charge, though?"

"What does this have to do with Julian?" Devon asked.

"We're trying to determine what role, if any, the estrangement with your parents might've played in your uncle's death," Jeannie said. "This information helps us to paint a picture."

After a long pause, Austin said, "My mom was in charge when we were at home. I can't really say how it is between them now. She's pursued the goal of writing her book and having her own show for many years. It's taken a lot of her time."

"Is she a conservative Christian?" Jeannie asked.

"Yes," Devon said. "In recent years when Julian's name came up, she was fond of quoting Leviticus, who preached that it's an 'abomination' punishable by death for men to have sex with other men the way they would with women."

"Do either of you believe that?" Jeannie asked.

"We came of age in a different time," Austin said. "A more tolerant time."

"So that's a no?" Jeannie asked.

"That's a no," Austin replied. "We loved our uncle and supported him the same way he supported us."

"But you did that behind your mother's back," Sam said.

"We love them both," Devon said. "We were in an awkward position. Our goal was to keep the peace. It was better that she didn't know."

"Can you think of anyone who might want to harm him? Any enemies or rivals?"

Devon shook his head. "We've been wracking our brains trying to think of who could've done this to him. He had strong opinions and ideals, but he had respect for other people's beliefs, too. That kept him from attracting a lot of overt enemies."

Unlike your mother, Sam thought, *who has no respect for others' beliefs and has attracted an army of enemies.*

"You said he was nervous about the hearings," Jeannie said, "but did he express any worries about his safety or the controversy surrounding his nomination?"

"Not about his safety so much," Austin said.

"He'd declined Secret Service protection," Devon added.

"It was offered?"

Devon nodded. "He had some reservations about the protestors. He was afraid they'd be disruptive, but I'm sure he never suspected someone would want to kill him."

"Where were you both the night before last?" Sam asked.

"*We're* suspects?" Devon asked.

"We need to rule you out," Sam said.

Austin sat up a little straighter at the talk of alibis. "I was with my girlfriend at her place."

"We'll need her name and number." Sam turned to Devon. "And you?"

"I was here."

"Alone?"

"Most of the night. My roommate got home from work around one. He's a waiter."

"And did you see him? Talk to him?"

Devon's eyes darted to his brother. "Yes."

Sam's radar went on alert. "Is there something else, Mr. Sinclair? If so, this would be the time to tell us."

Devon's entire body went rigid with tension.

"Tell them, Dev," Austin said softly.

"Shut up," Devon snapped. "It's got no bearing on what happened to Julian."

"Mr. Sinclair, anything you tell us will remain confidential unless it directly affects the case."

"We've told you everything we know," Devon said, sounding more desperate.

Sam stared him down. "Except?"

Devon glared at his brother. "My roommate, Tucker. He's my... We're involved."

"And I take it your parents are unaware of this?"

"Yes," Devon said through gritted teeth. "And so are his. We'd like to keep it that way."

"How long have you been aware of your brother's orientation?" Jeannie asked Austin.

"Always."

"And your parents have no clue?" Jeannie asked.

"I've gone to great lengths to keep my private life private," Devon said.

"Did your uncle know?" Sam asked.

"Yes," Devon said softly. "He was the only one in my life who understood. In a lot of ways, other than my brother, Julian was my best friend."

Austin rested a comforting hand on his brother's shoulder, the two of them united in their grief.

Sam stood up, and Jeannie followed suit. "Is your roommate home at the moment?"

Panic-stricken, Devon looked up at her. "No, why?"

"We need to confirm your alibi. A formality. Can we get his name and number?"

Reluctantly, Devon got up and wrote down the information. Handing the piece of paper to Sam, he said, "You don't need to tell him I told you about us, do you?"

"I don't see any need to mention it."

"Thank you," he said, relieved.

Austin handed her a sticky note with his girlfriend's name and number.

"One other question," Sam said. "Were you Julian's heirs?"

"Yes," Austin said. "We'll each inherit half his estate."

"I know I speak for my brother when I say we'd give up every dime we stand to gain to have him back," Devon said.

After witnessing their devastation, Sam believed him.

OUTSIDE, SAM RELEASED a long deep breath. "Wow. I don't envy that kid the road he has ahead of him."

"Me, either. That mother is a piece of work."

"I'd like to dig a little deeper into Diandra Sinclair's background. We also need to take a closer look at Julian's cell phone and email records. He had arranged a late-night meeting with someone. I want to know who it was."

"The cell records didn't show any activity after he arrived at the senator's house for dinner, so whatever he was up to, it was planned before he went to dinner."

"Let's find out what it was. I also want to know why the Secret Service saw fit to offer him protection." Sam checked her watch. "Damn it. I don't have time to do much of anything before that stupid hearing. I guess I'll run by and check on Cruz real quick."

"I'll go with you." When they were in the car, Jeannie

looked over at her. "I hope you know everyone thinks this thing with IAB is totally bogus, Lieutenant. Stahl is out for revenge because they gave you his command."

Sam's stomach kicked into gear when she thought about the hearing. "He's had it in for me long before now. And let's face it, I handed him a gift by hooking up with Nick in the middle of O'Connor."

"It's going to be fine."

Sam wished she could be so confident.

"What does Nick say about it?"

"I haven't told him."

"Why not?"

Sam shrugged. "He's got enough going on without having to worry about me getting in trouble because of him. There's no need for him to know about it."

"If you say so. Besides, you're probably right. He's been through an awful lot lately."

"Exactly." But recalling their conversation in the shower, Sam couldn't help but feel guilty for keeping it from him.

TWENTY-TWO

SAM WAITED OUTSIDE the Internal Affairs hearing room.
They were running late, which had sent her stomach into
a spiral. She focused on breathing: in through the nose,
out through the mouth. It wouldn't have been so bad if
she knew she'd done nothing wrong and could chalk this
up to a witch hunt by Stahl.

But that wasn't the case.

She had screwed up by getting involved with Nick
during the O'Connor investigation. He'd found the body,
which made him a material witness. She should've stayed
as far away from him as she could get until the case was
closed. That he had been instrumental to her successfully
closing the case might not matter to the board.

Though she had participated in many IAB hearings
during her career, she'd never been the subject of one,
even after the fiasco with the Johnson case. An internal
investigation had cleared her of any wrongdoing in the
death of young Quentin Johnson in the crack house shooting, but the department psychologist had recommended
a thirty-day administrative leave. The penalty this time
could be much stiffer.

Deputy Chief Conklin, Sam's delegate to the three-
person panel, came out to get her. "Lieutenant? We're
ready for you."

"Oh. Okay."

Inside the room, Conklin joined Stahl and Captain Andrews from the bomb squad at the head table. The three

of them would determine her fate. Chief Farnsworth and Captain Malone were also in attendance. A stenographer was set to record the proceedings.

"Before we begin," said Stahl, who was clearly enjoying this, "I'd like to once again protest the appointment of Deputy Chief Conklin to this panel. He maintains a close personal relationship with the lieutenant's father, and his participation here is a conflict of interest."

"As I've told you before, Lieutenant," Conklin said, "find me anyone in this department—besides yourself of course—who doesn't hold retired Deputy Chief Holland in the highest regard. Per the officer bill of rights, Lieutenant Holland can choose anyone she wishes to act as her delegate to this panel. You're wasting everyone's time with this protest."

"I agree," Andrews said. "Let's move on."

Stahl levied a hateful stare in Sam's direction. "Very well, Lieutenant Holland, raise your right hand." He swore her in and gestured for her to be seated. "You've waived your right to representation?"

"I have." She saw no need to suck someone else off real police work when she was more than capable of defending herself.

"And you're aware of why you're here today?"

"You believe I exercised poor judgment in becoming romantically involved with Nicholas Cappuano during the O'Connor investigation."

Stahl stared at her. Clearly, he hadn't expected her to be so forthcoming. "That's correct," he stammered.

Sam noticed that Captain Malone had a hand over his mouth as if trying to hide a smile.

Stahl cleared his throat. "And to that you say?"

"I can't deny that I become close to Mr. Cappuano during the investigation, or that he was enormously helpful to me and Detective Cruz as we worked to close that case," Sam said, thrilled to realize she was ruffling Stahl.

"Did you know Mr. Cappuano before the O'Connor investigation?"

Ignoring the grind in her stomach, Sam said, "Yes."

"Please elaborate."

"We met six years ago at a party. We spent one night together and didn't see each other again until Senator O'Connor was found murdered."

"And why did you never see him again?"

"A series of misunderstandings."

"Did you disclose this prior relationship with the witness to your superior officers?"

"I did not."

"Why not?"

"It wasn't relevant. It was one night six years ago."

"Did it occur to you at the time that your failure to disclose the relationship might endanger the investigation?"

"No."

"At no time did you think, maybe I ought to tell someone that I know this guy? That I slept with this guy?"

"As I said, since the relationship spanned one night six years earlier, I didn't see how it was relevant to the investigation. Mr. Cappuano was a tremendous asset and saved us a lot of time we would've wasted figuring out who the players were."

"When did you clear Mr. Cappuano of any possible culpability in the senator's murder?"

"Right away. He had an airtight alibi, no motive and his heartbreak over the loss of his friend and boss was genuine. At no time was he a suspect."

"Even after you learned that he was the beneficiary of a two-million-dollar life insurance policy left by Senator O'Connor?"

"Mr. Cappuano was never a suspect."

"At what point during the investigation did your relationship with Mr. Cappuano become personal again?"

"The first night."

Stahl's eyes lit up with glee.

Sam worked to keep her tone calm and even. "He called me when he realized someone had been in his house."

"So the first night of the O'Connor investigation, you went to Mr. Cappuano's home?"

"That's correct."

"Located where?"

"At that time it was in Arlington, Virginia."

"Which is well outside your jurisdiction."

"I had given him my card with instructions to call if he thought of anything that might help the investigation. When he arrived home and discovered disarray, he did as I asked by calling me. After I got to his house and confirmed that someone had entered the home, I called Arlington police."

"And your relationship took a personal turn that night?"

"I waited with him while Arlington investigated. During that time, he provided more background on the O'Connor family relationships. After the police left, we discussed our personal relationship, which he wished to resume. I told him it would have to wait until the investigation concluded."

"Did it?"

A sharp pain in her stomach stole her breath. This is where things got dicey. "Despite my intentions, the relationship later became serious."

"Did you disclose that to your superiors?"

"I did not. It still had no bearing on the investigation."

"How did your relationship with Mr. Cappuano become public?"

"When my ex-husband planted crude bombs on both our cars. The bomb on my car exploded, injuring both Mr. Cappuano and myself."

"This occurred where?"

"In front of Mr. Cappuano's Arlington home."

"You were there for what reason?"

Sam swallowed the ball of panic forming in her throat. "I had spent the night there."

"How many days into the O'Connor investigation was this?"

"Three."

"That didn't take long."

"Can the editorializing, Lieutenant Stahl," Conklin said.

With a smarmy smile, Stahl said, "Lieutenant Holland, did your superiors confront you about the relationship after the bombing?"

"I discussed it with both Captain Malone and Chief Farnsworth, both of whom accepted my explanation of how the relationship transpired and how helpful Mr. Cappuano had been to the investigation."

"What is your relationship today with Mr. Cappuano?"

"*Senator* Cappuano and I are in a committed relationship as you and everyone in Washington knows."

"Do you think the very public nature of your relationship with the senator could be seen as a detriment to your duties as a police officer?"

"In a perfect world, the media would have no interest in us. Unfortunately, I don't live in that world."

"Do either of you have any questions?" Stahl asked Conklin and Andrews. Both declined. "In light of Lieutenant Holland's testimony and her inappropriate relationship with a material witness, I recommend two weeks unpaid suspension and reduction in rank to detective."

Sam suppressed a gasp. Two ranks! That couldn't happen. But she refused to give Stahl the satisfaction of an emotional outburst.

"The panel will consider the recommendation in executive session," Conklin said. "Lieutenant Holland, we appreciate your candor. You'll be informed of our decision."

"Thank you, Deputy Chief Conklin. If I may, I'd like to say one more thing—obviously, I don't wish to lose my current rank, but I want you to know that if I had the O'Connor investigation to do over again, I wouldn't change a single thing. That's all."

She got up and left the room. It was out of her hands.

NICK AND CHRISTINA returned to his office after a marathon meeting of the Senate Homeland Security and Governmental Affairs Committee. Once they had gone over their notes and made a to-do list, she got up to leave.

"Thanks again for going with me earlier," he said. "And yesterday, too."

"Lots of drama lately."

"Yes."

She looked at him as if there was something else she wanted to say but had thought better of it.

"What's on your mind, Chris?"

She studied him for a long moment. "Are you going to, you know, go running out of here every time something happens with her?"

"I don't know," he said, caught off guard by the question. "Maybe. Do you have a problem with that?"

"No, it's just that you might not always be able to. You have so many commitments and obligations now. It's different than before."

"I'm well aware that my role has changed. We're just going through a period of transition. On multiple fronts." He paused before he added, "I know you've had a lot on your plate doing two jobs over the last month, but Terry will be starting soon. It should get better then."

"I guess we'll see how that works out. You have a nice evening, Senator."

"You, too."

For a long time after she left, he sat and stared at the painting of the Capitol that Sam had given him for Christmas. He thought about what Christina had said and acknowledged that she made a good point. It wouldn't always be possible for him to go running when Sam was in trouble—not that she expected him to. But he couldn't imagine sitting through a committee meeting, for instance, if he knew someone was holding her hostage.

They were definitely navigating uncharted waters here, and everyone was going to have to make some adjustments. He finally had time to pick up that day's *Washington Post,* which had devoted much of the front page to Julian's murder. At least they had taken a break from reporting about his romance with Sam. As Nick read the coverage about Julian, he was once again filled with sadness over the loss of his friend.

Suddenly, he remembered an op-ed piece that had run the week before in which Tony Sanducci, a leading abortion protestor, had spouted off about Julian's nomination and the setback it could represent to the rights of the unborn. He had urged his followers to take any steps necessary to stop the nomination. Nick wondered if Sam had thought to talk to Sanducci. Nick reached for the phone to call her, but got voice mail.

"Hey, babe, it's me. Listen, I was thinking you ought to check out an editorial that ran in the *Post* a week or so ago. Tony Sanducci went off about Julian. Might be a good lead. I'll send a link to your email. I'll be home in an hour or so. Maybe we can take another shower or something." The memory of their earlier shower made him smile. "Love you."

SAM EMERGED FROM the hearing and went straight to the restroom. The pain in her stomach bent her in half. In a cold sweat, she closed the stall door and rested against it, fighting for every breath.

She'd meant it when she told the board she wouldn't change a thing about the O'Connor investigation. Nick was, without a doubt, the best thing to ever happen to her. How could she regret falling in love with him? How could she regret the magic his love had brought to her life? But to be busted down to detective, just as she achieved her longtime goal of making lieutenant…

"God," she whispered, the enormity of it almost too much to bear.

She took another ten minutes to pull herself together. Determined to get out of there on time for once, she returned to the detectives' pit, where a crowd waited for her.

Gonzo pounced first. "Lieutenant, how did it go?"

"Are you all right?" Jeannie asked.

"Stahl's an asshole," Arnold chimed in. "This is all about you getting his command."

Sam held up her hand to stop them. "I appreciate the support, Arnold, but this is about me hooking up with a witness during a homicide investigation. While Lieutenant Stahl may have ulterior motives, he's entirely within his rights to call for an IAB inquiry."

"It's so *fucked up,*" Gonzo said, his face tight with dismay. "The senator was instrumental in you closing

O'Connor as fast as you did. That should count for something."

"We'll see if it does," Sam said, resigned now to whatever fate awaited her. "In the meantime, where are we with Sinclair?"

"I'm digging around in Diandra's background like we discussed," Jeannie said. "I should have a report for you in a couple of hours."

"We aren't authorized any O.T. on this one," Sam reminded her.

"I'll do it on my own time," Jeannie said.

Sam sent her a grateful smile, knowing Jeannie had been moved by Nick's devastation after hearing about Sinclair. The brotherhood—or in this case sisterhood—among her fellow officers had always been Sam's favorite part of the job. Luckily, there were a lot more like Jeannie and Gonzo and Cruz than there were like Stahl.

"I'm going to head home," Sam said. "Shoot your report to my email. I'll be working later."

"Will do, Lieutenant," Jeannie said. "Try not to worry too much. Conklin and Andrews know you're a great cop and a gifted detective. It's going to be fine. I'm sure of it."

"It'd better be," Gonzo added.

"Watch your blood pressure, Gonzo," Sam said, amused by his anger on her behalf. "I appreciate the support, you guys. Let's not allow it to be too much of a distraction. If you need me I'll be on the radio or call my cell."

She left them talking about the injustice of the IAB hearing. Their overwhelming support helped to boost her spirits. On the drive home, she listened to the voice mail from Nick and decided to stop at the store so she could surprise him with a home-cooked meal. After she stashed the makings for linguine and clam sauce in his refrigerator, she went over to check on her dad.

"Anyone home?" she called.

"In here," Skip replied from the kitchen. "Is that my wayward daughter who used to live here?"

"Very funny." Sam bent to kiss his cheek. "I still live here."

"I've been wondering why that is when you've gotten a much better offer from the handsome guy down the street."

"I'm thinking about the handsome guy's better offer."

"Are you now?"

She shrugged. "It is a pretty good offer. And he does have a Jacuzzi."

"You're so easy," Skip said, laughing. "I hope you're not holding out because of me. I'm in good hands with Celia. There's no need for you to be here if you'd rather be somewhere else."

"I'm just trying to take it slow," Sam said. "I don't want to rush into anything."

"Understandable. After all, if you were to rush in, you might end up on the front page of the *Post* every other day, and that would kind of suck."

"You're very funny tonight, Skippy." Sam reached for a soda in the fridge. "What's the occasion?"

"You gonna tell me about it?"

She paused in the midst of opening the bottle. "What?"

He shot her a "you know" look.

Swallowing hard, she said, "How did you hear about it?"

"The question is, why didn't I hear about it from you?"

"I've been in major denial mode."

"What did Stahl recommend?"

"Two weeks unpaid suspension, reduction to detective."

Skip winced. "No way Conklin will let that happen."

"Nothing I can do about it now. I was straight up with them in the hearing, told them exactly how it went down."

"That's the best strategy, which I would've told you if you hadn't kept me in the dark—again. Becoming kind of a disturbing pattern between us."

The comment went straight to her heart because he was right. They'd always been in sync with each other, and she hadn't been holding up her end of the deal lately.

"If you treat me like an invalid, that's how I feel, Sam. I don't want you thinking you have to protect me from this crap. It doesn't get much more crappy than living like this."

"I'm sorry." She dropped into one of the kitchen chairs. "I don't mean to keep stuff from you. I was hoping this was gonna go away before it got this far."

"Should've known better with Stahl involved."

"I know."

"Did you tell Nick?"

Sam looked up at him with a rueful expression.

"Sam! Are you *kidding me?* You've got IAB poking into your relationship with him and you don't think he needs to know that?"

"He's been so down about John and now Julian and wound up about what happened to Cruz. And then the whole mess with Reese today. I was afraid it might be one thing too many, you know?"

"You're playing with fire, baby girl. That man is one to be reckoned with. If you think he's going to put up with you keeping things from him, you're deluding yourself."

Sam knew he was right. "I'll tell him tonight. It'll be

fine." She got up and kissed him. "I've got to go. I'm making dinner."

"You? *Cooking?*"

"You really ought to consider a career in stand-up comedy—without the stand-up part of course."

"Now who's being funny? Let me know the minute you hear."

"I will. Try not to worry too much. Whatever happens, Nick was worth it."

"That's a good way to look at it."

"It's the *only* way to look at it. I'll see you in the morning."

After she packed a bag of clothes for the next day, she walked back over to Nick's, thinking about what her father had said. At this point, Nick would probably be furious that she'd waited so long to tell him about the IAB hearing. She'd have to see how the evening unfolded to determine if there'd be a good time to tell him. In the meantime, after dinner she would look into Sanducci.

TWENTY-THREE

BY THE TIME Nick got home an hour later, Sam was ready for him. She had enjoyed playing house in his primo kitchen and had even indulged in a little fantasizing about what it might be like to really live there rather than just spending most nights in his bed. Her trip down fantasy lane had also helped to keep her mind off the outcome of the hearing. Shouldn't she have heard something by now?

"Hey, babe," Nick called when he came in. "Sorry I'm so late. I got sucked into a Democratic Caucus planning meeting." He stopped short at the kitchen door. "Did you *cook?*"

"Yep," she said, standing at the stove. "You don't need to sound *that* surprised."

He slid his arms around her from behind and kissed her neck. "I didn't think you knew how to turn on the stove."

She pushed her butt into him. "I know how to turn on a lot of things."

Laughing, he tightened his hold on her. "You sure do." He buried his face in her hair. "I'm so damned glad to see you, Samantha. After everything today with Reese. I can't stop thinking about it."

She turned to face him and curled her arms around his neck. This would be a great time to tell him about the IAB hearing, except that he looked like himself again for the first time in days. Was it such a crime to want him to relax and enjoy the evening? "Everything's fine."

He dipped his head to kiss her. "It is now that I'm with you. I love finding you here when I come home."

She divested him of his tie and released his top buttons. "I decided to leave work on time for once."

"What's the occasion?"

Another golden opportunity. "No occasion. I just felt like cooking." She reached for the check she'd found on the counter earlier and waved it at him. "Got anything you want to tell me?"

Staring at the check, his face became unreadable. "You knew about that. You signed for it."

"What're you going to do with it?"

"Part of me wants to give it all away."

Her heart went out to him. The pain of John's loss was still so present. "What would John want you to do with it?"

"He'd want me to enjoy being a millionaire for a while," he said without hesitation.

"Then that's what you ought to do."

"How can I enjoy it when he had to die for it to happen? How do I do that?"

Sam reached up to run her fingers through his hair. "He loved you, Nick. He'd want you to be happy."

"I talked to Graham today, told him I'd gotten the money. He said he'd invest it for me if I wanted him to."

"Why don't you do that? Give it to him and forget about it."

"I guess I will. We have everything we need, right?"

"And then some."

He surprised her when he lifted her onto the center island and stepped between her legs. "Do we have to eat right now?"

"You're turning into a regular sex fiend, Senator," she said, relieved by the return of his playful mood.

"It's your influence." He zeroed in on her neck.

She tilted her head to give him better access. "I need to go back to work after dinner."

"Always with the work," he said, exasperated. "I'm proposing a bill requiring one night a week with no work, no commitments, no obligations, just you and me. We'll call it the Cappuano-Holland To Hell With Work Law." He kissed her. "All those in favor?"

"Mmm," she said against his lips. "Me. Definitely in favor. Holland-Cappuano has a better ring, though."

He smiled. "Passed. Unanimously." Framing her face with his hands, he delved deeper, teasing with his tongue. "Speaking of rings, you know what sounds even better? Cappuano-Cappuano."

Taken aback, Sam stared at him.

"Someday?" he asked with a hopeful, sheepish grin that made her melt.

"Maybe," she stammered. "Someday. But I'm not changing my name."

"Mmm. Progress." His pleasure came through in a deep, passionate kiss.

Her cell phone interrupted them.

She pulled back from him to reach for it.

"We have a law!"

"Sorry," she said. "I really need to take this. Holland."

"Hey, it's Conklin."

Sam held her breath. "What's up?"

"I just now got out of the deliberations."

"Wow."

"Yeah, to call it heated would be an understatement. The suspension was reduced to two days unpaid, effective immediately. That was the best I could do."

She could live with that. Swallowing hard, she said, "And the other?"

"We're meeting again in the morning to discuss it."

Her heart sank. "What's the hang-up?"

"Andrews wanted to think on it overnight."

Sam kept an eye on Nick as he checked the pots on the stove. "That doesn't sound good."

"I'm sure it'll be fine. He's a reasonable guy. You're going to need to watch out for Stahl, though. He really has it in for you. The two-day suspension infuriated him."

"Well, thanks for letting me know."

"I'll call you as soon as I have more."

Sam ended the call and clutched the phone to her chest. Her heart raced with anxiety. And then Nick turned and smiled, chasing away her worries.

"Everything okay, babe?"

"Everything's just fine," she said, surprised to realize it was true. Everything was fine as long as she had him. He was indeed so totally worth it. She sent him a saucy grin. "You know that bill we passed before?"

He popped a bite of carrot from the salad into his mouth. "Yep."

"Can we make it effective as of tonight?"

"Absolutely."

She held out her arms to him. "To hell with work."

SAM WOKE UP the next morning to the feel of Nick's lips laying a path up her back. Keeping her eyes closed, she wallowed in the sensation until she remembered the suspension.

"Why'd you just get all tense on me?"

"No reason," she said, not ready to leave the bubble they'd been in since the night before.

"You need to get going. You're going to be late."

"I'm working from home today."

"How come?"

She bit back the guilt. "I want to dig into that lead you gave me yesterday, and I need to get to some other research that's easier to do at my dad's than at HQ. Plus I want to bounce a few things off him."

"Sounds like a good plan." He kissed her and got up. "Graham told me yesterday that Julian's funeral is Saturday in Cambridge. He's chartering a plane to take the family. He asked if we'd like to join them. I told him I'd check with you."

"That'd be good. If we haven't closed the case by then, I'll need to go to the funeral anyway."

"And if you have?"

"Then I'll go to be there for you." She studied his fine naked form. "I wish you didn't have to go to work."

He emerged from the closet with a suit and dress shirt. "Why?" he asked with a salacious grin. "What would you do with me if you had me to yourself all day?"

"It sure would be nice to find out. We haven't had a whole day off since we've been together."

Leaning over to kiss her once more, he said, "We'll have to fix that. Soon. But today, I have two hundred Girl Scouts coming from Norfolk to tour the Capitol and have lunch with me."

"I'm jealous," she said with a pout.

"Don't be. You're the only girl I love." He left her with a smile and went to take a shower.

Only Nick could've made her forget, even for a few minutes, that she'd been suspended from her job and faced a possible reduction in rank. Even one level would be a bitter pill to swallow. But two. *Ugh, I can't even think about it.* She reached for her cell phone to call Gonzo. "Hey," she said when he answered. "How are you?"

"Better question is how are *you?* I heard about the suspension."

"Could've been worse. Between us, I'm working from my dad's today. Can you put out the word that I'm looking for help with Sinclair?"

"Sure, no problem. The press is clamoring for info on the investigation. Rumor has it the chief is on the warpath. Wants an arrest and wants it now."

"Well, let's get him one. Do me a favor—do a run on a Tony Sanducci. He's a big-time abortion protestor. Meet me at my dad's around ten?"

"You got it. I'll round up the cavalry."

"Keep it on the down low." They both knew she'd be royally screwed if she got caught conducting department business while on suspension.

"Will do."

AN HOUR LATER, Nick was signing a stack of letters to constituents when Christina came in bearing coffee. He noticed she looked tired. "Late night?"

"Sort of. Tommy was in rare form last night."

"Please," Nick said. "Spare me the details."

"How's Sam?"

"Fine," he said, pleased that she'd asked. That, too, was progress. "She's seen a lot over the years, so she bounces back from something traumatic like what happened yesterday a lot faster than most people would."

"She must be pissed, though. Tommy was enraged over it."

Not sure what Christina was getting at, he said, "I think she was more disappointed that she wasn't able to talk Reese out of the gun in time. Apparently, she almost had him when SWAT showed up."

Christina looked at him like he was speaking Greek. "I mean over the suspension. Tommy said it was totally bogus. You helped them close the O'Connor case and now to have Internal Affairs investigating your relationship! Let's just hope the media doesn't catch wind of it."

Nick felt like she had punched him. "Yeah," he said. "Let's hope not." He stood up and reached for his new overcoat. "What time do the Girl Scouts get here?"

"At noon. Why?"

"I'll be back before then."

"Where're you going?" she asked, baffled.

"I'll be back."

"TONY SANDUCCI," GONZO said, "age thirty-nine, native of Cleveland, Ohio. He's been actively protesting abortion for the last decade. Suspected in several violent altercations at abortion clinics, but none of the charges stuck. His rich parents apparently hire a team of high-priced lawyers who always get him off.

"Married, four children, lives outside Cleveland but opened a storefront in the District, on New York Avenue, three weeks ago and has been operating out of there since then. Has a legion of loyal followers who read his daily blog by the thousands and take their orders directly from him. Works outside the boundaries of the mainstream movement, which says it disapproves of his tactics but doesn't do anything to stop him."

"Passive approval," Sam said.

"Exactly," Gonzo said. "His editorial in the *Washington Post* was a thinly veiled hate rant. It was clear that he'd do anything to keep Sinclair off the court."

"We need to talk to him," Sam said. "Let's figure out who his most faithful followers are, too. Those who inspire legions of zealots have people in their ranks who'd do anything for the leader. He may not have put out the word he wanted Sinclair killed, but reading that editorial, it'd be hard not to get that message."

"I can't believe the *Post* even printed it," Jeannie said.

"Freedom of speech," Skip said.

"I'd also like to know why the Secret Service offered protection," Sam said. "Did they know of specific threats?"

"When you have a million people descending on the city to protest a specific nominee, that warrants protection," Skip said.

"You gotta wonder if Sinclair had all the info about the threats when he turned down protection," Gonzo said. He held up a printout of the *Post* article. "Did he see this?"

"Good question," Sam concurred.

A knock on the front door interrupted them. She got up to get it and found Cruz on the porch.

"Hey," he said. "I hear we're working from the home office today."

"What're you doing here?" He was pale and drawn, and his arm was in a sling. "You're still on medical leave."

"Nothing wrong with my brain."

"Come in," Sam said.

He turned and waved to the driver of a car idling in the street.

Sam looked closer and saw that Elin had driven him. "Still seeing the phone-shutter-offer, huh?"

"I told you it's not going to happen again," he said through gritted teeth. "Can we drop it?"

"Eventually," she said with a grin, delighted to see him back on his feet.

"You okay after everything with Reese?" he asked.

"You know how it goes. Shit happens. He didn't shoot my dad."

"I heard that, too. We'll dig into the prior tenants the minute we close Sinclair."

She nodded, grateful for his unwavering support. "Let's get you up to speed."

The others greeted Cruz warmly and updated him on the case.

"Moving on to Diandra," Sam said. "What'd you find out, Jeannie?"

"She's fifty-six, grew up in Missouri. The dad was a fundamentalist Christian minister, the mother a homemaker. Diandra went to Princeton, studied English literature. Met Preston there thirty years ago. Two sons, Devon and Austin. Began spewing her special brand of hatred as a newspaper columnist seventeen years ago. Moved to TV thirteen years ago."

"Right around the same time as the rift formed with her husband's homosexual brother," Sam said. "Interesting timing."

Jeannie nodded. "I thought the same thing."

"I'd like to get her downtown for a more in-depth interview," Sam said. "I keep going back to the irrational hatred she had for Julian over his sexual orientation. It just seems so over the top to me."

"Conservative Christians are very clear on homosexuality," Jeannie said. "And growing up as she did with a minister father, this stuff was probably pounded into her head all her life. I looked into her father's background. He wrote a book twenty years ago about how homosexuality was going to unravel the fabric of our country. It made quite a stir at the time. Apparently, her book is an update of his."

"So she comes by her hatred naturally," Sam said, feeling the buzz that came from uncovering a juicy lead. "We definitely need to have another conversation with her." She growled with frustration. "Freaking suspension! I want to go at her myself."

"We can handle it," Gonzo said, looking to Jeannie, who nodded in agreement. "We can also talk to Sanducci."

"I can research his closest aides," Cruz said.

"With only one good arm?" Sam asked.

"Don't worry about it."

The front door swung open. Sam looked up and was startled to see Nick. "What're you doing here?"

"May I have a word with you?" He gestured to the porch.

She looked closer, and this time she saw anger. *Uh oh. What now?* "Sure." She got up and reached for her coat. To the others she said, "I'll be back in a minute."

Outside, Nick vibrated with tension as he paced the length of the porch.

Her stomach took a nasty nosedive. "What's up?"

He turned to her, hands on his hips, clearly furious. "Were you going to tell me?"

"Tell what?" she asked, even though she suspected. How had he heard?

Running a hand through his hair in frustration, he said, "I thought we were past this shit, Sam! I thought we were past the point where we kept stuff from each other."

"I was going to tell you—"

"When?" The single word reverberated through the quiet morning. *"When were you going to tell me?"*

"You've been so upset," she stammered. "About John and Julian, what happened to Cruz, and then the thing with Reese. There just wasn't a good time."

"That's bullshit and you know it. We were together all last night, after you'd been *suspended* for hooking up with me, and *you didn't think I needed to know that?"*

"Can you keep it down?" she whispered. "The people in there work for me."

"I don't care who's listening! How do you think it made

me feel to have my chief of staff tell me that my girlfriend, or whatever you are, was *suspended* from her job because of me? How do you think that felt, Samantha?"

"I'm sorry." She silently cursed Gonzo and Christina and Stahl. Goddamned Stahl. This was all his fault. "I just wanted to make it go away without letting it touch us. I was trying to avoid this very scene."

"If you'd have told me about it when it first happened, there might not have been a scene." He took a deep rattling breath, clearly trying to control the impulse to beat the crap out of something—most likely her. "I want to know how this happened. I want every detail, and I want it right now."

So she told him—about receiving the summons from Stahl to the hearing the day before to the phone call from Conklin. She left nothing out.

"This happened on your *first day* as lieutenant? That was before Julian was killed."

"You were still dealing with losing John and your own new job. I was thinking of you, Nick. I didn't set out to deceive you. I was trying to protect you." She took a deep breath to contend with the pain in her gut. "Remember when we talked about you becoming a senator, when I said I was worried about my shit landing all over you and making you look bad just as you got this great opportunity? This is exactly what I was talking about. I was thinking of you."

At that, some of his steam seemed to dissipate. "I don't expect you to protect me. I never asked you to do that."

"Can't help it," she said with a shrug. "I love you. I don't want to be responsible for causing you problems at work or anywhere else."

"And I'm not supposed to feel the same way? You're in trouble at work because of *me*. That kills me, Sam."

She reached for him, brought him close to her and rested her head on his chest. "I'll tell you the same thing I told my dad last night." Glancing up at his handsome, earnest face, her heart ached with love. "You're worth it. No matter what happens, you're so, so, *so* worth it."

Even though he seemed moved by her words, he shook his head. "We should've waited until the case was closed. You knew this could happen. You tried to tell me, but I wanted you so much. I didn't listen to you—"

"Don't." She rested her fingers on his lips. "I wouldn't change one thing about the way we fell in love. It's the best thing that's ever happened to me. *You* are the best thing. How could I regret that?"

"But if you lose your rank. I can't believe they're even considering that."

"It might be for the best."

He stared at her, incredulous. "How in the world can you say that?"

"Less responsibility, fewer hours, fewer demands." She made a huge effort to keep her tone light. "More time for you. Might be just what we need."

"No, it isn't. It can't happen. I'd never forgive myself if I caused that to happen to you."

"Let's not worry about it until it happens. Captain Andrews is known for being logical. He'll do the right thing."

"What if he doesn't?"

"We'll cross that bridge when we come to it." She forced a teasing grin. "You've got Girl Scouts coming to visit. You can't keep them waiting."

"Will you call me? The minute you hear anything?"

"I will."

"And no more keeping stuff from me?"

"No more keeping stuff from you. I promise."

TWENTY-FOUR

THE CONVERSATION WITH Nick stayed with Sam long after he went back to work. She was still getting used to the rules of a real relationship. When she was married to Peter, she'd made an art form out of keeping things from him. His propensity to overreact and overanalyze every little thing made him the last person she wanted to share anything with. Nick was nothing like Peter, but old habits were hard to break.

Chewing on her pen as she stared at the computer screen, Sam thought about Nick leaving the Capitol to come have it out with her when he no doubt had a million other things to do. That was another way he wasn't like Peter, who had loved to give her the silent treatment—sometimes for weeks on end—rather than taking the initiative to talk about whatever was on his mind.

The two men were so diametrically different it was pointless to compare them. Then why, she wondered, was she holding out on moving in with Nick? If she already knew he was nothing like Peter, and since he had proven as much—many times over—what was the hang-up? "Hmm," she said. "Definitely something to think about."

"Talking to yourself, boss?" Freddie asked, returning from the coffee shop on the corner with a tray containing two tall cups.

Sam stood up and reached for the tray. "I'm going to send you home if you keep pushing it."

"I went to get coffee." He flashed the smile that made

even the strongest of women go weak in the knees. "Relax, will ya?"

Sam took a sip of her coffee and was surprised by an unexpected surge of emotion. "You scared me," she said, her voice hoarse as she glanced over at him.

"I'm sorry."

"If you ever do anything that stupid again, I'll kill you with my own hands, do you hear me?"

"If I ever do anything that stupid again, I'll deserve it."

"At least you know you're stupid," she muttered. "That's something."

"Hey!"

"And what's the cell phone rule?"

"Believe me, I'm never going to forget that, either."

"Humor me."

"Shut the freaking phone off before you sneak up on a perp."

"Here I was thinking you were coming along so nicely, and then you go and screw up so monumentally. And to go in without backup! Don't even get me started on that!"

"Okay, I won't."

"I appreciate what you were trying to do and why you were trying to do it, but don't risk yourself like that again. You're no good to me dead."

"Gee, I'm really feeling the love, Lieutenant."

"Good." She met his chocolate-brown eyes with an intense stare. It was as close as she would ever come to telling him how she felt about him.

Freddie cleared the emotion from his throat. "So what happened with Nick before? I've never seen him so pissed."

"He heard about the IAB hearing—through the grapevine."

"Ouch," Freddie said with a wince. "I hate to say I told you so, but, I told you so."

"Shut up."

"You should've told him the day Stahl gave you the summons."

"While I appreciate your sage relationship advice, I'd much rather talk about you and your fuck buddy."

His face turned bright red.

"Ahh, *now* we're getting somewhere."

"That's not what she is," he stammered.

Sam raised a skeptical eyebrow. "Oh, no?"

He shook his head. "I like her."

"You like *banging* her."

"Do you have to be so crude?" he huffed.

Sam pretended to give that some serious thought. "Um, yeah. I do."

"Can you try to be serious for just a minute?"

She could see there was something he wanted to say so she did her best to wipe the smug grin off her face.

"I wasn't expecting to like her so much," he said haltingly. "It wasn't supposed to be about that."

"Oh, for Christ's sake, Cruz, you can't fall for the first chick you ever bang—"

His face lit up once again. "I've asked you not to use the Lord's name in vain, and she's not the first."

Sam shot him a look intended to remind him of who he was dealing with. "Whatever you say, stud. I just hope you're being careful. Women like her aren't looking for forever."

"Neither am I."

"If you say so."

"Why do you have to be so cynical? Isn't it possible that maybe she's the one for me?"

"No, it's not possible. Life doesn't work that way. You

can have some fun with her but be prepared for her to get bored and move on. That's how it goes."

"Are you prepared for Nick to get bored and move on?"

The barb shot straight to her heart. "That's different. We're older and ready for a serious relationship." God, at least she hoped so. "You need to test the waters a little more before you start thinking permanent."

"I tested the waters and ended up getting shot."

Snickering, Sam said, "That could really only happen to you."

"Glad to amuse you."

"Oh, you do. That you do." She laughed at the tortured expression on his face. "Thanks for the laugh, Cruz. I really needed that."

His scowl answered for him.

"Now let's figure out who Sanducci's disciples are."

GONZO PARALLEL PARKED on New York Avenue, in one of the rougher neighborhoods along a main artery into and out of the city. Since McBride had been working the case, Sam had asked him to partner up with Jeannie for the duration of the Sinclair investigation. He studied the storefront and then looked over at her. "Nice digs."

"I guess his parents are only willing to pony up for bail and lawyers, not real estate." Jeannie reached for the car door handle. "What time did you ask Diandra to meet us at HQ?"

"In an hour, so let's see what Sanducci has to say and get out of there."

"I'm with ya."

The office had the temporary feel of a campaign headquarters, but with the unpleasant decor of posters featuring aborted fetuses. Packing boxes were scattered about, the floor littered with Styrofoam noodles.

Gonzo turned away from the images when his stomach turned with disgust.

A blonde woman who seemed barely old enough to be out of high school greeted them. "May I help you?"

They flashed their badges. "Tony Sanducci, please."

"Um, sure. Just a minute." She returned five minutes later with an aging preppy who seemed better suited to the Yale campus than this squalid storefront. He flashed the matinee idol grin that guys like him used to skirt the rules. Gonzo hated him on sight. "Tony Sanducci?"

"That's right." He extended a hand.

Gonzo flashed his badge. "Detectives Gonzales and McBride."

Sanducci's hand fell to his side. "What can I do for you?"

"Going somewhere?" Gonzo asked, gesturing to the boxes.

"We don't have much of a cause here anymore. We're just waiting to see who Nelson comes up with next."

"Must've broken your heart to hear that Sinclair had been killed."

"I didn't want him to be on the Supreme Court, Detective, but that doesn't mean I wanted him dead."

"Didn't you?"

The amiable smile faded. "I'm afraid I don't understand."

Gonzo read him some of the more inflammatory passages from the *Post* article.

"So?"

"Where were you the night Sinclair was killed?"

Taken aback, Sanducci said, "I was here all night. I have a cot in the back where I stay when I'm in the city. Helps to keep the expenses down."

"By yourself?"

Sanducci cast a quick glance at the teenybopper who ran the office. It was fleeting, but Gonzo saw it.

"That's right."

"Would you like to continue this conversation downtown, Mr. Sanducci?"

He ran his hand through well-coifed dark hair. "Listen," he said in a low voice. "I have a wife, four children. It's a fling. Means nothing."

Gonzo wondered if it meant nothing to the child he was sleeping with. "What's her name?"

"Does she really have to be brought into this?"

"Yeah, she really does."

With a deep sigh, he said, "Cindy, can you come over here for a minute, please?"

As if God himself had summoned her, Cindy came scurrying across the big open room.

Gonzo wanted to barf at the worshipful gaze she directed at Sanducci.

"Yes, Tony?"

"Honey, would you mind telling these fine police officers where you were the night Julian Sinclair was killed?"

Her eyes bugged, and for a moment she seemed too stunned to speak.

"It's okay," he said. "Go ahead."

"We were… I was…here."

"You were together all night?"

Humiliation radiated from her. "Yes."

"And your full name?" Gonzo asked.

"Cynthia Kaine." She spelled her last name.

Glancing at Sanducci, Gonzo said, "And how old are you, Cindy?"

"Eighteen."

"And how old are you, Mr. Sanducci?"

"How is that relevant?"

"Answer the question."

"Forty-four."

Gonzo made sure the disgust showed on his face. "I see."

Jeannie had Cindy write down her address and phone number before dismissing her.

Sanducci gave Gonzo a "guys will be guys" smile that Gonzo wanted to punch off his smug face. "We can keep this between us, right?"

"I'll need a list of your employees, members, followers, whatever you call them."

"That list is private," Sanducci sputtered.

"Then we'll get a subpoena. Until it comes through, we'll put you up downtown. Your choice."

Sanducci fumed for a long moment. "Cindy," he said through gritted teeth. "Print out the A list."

She stared at him.

"While you're at it," Gonzo said, "print out the B, C and D lists, too."

Sanducci's lips turned white and his cheeks flamed with color. "Do it."

Cindy got busy at her workstation.

"Must've been a letdown," Gonzo said, nodding to the posters and pickets lining the wall, "to make all these plans and then have nothing to protest."

Sanducci shrugged. "There're others on Nelson's short list who we don't want on the court any more than we wanted Sinclair. That's why we're still here."

"Will you have them killed, too?"

"I don't know what you're talking about!"

"Don't you?"

"I didn't kill anyone!"

"Maybe you suggested to one of your followers that it would be better if Sinclair was dead?"

"I told you," Sanducci said, his preppy veneer crumbling. "We didn't want him on the court. That was it."

Gonzo took the lists Cindy handed to him. "Stay local," he said to Sanducci on his way out the door.

On the sidewalk, Jeannie took a deep breath of fresh air. "I need a shower," she said, shuddering.

"Me, too."

"But he didn't kill Sinclair."

"No, but maybe someone on these lists did." He checked his watch. "We have just enough time to drop them off to the lieutenant and Cruz before our meeting with Diandra Sinclair."

"You read my mind, Detective."

"THIS IS SUCH bullshit," Sam said as she paced the length of her father's living room, gripping the lists Gonzo had brought her. "I'm stuck here when we're finally getting somewhere on Sinclair."

"Want me to make a phone call?" Skip asked.

"No," she said with an emphatic glare. "Don't even think about it. That won't help."

"You could make the call," Gonzo suggested. "Farnsworth is the only one who can override IAB. Tell him you'll serve out the suspension when we close Sinclair."

"Stahl would accuse me of using my connections."

"So what?" Freddie said. "If it'll get you back on the streets when we need you, why not do it?"

"Perhaps," Jeannie said with a mischievous grin, "you could lead Farnsworth to believe that it was *his* idea to defer the suspension."

"Oh." Sam snapped her fingers. "I like how you think." She reached for her cell phone to call the chief and put the phone on speaker so the others could hear.

"Lieutenant," Chief Farnsworth said when his assistant put Sam right through. "I believe you're on vacation today."

"Is that what we're calling it?"

"What can I do for you?"

"You can get me back on the streets. Sinclair is hot right now. It's not doing the department any good to have me stuck at home."

"While I agree with you, IAB—"

"Screw IAB! I'm in the middle of a case! I'll serve out the suspension after we close Sinclair. Hell, I'll give you four days unpaid at the end. We've got all kinds of leads I could be following, suspects to interview."

"You have plenty of qualified people working for you, Lieutenant. Delegate."

"They need me, Chief. Let me finish this case, and then I'll serve my sentence in silence. You won't hear a word from me."

"That'll be the day," he muttered. After a long moment of silence during which Sam's stomach pinged with pain, he said, "You'll have trouble with Stahl."

"I already have trouble with Stahl, but if you were to say *you* called *me* and ordered me back to work to close Sinclair, well then, there's not much he can say."

"You think you're very clever, don't you?"

"Actually, in this instance, Detective McBride is the clever one."

"Whose idea was it to allow women on the force?"

She smiled. "Is that a yes?"

"I'm ordering you back to work until Sinclair is closed, at which time you'll serve a *three*-day suspension. The extra day is for manipulating your favorite Uncle Joe."

Sam smiled. "You're the best." She swallowed hard before she added, "Any word from the deliberations this morning?"

"Not yet. I'm sure you'll hear from Conklin the minute he has any news."

What was taking so long? "Yeah."

"Get me an arrest, Lieutenant. The press is on me like white on rice."

"I'm all over it." She ended the call and turned to the others. "Let's go."

TWENTY-FIVE

"You're invited to Governor Zorn's sixtieth birthday," Christina said to Nick. "They'd also like you to say a few words."

"I promised the governor's wife I'd do that. Tell them yes."

"Just you?"

Nick thought of Sam and the possible outcome of the IAB proceedings. If he didn't hear something soon, he might just lose his mind. "I don't know if Sam can make it or not. Depends on her schedule."

"So what do I tell them?"

"I guess the standard answer going forward will be one for sure, two maybe."

"Allrighty," Christina said, even though her disapproval was apparent. "President Nelson sent you an invite to the state dinner with the Canadian prime minister. You can't be vague on that one. Either she's going or she isn't."

Nick tried to imagine Sam at a White House function. The idea of it made him smile. "I'll see if I can talk her into it."

"We have to let them know by next week. The next thing is this slew of interview requests we've received. Trevor and I agree that you probably need to pick one and do it. You can't just ignore them all." She handed him the list. "But there's one thing."

"What's that?"

"They want both of you."

"Both of who?"

"You and Sam."

"Are you serious?"

Christina nodded. "I know you're painfully aware that the media is enthralled by the two of you. They're clamoring for the first joint interview."

"She'd never do it in a million years."

"Even if you asked her to?"

"She's up to her eyeballs in the Sinclair case." *Not to mention the IAB situation,* he thought to himself. "I can't imagine asking her to sit down for an interview."

"Maybe if you do it," Christina said, "they'll move on to something else and leave the two of you alone."

"You really think so?" Nick asked, skeptical.

"Not really, but it's worth a shot."

"I'll think about it," Nick said, trying to imagine broaching the subject with Sam.

One of the receptionists came to the door. "Senator, Judson Knott is here. He wonders if he might have a few minutes."

Nick glanced at Christina who shrugged. "Not on the schedule."

"Sure," he said. "Show him in."

The chairman of the Virginia Democratic Party stepped into the office, full of apologies for showing up without an appointment.

"It's no problem, Judson," Nick said. "My door's always open for you." To Christina, Nick added, "Would you mind giving us a minute?"

When they were alone, Nick asked if he could get Judson some coffee.

"No, thank you, Senator. I'm fine. I've just come from breakfast with Richard and the rest of the party leadership. I wonder if your ears were ringing."

"Sir?"

Judson flashed a big smile. "You were the hot topic of conversation. The way you've come in and hit the ground running, getting O'Connor-Martin passed. Your approval ratings are higher than anything we've ever seen. You don't see numbers like yours. Ever."

"I'm sure it's just the sentimental bump from Senator O'Connor's loyal base."

"It's much more than that, Senator. You've struck a chord with people in the Old Dominion, and your romance with the pretty police officer hasn't hurt anything."

Nick scowled. He'd never understand why people were so interested in them.

"That leads me to the reason I'm here." Judson shifted in his seat, seeming uncomfortable all of a sudden. "I know we said we needed you for a year and that we'd run Cooper in the election."

"I hope his wife is doing better," Nick said.

"We heard just yesterday that her cancer is in remission."

"Well, that's a great relief."

"Indeed. However, the party is no longer interested in him as our candidate for your seat."

"Why not?"

Judson gave him a "come on, Senator, you're a smart guy" look.

"Wait a minute. You said one year and out. We had a deal."

"Why in the world would we go looking for another candidate when we have the perfect guy already in office? You're our man, Senator. You're the one the party wants. The *only* one."

All Nick could think of in that moment was the far

more important deal he had made with Sam when he accepted the position in the first place—one year in the Senate. "I, ah, I don't know what to say."

"Say yes. You're a natural and the very best thing that's happened to our state in years. We're invested in you for the long haul."

"I appreciate that, Judson. I really do. But I need to give this some thought."

"We'll need a decision in the next week or two. Campaign season is right around the corner."

The idea was so overwhelming that Nick couldn't begin to process it. A lengthy campaign, the prospect of a six-year term that he won on his own merits. "Have you talked to Graham about this?"

Judson shook his head. "He wasn't at the meeting today. He's taking Sinclair's death real hard. Such a tragedy, and right on top of losing his son. Well, I guess I don't need to tell you."

"No, sir."

"I have no doubt, however, that Graham will fully support your candidacy. You know he's your staunchest supporter." Judson got up. "You'll think about it?"

Nodding, Nick stood and offered his hand. "I'll be in touch."

"MRS. SINCLAIR, HOW long have you harbored a hatred for homosexuals?"

Diandra blanched at Sam's question. "I don't *hate* anyone, Lieutenant."

"All right then, how about you tell me your views on homosexuality."

"I find it to be an abhorrent lifestyle. However, I have no ill will for people who choose this way of life."

"What about it do you find so abhorrent?"

"Leviticus 20:13, states, 'If a man lies with a male, as with a woman, both of them have committed an abomination: they shall surely be put to death; their blood shall be upon them.' I tend to agree with him, and I was under the impression that as an American, I'm free to pursue my own beliefs."

"He was a hell of a guy that Leviticus, wasn't he Detective Cruz?" Sam said.

"In our time, he'd be considered a bigot," Freddie said with a pointed look at Diandra.

"I'm not a bigot, Detective. My beliefs are grounded in scripture."

"Your friend Leviticus also recommends stoning for married couples who engage in intercourse during the woman's period," Freddie said. "I sure hope you've never done *that*."

"It's not the same thing," Diandra snapped. "A woman's period is a *natural* event."

"How do you reconcile the unnatural 'abomination' with the commandment to love thy neighbor?" Freddie asked. "And Jesus himself said, 'If the world hates you, keep in mind that it hated me first.'"

Diandra glared at him.

Fascinated by the debate, Sam was reluctant to interrupt but needed to get back to the investigation. "Do either you or your husband own a gun?"

Diandra was clearly caught off guard by the change in direction. "We have a gun we keep locked in the house for protection. I've attracted my share of detractors."

"You say that you have no hatred for homosexuals, but would you say you hated your brother-in-law Julian?"

Diandra's posture lost some of its rigidity. "I was once very close to Julian. We lived for many years in Boston while Preston completed graduate studies at Harvard. We spent a lot of time with Julian."

"Yet you never had any idea that Julian was gay?"

She shook her head. "It came as a total shock to me. Like I said the other day, we'd allowed our young, impressionable sons to spend time in his home, to sleep there." She shuddered. "God only knows what they were subjected to."

"Did you suspect that he abused them?"

Diandra's eyes flashed with anger. "Of course not! He would never harm them. He loved those boys. I never doubted that."

"Did Duncan spend the night with Julian when the boys were there?"

"Not that I was ever aware of."

"So your brother-in-law, who was clearly devoted to your sons and who seemed to go to some lengths to keep his orientation hidden from them, was none-the-less banished from their lives?"

"You don't understand, Lieutenant."

"Then make me."

Diandra folded her hands on the table and focused on them. "Times were different then. People were less accepting of alternative lifestyles. Preston and I were building our careers, pursuing our goals—"

"And there was no room for his gay brother in the midst of all that ambition?"

"We didn't want our sons to be influenced."

"You're aware that you can't 'catch' homosexuality, aren't you?"

"That's a matter of opinion."

"Actually," Freddie said, "there's quite a lot of science to support that sexual orientation is something we're born with."

"I don't believe that."

"Mrs. Sinclair, if one of your sons happened to be gay—"

"Don't be outrageous, Lieutenant! My sons are normal, well-adjusted young men."

Oh, how Sam wished she could pop this woman's sanctimonious bubble. But since she had promised discretion to Devon, she bit her tongue. "Let's just speculate for the sake of argument that one of them is gay, would you exile him from your family and your life?"

"There's no point in speculating on something that could never happen."

"Humor me."

"I love my sons," Diandra said, her hand trembling ever so slightly.

"Unconditionally?"

"Yes," she stammered. "Of course."

"So if Devon or Austin came home one day and said, 'I love you, Mom, but I'm gay,' you'd be okay with that?"

"I'd be very disappointed—and shocked after the number of girlfriends my boys have had."

Devon has done a hell of a job hiding who he is, Sam thought. "What would it have meant to your book deal if Julian's orientation became public during the nomination hearings?"

Flustered, Diandra said, "It would've had no bearing."

"Embarrassing?"

"Somewhat. Who wants their family members' sexual predilections discussed publicly?"

"Were you under any pressure to avoid scandal in these final weeks before your book is published?"

"Do I need a lawyer, Lieutenant?"

"As I advised you at the outset, you can request an attorney at any time. However, you're not currently under arrest. We've asked you to cooperate with our investigation."

Diandra took a long sip from the glass of water Sam had provided at the beginning of their interview. "It's understood that I am to stay above any scandal."

A knock on the door interrupted them.

Sam nodded at Freddie to get it.

He came back in a minute later and gestured for her to join him and Captain Malone in the hallway. "A pizza delivery guy just found Devon Sinclair and his roommate shot in their home."

"Oh, shit." Sam glanced over her shoulder at Diandra in the interrogation room. "DOA?"

"Both were shot," Malone said. "One was DOA. We don't know yet which one."

"At least we can confirm she didn't do this one," Sam said.

"Right," Freddie said. "That was my first thought, too."

Steeling herself, she returned to the interrogation room. "Mrs. Sinclair, I'm sorry to have to tell you this, but there's been a shooting at your son Devon's home."

Gasping, Diandra stood up. "Dev."

"We only know there were two victims, one of them a fatality," Sam said.

Diandra sagged into the chair. "Oh, God, please. Not my Devon. Not my baby."

"If you'll wait here, I'll see if I can find out more."

Diandra nodded.

With Freddie following her, Sam emerged from the interrogation room and ran smack into Lieutenant Stahl.

"Lieutenant," Stahl said, his fat face shifting to a sneer at the sight of her.

Since he used her rank, Sam assumed she still had it.

"You've been suspended," Stahl said. "You have no business here."

"The chief called me back to close Sinclair," Sam said with a satisfied smirk.

Stahl's cheeks turned an unhealthy shade of purple. "You may think you've won this round, Holland, but you mark my words—I'll get rid of you if it's the last thing I ever do."

"Detective Cruz, did you hear Lieutenant Stahl threaten me?" Sam asked, her eyes fixed on Stahl.

"Yes, ma'am. I sure did."

"So if anything suspicious ever happens to me, you'll know just where to begin your investigation, right?"

"Yes, ma'am."

"This is not over," Stahl said, his spit hitting Sam's face.

She wiped it away. "Do you mind getting out of my way? I'm working a homicide here." Shoving past him, she signaled for Freddie to come with her.

"You might want to consider your allegiances, Detective," Stahl said to their backs. "I'd hate to see such a promising young career derailed."

Freddie spun around. "My allegiances, Lieutenant, are with my partner, the best cop on this force, so don't bother wasting your bad breath on me."

Stahl's eyes almost popped out of his fat head.

Sam took hold of Freddie's good arm and half led, half dragged him back to the detectives' pit. "You shouldn't have done that. He was baiting you."

"I knew that."

"It's bad enough he has it in for me. I don't want you sucked into it, too."

"Too late."

Captain Malone joined them. "You've heard the news? No reduction in rank?"

"Not officially until right now," Sam said, the relief almost as overwhelming as the worry.

"Apparently, Stahl about had an apoplexy when Andrews sided with Conklin," Malone said. "You've got a very significant enemy there, Lieutenant."

"I'm not worried about him." Sam grabbed her radio off her desk. "I've got another shooting in the Sinclair case to contend with."

"Word is the roommate, Tucker Farrell, was DOA on the scene," Malone said. "Devon Sinclair is being taken to GW Trauma."

Sam watched Freddie struggle into a coat. "Cruz, you're done for today. Arrange transport to GW for Mrs. Sinclair, and then call your ride to pick you up."

"But I'm fine!" he sputtered. "I'm good for a couple more hours."

"Call your ride," Sam said. "You did enough for the first day back."

"Oh, *come on,* Lieutenant!"

"Detective," Malone said in his quiet but effective way. "I believe your lieutenant has given you an order."

"Yes, sir," he mumbled, stalking off to his cubicle.

"Thanks for the assist," Sam said to Malone. Viewing the empty pit, she looked up at him. "I could use a partner. You game?"

His eyes lit up. "On a real case? Me?"

"If you can stand leaving your desk for an hour or two."

"I'm in. Meet you outside in ten."

"Make it five. Crime scene is waiting on us." On the way to the parking lot, Sam called Nick. "Hey," she said when he answered, "no reduction in rank."

"Oh, good," he said, releasing a long deep breath. "That's good."

He sounded so relieved that she laughed. "Yes, it is."

"I don't know if I could've lived with being responsible for you getting busted down to detective."

"We would've coped."

"I'm glad we don't have to."

"So am I. What're you doing?"

"Reading committee reports. That seems to be all I've done since I took office."

"Ah, the exciting life of a U.S. senator."

"Nonstop glamour. What's up over there?"

"I'm on my way to investigate a shooting at Julian's nephew's house."

"Oh, no. Which one?"

"Devon."

"Jesus. Is he dead?"

"No, but his roommate is. Devon's on the way to GW."

"I hope he's okay. Julian adored him. He was so thrilled when Dev decided to go to law school."

"Did you know Devon?"

"I never met either of his nephews. Because of Julian's rift with their parents, he kept his relationship with them quiet."

"But you knew he saw them?"

"He talked about them all the time, so I just assumed he did. This is all so unbelievable."

"I'm sorry. I know you're still upset about losing him."

"And now this. Do you think the two shootings are related?"

"I'm working under the assumption that they are."

"Which eliminates a lot of other suspects."

"Not entirely. This could be intended to throw us off the trail."

"True. I guess this means you'll be working late again."

"Right you are. I'll see you when I see you."

He paused, as if there was something else he wanted to say.

"Everything all right?" she asked.

"Yeah. We can talk later."

"Or not," she said, her tone rife with suggestion.

He laughed. "Be careful out there, Lieutenant."

"I always am."

TWENTY-SIX

FURIOUS AT BEING exiled, Freddie paced the sidewalk and waited for Elin to arrive. He hated being helpless and at the mercy of others. But since his car had a standard transmission, he couldn't drive until his shoulder healed. Right now, it hurt like a bastard, which meant he was due for another pain pill.

Elin pulled up in her sleek black Acura and leaned over to open the door for him.

"I can get it myself," he snapped.

"Yeah, nice to see you, too."

Freddie slammed the door and did his best to situate his injured arm. The pain left him feeling sweaty and sick.

"You look like shit."

"Thanks."

"The doctor told you to take it easy. It's too soon to be back at work."

"I've already got my mother and Sam bitching at me. I don't need it from you, too."

She abruptly pulled over. "Then why don't you get one of them to drive you home?"

Startled, he ventured a glance at her and was surprised to see that she was genuinely pissed.

"Yeah, I shut your phone off. Yeah, it's my fault you got shot. I get it. Now maybe you can get over it. If you can't, you'll have to find someone else to be your bitch. I've had enough."

"I don't blame getting shot on you," he said haltingly, stunned and unnerved by her outburst.

"Right."

"I *don't*."

"You could've fooled me. I put up with your crankiness when you were in the hospital and when you got home because I blamed myself. But I figure my debt is about paid up at this point."

Suddenly, Freddie didn't want to lose her. He wasn't ready for this—whatever it was—to be over. "You're right. I've been a shit to you, and I'm sorry." He brushed at imaginary lint on his jeans. "I wasn't prepared for this to be more than just…"

"Sex?"

Shrugging, he said, "I thought we'd have some fun, and then go our separate ways."

"No reason we can't."

"I don't want that," he said, reaching for her hand. "We haven't had nearly enough fun yet."

"So you want more sex, and then you'll cut me loose?"

"I don't know what you want me to say, Elin. I like you. I like being with you. That's the part I wasn't expecting."

She stared out the windshield. "I like being with you, too."

"You sound surprised."

"I was in it for the sex, too," she confessed.

"So you're using me," he joked. "I see how it is."

"You were using me, too!"

His eyes met hers. "All I know is that from the first time I met you during the O'Connor investigation, I wanted you. I thought about you, and I wanted you."

"I wanted you, too. Just as much."

"So what do we do now?"

"You're really done being a shit?"

Freddie winced. "I'm done."

She replied with a coy grin. "Then you wanna go home and have some fun?"

He hesitated.

"What?"

"The last time I had that kind of fun, it didn't work out so well."

"It worked out *great* until you got pissed and left."

"Yeah. I guess."

"So what's the problem?"

"I want to tell you, but you might think I'm weird or something."

"Don't worry. I already do."

"Very funny. I'm trying to be serious."

She made a poor attempt at a solemn face. "Please. Proceed."

"You met my mom." His heart raced with nerves and anxiety. When Elin nodded, he said, "It was just the two of us when I was growing up. Our church and our faith were important." He let his eyes wander over to her, petrified by what he'd find. "They still are."

"Okay. That's no big deal to me."

"When I was fifteen, I took a vow of celibacy."

"Oh."

"It was voluntary, and I stuck to it for a long time—a really long time. In fact, I only just recently—"

"Oh, my God! *You're not saying what I think you're saying!*"

He looked down at his good hand, which had rolled into a fist in his lap. "That's what I'm saying."

"Why didn't you tell me?"

"I *am* telling you."

"I mean before."

"What difference would it have made?"

"It just would've been nice to know." She studied him for a long time before her eyes widened. "You sought me out with that in mind, didn't you? You figured I'd be easy."

"No," he said quickly. "I figured you'd be fun. And you were. We had a lot of fun before we ever had sex."

"That's true."

"Are you mad?"

"I never would've guessed," she said with a shy smile.

"Really?"

"It was amazing."

"Yeah." He shifted to accommodate his instant erection. "It was."

"Why do you think I've put up with your crap the last couple of days?"

Clearing his throat, he said, "Because you want more?"

She bit her lip and nodded.

A hot ball of lust surged through Freddie and landed in his lap. "Your place or mine?"

SAM AND MALONE arrived at Devon's Dupont Circle townhouse at the same time as the medical examiner.

"We meet again," Dr. Lindsey McNamara said. "What've you got?"

Sam filled her in on what they knew. "I'm looking for a connection between Julian Sinclair's shooting and this one."

"If there's a connection," Lindsey said, "I'll find it."

"That's what I'm counting on."

Inside, the place smelled of pizza and death. Sam nodded to the officers who had arrived first on the scene.

"Called in by the pizza delivery guy, Mac Healy, age twenty-three." The patrolman gestured to the living room sofa where Healy sat with his head in his hands. "Shook up."

"We'll talk to him," Sam said.

"Tucker Farrell, age twenty-seven, shacked up with Sinclair, who owns the place," the patrolman continued. "Farrell's next of kin are his parents in Wilmington, Delaware." He handed her a slip of paper with their phone number.

"I'll call them," Sam said, her stomach knotting. She hated making those phone calls. "What about Sinclair?"

"Bullet wound to the back of the head. Paramedics left with him about ten minutes ago. He was found over there." He pointed to a puddle of blood just short of the doorway to the kitchen. "They said his condition is grave."

"The shooter took out Farrell first," Malone observed. "Sinclair was running away when he was hit."

"That's how I see it, too," Sam said. To the officer who'd briefed them, she added, "Thanks, Peterson. Good work." She crouched down to take a closer look at Farrell's chest wound. "Looks like a direct hit to the heart."

Lindsey nodded in agreement. "He bled out fast."

"Might've confronted the shooter," Malone said.

"It was close range," Lindsey concurred.

Sam stood up and went over to talk to the pizza guy. "Mr. Healy, I'm Detective Lieutenant Holland, my partner, Detective Captain Malone. Can you tell us what happened?"

Healy's eyes, flat with shock, were rimmed with red. "I already told them."

"Do me a favor, and run through it one more time," Sam said.

"I brought the pie they ordered." Healy gestured to

the red thermal bag sitting at his feet. "A large sausage and onion. Their usual."

"So they were frequent flyers?" Sam asked.

"Yeah, at least once, maybe twice a week. Anyway, I got here and the front door was wide-open, which was weird this time of year. I rang the bell a couple of times, but no one answered. I stuck my head in and saw a foot on the floor." He zeroed in on Tucker's body. "I started to run away, but then I thought he might need help so I came in. That's when I saw the other guy, on the floor over there." Shaking his head, he took a couple of deep breaths. "I kinda freaked and went outside to call 911."

"When you arrived, did you see anyone leaving or running on the street?"

"No. I didn't think anything was weird until I noticed the door open."

Sam took down his contact info and released him.

"What's next, Lieutenant?" Malone asked as they watched Lindsey follow Tucker's body out of the house.

"A bit rusty, are you, sir?" she said, smiling at his scowl. "Now we knock on doors to see if we can narrow down when the shots were fired and whether anyone saw someone fleeing the scene."

"What're you thinking?"

Sam studied the two bloody areas on the wood floor. "Not sure yet. We've got an uncle and nephew, both of them gay, one still in the closet, shot in the span of a few days. If I hadn't had Diandra in interrogation when this went down, I'd be getting a warrant for her arrest."

"Who else is there?"

"Preston and Austin Sinclair, father and brother of Devon, brother and nephew of Julian."

"Any chance this is unrelated to Julian?"

"Sure, there's a chance." She took a good look around

the latest crime scene. "But this doesn't feel random. It doesn't feel random at all."

"Not to me, either."

"We'll have to dig into Farrell's life to rule out anything there, but until we can talk to Devon Sinclair, we knock on doors."

"I'm following you," Malone said.

"I JUST DON'T get it," Freddie said, his heart racing. "This has never happened. Ever." He looked down at his limp penis and willed it to life. Not that he'd had much experience, but getting an erection had never been a problem. In fact, having too many of them in his sexually frustrated state had been more of an issue. He had no idea what the hell was wrong with him.

"Don't worry about it." Elin kissed and caressed his chest. "We can do other stuff."

"It's probably the pain drugs." However, it occurred to him that he'd been hard as stone in the car just a short time ago. Now here he was, naked and in a bed with the equally naked Elin, the subject of his most lurid fantasies, and *nothing* was happening? *How could that be?*

"I'm sure that's all it is."

But in the back of his mind, Freddie suspected the guilt had gotten to him. It had eaten away at him until even his manhood was guilty.

Elin sat up, straddled him and ran her hands from his belly to his pecs. "Don't think. Just feel. Close your eyes."

He did what she said, trying to clear his mind of everything except for what was happening right in front of him—and on top of him. Imagining Elin's pierced nipples and the heart-shaped tattoo, Freddie felt a surge of desire.

"That's it," she whispered, her lips cruising from neck to chest to belly. "Just feel. No thinking."

"No thinking."

She massaged his thighs, first with her hands and then with her lips.

Freddie moaned.

Dragging her breasts over his penis, she continued to whisper soft words of encouragement.

He concentrated on putting aside the guilt and the conflict. Even the throbbing in his shoulder couldn't dampen the surge of lust. "Elin." With his good hand, he reached for a handful of soft breast and ran his thumb over her nipple.

She gasped. "Now we're getting somewhere," she said, stroking him until he was hard and throbbing.

"I'm glad it's not broken."

Laughing, she bent to take him into her mouth. "Definitely not broken."

His hips seemed to have a mind of their own. "Mmm." He sighed. "That's so good." The sweep of her tongue, the heat of her mouth, the tightness of her throat had him teetering on the brink in no time. She continued to stroke him until he was so hard he was afraid if he moved, even the slightest bit, he'd lose it. Then she squeezed his balls, just enough to make him surge off the bed. Wincing, he shifted to accommodate his injured shoulder.

"Sorry." She sat up. "We need to make you more comfortable for what I have in mind." Piling up pillows behind him, she arranged him the way she wanted him.

Freddie's heart slammed around in his chest, anxiety battling overwhelming curiosity.

She straddled him and took him into her moist heat.

They hadn't gotten to this position the other night, even though he'd wanted to try it. God, it was even better this way, if that was possible. As she rode him, she kept her gaze fixed on his face.

"Like it?" she asked.

"Oh, yeah." As he climbed toward what would no doubt be another explosive climax, it occurred to him that he could very easily become addicted to this—and to her.

TWENTY-SEVEN

SAM AND MALONE worked the street for an hour but found no one who had seen or heard anything that could help them.

"I hate middle-of-the-day shit that happens when everyone is at work," she said, rubbing the back of her neck as she tried to regroup.

"Devon Sinclair and his roommate would've been at work, too, if his uncle hadn't been murdered," Malone observed.

"True. So who knew he'd be at home?"

"His family, friends, the pizza guy, coworkers, the roommate's coworkers. What'd he do?"

"He was a chef," she said, her stomach pinging when she remembered she still had to call Tucker's parents.

"Worth looking into."

"Let's see what ballistics gets us. I'd bet all the dough I have that it's going to be the same gun that did Julian, which rules out anything random." Sam's cell phone rang, but she didn't recognize the ring tone. "What the hell?" She glanced at the LCD. "Goddamn it."

"What now?" Malone asked, grinning at the expression on her face.

"I forgot about this freaking doctor's appointment. Nick programmed a reminder alarm into my cell. What a pain in the ass he is!"

"Sneaky bastard."

"I know!" Jamming the phone into her pocket, she

took a long measuring look at the deserted neighborhood. "I'll have to reschedule. I need to get over to GW to check on Devon's condition. Hopefully, he'll wake up and tell us who the shooter is. That'd save a whole lot of time."

"I'll go to GW. You're going to the doctor. You can meet me there after."

She stared at him. "You can't make me go!"

He raised an eyebrow, daring her to defy him.

"You can't! It's my personal business."

Scratching at the gray stubble on his chin, he sized her up. "I could take you off Sinclair if I wanted to."

"You wouldn't do that."

"Bet?"

"I can't believe this! We've got two homicides going here, and you're gonna pull rank on me over a doctor's appointment?"

"Whatever is taking you to the doctor must be significant enough for Nick to program a reminder into your phone. So you're keeping the appointment, and you can rejoin the investigation when you're done." He checked his watch. "You'd better get going."

"I should've left you where you belong—on desk duty." With one last furious glance at his laughing face, she stormed off to her car, leaving him to find his own way to GW. "Goddamned bossy men," she muttered. "Why can't they mind their own freaking business? It's my stomach. They don't need to be all up in my grill about it." Her cell phone rang again, and this time it was Nick. *"What?"*

"Hello to you, too, babe. Where are you?"

"In the car."

"On the way to?"

"I'm going! For Christ's sake, will you back off and

leave me alone?" He laughed, and she saw red. "What the hell is so funny?"

"You are."

"I'm too busy for this shit. I've got two bodies to contend with and no time for doctors."

"You'd better keep that appointment, Samantha. I mean it. You've put this off long enough."

"Stop bugging me! I don't need a freaking keeper!"

"Clearly you do or you would've taken care of this a long time ago."

"It doesn't bother me. It only bothers you."

"Yeah, you're right. It does bother me to see the woman I love crippled with pain on a regular basis."

"It's not that often," she said, ignoring the ache circulating in her gut as the conversation escalated into a fight.

"It's often enough. Now, stop bitching and drive. Call me when you're done. I want to know what he says. Oh, and tell Harry I said hi."

"Screw you. Tell him yourself."

"Love you, too, babe."

HARRY MADE HER wait thirty minutes in a cold exam room wearing nothing more than the stupid paper gown they'd made her put on—with *nothing* under it. God, she hated doctors. Due to all the crap she'd been through trying to get pregnant and then the miscarriages, one of them an ectopic pregnancy that had nearly killed her, she had stayed far away from doctors the past few years. And for good reason: they kept you waiting when you had more important stuff to do. Like hunting down murderers.

Maybe she'd send good old Harry a bill for *her* time. She smiled. Yes, that would make her feel much better, and it would piss Nick off, too. Sam loved a plan that killed two birds with one stone.

After a brisk knock on the door, Harry came in a few minutes later, full of apologies for keeping her waiting. Of course he was totally hot. Wasn't that just her luck? Why couldn't he have been homely? Then she wouldn't have cared about him poking around in her parts. That he was also Nick's good friend made this even more uncomfortable and embarrassing. Why in the world had she agreed to this? *Because Nick asked you to,* she reminded herself. *Yeah, well, right now I hate him.*

"It's so great to meet you." Harry shook her hand, his brown eyes sparkling with warmth. "I was sorry I couldn't make it to your New Year's party, but Nick's told me all about you."

"Oh, really?"

"Yep, and of course I've read about you two in the paper."

Sam scowled. "Hasn't everyone?"

He laughed, and she realized he had dimples. Cute dimples. *Great.*

Harry sobered, but his eyes continued to dance with delight. "I suppose I should call him 'Senator' now."

"If you do, I'll shoot you. I'm trying to keep him humble."

"Nick said I would like you, and he was right." He washed his hands and pulled up a stool. "So what brings you here today?"

"Just this deal with my stomach," she said as the organ in question took a nasty dive.

"What kind of deal?"

She took a deep breath to counteract the surge of pain. "It, well, it kind of runs my life. Whenever I get nervous or anxious about something, it acts up."

"Are we talking reflux or heartburn or pain?"

"Pain."

"On a scale of one to ten, where's it at?"

"Um, twenty?"

"Huh. Well, that's no fun."

Sam laughed. "Not so much. Nick's all freaked out by it."

"With good cause, I'd say."

"Figures you'd side with him. You guys all stick together."

"We have to. It's us against you. Let's go over your history, and then we'll take a look."

Despite her best intentions to hate him as much as she hated Nick at the moment, Sam liked him, so she decided to level with him about everything—from the miscarriages to the endometriosis that had stolen her fertility, she laid it all out there.

"Huh," he said again. "How long ago did you hear that you were unlikely to conceive again?"

"Three years."

"And have you been seen since then?"

"No."

His eyes widened. "For *anything?*"

She shook her head. "I basically swore off doctors after that last episode."

"I don't have to tell you that's kind of dumb, do I?"

"It's not like I planned it or anything. It's just that one year became two and then two became three…and here we are."

"Well, I'm glad Nick made you come see me. We'll fix you right up. You might be glad to know that since you began boycotting me and my kind, they've made some great strides in treating endometriosis-related infertility. Women who were told exactly what you were are now having healthy babies after some minor laser surgery."

Sam refused to allow her hopes to rise for even one

second. "I think that ship has sailed for me. I'm happy with my life the way it is."

"What're you doing for birth control?"

She looked at him, wondering if he'd heard her say she was infertile. "Nothing. There's no need."

"As long as you still have all your parts, there's always a chance of conception."

Sam pondered that, feeling a surge of hope for the first time in years. But then reality returned, and she pushed the idea from her mind. "It's not something I worry about. I've resigned myself to remaining childless."

"You don't have to decide anything today about the surgery. It's just something to consider." He stood up and encouraged her to lie back on the table. "Since you've been so neglectful of your health," he said with a teasing scowl, "I'm going to treat you to the full deal."

"That's what I was afraid of," she said, swallowing hard. "You're not *that* kind of doctor, so you don't need to worry about the 'down there' stuff."

He replied with a charming smile as he very unobtrusively gave her a breast exam. "I'm a general internist, so I can worry about *all* your stuff."

"Fabulous."

"Do you want a nurse in the room for the pelvic exam?"

She swallowed hard, again. "No, that's okay. I guess if you're Nick's friend, I can trust you." Grimacing her way through a thorough check of her abdomen, she added, "Isn't it weird to be poking and prodding your friend's girlfriend?"

"Nah. It's just like a mechanic looking at a car engine—you've seen one, you've seen 'em all."

Sam's mouth fell open. "Surely some are better than others."

"Oh, yeah, definitely. Now be quiet so I can listen to your heart."

He kept up a steady stream of chatter as he poked and prodded *everything*. She learned that Nick was a menace on the racquetball court, that he still played hockey whenever he could and that he was a regular chick magnet in the bars. She'd have to discuss that with him after she punished him for making her go through this exam in the first place.

"It's not the same since you took him off the market," Harry lamented, as he performed a Pap smear and pelvic exam. "The rest of us have to work a lot harder to get the women to notice us without him there."

She stared at the ceiling and prayed for mercy as he prodded her in places no man had ever gone before. "Sorry to interfere in your conquests," she said through gritted teeth. She was going to beat the living daylights out of Nick for this.

"He seems really happy, though. After his friend John was murdered, we were so worried about him, but then he started seeing you and things seemed better."

"It's been a tough month for him," she managed to say. "Julian Sinclair was a close friend of his, too."

"I know," he said, probing deeper.

How was it possible to go *deeper*? First, she planned to punch Nick square in the face. Then she would kick him right where he lived. Next she would stab him in the heart with a rusty steak knife.

Harry *finally* finished prodding, took off his gloves and told her she could sit up. "Everything checks out well, Sam, so let's talk lifestyle and diet. Are you getting enough sleep?"

She thought of the long hours she kept at work and the late nights she'd had recently with Nick. "Sometimes."

He frowned. "Diet?"

"I try to eat healthy, but it's hard sometimes with my job."

"How do you manage the stress?"

"I focus on breathing. In through the nose, out through the mouth."

"Well, that's one way to cope." Running through a checklist on his clipboard, he asked a bunch of questions. "Caffeine intake?"

"Some," she said tentatively. Her last doctor had freaked out about her diet cola addiction.

"What's some?"

"A few diet sodas every day. No biggie."

"How many is a few?"

"I don't know. I don't keep count."

"Guesstimate—two, three, six, ten? What do you think?"

"Six maybe."

His eyes widened. "Six cans or bottles?"

"Um, bottles usually."

"You drink six twenty-ounce bottles of diet soda a day? *Every day?*"

Sam squirmed under the heat of his stare. This was worse than when he'd had his hands in her unmentionables. "I don't always finish them."

"Six twenty-ounce bottles is one hundred twenty ounces of soda. In other words, a gallon."

"Wow, all this and you can multiply, too."

"I'd say we've found our culprit. The acid in the soda is no doubt eating away at the lining of your stomach. If you don't already have an ulcer, you're probably well on your way to one."

"I need the boost. I can't function without it."

"Sure you can. You've just convinced yourself you can't. It's all psychological."

So now he was calling her crazy? Nick would get another punch for that.

"Here's the deal—I can do a series of invasive tests to rule out anything sinister, or you can give up the soda for a couple of weeks and see if that solves the problem."

"Define *invasive*," she said, swallowing a gulp.

"Down the gullet, up the kazoo—we'd come at you from both ends."

Sam narrowed her eyes, using her best cop stare to intimidate him.

He never even blinked, the bastard.

"I can see why you and Nick are such good friends."

Laughing, he said, "I take that as a compliment. So what do you say?"

"Fine! I'll give it up! But when Nick calls begging you to assist in his suicide, you'll have only yourself to blame. I'm a total gorilla without my caffeine."

"You'll just have to replace it with something equally stimulating, such as exercise or more sex."

"Not possible," she grumbled.

Harry flashed her a dirty grin as he typed something in to the computer. "No wonder why my buddy is looking so... what's the word? *Satisfied* lately."

Sam glared at him. "I hate you. Almost as much as I hate him—and that's a lot."

"You'll thank us both when you stop having crippling stomach pain." Before he left the room, he handed her his card. "If you want some more information on the endometriosis treatment, call me. Otherwise, come back in a month so we can see how the soda famine works out. If you have any problems in the meantime, or if the stomach pain continues to be bad, call me. You'll get the Pap results in the mail."

"Thank you. I think."

He left her with one last charming smile. "I can see why Nick loves you."

Now that wasn't fair! Just when she was starting to seriously hate him he went and said that! She got dressed while pondering life without soda.

This was not going to be pretty. Not one bit.

TWENTY-EIGHT

GASPING FOR AIR, Freddie used his good arm to reach up to see if the top of his head had blown off. Everything was still where it belonged, but nothing would ever be the same. He'd had no idea it was possible to come that hard and live through it.

"So," Elin said, peppering his chest and neck with kisses, "did you like it?"

He tried to form the words, but there were none.

She laughed. "I'll take that as a yes." Her hand traveled from his chest to his waist, heading south.

Freddie stopped her.

"What's wrong?"

"Nothing." It took every ounce of energy he could muster to sit up and look for his clothes. If he stayed, he had no doubt they'd be going at it again in no time. He was more than a little appalled by how ferociously he wanted her—he wanted her in every way it was possible to want a woman. Would he ever get enough? Probably not and that was the problem. It hadn't occurred to him that once he did this for the first time, he'd discover an insatiable appetite for more. He was in danger of becoming someone he barely recognized.

"Where're you going?" she asked.

"I need to go home. I'm working tomorrow."

"You're still on medical leave."

"I feel good enough to work." He didn't add that he was anxious to follow up on the people who used to live in Clarence Reese's house. If he couldn't do anything else to help Sam right now, he could do that.

Struggling into his shirt, he attempted to close a few buttons over the bulky sling that held his injured arm.

"Why don't you just stay?" Elin asked, her voice full of petulance.

"I need clothes for the morning, and I've got some stuff I have to do at home."

"Did I do something wrong again?"

"Of course not," he said, but his protest fell flat even to him. "It was amazing." And that, he thought, was the problem. It was just too damned good.

Freddie pushed his second leg into his jeans and tugged up the zipper. Doing things with one hand definitely sucked.

"I wish you wouldn't go," Elin said softly.

He glanced over and was stunned and unnerved to find her big eyes swimming with tears. Reaching for her hand, he brought it to his lips. "I had a good time tonight."

She took back her hand and started to get up. "I'll drive you home."

"No need. I'll grab a cab."

"Oh. Okay. Whatever."

"Elin…"

"Don't. Don't bother giving me the whole 'it's been fun, but it's over' speech."

"Who said anything's over?"

"The handwriting's on the wall."

"Well, it's not my handwriting. I'm going home because I have bills I need to pay and laundry to do. On top of that, my pain pills are there, and my shoulder's killing me." Making sure he had her full attention, he added, "I'm *not* going home because you rocked my world."

A hint of a smile graced her pretty pink mouth. "I did?"

He bit his lip and nodded. "Totally."

"So you might want to do it again sometime?" she asked, her smile now coy.

Leaning in to kiss her, he captured her bottom lip between his teeth. "Definitely. I'll call you."

Her smile faded.

"What?"

"Guys always say they'll call when they have no intention of calling."

"They do?" Freddie asked, genuinely surprised.

She nodded. "Universal code for a blow off."

Clearly, he still had a lot to learn about such things. "Well, that's not how *I* intended it. I *will* call you." He pulled the covers up over her and kissed her once more. "Get some sleep."

"You, too."

Freddie moved through the dark apartment, collected his coat and locked the door behind him. Once outside, he took several long deep breaths of cold air before glancing up at her window. He'd wanted exactly what he'd gotten from Elin. So why was it that he couldn't shake the feeling that he was in *way* over his head with her?

SAM LEFT HARRY'S office and went straight to the trauma unit at George Washington University Hospital, where she learned that Devon Sinclair was in surgery, and the outlook was grim. Of course it would've been too simple for him to be awake and alert and able to tell her who'd shot him and his lover. That kind of luck was apparently restricted to TV cops.

In the waiting room, Devon's brother, Austin, tried to comfort his inconsolable mother while weeping bitterly himself. "How could this have happened?" Austin asked. "Who would shoot Dev? Or Tucker?" He looked up at Sam. "God, I can't believe Tucker's dead."

Diandra's shoulders shook with sobs.

"You have no idea who might want to harm either of them?" Sam asked Austin.

"No. No one. They both had tons of friends. Everyone liked them."

"We can't…" Diandra couldn't seem to form the words she needed. "We can't find Preston."

Sam straightened, her spine tingling. "What do you mean?"

Diandra wiped her face with a tissue Austin handed her. "He's not answering his cell, his colleagues haven't seen him all day. I can't imagine where he could be. He needs to know about his son."

"I'll see what I can do to locate him."

"We'd appreciate that," Austin said.

Sam handed him her card. "When your brother wakes up, will you please call me?"

He nodded.

"I'll, um, hope for the best for Devon," she said, hating the way she sounded. She never knew what to say in these situations.

"Thank you," Austin said.

As Sam walked to the car, her sister Angela called. "Hey, Ang. What's up?"

"Are you anywhere close to heading home?"

"Getting there."

"Can you stop by on your way?"

"What's going on?"

"I just want to see you and so does Jack," Angela said, referring to her son.

"Sure, okay. I'll be there as soon as I can." Wondering what was going on with her sister, Sam spent the next hour looking for Preston Sinclair at his office and home. She confirmed Diandra's assertion that no one had seen him all day. When she ran out of places to look, she called in an APB to dispatch, ensuring that every cop in the city would be looking for him with orders to contact her the moment he turned up. Before she could chicken out, she also made the horrible, unimaginable call to Tucker Farrell's parents.

Afterward, her hands were sweaty, her stomach growled and her caffeine level had plummeted. Under normal circumstances, she'd be stopping for a diet cola right now. Her stomach might be benefiting from the soda famine, but her blood pressure was soaring. When she got her hands on Nick…

The cell rang again. Sam took her eyes off the road to glance at the caller ID. "Speak of the devil." She flipped the cell phone to speaker mode. "What?"

"Hello to you, too."

"I'm working here."

"You're in a fine mood. What time will you be home?"

Home? Where was that these days? "An hour or so. I have to stop at Angela's on the way."

"How's Devon?"

"In surgery. Doesn't look good and now his father has gone missing. I'll need to go back to work tonight."

"No problem. I'll feed you and send you on your way."

"Fine."

"Are you going to tell me what Harry said?"

"Nope."

"I'll get it out of you."

"Give it your best shot."

"Oh, I will. You can count on that."

Closing the phone, she tossed it into the passenger seat

and headed for Angela's house, where she was greeted by five-year-old Spider-Man.

"Spidey!" Sam scooped him up and swung him around.

Jack squealed with delight.

"Where's your mama?"

"In the house." Jack kissed her noisily on the mouth. "Where ya been, Sam?"

"Oh, here, there, everywhere."

"Did you shoot anyone?"

Sam poked his ribs as she carried him inside. "No, silly."

He touched the bandage on her chin. "Didja get beat up?"

Laughing, Sam said, "Not this week."

"Boring."

"*So* boring." She put him down and kissed her sister's cheek, noting that Angela looked pale and drawn.

"Jack, go get changed for dinner and *wash* your hands with real soap, not just water."

"But, Mom! Sam just got here."

Angela narrowed her eyes and pointed to the stairs. "Go."

Jack stomped off, grumbling under his breath.

"He's killing me." Angela sagged into a kitchen chair. "He never runs out of gas."

"You look like you have."

"I'm exhausted."

"What's wrong, Ang? You're scaring me."

After a long pause, Angela said, "I'm pregnant."

Sam took a moment to absorb the instantaneous burst of jealousy. "Really? How far along?"

"Almost three months."

"And you haven't told me?"

"It's hard, Sam. With all you've been through and everything."

"That doesn't mean I can't be happy for you. Who loves Jack more than me?"

"Only me and Spence."

Sam hugged her. "And I'll love this one just as much. I promise."

Angela's eyes went bright with tears. "Fucking out-of-control hormones."

Sam laughed and reached for her sister's hand. "Are you going to find out what you're having this time?"

"I want to, but Spence doesn't."

"Well, find out and tell me!"

Angela's pretty face softened into a smile. "You're sure you're okay?"

"I'm happy for you. You know that." Sam pushed around a toy car Jack had left on the table. "I saw a doctor friend of Nick's today. He told me about some new laser treatment that's working wonders for women who've had endometriosis. But I don't know."

Angela gasped. "What don't you know? You have to do it!"

"It's not that simple. I don't think I could go through that again."

"You have to! You have to at least try!"

"I shouldn't have told you."

"What did Nick say?"

"I haven't talked to him about it. I don't want to get his hopes up."

"Or yours."

"Or mine."

"Sam, if there's a chance, even the *slightest* chance, how can you *not* try?"

"I just heard about it a couple of hours ago. I haven't had time to even process it yet."

"Will you tell Nick?"

Sam shrugged. "I'm mad at him right now."

"Why?" Angela asked, alarmed. "What'd he do?"

"He made me go see his doctor friend Harry, who poked and prodded me in ways and places I've never been poked or prodded before."

Angela howled with laughter. "Oh, the nerve of him! You have to dump him. Immediately!"

Sam shot her a dirty look. "Harry says I have to give up soda. Entirely. Because of my stomach."

Angela stared at her sister. "Shut up. No way."

"Yes way. I'm already going through withdrawal. And it's all Nick's fault."

"Seriously. He must be punished."

Sam stood up. "I'm glad you agree. I've got to get on that. Tell Jack I'll see him this weekend."

"I predict you'll be horizontal under Nick in—" she consulted her watch "—twenty minutes."

Rolling her eyes, Sam headed for the front door. "Whatever," she called over her shoulder. "I'm not the one who's knocked up."

"Yet," her sister shot back.

Sam headed for her car, refusing to even entertain the possibility. She couldn't go through that again. She just couldn't.

SAM PARKED BEHIND Nick's car on Ninth Street and headed for her dad's.

"Lieutenant!"

She spun around and groaned when she saw Darren Tabor from the *Washington Star* rushing down the sidewalk. "What do you want, Darren?"

"A few minutes of your time."

She kept her back to him. "I'm busy."

"How close are you to an arrest on Sinclair?"

"Which one?"

"Both."

"Not as close as I'd like to be."

"Any suspects?"

Sam stopped and turned to him. "If I was giving out exclusives, what makes you think you'd get one?"

He flashed a smarmy smile. "In other words, you got dick, right?"

"In other words, I'm not telling you."

"How's the senator?"

She rolled her eyes. "Go home, Darren, and get a life."

"Rumor has it you've got some interesting skeletons in your closet, Lieutenant. But that doesn't surprise me."

"What the hell is that supposed to mean?"

He shrugged. "Just rumors."

"I work in facts, not rumors. I'm going home. I'd suggest you do the same."

"Have a nice evening, Lieutenant."

Anxious to get away from the pesky reporter, she dashed up the ramp to her father's house and opened the door to a dark, empty house. Unaccustomed to her father being out when she wanted to see him sent her even further out of sorts.

So many details and thoughts and ideas were bouncing around in her mind that she couldn't make sense of or process any of them. And what the hell had Tabor been spewing about? Rumors? What did he have on her? She probably didn't want to know.

The case was stalled, her body craved caffeine and despite what she'd told Angela, all she could think about was the possibility of being pregnant again. Now she also had to ponder what Tabor had been talking about. He'd been particularly harsh in his reporting about her after a child had been killed in a crack house during a raid she'd supervised. He was the last reporter in town she wanted poking into her business.

Sam decided she needed some time to herself before she saw Nick. Upstairs in her room, she unclipped her hair, stretched out on the bed and stared up at the ceiling, hoping to quiet the chaos in her mind so she could think. Beginning with the discovery of Julian Sinclair's body, she worked her way through each aspect of the case. The shooting of his nephew had to be related. How could it not be? But why? What possible connection existed between the two men that would generate a motive for shooting both of them? Both were attorneys, both were gay, both were successful men. Where was the motive?

Going on the assumption that the two shootings were related, her most promising suspect had vaporized that afternoon when Devon Sinclair had been shot while his mother was being interviewed.

Sam combed her fingers through her hair and wondered where Preston Sinclair had gone. Could there be a third Sinclair victim waiting to be discovered dead or injured? Sam's gut told her it was all related to Diandra and the rift that had festered for years in their family. But how? Where was the connection? As far as Sam could tell, Diandra hadn't seen her brother-in-law in more than thirteen years. How would she know his schedule or his whereabouts?

If she had wanted him dead, wouldn't she have killed him years ago when she discovered his closet homosexuality after her sons had spent time alone with him? Her sons had confirmed her rage at learning that their uncle was gay.

Sam sighed, her head aching from the strain and the caffeine withdrawal. She dug her cell phone out of her pocket and called Jeannie McBride.

"Hi, Lieutenant. What's up?"

"Are you at HQ?"

"Yes, ma'am."

"Do me a favor and re-run the financials of Preston and Diandra Sinclair, only this time go back more than a year."

"Sure thing."

"While you're at it, get me both their sons, too. Devon and Austin Sinclair."

"Will do. Am I looking for anything in particular?"

"A large payment or transfer. Anything that stands out." Sam knew Diandra hadn't pulled the trigger on her son but couldn't rule out her hiring someone else to do it. But why would she have done that?

"I'll get right on it," Jeannie said.

Sam checked her watch and winced when she realized Jeannie's shift was long over. "Thanks. I hope I'm not screwing with your plans."

"No worries. My boyfriend's working late tonight, too."

Sam knew she should ask, that she should show some interest. "What, ah, what does he do?"

"Finance stuff. Investments, portfolio management. Nothing I really understand and nothing quite as exciting as dating a United States senator."

"That's funny, Jeannie. Really. Very funny."

Jeannie laughed. "Just speaking the truth, Lieutenant."

"Call me if you get any hits on the financials."

"Will do."

Sam hung up and continued to stare at the ceiling. Her thoughts wandered to what Harry had said about the endometriosis treatment. Half of her wished she'd never been told it was even possible. She knew herself well enough to accept that she would obsess about it endlessly until she decided whether or not to pursue it.

"There you are."

Startled out of her thoughts, Sam looked up to find Nick leaning against the door frame. As her eyes met his, she was overcome by a sense of rightness and absolute truth. He would make one hell of a father.

TWENTY-NINE

NICK CAME INTO the room and stretched out next to her. "Everything okay?"

It is now, she thought. *The second I saw you, I felt better. How was that possible?* She worked up a smile for him and laced her fingers through his. "Yeah."

He brought their joined hands to his lips. "Will you do something for me?"

Anything. Anything at all. "Sure."

"I get that you're planning to torture me about how it went with Harry, but will you tell me if there's anything seriously wrong—"

Seeing the worry etched into his face she leaned over to kiss the words off his lips. "There's nothing to worry about."

"You swear?"

"What is this? Fifth grade?"

He released a long deep breath that sounded full of relief. "All day today, I just kept thinking, what if it's something really bad and all this time she's been ignoring it?"

"Your caring concern is ruining my plans to stab you with a rusty steak knife for subjecting me to the most thorough poking and prodding of my life—and as someone who's been through infertility testing, that's saying something."

He winced. "A rusty steak knife, huh?"

"That was just one of my many plans for you."

Shifting so he was on top of her, he pinned her hands

to the pillows and kissed her. "What were some of your other plans?" he asked with a lascivious smile.

All at once, she remembered Angela's prediction. Here she was, horizontal under Nick exactly twenty minutes after she left Ang's house. Sam laughed at the accuracy of her sister's statement.

His eyebrows knitted with confusion. "What's so funny?"

She got him to release her hands and looped her arms around his neck. "We are."

Between kisses, he said, "How so?"

"One minute I'm stabbing you with a rusty steak knife and the next you've got me right where you want me."

"Mmm," he said against her lips, delving deeper in sweeping thrusts of his tongue that drove her crazy.

Sam curled her legs around his and pushed hard against his erection, drawing a deep groan from him. She drank him in, the scent of soap and cologne that was all Nick, the corded muscles pressing against her, the heavy weight of his arousal.

He tore his lips free and focused on her neck. "Are you going to tell me why you're over here contemplating the ceiling when you could be home with me eating the chicken I made you?"

Sam closed her eyes and gave herself over to the sensation of his lips on her neck. His softly spoken words sent a shiver of desire all the way through her. "I just needed some time to think."

"I was waiting for you. I looked out and saw your car on the street."

He was hurt that she hadn't gone to him first. She could hear it in his voice. "Make love to me, Nick."

Surprised, he raised his head to meet her eyes. "Let's go home," he said, starting to get up.

She stopped him. "No. Here. Right now."

Wincing, he said, "You know I hate having sex in your father's house."

"At least he's not here this time."

"I still say he's got this room wired. He'll know."

Unbuttoning his shirt, she fastened her teeth on his nipple.

He gasped. "Sam! The door's wide-open."

"So? No one's here." She slipped her hand inside his pants and wrapped her fingers around him.

"God," he whispered, shuddering in surrender to her stroking hand.

"I want you. Hurry."

In their haste, they pushed clothes aside rather than removing them.

"Now," Sam said, her eyes closed as she guided him to where she needed him more than the next breath.

"Look at me."

She glanced up to find the hazel eyes she loved so much hot with desire and love. Tightening her hold on him she urged him on and released a long, satisfied sigh when he finally filled her. Without breaking the intense eye contact, she wrapped her legs around his hips to keep him still. Watching him, she reveled in the battle he fought with his control. A bead of sweat formed on his forehead, a muscle in his cheek twitched with tension.

"*Sam.* Come on."

When she released him, he seemed to go a little crazy, driving them both to a fast, explosive finish that left her feeling both drained and energized.

"Jesus," he muttered into her neck several minutes of heavy breathing later. "Are you trying to kill me?"

Aftershocks rippled through her as she tried to catch her breath, the weight of him on top of her filling her more than the physical act ever could with a sense of safety and security. "I was planning to kill you, but now I'm thinking I'll keep you around."

Rolling off her, he laughed. "Gee, thanks."

Sam reached for the blanket at the foot of the bed and covered them. Nuzzling his soft chest hair, she said, "I'm supposed to be working tonight."

"Well, don't blame me for getting sidetracked. I just came over to tell you dinner's ready, and then suddenly your hand was in my pants. What was I supposed to do?"

"Exactly what you did."

"What's wrong, Sam?"

"Nothing."

"Something."

He knew. He always knew. "The case. It's got me stumped. I can't seem to find my usual mojo on this one. Too many distractions."

"After what happened with Reese, I can see why you'd feel off."

"It's not that. I'm okay with that."

"How can you be okay with being kidnapped, held hostage at gunpoint, threatened? Not to mention watching him kill himself right in front of you."

She shrugged. "I'm a cop. Shit happens. You roll with it or you can't get up the next day and do the job."

"Still, it has to have *some* impact."

"It's not what's screwing me up on Sinclair. None of the pieces fit. I keep trying to make them fit, but they don't. Now Julian's brother Preston has gone missing, too."

"That's weird."

"Tell me about it! First Julian is shot and it looks like it's connected to the Supreme Court nomination, but then when his nephew and the nephew's roommate are shot, too, where's the connection? No matter how I spin it, I can't see how anyone would have a beef with both of them."

"So you don't think Julian's murder is related to the nomination?"

"Not if the same shooter did his nephew."

"How soon will you know that?"

"We've put a rush on the ballistics report. In the next day or two, I hope."

"Did you hear that the family postponed Julian's service?"

"No, but I figured they would."

"The nephews were planning it. Graham called earlier to let me know that Austin wants to wait until Devon recovers."

"*If* he recovers. It sounded pretty bad when I was at the hospital." She paused, contemplating how this changed her plans for the weekend.

He massaged her shoulder. "Since you're waiting on ballistics and now we don't have to go to Boston, maybe you could take some down time to recharge?"

She smiled up at him. "I thought that's what I was doing."

"I mean *real* down time. An actual night off with a full eight hours of sleep and everything."

"I need to get in some computer time after dinner."

"That can be arranged."

Pressing her lips to the soft skin under his jaw, she said, "How was your day?" She didn't see so much as feel the change in him, the tensing of previously relaxed muscles.

"Fine."

"And?"

"And what?"

"And what else?"

Laughing softly, he hugged her even closer to him. "I should be freaked out by how well you read me."

"Likewise. Spill it."

"Let's talk about it after dinner." He helped her to sit up and located her bra under the blanket. Handing it to her, he watched her put it on.

Her cheeks heated under the intensity of his stare. "Stop looking at me like that."

"Why?"

"Because. It leads to trouble."

One minute she was attempting to hook her bra, the next she was once again spread out beneath him.

"I love your brand of trouble," he said, capturing her mouth in a deep, sensual kiss that started her motor running all over again.

She sighed against his lips. "At this rate, I'll never get anything done tonight."

"You'll get me done."

Sam laughed. "I thought I'd already checked you off my to-do list."

Smiling, he kissed her nose and then her lips. "Consider this an encore."

"So WHAT GIVES?" she asked as they lingered over a second glass of wine after dinner. The sex, the food, the wine, *him*. The combination had mellowed her after the crazy day, even if the tabloid reporters positioned outside his house had rattled her on the way in. This is what had been missing from her life before he'd come into it. Balance. In the past, she would've been too focused on the case to take a moment for herself in the midst of it.

He sat back in his chair, suddenly interested in the play of his fingers over the stem of his wineglass.

"Uh-oh," Sam said, watching him. "This doesn't sound good."

"I haven't said anything yet."

"Exactly." She noticed the tension had returned to his face, and her stomach twisted with fear.

"They want me to run."

"For?"

"The Senate. In the general election in November."

Sam sat perfectly still, processing what he had said. She didn't allow an ounce of emotion to show on her face.

After a long moment of silence, he glanced at her. "Say something, will you?"

"You said a year. You said we can do anything for a year."

"I know what I said. It was the truth at the time."

"And what's the truth now?"

"I don't know yet. I guess that depends on you."

"On *me?* Why on me?"

He reached for her hand, linked their fingers. "Because I promised you a year, and this would obviously be much more. Seven in fact. Much of this year campaigning and then six years in office if I win."

"You'd win," she said in a dull, flat tone. "That's why they want you to run. No one can beat you."

"So they said." He scooted his chair closer to hers and brought their joined hands to his lips, a gesture so totally his that Sam's heart ached with love. "Has it been so bad?" he asked with a cajoling smile. "This last month?"

"It hasn't even really started yet. And the press. They're outside your house and chasing me down the street."

"I know they're a pain, and you hate the intrusion. I do, too. But they'll lose interest in us. Eventually."

She pulled her hand free of his and got up to pace the kitchen. "They won't, Nick. It's only going to get worse."

"I don't have to do it. I can say no to them. There's plenty of other stuff I can do that would simplify things for us."

The statement stopped her in her tracks and served to clarify the debate—at least for her. She turned to him and studied the handsome, earnest face she loved more than anything. "Is that who we're going to be?"

His eyebrows knitted with confusion. "What do you mean?"

"Are we going to be people who do what's easy? Or are we going to be people who take a chance to be more than we thought we'd ever be?"

He stood up and held out his hands to stop her from pacing. "What are you saying?"

She smiled as a sense of peace came over her. "Run, Nick. This is your destiny. It's who you were meant to be."

Perplexed by her sudden change of heart, he tilted his head with inquisition.

"You don't see it, do you?" she asked.

"See what?"

"The way you've changed in the last month. How you carry yourself, the confidence."

He released a choppy laugh. "Yeah, right. I feel like a total fraud. As if I'm playing the part until the real guy gets back."

"No," she said, shaking her head. "You *are* the real guy. You're a United States senator, Nicholas Cappuano. That's who you are now."

"But, Sam, the press…"

"We can handle them. We'll toss them an occasional bone to keep them off our backs."

His hands landed on her shoulders. "Are you sure, babe? We don't have to decide anything tonight."

"I've never been more sure of anything in my life, except that I was meant to spend it with you. Run. Win big. Make me proud. Just don't expect me to make any speeches."

"I wouldn't dream of it." His grin lit up his face. "You never cease to surprise me, Samantha. Just when I think you're going to freak, you go all Zen on me."

Flashing her most dazzling smile, she went up on tiptoes to kiss him. "It's my goal in life to keep you guessing."

"So far, you're succeeding brilliantly."

When he tried to kiss her with more serious intent, she dodged him. "No way, buster. I have to get back to work."

"All right," he said with a dejected sigh. "Be that way. I cooked *and* I get stuck with the dishes. I see how this is going to be."

"Such is the glamorous life of a United States senator. And by the way, no one said we were running a democracy at home, too."

"She giveth and she taketh away."

Laughing, she refilled her wineglass and took it with her. Over her shoulder, she said, "Come visit me when you finish kitchen duty."

"Yeah, yeah."

THIRTY

SAM WANDERED INTO the cozy study that Nick had put together with his unique blend of style and practicality. She marveled at how quickly he had made this big empty house into a warm, inviting home. His outstanding taste and sense of style were just two more reasons to love him. Sam had to admit that it no longer seemed preposterous to imagine living here with him.

"Huh," she said, resting her chin on her fist as she absorbed the astounding revelation. "Wonder when that happened?" Over time. That's when it had happened. He hadn't pushed. Instead, he'd allowed her to come to her own conclusion in her own time. "Crafty of him." She decided to wait until she closed Sinclair to act on the decision she seemed to have made at some point over the past few weeks. "Wonder what he'd say if I just show up with all my crap and say, 'Hi, honey, I'm home.'" The idea of disrupting his finely tuned sense of order had her chortling with laughter.

Scooting the leather chair up to the desk, she checked things out. Of course, Nick being Nick, everything was exactly where it belonged, which all but dared her to mess with it. Feeling a little reckless after the conversation they'd just had, she moved a few items around on his impeccable desk while waiting for the computer to boot up.

Delighted with her handiwork, she tried to focus on the computer and the long list of names she needed to run. But rather than log into the police department system, she opened the internet browser and did a search for endometriosis treatment.

That's where Nick found her fifteen minutes later. "What're you looking at?" he asked, massaging her shoulders from behind. "And *why* do you have to screw around every time you sit at my desk?"

Startled, Sam attempted to minimize the window but clicked the wrong button and made it larger.

Nick leaned in for a closer look. "'Laser surgery offers revolutionary hope to endometriosis sufferers,'" he read from the screen.

She closed the window and attempted to shake him off.

"Hey! I was reading that."

"And now you're not."

"What did it say?"

Sam could hear the excitement in his voice, which is exactly why she hadn't mentioned it earlier. She couldn't bear to get his hopes up only to see them dashed the way hers had been by two miscarriages when she was married to Peter. "Nothing. It's nothing."

"It's not nothing." He spun the office chair around, forcing her to look at him. "Talk. Now."

"There's nothing to say."

He raised an eyebrow to let her know he wasn't buying it.

"It's just this thing Harry mentioned. It probably doesn't even apply to me, so there's no need to get all worked up over something that'll never happen."

His eyes widened with understanding. "He said there's something you can do—something *we* can do—didn't he?"

"See? You're already excited, and I can't deal with that!"

"Maybe if you just told me what he said, rather than expecting me to decode your ramblings, we could have an honest conversation here."

Sam folded her arms in defense against the gamut of emotions storming around inside her. "He mentioned a new treatment for endometriosis. Surgery that's been apparently yielding great results."

"And you're going to try it?"

"I don't know! I just heard about it today."

"Why wouldn't you?"

"Because! You have no idea how awful it was to go through three miscarriages. I thought this door was closed to me, and I've made peace with that. Now there's this tiny little crack, letting it all in again." She looked up at him. "I don't know if I'd survive if it happened again, Nick."

He dropped to his knees in front of her. "Then don't do it. Close the door, put the lock on and we'll go on with our lives as if we never heard about this. When we're ready, we'll adopt or hire a surrogate. Whatever we have to do."

Astounded, she stared at him. "You'd do that? Even if it might be possible for us to have our own?"

"I've told you before and I'll tell you again—*how* we have them doesn't matter one bit to me. That we have them—someday—that's what matters. As long as we're on the same page there, the rest is details to me."

Once again, she said a silent prayer of thanks to whatever higher power had arranged to have their paths cross again, years after they first met and connected on every possible level. He always knew just what to say to her, just what she needed to hear. "It's all I can think about," she confessed. "That I could have what Harry calls a simple surgery and then maybe..."

"Were you going to tell me?"

"I didn't want to get your hopes up only to see them crushed when it doesn't work out. And it *is* crushing. Take my word for it."

"I can't even imagine. But I can't help but remember what you said before."

"What?"

He shook his head. "Never mind. I don't want you to think I'm pressuring you, because I meant it when I said it doesn't matter to me if they're our biological children."

"Tell me anyway."

After another moment of hesitation, he said, "It's just what you said, about what kind of people we're going to be. Are we going to do what's easy or are we going to take some chances?"

Sam released a jagged deep breath. "We're not talking about a job, Nick. This is *much* different."

"Is it? Is it really?"

"So you're only *saying* you'd be okay adopting?"

"No, babe. I mean it. But I'm not thinking about me. I'm thinking about you, and I know this is something you want so badly, even if you'd never admit it. You say you've made peace with it, but you haven't. Not really. How could you?"

She didn't want to cry, but the tears seemed to have a mind of their own. They came in a great torrent that reminded her of the aftermath of her third miscarriage. This subject could be counted on to make her cry every time it came up.

Nick wrapped his arms around her and held her until she got it all out. "It's okay, Sam," he whispered, stroking her hair. "I'm here now, and no matter what happens, we'll deal with it together. Whatever you want to do is what we'll do."

"I don't *know* what I want to do," she said, sobs hiccupping through her. "I can't even talk about this without bawling my head off. Can you imagine what a mess I'd be if I had the surgery and managed to get pregnant? I'd spend the whole time panic-stricken, waiting to lose it."

"I can't picture that. The Samantha I know and love is ballsy and fearless and so courageous it often takes my breath away."

Touched by his faith in her, she attempted a smile. "You haven't seen her pregnant."

"I'd *love* to see her pregnant, but only if it's what *she* wants." He leaned in to kiss her and wipe away the remaining tears. "I love you, no matter what, and I'll support whatever you decide to do."

"Thanks," she said, "for getting me, and for understanding how this would hit me without needing me to draw you a map."

"Don't put pressure on yourself to decide anything right away. We've got plenty of time."

"My eggs aren't getting any younger."

"Puhleeze, you're a spring chicken." He kissed her again. "Are you going to tell me what else Harry had to say?"

"Do I have to?"

"Uh-huh."

"He said to say hi to you," she said with a big smile.

"Fabulous." He poked her ribs. "What else?"

She made a face at him. "He's making me give up soda."

Nick's mouth fell open. "You're kidding."

"I wish I was. Be prepared to see me at my very worst, starting tomorrow morning when I don't get my daily kick start."

"Thanks for the warning."

"You think it's funny now."

"So that was it? Just give up the soda and see what happens?"

"For now. He was very thorough, your pal Harry. I hope you're not planning on having him over or anything. I doubt I could make eye contact."

Nick hooted with laughter. "That sounds like a dare."

"*Don't* you dare!"

"Do you feel better, babe? About the other thing?"

She exhaled a long deep breath infected with the hitches that follow a good cry. "Yeah." Rolling her shoulders, she sat back in the chair. "But I feel all revved up. You know what I'd really like to do?"

He raised a swarthy eyebrow. "Again?"

Laughing, she gave him a little shove. "Get your mind out of the gutter. I want to go back to Julian's hotel room and take another look. Sometimes when I'm stuck it helps to start all over."

"How about I go with you?"

"You don't want to do that."

He reached out to help her up. "There's nothing I'd rather do, and besides, maybe I'll be the one who figures this whole thing out."

She rolled her eyes at him. "Whatever. Stick with me, rookie. I'll show you the ropes."

Nuzzling her neck, he said, "Oh, ropes. That sounds promising."

SAM PUNCHED IN the police code to unlock the hotel room door. Inside, she flipped on the lights and took a long look around at the large, elegant room where everything was neat and orderly.

"Looks like he was never here," Nick commented, "but I can smell his cologne."

Sam turned to him. "If it's too hard for you to be here—"

He rested an index finger on her lips. "I'm okay."

Even though crime scene detectives had already done it once before, she went through the room again with methodic precision. She checked suit coat pockets, zippered linings in the suitcases and briefcase, and poked through the shaving kit in the bathroom but found nothing out of the ordinary.

"Are all your friends as anal-retentively neat as you and Julian?" she asked.

Nick sat at the desk and flipped through Julian's date book. "Not all of them." He turned to the page from the day of the murder. "Lunch with Trip. That would be Ackerman, chairman of the Senate Judiciary Committee."

"We couldn't figure out who that was." Sam marveled at how quickly he had given her a lead to follow.

"Prep school nickname. They probably went over how the nomination hearings would go, and he answered any questions Julian had. Will you talk to Ackerman?"

"First thing in the morning." She leaned in to kiss his cheek. "Thank you."

"I told you I'd figure this out for you."

She laughed. "Don't get all full of yourself quite yet."

"What do you suppose this refers to?" He pointed to an entry in the book that said, "P/a.d."

"No idea. I wondered if the *P* referred to his brother. Preston said he'd been in touch with Julian and hoped to see him while Julian was in town."

"What could *a.d.* stand for?" Nick asked.

"After Diandra goes to bed?" Sam ventured. "Austin and Devon?"

"After dinner?"

"Could be. I just wish we had tape of what happened after Graham and Laine dropped him off."

"Is it possible he managed to get back to his room but didn't leave again on foot?" Nick asked.

"What do you mean?"

"He could've been taken out in a laundry cart, for instance. I saw that in a movie once."

"So you're saying someone came in here, tied him up, tossed him in a laundry cart and wheeled him out without anyone seeing a thing?"

"Could've happened."

"We can't even prove that he came into the hotel after they dropped him off. In this fictional scenario of yours, did Julian go willingly? Did he just hop into the laundry cart and say, 'Tie me up and take me for a ride'?"

"Of course not."

"So then where's the struggle?" She gestured to the immaculate room. "Wouldn't a lamp be toppled or the bed covers rumpled or *something* disturbed?"

"Not if the attacker had a gun pointed at Julian. He'd do whatever he was told to stay alive."

Sam hated to concede the point. "That's possible. A gun would explain the lack of struggle."

Nick's grin lit up his face. "See, I'm a natural."

"You're still a rookie, though."

"So then teach me, master."

Hands on her hips, Sam surveyed the room, trying to imagine how it had gone down. "I'd love to have the background check the administration must've done on Julian."

Nick reached for his cell phone.

"What're you doing?"

"Getting it for you."

She watched in silent amazement as he called the

White House deputy chief of staff at home and requested a copy of the vetting document on Julian Sinclair.

"He's emailing it to you," Nick said when he hung up. He looked up to find her staring at him. "What? We play racquetball together. He's a friend."

"Who *isn't* your friend?"

"Are you complaining?"

"Nope. You might be pretty useful to have around, rookie."

"Is that your ass-backward way of saying thank you?"

"I'm sure I'll think of *some* way to thank you—but not until we're off duty."

His eyes went hot with lust.

"Don't even think about it." As Sam took a step back from him her cell phone rang.

"Hey, Lieutenant," Jeannie McBride said. "I went through two years' worth of financials on all the principal players. The only interesting thing I found was a ten thousand-dollar wire transfer from Diandra Sinclair's personal account to an account in the Cayman Islands."

"Owned by whom?"

"I'm still trying to figure that out. The bank is closed right now, but I've left messages. I also tagged the Cayman police to make them aware of our investigation."

"Good work, Jeannie. Go on home. We can pick this up in the morning."

"It's something anyway."

"Absolutely. I appreciate you staying late. Any sign of Preston Sinclair?"

"Not that I've heard."

"Thanks again, Jeannie."

"Have a good night, L.T."

Sam ended the call and filled Nick in on what she'd learned.

"What do you suppose it means?"

"She could've paid someone to off her brother-in-law."

"If she did, why wait until he's here for nomination hearings? Everyone knew he was on Nelson's short list for the court. His nomination was hardly a surprise."

"Who knows? Maybe she had someone on retainer in case it ever got this far. At any rate, I'd like to speak to her again. What do you say we hit GW on the way home? I want to check on Devon, too."

"It's not exactly on the way."

"No grumbling, rookie."

"I'm just saying…"

Patting his cheek, she said, "I can always drop you off at home if it's getting too late for you."

"And miss all this excitement? No way. Besides, you promised me a reward for getting you that background check. I intend to collect."

Closing and locking the hotel room door, she shot him a look full of innocence. "I was planning to make you an ice cream sundae. My nieces and nephews love my sundaes. Is that what you had in mind?"

"Not exactly," he muttered. "Although you can feel free to include hot fudge and whipped cream in my reward."

Somehow he always managed to get the last word.

THIRTY-ONE

HEADLIGHTS FILLED THE rearview mirror with a bright glare.

Sam winced at the light and slowed down. "What the hell?" she said to the car behind them. "Get off my ass."

Instead of backing off, though, the other car tagged her back fender.

"What the fuck?" she cried.

Nick spun around for a better look and nearly lost the top of his head to the bullet that shattered the back window and lodged in the windshield.

She pushed his head down and hit the gas.

Nick pushed back. "Goddamn it, Sam! Let go of me!"

"Keep your head down and hold on!" She released him, called for backup and slammed on the brakes, spinning the car around to face the shooter. She drew her weapon, turned on her emergency lights and opened the car door.

"Where are you going?" Nick cried, grabbing her coat. "Get back in the car!"

She tugged herself free and got out.

The driver of the other car revved the engine and came at them, smashing into her car and narrowly missing Sam, who dove for cover in her car. Slamming the car into Reverse, tires smoked as the attacking car backed up and bounced off a parked car before it took off in the other direction.

Sam jammed her car into Reverse and turned around

to give chase. "Damn it, I couldn't see who it was with the glare of the headlights."

"Jesus Christ," Nick muttered, clinging to the handle above the window as Sam took a corner on two wheels.

"Get down!" she cried.

"What about you?"

"I'm driving."

Another shot blew the driver's side-view mirror off her car.

"Son of a bitch," she muttered.

"Who the hell would be shooting at you?" Nick asked, his heart pounding, adrenaline and fear coursing through him. Thanks to the shattered windows, the temperature inside the car plummeted as the speedometer climbed to eighty-five. Lights flashing, they flew through deserted streets, dodging parked cars and the occasional pedestrian.

"Get the fuck out of the way!" Sam screamed at one of them. "Could be anyone. I've made lots of 'friends' during my twelve years on the force." Her eyes darted to the rearview mirror. "Where the hell is my backup?" Reaching for her radio, she made a second more urgent call for help.

Zipping through red lights on Fourteenth Street, Nick braced for side impact. Watching her, he saw concentration, determination and a complete lack of fear, which made him feel like a total wimp since he was scared shitless. "You're one ballsy chick, Holland."

"Just doing my job, Senator. Oh, fuck!" She grabbed his coat. "Get down, Nick!"

The shooter in the other car had turned around to aim the gun at them. They dropped down in their seats, and Sam eased off the accelerator—slightly. The shot took out their left front tire, sending them into a spin that Sam tried valiantly to control. She let out a scream when the car suddenly launched into a series of bone-jarring flips, coming to rest upside down.

Since the front end didn't hit anything, the air bags didn't deploy, and at some point during the spin, Nick took hard hits to his forehead and shoulder. Shaking off the stars that danced in his eyes, he hung upside down, held in place by a seat belt. Once he could see straight again, he looked over at Sam. Blood dripped from an open wound on her forehead, and she was out cold.

"Sam!" He managed to release his seat belt and fell to the ceiling of the car. Catching a whiff of gas, his heart kicked into overdrive. "Sam! We've got to get out of here!"

The glow of a flashlight appeared outside the scrunched passenger window. Nick saw a badge on the chest of the officer who leaned into the car. "Are you folks all right in there?"

"I am, but Lieutenant Holland is hurt, and I smell gas."

"I do, too. Try to stay calm. The fire department's extrication unit is on its way."

Based on the amount of blood coming from the cut on her head, Nick decided that releasing her from the seat belt was more important than keeping her still. He worked his way under her so he could catch her when she fell. Even though his shoulder throbbed and he trembled from shock as well as the frigid temperature, he broke into a sweat from the effort it took to free her from the belt.

Her dead weight landing on him forced his side into the shift handle. Nick cried out in pain and wondered if he had broken a rib.

Through the smashed window on the passenger side, the officer peered into the one-foot space.

"Can we get her out?" Nick asked.

"It's not big enough."

"Not for me," he said, gagging on the gas fumes that filled the air. "But she might fit." Grimacing at the pain coming from his shoulder and ribs, he shifted her closer to the window while using the sleeve of his new overcoat to wipe the blood off her ghostly pale face. "Babe," he whispered, kissing her cold lips. "Wake up."

"Is she breathing?"

Nick put his face down close to hers and went weak with relief when he felt a whisper of air hit his cheek. "Yeah." In the distance, he could hear sirens. "I want to get her out of here."

"The opening is too small. Hang tight, Senator. Rescue is almost here."

His own head throbbing, he rested it on Sam's chest, comforted by her faint but audible heartbeat. "What's your name?"

"Montgomery. Officer Montgomery."

"Did they get the guys that shot at us?"

"I haven't heard yet, but I can check."

"Yeah." Nick's chest ached from the effort it took to breathe. "Do that." His eyes burned closed, but he fought the blackness, knowing if he had a concussion he should stay awake. "Samantha. Wake up, honey. Please wake up." He wiped more blood from her forehead. "Montgomery, do you have something I could use on her wound?"

The patrolman handed him a clean handkerchief.

"Thanks." He pressed the cloth to Sam's forehead while talking softly to her. The gas smell seemed to be getting stronger, and Nick was convinced the car was going to explode any second. "You should back up. Get away from the car. Just in case."

"I'm not going anywhere," Montgomery said.

"Lieutenant!"

"Who's that?" Nick asked.

"Detective Gonzales. Are you all right, Senator?"

"I am, but Sam's not."

"Fire's here," Gonzo said. "They'll get you out."

"Someone shot at us," Nick said. "That's how this happened."

"We got 'em. They crashed on the bridge."

"Good," he said, relieved. "That's good. Why were they shooting at us?"

"We think it might've been a gang initiation thing. Extra credit for shooting the famous lady cop. Triple extra credit for getting the senator, too. They're still sorting it out."

"Fabulous," Nick muttered.

The fire department sprayed flame retardant foam on the car. Nick closed his eyes and mouth and covered Sam's face with the handkerchief. In deference to the frigid cold, the EMTs passed a blanket in to Nick. He spread it out over Sam and snuggled up to her to share his body heat.

"Babe," he said, dropping kisses on her face. "Wake up. I need you." Sparks from the Jaws of Life rained down on them. Nick drew the blanket up to protect her face.

Twenty minutes later, the firefighters peeled back the side of the car. Hands landed on Nick's shoulders.

"Take her first," he said.

"We need to get you out so we can reach her, Senator."

Nick kissed her cold lips. "The paramedics are going to take me now, but I'll wait for you outside."

He had never felt more helpless than he did leaving her unconscious in the car. Once he was on a gurney, paramedics swarmed around him, assessing his injuries. He couldn't see what was happening with Sam. "I'm fine," he said, trying to sit up. His head swam, his side felt like it had been stabbed with a knife, and his shoulder seemed disconnected from the rest of him.

"Whoa, Senator." One of the paramedics held him down. "You have to stay still."

"I need to see her!"

"We're taking good care of her. Don't worry."

Don't worry. Sure. "Gonzo!"

"Right here, Senator."

"What's going on with Sam?"

"The paramedics are working on her."

"Did they get her out?"

"Not yet. Looks like they're stabilizing her before they move her."

"God," Nick whispered. "Don't let her die. Please don't let her die. If she does, I will, too."

Gonzo placed a hand on Nick's uninjured shoulder. "Hang in there, man. She's tough. She's going to be fine."

Nick wanted to believe him, but the hitch he heard in Gonzo's voice told him he wasn't the only one who was frightened for her.

THEY WERE TRANSPORTED in separate ambulances. Halfway to the hospital, Nick's lung collapsed. He'd never, in all his life, experienced pain quite like that. As he gasped for air, the paramedics moved quickly to insert a chest tube to re-inflate his lung. The minute he could breathe again, he asked what was happening with Sam.

"She's stable, Senator."

"Is she awake?"

"Not yet."

Nick realized his mouth had dried up, and his head buzzed. "What'd you give me?" His tongue suddenly felt too big for his mouth.

"Something for the pain."

"Don't give me any more. I need to stay alert."

"It's gonna be bad."

"No meds." Nick tried to move his left arm and gritted his teeth against the agony. "Will you call and check on her? Please?"

The older of the two paramedics nodded to his partner, who reached for his radio.

"Nothing new," the younger paramedic reported a few minutes later.

They pulled up to GW Trauma, where a swarm of reporters had gathered outside the E.R. Nick heard the paramedics radioing to the police, asking for help with the crowd. Even from inside the ambulance Nick could hear Gonzo screaming at the reporters to get the hell out of the way. For the first time in more than an hour, Nick smiled.

"We're going to put this over your face to preserve your privacy," one of the paramedics said, draping a clean white towel over Nick's head.

"Make sure they do the same for Sam," he said. "She'd hate to be photographed when she's out cold."

"Of course, Senator."

"You could probably call me Nick at this point." He hated the way everyone fawned over him these days. It was the one thing about his new life that didn't sit well with him. It wasn't like he'd run for office and won. No, his friend had been murdered, and he was just filling in for him. Maybe he'd feel differently if he won in November. Until then, it just seemed weird to be afforded respect he'd done nothing to earn.

The next couple of hours passed in a blur of pain, doctors, nurses, X-ray technicians and needles.

"How're you feeling, Senator?" the doctor in charge asked.

"Like I got hit by a bus." Nick wished he hadn't been so obstinate about the pain meds. He hurt everywhere, and his chest felt like an elephant was sitting on it. Every breath required supreme effort.

"The X-rays show a broken clavicle and a fractured rib, both on the left side in case you didn't already know that."

"How's Sam?"

"We're talking about you."

"I don't care about me. Tell me what's going on with her."

"The plastic surgeon put forty stitches in her hairline. Remarkably, she doesn't seem to have any other injuries besides a severe concussion."

"Is she awake?"

"No."

"Is that normal? Shouldn't she be awake by now?"

"Head injuries are tough. It can take an hour or a day, but she should be fine."

Should be wasn't good enough for him. "I need to see her."

"I'll arrange that after orthopedics deals with your shoulder and wraps your ribs. I don't want you to move around too much until then. The fractured rib is what caused your lung to collapse."

Nick winced at the reminder of that painful ordeal. "You're sure she's okay?"

"Right now she's stable. That's all I can tell you."

Nick studied the doctor's face, trying to see what he wasn't saying. "I need to call her dad."

"I believe Detective Gonzales took care of that. There's quite a crowd forming in the waiting room."

"I'm sure the entire MPD is here."

"Some of them are asking for you, too. People are here from your office, and we received a frantic phone call from your father. He said to tell you he's on his way."

"Oh. Okay." Nick was surprised and touched by his father's concern. "Is Captain Malone out there?"

"I can check, but you have to rest and take it easy."

"I need to see him. It's important."

"I'll send him in."

Malone came into the room a few minutes later. "How're you doing, Senator?"

"If one more person calls me that tonight, I'm going to lose it. My name is Nick."

Malone's solemn expression shifted into a small smile. "Are you okay, *Nick?*"

"I will be. Sam, on the other hand, I'm worried about."

"She's in good hands," Malone said, but Nick could see the concern etched into the older man's face.

"When she wakes up, she'll be freaking out about the Sinclair case. We were on our way here when this happened." He filled Malone in on Sam's theory about Diandra possibly paying someone off to take out Julian and mentioned the wire transfer Detective McBride uncovered.

"How does the son's shooting fit into that?"

"She wasn't sure yet. She was waiting for ballistics to see if the same gun was used in both shootings. She felt like she was getting close to some answers. We also figured out that Julian had lunch with Senator Ackerman, chairman of the Senate Judiciary Committee, earlier in the day he was killed. Sam was going to talk to him in the morning."

"Don't worry. I'll put Gonzales on that. He's been a

mess since he saw you two in the wreck. This'll give him something to do with his considerable energy."

"There was an officer there. Montgomery. He was a big help to us. If there's anything you can do for him…"

"I'll make sure he's recognized."

"Good," Nick said, his energy flagging. He closed his eyes for a brief moment. When he opened them, Malone was gone and Skip Holland had taken his place. "Hey," Nick said. His voice sounded gravelly, so he cleared his throat.

"How're you doing?"

"Okay." He shifted in the bed, trying to find a more comfortable position. Pain radiated from his head, ribs and shoulders, briefly taking his breath away.

"You don't look okay."

Gritting his teeth, he sucked in a deep breath. "How's Sam?"

"The same. Celia, Angela and Tracy are with her. I wanted to check on you."

"Thanks, but I'm fine. I'm sure you want to get back to her."

"I hear your dad is on his way."

"So they say."

"Then I'll stay until he gets here."

THIRTY-TWO

NICK AWOKE A few hours later and insisted on being taken to Sam's room. They'd given him a pair of scrubs to wear since his clothes had been cut off in the E.R. Because he was more comfortable standing than lying down, he hovered next to Sam's bed, staring at her pale face, willing her to wake up. Her sisters had encouraged their father to go home when he showed signs of tiring. Nick's own father spent a couple of hours with him until Nick sent him home, too.

"You really ought to get off your feet, Nick," Sam's sister Tracy said at two in the morning.

"I'm fine." In truth, he hurt from the top of his head to the end of his toes and everywhere in between. But until Sam woke up, he couldn't think about anything but her.

The door opened, and Freddie Cruz stuck his head in.

"Come in," Nick said.

"How is she?"

"The same."

Freddie approached the bed and rested his hand over Sam's. "Why doesn't she wake up?"

"I don't know. They keep saying she will."

"When?" Freddie glanced at him. "That was a stupid question. Sorry. How are you?"

"I've been better."

"Why aren't you in a hospital bed?"

"Because I need to be with her."

Sam's sister Tracy squeezed Nick's uninjured arm.

"Ang and I are going to find some coffee. Can I get you something?"

He shook his head.

"Are you sure?"

"Yeah, thanks." Shifting his injured arm in the sling the orthopedic doctor insisted on, he gasped at the shaft of pain.

"Nick, why don't you sit for a while?" Angela said.

He bit back the urge to snap at them. "I'm fine," he said through gritted teeth.

"We'll be right back," Tracy said, shepherding her sister from the room.

"Take your time," Nick whispered after the door closed behind them.

"Getting on your nerves, are they?" Freddie said.

"They can't take care of her, so they're determined to take care of me."

"You look beat up, man."

"Tell me something I don't know."

"Um, the media has taken over the hospital lobby?" Freddie said with a sheepish grin.

"Ugh. Bloodthirsty vultures."

"It's a big story—the lady cop and the dashing senator in a car crash."

Not wanting to think about the morning's headlines, Nick linked his fingers with Sam's and brought her hand to his lips. "I wish she would just wake up!" When his outburst failed to stir her, Nick tightened his grip on her hand. "How's your shoulder?" he asked Freddie.

"Better. I'm finally free of the sling."

"Now it's my turn." Brushing the hair back from Sam's face and trying desperately to get his mind off his worries, Nick said, "So I hear you have a girlfriend."

Taken aback, Freddie sputtered. "Ah, um, well, I guess."

Nick laughed softly. "Well, do you or don't you?"

"I have no idea."

The younger man's exquisite discomfort provided Nick with some badly needed entertainment. "What would she say?"

"Probably that I'm a jerk."

"Why's that?"

"Because I haven't seen her or talked to her since the last time we, you know…"

"Ah," Nick said, enjoying this more with every passing moment. "And why's that?"

"This isn't really the time to have this conversation."

"Give me something to think about other than why she won't wake up."

Freddie looked down at Sam for so long that Nick wondered if he was going to say anything.

"It's just, you know, things got kind of intense sort of fast."

"You're in love with her."

"No! I'm not. I don't mean intense like that."

"Then how?"

After another long pause, Freddie muttered, "This is so embarrassing."

"Just say it."

"I've discovered I like sex. I mean I *really* like sex."

Despite the pain it caused him, Nick laughed so hard he wondered if he'd broken a second rib. "And that makes you different from every other guy how exactly?"

"You don't understand," Freddie said, taking a sudden and fervent interest in Sam's blanket.

"What don't I understand?"

"This thing, with Elin, it's, um, kind of out of character for me. It's like I've lost my mind and now my dick's doing all the thinking for me."

"You sound like a teenager who just got laid for the first time," Nick said.

"Well…"

Nick stared at him, incredulous. "You're not saying—"

"Look, I took a vow, okay? It was important to me, but then I met Elin and I've become someone I don't even recognize. All I can think about—morning, noon and night—is sex."

"You're making up for lost time," Nick said, hiding his surprise at Freddie's confession. "That's all it is."

"So there's not something wrong with me for wanting it *all* the time?"

"No," Nick said, laughing. "Welcome to the club. What does she think of your, um, urges?"

"She's always willing to accommodate them," Freddie said, flushing with discomfort.

"Lucky you. You managed to hook up with the woman we all dream about first time out of the gate."

"You'd better watch what you're saying, Senator," Sam mumbled.

Nick gasped. "Sam. Babe, open your eyes."

"Only if you two are done talking about Cruz's raging hormones."

"Oh, *shit*," Freddie whispered, his eyes wide with horror. "How much did you hear?"

The left side of her face lifted into a small smile but her eyes remained closed. "Enough to torment you for the rest of your natural life."

Weak with relief, Nick bent down to kiss her. "Oh, Samantha, I'm so glad to hear your voice."

"That'd better be Nick kissing me."

"Don't worry. It's me. How do you feel?"

"Like my head is going to explode." She finally opened her eyes and looked up at him.

Nick had never been so happy to see her light blue eyes, even if they were heavy with pain.

"I, ah, I'd better go," Freddie said, backing out of the room. "I'll let you get some rest, Lieutenant."

"Call Skip's house," Nick said. "Let them know she's awake."

"Will do," Freddie said.

The moment the door closed, Sam laughed and then grimaced at the pain even that small movement caused her. "Clearly, he lost his mind along with his virginity."

"Try to stay still." Nick lowered himself gingerly to the edge of her bed.

"You're hurt," she whispered. "What happened?"

"You don't remember?"

"We were in the car." She closed her eyes and took a deep breath. "Someone shot at us. I can't remember anything after that. Wait! We were going to see Diandra."

"Don't worry. Gonzo and Jeannie are on it."

"Oh, good. So what happened? Did we crash?"

"We chased them, but they shot out one of our tires and the car went airborne and flipped a couple of times. We landed upside down." Reliving it, his throat closed when he thought about what could've happened, what had *almost* happened. Overcome, he rested his hand on her chest, taking comfort in the steady beat of her heart. "You were bleeding like crazy, and you wouldn't wake up."

She reached up to caress his hair.

"Scared the shit out of me."

"What did you hurt?"

"Broke my collarbone and a rib. No biggie."

"Nick," she said on a long sigh. "I'm so sorry. I

never should've chased them when you were in the car with me."

"Why not? Would you rather they'd gotten away after shooting at us?"

"I'd rather you hadn't gotten hurt because of me."

"While your driving clearly leaves something to be desired, they weren't just after you." Smirking, he filled her in on what he'd heard about the gang initiation. "I was worth triple extra points. You were just *regular* points."

"And you're quite proud of that, aren't you?"

"You know it."

"I hope you're not so freaked out that you're going to run away again."

The genuine worry on her face made his heart ache, and he reached for her hand. "I can't. I made a promise. Remember?"

"Yeah. I remember." Her fingers tightened around his. "You can't run. Ever again."

"Your scar is going to be more gnarly than mine," he said, referring to the scar over his eyebrow from the bombing incident involving her ex-husband.

Her lips lifted into a smile. "Lay down with me."

"I don't know if I can."

"I'm so tired, but I can't sleep without you."

After hearing that, nothing could keep him from trying. "I'll give it a whirl." Moving very carefully, he eased himself down on his right side and attempted to find a comfortable position for his left arm. By the time he got settled, he'd broken into a cold sweat.

"You're hurt bad, Nick." She wiped the sweat from his brow.

"I'm much better now that you're awake."

"Your chest sounds all wheezy."

"My lung collapsed in the ambulance. That kinda hurt."

"I'm so sorry."

"It's not your fault, Samantha." He brought their joined hands up to rest over his heart and finally allowed himself to give in to the exhaustion. "I thought I knew exactly how much I love you, but I found out tonight that it's way, way more."

"So does that mean you want me morning, noon and night?" she asked, mocking Freddie.

Nick cracked up. *"Don't make me laugh,"* he moaned, his ribs burning from the movement. "I'm begging you."

"Is that a yes?"

"You bet it is."

FREDDIE LEANED AGAINST the wall outside Sam's room, his heart racing. *I can't believe I just had that conversation with a United States senator. And Sam was listening! I'm never going to hear the end of this.* He wanted to curl up and die of embarrassment. *They must think I'm a freaking idiot!*

"Everything all right, Detective?"

Startled out of his thoughts, Freddie straightened at the sound of Captain Malone's voice. "Yes, sir. Lieutenant Holland is awake."

"That's great news."

"I'm going stir-crazy sitting around. There's got to be something I can do to help in the Sinclair case."

"The doctor cleared you?"

"Not technically, but I feel fine."

"You can come back when the doc says you can."

"I'm not due to see him until next week, but I'm ready to come back."

Malone studied him for a long moment. "All right.

Desk duty only. Check in with Gonzo in the morning. See what he needs on Sinclair."

"Great," Freddie said, releasing a sigh of relief. "Thank you."

"You're sure you're all right? You look kind of funny."

The conversation with Nick came back to him in a rush of humiliation. "I'm fine."

"Go home and get some sleep."

"Yes, sir." Freddie decided to get the heck out of there before the captain changed his mind about letting him go back to work. In the lobby, reporters came swarming at him.

"Detective, what can you tell us about the condition of the lieutenant and the senator?"

"No comment." He pushed through them, amazed to realize they had doubled in number since he'd arrived two hours earlier.

"Are they alive?"

"Yes. That's all I'm saying."

"Have you recovered from being shot by Reese?"

"I'm fine." After only two minutes in the scrum, Freddie couldn't imagine how Sam and Nick stood the constant intrusion. Outside, the cold air was a welcome relief. Keeping his head down, he headed for his car. One of the reporters chased after him. Freddie saw it was Darren Tabor. Knowing Sam couldn't stand him, Freddie kept walking.

"Detective. I just need a minute."

"You're not getting anything out of me."

"Wait, Freddie. Seriously, I need to talk to you."

Tabor's use of his first name and his urgent tone got Freddie's attention. "You have one minute."

"There's a rumor floating around about Lieutenant Holland."

"I don't want to hear—"

"They're saying she had an abortion years ago."

Freddie stared at him. Shaking his head, he started to walk again. "That's ridiculous. Everyone knows how badly she wants kids."

"This was when she was in college. The source is solid."

"So what're you going to do with it?"

"It's not me you need to worry about. It's one of the tabloids."

"Why are you having a sudden burst of conscience? After the way you savaged her during the Johnson case, I expect less from you."

"I deal in news, not gossip." Tabor grabbed his forearm. "Freddie. This is going to blow up big-time in the next day or two. Someone needs to warn them."

The idea of someone intentionally hurting Sam—and Nick—killed him. "Why now? I don't get it."

"A former receptionist from the clinic sold the story to the *Reporter*. Apparently, she made a killing thanks to their popularity."

Freddie felt sick. "How do you even know about it?"

"A buddy of mine is a photographer for the *Reporter*. He told me on the Q.T."

"So why do you care so much about giving them a heads- up?"

"I don't always agree with her, but she's a straight shooter. She doesn't deserve this. No one does."

"Thanks for letting me know. I'll take care of it."

"If, you know, the next time you guys need to use the media to advance your agenda, maybe you'll consider giving me a call?"

Nothing was ever free. "We'll keep that in mind."

Darren turned to walk away.

"Tabor."

"Yeah?"

"Thanks for the heads-up."

"No problem."

Freddie opened the door to his rattletrap Mustang and got in. He sat there for a long time processing what he'd been told. Tension gripped him as he thought about Sam, who'd been so much more than a partner and mentor. She was like a ball-busting older sister who he'd come to love over the past year of working closely with her. And Nick. Lately, he'd begun to feel like a friend, too. Even though he had a lofty job now, there was nothing lofty about him. Tabor was right when he said Sam didn't deserve this. Neither of them did.

Under normal circumstances, he'd go directly to Sam, tell her what he'd heard, and offer his help. But since she was in a hospital bed recovering from a serious head injury, that wasn't an option. What to do? He thought about going to Skip Holland, but due to the nature of the situation, he dismissed that idea.

Nick. He had to tell Nick, but remembering the crowd in the lobby, he didn't want to go back in there.

Freddie dug his cell phone out of his coat pocket and called Gonzo.

"Yeah. Gonzales."

"Gonzo. Wake up."

"I just got home," Gonzo mumbled. "Got to be back in two hours. This'd better be good."

"Is Christina with you?"

"What's it to you?"

"Can I talk to her?"

"What the fuck, Cruz?"

"It's important."

After a long pause, Gonzo said, "Hang on."

Freddie could hear Gonzo waking her up.

"This is Christina."

"I'm sorry to disturb you." He swallowed hard. "This is Detective Cruz. I'm Lieutenant Holland's partner."

"Yes, I know."

"I was wondering if you could give me the senator's cell phone number. It's urgent that I reach him."

"He's in the hospital. You know that. I saw you there earlier."

"I just left him with Sam, but the hospital is overrun with media, and it's very important that I speak to him tonight. In fact, after I talk to him, he's probably going to want to talk to you."

"What's going on, Detective?"

"May I please have the number?"

"Fine," she said, rattling it off.

"Thank you." Freddie ended the call before she could grill him some more. His stomach grinding with nerves, he dialed Nick's number and pressed send. It rang four times before going to voice mail. Since he knew Nick was injured and moving slowly, he called back.

He answered on the third ring. "Hmm, Nick Cappuano."

"Senator. It's Freddie Cruz. Are you awake?"

"No."

"Senator. Wake up. I really need to talk to you."

"There's nothing wrong with you, Freddie. I told you that."

"Senator! Listen to me. Come down to the parking lot outside the Emergency Room, but don't go through the lobby. It's full of media."

"You've got to be kidding me," Nick said. "I can barely move."

Freddie hated to ask him to come outside, but he

couldn't take a chance on Sam overhearing what he had to tell Nick before they could figure out how to handle it. "It's about Sam. You have to come, Nick."

Freddie could tell that Nick was now fully awake. "I'll be right there."

"I'll wait for you in my car."

THIRTY-THREE

FIFTEEN MINUTES LATER, Nick opened the passenger door and grunted from the effort it took to lower himself into the car. Glancing over at Freddie, he said, "This had better be good."

Freddie flipped on the inside lights so they could see each other in the murky predawn. "The *Reporter* is going to run a story that Sam had an abortion years ago."

Nick's pale face drained of what little color it had left. "What? What did you say?"

"It's not true. It can't be true. She could never—"

Nick sat perfectly still. "Tell me what you know. Everything you know."

Freddie relayed Darren Tabor's warning.

"Patient records are private. They couldn't possibly get the record."

"Are you saying it's true?" Freddie asked tentatively.

"I can't talk to you about this. I'm sorry. It's her personal business."

"Which is about to be splashed all over the news."

"Oh, my God. This can't be happening."

"You need to warn her."

"No." Nick shook his head. "She's hurt. I don't want her to know about this." He reached for the door handle. "I'll take care of it."

"What're you going to do?"

"I don't know yet."

"Call me if I can help."

With a quick nod, Nick worked his way out of the car and disappeared into the night.

Freddie sat there for a long time. He didn't envy Nick the task he had before him, but he did envy his love for Sam. What they seemed to have was something most people only dreamed about. Freddie started the car to head home, but home held zero appeal. Even though he knew he had no right, he called Elin.

"Hey," she said, sounding sleepy and sexy.

He yearned for her. "Sorry to wake you."

"S'okay."

"Can I come over?"

"Now?"

"Yeah."

With only the briefest of hesitations, she said, "Okay."

"I'll be there in a few minutes."

When she opened the door to him ten minutes later looking adorable and disheveled, he realized he'd missed her. Not the sex. *Her.*

"I'm sorry. I acted like an idiot."

She looked up at him with those bottomless blue eyes. "I missed you."

He reached for her, and she dissolved into his embrace. With one arm around her, he walked her into the bedroom, dropped his clothes into a pile on the floor, crawled into bed with her in his arms and fell instantly into a peaceful, dreamless sleep.

NICK STARED OUT the window in Sam's room but could see nothing through the rage. That someone could do this to her… He checked on her, confirmed she was still asleep and stepped out of the room. Scrolling through the numbers on his phone, he found his attorney friend Andy, one of the guys he played basketball with. Andy and his wife had recently had a baby, so he hesitated to wake them up. But then he thought of Sam, sobbing at the Lincoln Memorial the night she told him her darkest secret, and made the call.

"I'm sorry to bother you, Andy. It's Nick Cappuano."

"Senator," Andy said, sounding groggy and surprised to hear from him—especially at that hour. "Are you all right? I heard about the accident."

"I'm banged up, but I'll survive. Sam's a little worse off."

"Sounds like it was quite a wreck."

"Yeah, it was. So listen, I've got a problem I could use your help with."

"Sure, Nick, er, Senator. Whatever you need."

"Nick is fine, and it's about Sam." Nick told him about the tabloid. "Tell me there's something we can do. An injunction. Something. If this comes out, it'll kill her."

"Is it true?"

Nick hesitated, hating this more with every passing second. "Yes and no. She had an appointment for the procedure, but miscarried beforehand. It sounds like the source only passed along the first half of the story."

"If it's true, it's harder to claim libel. And since she's a public figure, that further complicates things."

"How can that be? This is her private medical history that someone sold to a tabloid for personal gain. How can that be legal?"

"You can file for an injunction since medical records are private, but I doubt you'd get it in time to stop publication."

Nick released a ragged deep breath. "So because she's with me, because I'm in the Senate now and we've gotten all this attention, she forfeits her basic right to privacy?"

"It's more like it can be taken from her without no-

tice. I can file for an emergency injunction in the morning. The best we can hope for is a sympathetic judge
who will move swiftly. Be advised, though, the injunction will make news, too. It'll all but confirm that the
story is true—and in this case, partially true is enough
to be damaging. She can also sue the asses off the clinic
and the tabloid—and she absolutely should—but again,
that'll only perpetuate the story."

Nick ran a hand through his hair. "I can't believe this
is happening."

"You'll want to get with your staff to figure out how
to respond from a political standpoint."

"There's no way I'm dignifying this with a response."

"Your communications people will no doubt advise
otherwise."

"This has nothing to do with my job."

"It has everything to do with it, Nick. We're talking
about the most divisive issue of our time. The public will
be looking for your position on this."

"I love her, I support her right to choose. I support
every woman's right to choose."

"Then that's what you say."

"I can't protect her, Andy." The helplessness overwhelmed him. "I hate that I can't protect her from this."

"I haven't met her, but from what I've read about her
in the papers, I can't imagine that she'd expect you to
protect her."

"That doesn't mean I don't want to," Nick said. "Could
I offer the tabloid more money than they paid for the
story not to run it?"

"No doubt that would get out, too, adding gas to the
story's fire."

Nick sighed. "I'm really sorry I woke you up."

"I'm glad you called. I'm heading to the office now.

I'll get that injunction filed first thing and let you know when it's done."

"I really appreciate your help. Send me the bill for your time."

"Don't worry about it. I'll be in touch."

SAM FLOATED SOMEWHERE between dreams and nightmares. Victims and perps and hideous crimes cycled through her mind. Scenes from the Sinclair investigation flashed one by one, parts and pieces that refused to add up to a whole. Julian's body in Lincoln Park, his estranged brother and sister-in-law, the beloved nephews, one of them shot, his roommate killed. Preston Sinclair missing. Where had he gone? Why had he gone? What was she overlooking?

She could feel the answer circulating close to the surface. If only she could find the final pieces to the puzzle. If only she could find Preston.

The pulsing pain coming from the cut on her head interrupted the flow, demanding her full attention. Her eyes fluttered open. "Preston."

Nick turned from his post at the window. "What's that, babe?" In obvious pain, he moved slowly to the bedside and lowered himself down.

"It's Preston."

"What is? I don't follow."

"Preston shot Julian and Devon."

Nick curled a lock of her long hair around his finger. "What? Why?"

"To protect Diandra. I can't believe I didn't figure it out sooner."

"But why would he shoot his own brother and son?"

"Think about it. For thirty years, he lives with this domineering woman who has unpopular beliefs that caused him to be estranged from his brother. He had to make a choice—her or Julian. She was his choice. Now here she was, weeks away from her book being published, and Julian was going to steal the limelight from her. Everything about his life was going to come out, and Diandra would be embarrassed. She might even lose her TV gig. What if the publisher got squeamish about taking on a new Supreme Court justice and cancelled her book? She wouldn't have wanted to risk it."

"So he lured his own brother out of a hotel, hog-tied him and shot him in Lincoln Park?"

"Julian never went into the hotel." The whole thing clicked into focus with such amazing clarity it was all she could do to keep up. "That's why we couldn't find him leaving on the tape. Graham and Laine said they dropped him off at the hotel, but neither of them could confirm they saw him go in the door. No one in the hotel could recall actually seeing him after he returned from dinner."

"So he snuck off and met Preston somewhere?"

"They'd been in touch. Preston said he hoped to see his brother while he was in town."

"Do you think he intended to kill Julian?"

"Yeah, I do." Sam stared at a spot on the far wall, imagining the crime going down.

"Did Diandra know?"

"She planned the whole thing. She would've been freaking out about the timing, Julian coming to town for contentious hearings just as her book was released. She worried that she'd lose her TV show. How could she continue to spew hate and venom about gays when her Supreme Court justice brother-in-law was one of them? She worked on Preston until he saw no other option but to get rid of his brother. No one would suspect him. They hadn't spoken in years."

"What about the money in the Caymans?"

"She did that as a backup. In case Preston couldn't do it. She probably had someone else lined up."

"How do you explain their son being shot?"

"Austin might've told their father what Devon confessed to us when we interviewed him."

"I don't get why Austin would tell their father that."

"Who knows? Maybe he was rattled from being interviewed by cops. Maybe Preston somehow pressured him into recounting everything they told the cops. Hard to say. However it happened, Preston found out Devon was gay, and all he could see was how it would affect Diandra."

"So she didn't know Preston intended to shoot Devon?"

"She had no idea." Sam recalled Diandra's reaction to the news about her son. "But she knew right away that Preston had done that, too. What she doesn't know is why."

"He's gone mad, and she drove him to it."

"Yes, he pulled the trigger. Both times. He was the one with the gun, but I'll bet we can prove she was an accessory to Julian's murder."

They stared at each other, adrenaline pumping through them.

"I think you've got it," Nick said.

"It took a knock to the head and forty stitches, but yeah, looks like we've got it nailed. Finally. Is Captain Malone still here?"

"He's asleep in the waiting room."

"Would you mind getting him for me?"

"Sure."

While he was gone, Sam closed her eyes in an effort to calm the pounding pain in her head. It had definitely gotten worse overnight. The smallest of movements made her nauseous.

Nick returned with Captain Malone in tow.

"How're you feeling, Sam?" Malone asked.

"As long as I don't move, I'm fine."

"Ouch. Nick tells me you've managed to crack the Sinclair case from your hospital bed." His face lifted into a proud smile. "Only you, Holland."

Sam told him her theory. "Here's what needs to happen. We need to get Austin Sinclair away from his mother. Get him to confirm that he told his father about Devon being involved with his roommate, Tucker. I need to know how and when that happened." A blast of pain reminded her of the need to stay still.

"Take it easy, babe," Nick said.

She took a shallow breath, fought back the nausea and continued. "We have to find Preston. He's armed and unhinged. We need to get him before he hurts someone else. If he has any capacity left, he's probably aware of what he's done and feeling desperate about his son. Maybe we can use Devon to somehow lure him in."

"What about the wife?" Malone asked.

"Have Cruz trace the purchase of the rope that was used to tie Julian. I'll bet my life she bought it. She set this whole thing up. She convinced her husband that killing his brother was the only way. The brothers were estranged because of her. She violently disapproved of Julian. He came to town for Supreme Court nomination hearings just as she was due to realize the dream of a lifetime by seeing her book published. No way was she going to let him deny her that. When Preston found out about Devon, he went off on a rogue mission to neutralize that threat, too."

"He shot his own son," Malone said, incredulous. "Preston saw him as a threat to the wife and took action."

"Yes," Sam said. "His lawyer will argue diminished capacity, and it'll probably fly. He'll end up in the psych ward. She's the one I want behind bars. She didn't pull the trigger on Julian, but she made sure her husband did."

"We'll get them both," Malone assured her. "You worry about getting better."

"I hate that I can't go after them myself."

"I'm sure you do, but we've got it covered."

"Keep me posted?"

"You know I will."

AFTER THE CAPTAIN left, Nick could see that Sam's burst of energy had faded and the pain had her full attention.

Clutching her hand, he studied her precious face, aching from what he needed to tell her. If he had his way, she'd never know about the tabloid. But they had a deal about keeping things from each other, so he owed her nothing less than the truth, even if telling her would break his heart—and hers.

"What?" she asked. "What's wrong? Is it Julian? I know it's so hard for you to hear about how he was killed."

"No, babe. It's not Julian. Something happened while you were asleep before, and I wish I didn't have to tell you this."

"Not my dad," she said in a small voice.

With his good arm, Nick hugged her as best he could. "No, honey." Holding her against him, he pressed his lips to her temple and very softly, very gently told her about the tabloid.

As his words registered, she stiffened in his arms. "No," she whispered.

"I'm so sorry, Sam. I'd do anything in my power to protect you from having to deal with this. My lawyer is filing for an emergency injunction this morning, but he doesn't think it'll happen in time to stop the publication."

"My dad," she said, frantically. "I have to tell him before he reads it in the paper." She struggled free of Nick's embrace, and then nearly fainted when her head injury fought back.

He eased her to the pile of pillows. "Sweetheart, you can't go anywhere right now."

"I have to tell him."

"I'll call Celia. She'll bring him here. I'll make sure she brings him in a side door so no one gets to him before you do." He brushed the hair back from her face. "It's going to be okay, Sam. You didn't do anything wrong."

"Everyone will know what I was going to do," she whispered.

"How about we steal their thunder?"

"What do you mean?"

"We could release a statement that tells the story your way, on your terms, rather than waiting for it to explode in the *Reporter*. We could pull the legs out from under them."

"Come right out and admit it? I don't know if I could do that."

"Tell your story, Sam. Tell the same story you told me. We'll issue a joint statement saying this is the only thing either of us will ever have to say on the issue. And then we'll sue the asses off the clinic, the woman who stole your record and the *Reporter*. I'll bet you all can come up with something to charge her with criminally."

She looked up at him. "How do I make a statement?"

Proud of her courage, he said, "Christina and Trevor

are on their way over here now. We'll take care of everything."

"You can't be involved with this, Nick. You're running for office. This'll be a nightmare for you."

"Of course I'm involved with it. I told you before I ever accepted this job that you come first and you always will. Political fallout is the very last thing on my mind right now. This is happening to you because of me and my job. You have to let me fix it. I *need* to fix it, Sam."

Biting her lip, she studied him for a long time. "Okay."

Nick called Celia and asked her to bring Skip over as soon as possible. Returning the phone to his pocket, he reached for Sam's hand and brought it to his lips. "It's going to be okay. I promise."

THIRTY-FOUR

"NO WAY, SENATOR," Christina said. "You can*not* go out there and read this. It's political suicide to attach yourself so vocally to this issue."

"I'm attaching myself to her, not the issue."

Astounded, Christina stared at him. "Are you really that naive?"

Trevor cleared his throat.

"Speak," Nick said.

The communications director glanced at Christina. "I, um, I agree with the senator." Before she could pounce, he said, "The entire region is caught up in their romance. People will respond to him sticking up for her."

"You've lost your minds—both of you," Christina retorted. "He's a *United States senator* who's going to tell the world that his girlfriend planned to have an abortion before a well-timed miscarriage saved the day. An *abortion!*"

"I'm going to say that fifteen years ago, when she was still a student, my girlfriend planned to have a legal medical procedure to end a pregnancy she was unequipped to handle at that time in her life. I'm going to tell them she miscarried before the procedure was performed and she's regretted the decisions she made at that time ever since. I'll say I love her, I support her and I support the right of all women to choose. Then I will tell them that neither the lieutenant nor I will have another word to say about this. Ever."

"Why can't someone from her family read the statement?" Christina asked. "Why does it have to be you?"

"Because I *am* her family, and this is happening to her because of me."

"How do you figure?"

Nick rolled his eyes. "Seriously, Christina? You don't see the connection?"

Trevor cleared his throat again. "If he hadn't agreed to finish Senator O'Connor's term, no one would care about Lieutenant Holland's past."

"Thank you, Trevor," Nick said, his eyes fixed on Christina.

"Fine." She handed him the statement. "Have at it. Just don't say I didn't warn you when the party tries to run you out of town on a rail."

"Unfortunately for them, I'm all they've got." Turning to Trevor, he said, "Let the media know I'll be making a brief statement in the hospital lobby at ten."

"Will do, Senator."

"Relax, Christina," Nick said. "It'll be fine."

Her expression rife with trepidation, she said, "Sure it will."

FROM HER BED, Sam heard the whir of her father's chair coming down the hallway. Pushing herself up, she winced when pain bounced off every corner of her skull. She had a whole new respect for concussions.

Celia held the door open for Skip. "Morning, honey," Celia said. "How are you today?"

"Fine as long as I don't blink."

"You need to stay very still, which of course will be a challenge for you," Skip said, his sharp eyes assessing his daughter's condition.

"Did you have any trouble with the media?" Sam asked.

"Nope," Skip said. "We came in through the Emergency Room."

Sam's stomach tightened with the familiar pain, although she had to admit it wasn't as sharp since she gave up soda. Then again, *she* wasn't quite as sharp, either. "There's something I have to tell you."

"Why don't I wait for you outside, Skip?" Celia said.

"No," Sam said to her future stepmother. "Stay. Please."

"All right." Celia moved to the bedside and rested her hand over Sam's. "Are your injuries worse than they thought?"

Sam tuned in to the worry on both their faces and hated that she'd caused it. "No, nothing like that. It's about something that happened years ago, something shameful. The media has caught wind of it."

"Whatever it is, Sam, we love you," Skip said, but she could see the trepidation on his face. "You know that."

Sam cleared the emotion from her throat. "Yes, I do, and that's why I never wanted to disappoint you."

"And you never have. What's wrong, honey?"

"Do you remember the French guy I dated in college? Jean Paul?"

"Vaguely. As I recall, there was no shortage of young men interested in my little girl."

Sam wouldn't have believed it possible to smile just then. Taking a deep breath, she told them about the terrible decision she'd been forced to make, the miscarriage she'd suffered and the consequences she had lived with every day since. "I didn't know what to do, Dad," she said softly. "I felt like I had no choice."

Both Skip and Celia seemed stunned.

Nick stepped into the room, came over to the bed and slipped an arm around Sam. Kissing her temple, he whispered, "You okay?"

She closed her eyes for a moment, absorbing the tender comfort only he could provide. "Yeah."

"Why are you telling us this now?" Skip asked, his expression unreadable.

"Because it's about to hit the news," Nick said.

Celia gasped.

"Someone from the clinic sold the story to one of the rags and told them I went through with it. We have no idea what they'll actually report, but we suspect it won't be the truth."

"But that's illegal!" Celia huffed.

"You have to do something," Skip said, his eyes darting from Sam to Nick and then back to her.

"We're doing what we can," Nick assured him, outlining the plan.

"Still," Sam said softly, "everyone will know." After a long pause, she glanced at her father. "Say something, Dad. Please."

"I'm sorry you didn't come to me when this happened."

"Don't you remember how it was then? Mom had left, Tracy had just had Brooke, everyone was upset and stressed. I thought it was my only option. And then I lost the baby. Not a day has gone by that I haven't wondered what might've been."

"I have no doubt."

"This is embarrassing to you. I'm sorry."

"Don't be ridiculous," Skip said tersely. "I couldn't care less what anyone thinks. All that matters is that you're okay."

Nick squeezed Sam's shoulder.

Overwhelmed, Sam said, "It's mortifying to have everyone know about my personal business, but I don't want you to worry, Dad. We'll get through this." On top of her other regrets, she hated that her past was going to cause political grief for Nick.

"I think it'd be best if you leave before the press conference," Nick said to Skip and Celia. "I'd hate for them to get ahold of you."

"We'll take our chances," Skip said.

"I'd rather you go," Sam said softly. "If you stay, I'll be worried about getting you out of here."

"Sam's right," Celia said to Skip. "We can come back tonight."

"Absolutely." Sam sat up slowly. Leaning down, she kissed her father's cheek and hugged Celia. "I'll see you later."

"Sam." When he had her attention, Skip said, "There is nothing, and I mean *nothing,* you could ever do or have ever done that would disappoint me or make me love you less. *Nothing.* Do you hear me?"

"Yes," Sam said softly. "Thank you for saying that."

To Nick, Skip said, "Go out there and give 'em hell, Senator."

"I will. Don't worry."

After Skip and Celia left, a nurse came in. "That very cute partner of yours called to check on you," she said as she scanned Sam's monitors. "He said he didn't want to wake you up by calling, and he'll be here shortly."

"Good," Sam said, drained by the conversation with her father. Her head pounded, and her mouth was dry as the desert.

"Is he single?" the nurse asked with nonchalance. "Your partner?"

"He's seeing someone."

"Oh, well. My loss. He's *adorable*." Under her breath, she added, "So is your guy." She glanced at Nick, who stared out the window at the gray, frigid day. "Yum."

Sam smiled but her heart ached at the thought of what he was about to do for her.

AN HOUR LATER, Sam watched on television as Nick stood before the press to read the statement she had approved. Off to the side, Christina and Trevor watched anxiously. "I have a brief statement, and then neither I nor Lieutenant Holland will have anything further to say on this subject."

The gathered reporters all but salivated with anticipation.

Sam muted the TV. She couldn't bear to listen. Fixating on Nick's handsome, serious face, she noted how pale and drawn he appeared. He'd suffered serious injuries of his own the day before, and yet taking care of her was his top priority. Despite the firestorm his announcement would set off in both their lives, she wasn't as freaked out as she would've been without him by her side.

Anxious to think about anything other than what Nick was saying to the press and the pounding in her skull, Sam wondered if they'd found Preston yet. Where in the hell would he go? A man like him, used to the creature comforts, wouldn't last long on the streets. Had he checked in to a hotel? Had anyone thought to look into that?

"I need to get back on that case." She pushed herself up as slowly as she could and then took a moment to contend with the accompanying swell of nausea.

Freddie tapped on the door and came in. "Morning, boss. How're you doing? *What* are you doing?"

"I gotta get out of here, Cruz."

"No way, Lieutenant." He stepped over to the bed and rested his hands on her shoulders, clearly intending to re-settle her in the bed. "You're supposed to be still."

Gritting her teeth, she snarled at him. "Remove your fucking hands and get that bag of clothes over there." She pointed to the bag Celia had brought. "Hurry up. Before Nick gets back."

Startled by her tone, Freddie jumped back, jostling her in the process.

"The *clothes,* Cruz." It was all she could do to get the words out. "Now."

"If you ask me to dress you, I'll quit the force."

"Dream on. Go out to the nurse's station and sign for my personal effects. Tell them I'm twitchy without my gun since a bunch of gang punks put me here. What if they show up to finish the deal?"

"They aren't going to give me your stuff."

Sam closed her eyes, seeking mercy from the pain. "Ask for Holly," she rasped. "For some unknown rea-son, she thinks you're adorable. Charm her, but make it snappy." She glanced at the TV and saw Nick stepping away from the podium. "We're running out of time."

With a wary glance at her, Freddie put the bag of clothes on the bed and left the room.

Swallowing the sickening waves of nausea, she got dressed in a sweat suit and sneakers. Thankfully, Celia had also brought a warm parka.

Freddie returned a few minutes later with a satisfied smirk on his face. A plastic bag containing her gun, badge, cuffs and wallet landed on the bed next to her.

Sam jammed the gun into the back of her sweats, put the other items in her coat pockets and stood up. Just as quickly, she sat back down when her head exploded in protest.

"Sam—"

"Shut up," she growled. With one hand on the bed, she pushed herself back up and took a second to contend with the now-predictable burst of pain. Reaching up, she snatched the knitted skullcap off his head and dragged it over her injured dome, tucking her long hair inside. "Let's go."

"That's okay, I wasn't using that."

"I need it more than you do."

"Nick's gonna kill me for this," Freddie muttered.

"No, he's gonna kill *me*. So let's make it worth it."

Moving down the hallway, dodging nurses, Sam discovered her body hurt everywhere. The diagonal seatbelt bruise, stretching from shoulder to hip, protested every movement. Apparently, she'd also managed to hurt her knee, but no one had noticed that thanks to the head injury.

At the elevator bank, she pressed the up arrow.

"Where're we going?" Freddie asked, puzzled.

"To see Diandra. Did you get anything on the rope that was used to bind Julian?"

"Diandra purchased a spool of rope from the Home Depot in Gaithersburg two weeks before Julian was murdered. Gonzo is getting a warrant to search the house for the rest of it."

Sam wished she had the strength to dance a jig. "Excellent! I knew it. What else have you heard today?"

"Gonzo talked to Austin. Devon is still critical. Could go either way. Austin confirmed that he told his father about your conversation with Devon."

"Bingo. I knew it. Preston heard Devon was gay, and lost it. We *have* to find him. He's the key to this whole thing."

They rode the elevator to the ICU, where Sam flashed

her badge and asked for Diandra. "It's critical we speak to her," she told the nurse on duty. They were granted entry to Devon's room where Diandra sat hunched over her son's bed.

"Mrs. Sinclair," Sam said from the doorway.

The face that looked up was barely recognizable as the stylish, put-together woman who made her career as a TV commentator. When Sam first met her, Diandra believed she had the situation fully under control. Her husband had done her bidding and taken out his inconveniently nominated brother. Everything was right in her world. Until the moment Preston went too far and shot their son. That, most definitely, had *not* been part of Diandra's plan.

"What do you want?" Diandra asked, her voice and posture defeated.

"How is he?"

"How does he look?"

"Not too good. May I speak to you outside for a moment?"

"I don't want to leave him."

"It'll only take a minute."

Diandra bent to press a kiss to Devon's forehead. In the hallway, she crossed her arms and leaned back against the wall, exhaustion all but rippling from her.

Aware of the nurses clustered around the monitoring station a few feet away, Sam kept her voice low. "Where's Austin?"

"He went home to change."

"What about Preston?"

"I have no idea." Clearly her concern from yesterday had morphed into anger overnight.

"Where would he go?"

Diandra shook her head. "I wish I knew. He doesn't even know about Devon."

So, Sam thought, *still in denial, are you, Diandra? Still not sure your husband could really shoot his own son? Still not aware of just how much power you exert over Preston or how far he'd go to ensure your happiness?* Being on top—or thinking you were on top—made the fall that much harder and longer. This woman had a huge fall coming her way, even if Devon survived.

"We'd like to speak to him." Sam nudged Freddie. "Give her your card. Call Detective Cruz if you hear from him. Do you understand?"

"What does Preston have to do with anything?"

"I don't know yet. That's why I want to talk to him."

"What's wrong with you?" Diandra asked, zeroing in on Sam's face. "You're trembling and ghostly pale."

"She was in a car accident last night," Freddie said.

"And you're working on Devon's case?"

"I'm working on both cases—Devon's *and* Julian's."

Diandra appeared startled to hear that. "What does one have to do with the other?"

Sam took a moment, sized up the other woman, measuring her every movement. "I don't know yet." Despite what the motion cost her aching head, she leaned in closer. "But I'm going to find out, Diandra. You can bet your ass I'm going to find out. Detective Cruz? Let's go."

Emerging through the ICU double doors, Sam gripped Freddie's jacket to keep from falling down. Her legs had the consistency of cooked spaghetti. "Get on the horn with the lab," she whispered. "Tell them they have one hour to get me the report on the weapon used on Devon. I already know it was the same gun that did Julian. I just need confirmation. One hour."

"Lieutenant, maybe you should sit for a minute."

"Not 'til we're out of this place. Get me out of here without going anywhere near the lobby."

"Can I ask you something?"

"Yeah."

"Why didn't you nail her just now? You've all but got her on accessory to murder."

"Because we still need to sew up a couple of loose ends, and then I'm going to let Preston nail her. It's the least of what he owes her. All we have to do is find him." She staggered, and Freddie tightened his hold on her. "Make the call."

Freddie gripped her arm while dialing the cell phone with his free hand.

THIRTY-FIVE

"WHERE THE HELL would he go?" Sam asked the minute they were safely in Freddie's Mustang. Refusing to puke in the hospital parking lot where the press might see her, she fought back a vicious wave of nausea. "You're sure they checked all the hotels?"

"Every one within twenty miles of the city. The theory is he wouldn't go much farther knowing his son was wounded."

"And Austin couldn't think of anywhere else his father might be?"

"Only places we've already looked."

Sam punched the door and then instantly regretted it. Gasping from the pain that rippled through her in sickening waves, she closed her eyes and took shallow breaths through her nose.

"Damn it, Sam. You should be in the hospital."

"Drive. Now."

"Where to?"

"Out of this fucking parking lot! Before we get snagged!"

"Jeez, you're bitchy when you're in pain."

"I'm always bitchy."

"True."

"More so since I quit soda."

"*Very* true."

"So how's that whole 'I'm a crazy horn dog after all' thing going?"

"You're never going to forget that, are you?"

"Not in this lifetime." She rested her head back against the seat, pleased that at least something in her life had returned to normal—or what was passing for normal these days. Ever since the moment she first walked into John O'Connor's apartment and encountered Nick's grief-stricken face, her life had changed forever. Imagining the news of her long-ago near-abortion whipping through the city, she released a jagged sigh. "So, Nick said Darren Tabor spilled the whole thing to you."

"Yes. He was actually extremely cool. For him."

"Good of him to tip us off." She knew she had to ask, that this would be the first of many times she'd have to revisit the most painful moment of her life, a moment she thought she'd left behind a long time ago. "Are you disgusted with me?"

His eyes darted from the road to her and back to the road. "Of course not."

"Not even a little?"

His jaw tightened with tension. "You must've had no choice."

"I really didn't. But I know your faith runs deep. You should feel free to speak your mind, Freddie."

"I already have."

The tone of his voice indicated the conversation was over, that there would be nothing more said about it. Ever. He no doubt had strong feelings about the issue, but apparently he had strong feelings about her, too.

"You know what's disgusting?" she asked, looking to lighten things up.

"What's that?"

She kicked at the candy wrappers, chip bags and soda cans on the floor of his car. "Your disgusting eating habits."

"I'm a growing boy," he said with that charming smile of his. "I need my sugar."

"It's gross."

"You're just jealous because you wish you had my metabolism."

"I continue to hope I'm around to see your crappy diet catch up to you." The old car hit a huge pothole, and Sam gasped. "*Dude.* Watch the bumps."

"Um, do you think maybe you could tell me where we're going?"

"Just drive. Let me think. Where are you Preston? Where's the last place you think we'd look for you?" She let the thought run around in her mind for several minutes. "Call Gonzo. I want the log from Devon's house."

Dialing while driving, Freddie passed along the request.

Keeping her eyes closed, Sam said, "Ask him if Preston Sinclair came to the house after the bodies were found."

A minute later, Freddie confirmed that Preston had, in fact, come there looking for his son while crime scene processed the house. According to Gonzo's report, Preston acted suitably distraught and left after packing a bag for his son. He said he was going straight to the hospital. While they were on the phone, Gonzo also confirmed the same gun had been used in both Sinclair shootings.

The buzz of all the pieces falling into place rippled through Sam's battered body. "I *knew* it! Dupont Circle. Stat."

"There might be bumps."

"I'll risk it."

RIPPED TO SHREDS by what he'd just endured with the media, Nick returned to Sam's room to find it empty. "What the hell?"

Storming down the hall to the nurse's station, he inquired about her.

"She was in her room, Senator. I was just in there."

His ribs ached, his collarbone was on fire and his nerves were totally shot. Making a supreme effort not to rip the nurse's head off, he bit back a nasty retort and summoned a calm tone. "She's not there now. I want to know where she is."

"So do I." The nurse picked up the phone and called for security. "If she's in this hospital, they'll find her."

"Thank you."

He returned to Sam's room, dug his cell phone out of his pocket and called her. Hearing the tune of "Living on a Prayer" coming from under the pillow made him want to throw his own phone across the room. Then he noticed the bag Celia had brought.

Empty.

"Goddamn it, Sam. *Goddamn it!*" He reached under the pillow for her phone, scrolled through the numbers, found Freddie's and pressed Send.

"I BET HE was in the house just long enough to unlock a window or door," Sam said.

Freddie pulled up to the townhouse and parked. "So you think he came back after the cops left?"

"That's exactly what I think." Sam reached for the door handle.

Freddie's hand on her arm stopped her. "What's the plan, boss? To go in there balls to the wall and ferret him out?"

"Well, yeah. Exactly."

"Um, no offense or anything, but a certain lieutenant near and dear to me recently ripped me a new one for going in without backup."

"You have backup. You have me."

"Again I say no offense, but I'd rather go in with my fat Aunt Doris than you in the condition you're in right now."

"Ouch. I'm hurt."

"Yes, you are, and I'm not going in there with just you to apprehend a man who's already shot his own brother and son." Stretching his injured shoulder, Freddie added, "I'd like to think I've learned my lesson. The two of us are hardly equipped at the moment."

"Christ, you're such an ass pain, Cruz. Call it in, but the collar's mine, you got me?"

"I got you, and I've asked you not to take the Lord's name in vain."

She growled at him.

Just as he reached for the radio to call for backup, his phone rang. Checking the caller ID, he glanced over at her. "Funny. It's you."

"Shit. It's probably Nick, and I'll bet he's pissed."

"*Gee,* do ya think?"

"Your sarcasm is of no use to me right now."

"Am I answering?"

Sam stared at the phone. "No. I'll call him after this goes down. Get the backup here before Preston slips through our fingers."

"You are so dead when Nick gets ahold of you. I hope I get to watch that."

"Shut up and call!"

THE SWAT TEAM scampered out of two black vans. They moved with the precision of a NASCAR pit crew, each member knowing exactly what they were supposed to do and when they were supposed to do it. Early in her career, Sam had considered SWAT but decided against it when she realized they did a lot of waiting for situations to arise while detectives were constantly in the thick of things.

With officers in place on the roof, in the street and on the ground they stormed the front door.

"Damn," Freddie said reverently. "I never get tired of watching them in action." A rumble of activity lit up the radio, and he reached for the door handle. "They're coming. Stay here."

"Screw you." Sam got out and was hit with another wave of nausea that nearly brought her to her knees. She forced the stars from her eyes and watched them bring a broken, bawling, handcuffed Preston Sinclair out of his son's house.

The SWAT lieutenant handed her a 9-millimeter handgun zipped into a plastic bag. "We got there just in time. He was going to off himself."

Malone and Gonzo arrived on the scene.

"I'm not even going to ask what the hell you're doing here, Holland," Malone said. "But why am I not surprised?"

Sam took the bag containing the gun. "Got the guy, got the weapon," she said with a smug smile. Even that small movement cost her. To Gonzo, she added, "Get him to HQ, put him in a room and stay with him until I call you. Don't even step out to take a leak, got me?" She handed him the gun. "Have Jeannie trace it. I want proof that Diandra bought it. Get it for me."

"Yes, ma'am." Gonzo took Preston by the arm and escorted him to the car.

Malone raised an eyebrow as he studied Sam. "What're you up to, Holland?"

"I need someone to pick up Diandra Sinclair at the GW ICU."

"That doesn't answer my question."

"I'll do it." Freddie flagged down a uniformed officer directing traffic around the scene. "We'll take his squad car and leave my car here. I'll meet you at HQ."

"Don't bring her in until I tell you to. Wait for my call."

"Got it." His face full of concern, Freddie turned to Malone. "Captain, you'll escort Lieutenant Holland back to HQ?"

"I'll escort her back to the hospital," Malone said.

"Then I'll grab a cab," Sam said, raising her chin—painfully—in defiance, "but either way, I'm going to HQ." The blinding light of the sun over his shoulder brought tears to her eyes, but she didn't look away.

"Fine, but the minute you finish this, you're on medical leave until I say otherwise."

"Fine."

"Fine," he retorted as he led her to his car. "You may be aware that there's a very unhappy United States senator looking for you."

"So I've heard." Closing her eyes, she rested her head against the seat. "Do me a favor? Help me dodge him? I need an hour to finish this, and then I'll take my punishment and my suspension and whatever else you all want to dole out."

"I'll look forward to seeing that."

"You and everyone else." She glanced over at him. "So, nothing to say? About the other thing?"

Malone shrugged. "None of my business. None of anyone's business."

"Is HQ all abuzz with it?"

"Maybe."

She sighed.

"Give it a day, maybe two—and you'll be on leave for most of it. It'll blow over."

"It's horrifying," she said softly. "That they all know."

"What's horrifying is that your privacy has been breached this way just because of who your boyfriend is."

"Yeah."

"But he's worth it, right?"

"He really is."

Malone smiled. "But that doesn't mean we won't nail the bitch who sold your medical record to the rag."

The unexpected laughter had Sam reaching for her head with both hands. "Oh, my God, don't make me laugh. *Please.*"

ON THE WAY to HQ, she used the captain's phone to call ahead to the U.S. Attorney's office. Hope Dobson, one of the three identical triplets who served the District as assistant U.S. Attorneys, answered. Sam laid out the case against Preston and detailed Diandra's role.

"Do you believe she knew he was going to kill his brother?" Hope asked.

"Not only did she know, she put him up to it, and I'm going to prove it. Can you be in the detectives' pit in thirty minutes? There's gonna be one hell of a show. You won't want to miss it."

"I'll be there."

"Thanks, and Hope? She's the main event as far as I'm concerned. Preston is diminished capacity all the way. He's totally under the control of his wife. It's disturbing."

"I'll see what I can do. How does the son's shooting fit in?"

"All your questions will be answered very soon. I'll let you hear it from the horse's mouth." She ended the call and handed the phone to the captain. "You might want to let the chief know this is going down."

"Again I ask, what are you up to, Holland?"

"Just closing a case, sir," she said, indulging in the

chance to close her eyes and sink into the seat for just a minute. Among her many other woes, the line of stitches at her hairline was on fire. One minute of complete stillness to soothe her aching head and body. That was all she needed.

Captain Malone nudged her awake when they arrived at HQ. "This is insane, Holland. You need to be in the hospital."

Forcing herself to wake up, Sam tried to shake off the grogginess and gasped from the ricochet of pain. "Give me thirty minutes, and I'll wrap this one up with a bow on top just for you."

He cast a wary glance at the throng of media gathered outside the main door to HQ. "We need to go in through the morgue."

That would mean a longer walk to the pit—a much longer walk. "That's fine," she said, gritting her teeth. Anything to avoid the savages looking to take another piece out of her wounded hide. "Actually, I'm glad to see them here. They'll help my plan." She smiled at the idea of Diandra Sinclair, in handcuffs, being marched through the scrum into HQ.

"Which you *still* haven't shared with me."

At some point during the interminable walk, Sam became aware of his hand on her arm, all but holding her up as he directed her down the long hallways.

In the pit, she was greeted with none of the usual hubbub she'd come to expect. Rather, a subdued silence had descended over her troops as they no doubt tried to process what they'd learned about her that day. Refusing to be distracted, Sam shrugged off her coat and reached for the handheld radio on her desk.

Malone lowered himself into the other chair in her office.

"Detective Gonzales, what's your twenty?" she asked.

"Interrogation A with Mr. Sinclair."

"Detective Cruz?"

"In the parking lot with Mrs. Sinclair."

"Detective McBride?"

"On the way to your office, Lieutenant, with the information you requested."

Sam put down the radio and smiled. "Excellent."

Jeannie knocked on the door a minute later and handed Sam a file. Inside was a copy of a gun license, registered to Diandra Sinclair.

"Good work, Detective," Sam said, trying not to worry about the fact that Jeannie couldn't seem to make eye contact with her.

AUSA Dobson stepped into the room, followed closely by Chief Farnsworth, who took one look at Sam and blanched.

"What, in the name of God, are you doing out of the hospital, Lieutenant?" he asked.

"Thank you," Malone muttered. "She's up to something, won't tell me what, but I take it we're in for a show, Chief."

"What've you got, Lieutenant?" Hope asked.

Sam sensed an odd vibe coming from the assistant U.S. Attorney and wondered how long it would take to "blow over" as the captain predicted. She handed Hope the file with the license.

"The owner of the store recognized her and remembers her buying the gun," Jeannie said. "Diandra told him she was buying it as protection against the crazies who take issue with her views. She told him she'd been repeatedly threatened. He's willing to testify."

"So she put the gun in her husband's hand and told him his brother had to go?" Hope asked.

"That's exactly what she did, but she got more than she bargained for when he also used the gun on their son." Reaching for the radio, she called Cruz. "Bring her in, but wait to un-cuff her until you get inside." Sam waited exactly two minutes before she called Gonzo. "Please escort Mr. Sinclair, un-cuffed, into the pit." To the others in her office, Sam offered a gracious smile. "Ladies and gentlemen, will you join me in the hallway?"

SECONDS BEFORE FREDDIE was due to bring Diandra in, Nick came around the corner, his handsome face tight and furious.

Sam raised a hand to stop him, using her eyes to implore.

He halted, noted the gathered group and stayed put.

Sam released a jagged sigh of relief. "Here we go," she said softly as Diandra and Preston approached each other from opposite sides of the detectives' pit.

As if gas had been thrown on a fire, Diandra took one look at her bedraggled husband and charged, just as Sam had hoped she would. Claws out, Diandra shrieked. *"What were you thinking?* You miserable excuse of a man! How could you shoot your *own son?"* She beat his chest with her fists. "Why? *Why?* We never said anything about Devon!"

His arms hanging loosely by his sides, Preston did nothing to defend himself against her tirade.

"Why?"

"He's gay," Preston said so softly it was almost inaudible.

As if he had struck her, Diandra stepped back from him. "What did you say?"

"Your son is gay. He and Tucker weren't just roommates. They were lovers."

"That's not true. You're making that up to get back at me for Julian."

Sam was pleased that Diandra seemed to have completely forgotten where she was and who was listening. This was even better than she'd hoped. Across the room, she met Nick's glance and was relieved to see that some of the rigidity had left his posture as he realized what was unfolding in front of him.

"I didn't want to," Preston sobbed. "I didn't want to do it, but you said Julian would ruin everything if he went before Congress and told the world he was a gay man. You said we couldn't let that happen. So when Austin told me Dev was gay, too, I just did what I thought you'd want me to do."

"You shot Devon, Dad?" Austin asked in a dull, flat tone. He stepped through the doorway, having obviously followed his mother from the hospital to HQ.

Uh-oh, Sam thought. He hadn't been part of the plan.

"Mom's book is coming out." Preston fumbled over his words. "She's getting her own show. She's worked so hard. Everything she's ever wanted is finally within reach. I couldn't let them ruin it for her. She was afraid they'd ruin it for her."

"I never said anything about Devon!" Diandra repeatedly slapped Preston's face.

Austin grabbed her from behind, pulling her off his father. "Leave him alone. For God's sake, Mom. Hasn't he done enough for you? Haven't we all done enough?"

Preston descended into brokenhearted sobs.

"I've certainly heard enough." Sam stepped out of the crowd and nodded to Freddie, who cuffed Diandra.

"What're you doing?" she cried, fighting him. "I didn't shoot anyone. He did! I was with you when he shot Devon! You know that!"

"Mrs. Sinclair, you're under arrest for accessory to the murder of Julian Sinclair," Freddie said. "You have the right to remain silent. Anything you say can and will be used against you in a court of law."

Realization seemed to settle on Diandra all of a sudden. *"You fucking bitch,"* she seethed at Sam. *"You motherfucking bitch!"*

"You have the right to an attorney," Freddie continued. "If you cannot afford an attorney, one will be appointed to you. Do you understand these rights as they have been read to you?"

"Fuck you."

"I'll take that as a yes."

Sam turned to Preston. "Mr. Sinclair, you're under arrest for the first-degree murder of your brother, Julian Sinclair, for the attempted murder of your son, Devon Sinclair, and for the murder of Tucker Farrell." She repeated the Miranda warning as Freddie cuffed him. "Do you understand these rights as they have been read to you?"

"Yes, ma'am," Preston said wearily.

He was so defeated that Sam felt her heart go out to a murderer for the first time in her career.

"Detectives Cruz and Gonzales, please escort Mr. and Mrs. Sinclair to central booking."

After they were gone, with Diandra shrieking and fighting the whole way, Sam turned to Austin. "I'm sorry."

"I just can't believe he shot Dev," he said, the shock echoing through his voice. "She had him so under her control that he honestly thought that's what she'd want."

Sam rested her hand on his arm. "Your brother needs you to be strong for him. If he recovers, he'll need you to help him through this, as well as the loss of Tucker."

Austin seemed to make an enormous effort to shake off the stupor. "Yes, you're right. I'll see about getting an attorney for my dad."

"What about your mother?"

Austin fixed cold eyes on the doorway into which his parents had been taken. "She's on her own." He glanced at Sam. "Thank you for getting justice for my uncle and my brother and Tucker. In a million years, I never could've imagined that my parents were involved, but with hindsight I should've known my mother had something to do with it. I should've known that."

"You had no reason to suspect either of them was capable of this. Go on back to your brother, Austin. That's where you need to be right now."

He nodded and turned to leave.

Nick stepped up to her and put his arm around her.

Sam leaned gratefully into his embrace.

With his good arm, he took the coat Captain Malone handed him and the two of them got her into it. "I have a serious bone to pick with you, Lieutenant," Nick said.

"So I've heard," Sam said, the burst of energy leaving her as suddenly as it had come.

Nick steered her toward the door.

"Hey! What're you doing? I've got to do the report!"

"I'm taking you home, Samantha, so shut up before I bend you over my knee and spank the life out of you right here in front of all your coworkers."

Since she didn't have the energy to fight him, she rested her head on his shoulder and let him take charge. "Mmm, that sounds like fun. Can we try that sometime?"

"I said to shut up," he growled but she could tell that she'd flustered him. She could hear it in his voice.

"Speaking of going home, I've been meaning to talk to you about that," she said, her voice thick with exhaustion.

"We'll get to it. When you can keep your eyes open."

"'K. Don't let me forget."

"Don't worry, babe. I won't."

EPILOGUE

AFTER TWO WEEKS of forced medical leave, all Sam wanted to do was get back to the action, but everyone seemed to be conspiring against her. Nothing infuriated her more than being mollycoddled by a bunch of overwrought men. All she'd managed to get done on her first day back was to confirm that Devon Sinclair was expected to make a full recovery. Malone and Cruz shoved her out the door at the stroke of five o'clock as if she wouldn't have had the good sense to go home on her own.

Home. Where was that exactly? Every time she'd tried to talk to Nick about moving in with him over the past two weeks, he'd dodged her, telling her they'd talk about it when she felt better. She was feeling *fine,* but if one more person treated her with kid gloves she was going to punch them. Her temper had been her biggest problem lately as she learned to live without caffeine. Her stomach, on the other hand, had been much better, which she hated to admit.

She'd been so bored during her leave that she'd even accompanied Nick to kick off his campaign in Richmond and to several events in southern Virginia. Following an initial burst of interest from the media about her long-ago almost-abortion, she and Nick had settled back into the usual grind of fending off just a small horde of reporters everywhere they went.

Buckling under enormous pressure, they had agreed to give Darren Tabor their first exclusive sit-down interview as a couple next week. Sam had major reservations about the idea and was doing it only to help Nick's campaign.

She parked on Ninth Street and contemplated where she wanted to be. Her dad's house was dark, as it often was these days as he and Celia finalized the plans for their Valentine's Day wedding. The thought of her father getting married on Valentine's Day made Sam want to gag, but they were so excited that she couldn't bring herself to object. She'd even grudgingly agreed to wear the red satin bridesmaid dress Celia had chosen for Sam and her sisters. Double gag.

While her dad's house was dark, Nick's was lit up like he was having a party. Sam locked her car and headed for Nick's. Inside, she found her sisters waiting for her.

"What're you guys doing here?" she asked, dropping her coat over the sofa. It drove Nick crazy that she couldn't hang it in the closet like a "normal" person, which was why she so enjoyed dumping it on his sofa.

"We're helping Nick with something," Angela said.

"With what?" Sam asked.

"Oh, a little project named Samantha," Tracy said as she linked her arm with Sam's and led her to the stairs. "Right this way, *Samantha*."

"He's the only one allowed to call me that," Sam snapped.

"When can you go back on caffeine?" Angela asked. "I liked you better with a bad stomach and a happy disposition."

"Bite me." In the doorway to the bedroom, Sam stopped and gasped. "What the hell?" Hanging on the closet door was the most exquisite ice-blue gown Sam had ever seen. She broke free of her sisters and pounced on the dress. "Oh, my God, is that *silk?* Where did this come from?" She let out a most uncoplike girlish squeal. "*Oh, my God!* It's Vera Wang? *Seriously?*"

"He said, 'the sky's the limit,'" Tracy reported, her face set in a grave expression. "We took him very, very seriously." She pointed to a box on the floor.

Sam screamed. *"Manolos!"* Tearing into the box, she withdrew delicate heels with beaded crystal accents—a perfect match with the dress.

"A delightful size nine," Angela said, gazing reverently at the shoes.

"I'm a nine-and-a-half," Sam reminded her.

"I know, but I'm a nine, and Spencer has this thing coming up at work, so don't stretch them all out with your big old hoofs, you hear me?"

"I'll see what I can do. And remind me to execute a warrant next week on your closet. I bet I'll find my missing Jimmy Choos there."

"You weren't using them," Angela retorted.

Sam sighed, unable to tear her eyes off the shoes. "This is better than sex."

"You need to have better sex," Tracy said.

"Not possible," Sam said. "What's this all about? I don't get it."

"He said to have you ready by seven, and he'll pick you up," Angela said.

"Pick me up? He lives here."

Tracy shrugged. "We're just doing what we were told. We were giving you five more minutes before we called to order you home."

"This isn't my home," Sam said, looking around wistfully at the bedroom where they'd spent so many blissful nights over the past month. Their near-death adventure in the car crash had driven their passion to all new heights. Sam hadn't known it was possible to feel so much. What was already amazing had ascended to stupendous lately, but she'd been frustrated—and baffled—by his refusal to let her tell him she was ready to officially move in. Whatever he had planned for tonight, Sam decided, there'd be no nookie until they had that conversation. She wasn't going to let him pull back from her now. No way. Not after everything they'd been through together.

"What do you suppose she's thinking about, staring at that big bed?" Angela asked Tracy.

"Her face got kind of red for a minute there," Tracy replied. "I bet I know what she's thinking about."

"All right, you two. That's enough. You've got ninety minutes to fix me up. Let's get busy."

SAM STOOD BEFORE the mirror. The dress fit as if it had been cut for her. The shoes, a little tight thanks to Angela's scheming, wouldn't cause blisters, but even if they did, they were worth it. The girls had corralled her impetuous curls into an elegant French twist and had even given her an emergency manicure and pedicure.

"Oh, wow," Nick said, releasing a low whistle from the doorway.

Sam turned to him.

"Wow," he whispered.

The sight of him in a tuxedo left her weak in the knees. "Not too shabby yourself, Senator."

He stepped into the room, reached for her hand and brought it to his lips. "You're beautiful."

"I'm not sure how I feel about you scheming behind my back with my sisters, although Vera and Manolo told me I should go easy on you."

His face lifted into the smile she loved so much. "Did they now?"

"Where's your sling?"

"Don't need it anymore." He made a big show of twirling his arm around, but she caught the grimace he tried to hide when his collarbone protested.

"It'll be back on tomorrow."

"If you insist."

"I do. Where're we going?"

"That's a surprise." He offered his good arm. "Shall we?"

Ready to go anywhere he chose to take her, Sam slipped her hand into the crook of his arm. "By all means."

HE HAD A limo waiting at the curb.

Sam stared at it, suddenly filled with trepidation, nerves and a strange sense of foreboding. What was going on? What did he have planned? Didn't he know she hated surprises? Shouldn't he know that by now? The dress and the shoes were one thing…

"What's wrong, babe?"

"Where're we going, Nick?"

He put his arms around her and brought her in close to him.

Sam was grateful that the press seemed to have taken the night off from stalking them.

"Trust me?"

"You know I do."

"Then let's go have some fun."

She tried her best to relax. "All right."

As the limo worked its way slowly through the congested city, he asked about her first day back to work, told her about a low-income housing bill he'd been asked to cosponsor and refused to say another word about where they were going. They glided along Pennsylvania Avenue, past the Old Executive Office Building and came to a stop in front of the White House.

"Nick?"

"Go with the flow, babe."

"You never said anything about the White House," she stammered.

"Didn't I?"

"You know you didn't!"

"If I had, would you have come?"

"No!"

"Exactly."

The driver came around to open the door for them. Nick scooted out ahead of her and held out a hand.

Sam sat stubbornly still, her heart racing and her stomach hurting for the first time in weeks.

"Samantha?" He gazed in at her. "Please?"

He never asked for anything, so something about that softly uttered "please" had her reaching for his hand.

"I'll deal with you later, mister," she growled.

"Yay. Something to look forward to."

"This was very sneaky," she said, oddly let down by the whole thing. She'd hoped for a rare night alone together with neither of their jobs interfering, and here they were at a work-related event, even if it wasn't your average work-related event. "Did my sisters know where we were going?"

"Nope. I was afraid you'd find a way to beat it out of them and refuse to come."

"What's the occasion?"

"State dinner for the prime minister of Canada."

As they were sucked into the crowd, Sam's stomach hurt worse than it had in weeks.

"What's wrong?" he asked, his lips brushing her temple.

"Stomach."

He swore under his breath and directed her to a bench
outside the security area. "I shouldn't have forced this on
you. I'm sorry. I just figured once you were here you'd
love it, but if you had to think about it, you'd freak. I'm
sorry."

Brushing her fingers over his hair, she leaned in to
kiss him. "You handled me just right. I will think this
is very cool, and yes, I would've freaked if I had known
where we were going."

Clutching her hand, he said, "Then what's wrong?
Why do you still look so worried?"

"It's just that all these people, even the president and
first lady. They know. About me. About what happened
years ago."

"Sam, honey, no one will be thinking about that tonight. I promise you. Let's just go in there and act like
we belong there. Can we do that?"

"I guess so."

"We don't have to. If you don't feel up to it, we'll go
somewhere else and have dinner, just the two of us."

"You can't diss the president of the United States," she
said with a droll smile.

"Oh, no? Watch me."

"Thank you for being willing to bolt, but that's not
necessary." She stood up and held out a hand to him.
"Let's go, Senator. Duty calls."

He flashed her that one-in-a-million smile, and her
nerves disappeared. As long as he was right there with
her, she could get through anything. Even a state dinner
at the freaking White House.

HOURS LATER, THEY had been wined and dined and daz-
zled by the pomp, the ceremony, the sheer magic of the
White House. Sam had to admit that she was glad she'd

come, even if this was *so* not her scene. It was something she'd remember always.

And now, as a reward for her astounding patience with the formal aspects of the evening's program, she had Nick's arms tight around her as they moved together on the crowded dance floor.

She looked up at him. "I need to talk to you about something."

"I know. Can we do it a little later?"

"As long as we do it tonight, that's fine."

"Oh, we'll do it, all right."

Laughing, she poked him in the belly. "Do you ever think about anything else?"

"Not really, and definitely not since the first second I saw you in that dress."

Over his shoulder, one of the White House valets seemed to be trying to get his attention. "Friend of yours?" Sam asked, nodding to the other man.

The valet gestured them over to where he stood by the door to the ballroom.

Baffled, Sam held Nick's hand and followed him.

"Everything's all set, Senator. Right this way."

"Thank you, Mike."

The older man's smile lit up his face. "You're quite welcome, sir."

"What's going on, Nick?"

He brought his lips down close to her ear. "Just come with me, and try not to make a scene, okay?"

She scowled at him but did as he asked. They followed Mike through several corridors before coming to a stop at a set of French doors.

Mike opened them and gestured for Sam and Nick to go out ahead of him. "I'll wait for you right here, Senator." He flashed another dazzling smile. "You take your time now, you hear?"

Nick shook his hand on the way by. "Thanks again, Mike."

"My pleasure, sir."

Outside, Nick slipped his tuxedo jacket over Sam's bare shoulders.

Steeped in his essence, Sam burrowed into his warm jacket as the faint scent of something else filled her senses. Roses. Even out of season, the fragrance drifted lightly through the air. She gasped. "Oh, Nick, is this the Rose Garden?"

"It is. What do you think?"

The light of a three-quarter moon silvered the leaves and grass in the garden where the roses lay dormant for the winter.

"It's amazing. How did you do this?"

"I told you. The deputy chief of staff is a buddy of mine."

"Who *isn't* a buddy of yours?"

His sheepish grin touched her heart.

"What're we doing out here?"

"Come over here, and I'll tell you." He led her to a stone bench along one of the walkways and sat next to her. "Are you warm enough?"

She nodded.

"I had a meeting today with the chair and vice chair of the Democratic National Committee."

"What did they want?"

"To gauge my interest in a run for the White House in four years."

Sam's mouth fell open. "They did not."

He laughed at her reaction. "They really did."

"But…I don't get… I mean… *Wow.*"

"Yeah," he said, chuckling again. "That's what I said, too."

"What did you tell them?"

"I suggested they talk to me in a year or two when I have a chance to see how things go in the Senate. My numbers are really good right now, but I'm just getting started. Who knows what they'll be a year from now?"

"I'm sure they'll be higher than ever."

"You have such faith in me, Sam."

"Of course I do. There's nothing you can't do when you set your mind to it."

"Only if I have you by my side." All at once, he dropped to his knees in front of her.

Sam gasped and raised a hand to her chest to keep her galloping heart from leaping through fevered skin.

"Samantha, I love you so much. Since you've been back in my life, I feel like anything is possible." He glanced at the grand old house behind them. "Even things I never dreamed of. Our life together will be crazy and chaotic and wonderful. Will you marry me and take the trip of a lifetime with me?"

"Yes," she said. *"Yes!"* As he gathered her in his arms, she had no thoughts about the past, about the marriage that had failed or anything other than what was right in front of her—the love of her life.

He reached for the inside pocket of the coat she wore and withdrew a dazzling square-cut diamond ring that took her breath away.

"I can't wear that to work," she said as he slid it on her trembling finger.

Smiling, he said, "I wouldn't expect you to. But you *will* wear the other one after you say 'I do,' you got me? I want the whole world to know you're taken."

Framing his face with her hands, she touched her lips

to his. "I've been trying to tell you I'm ready to move in with you."

"I know," he said, returning to the seat next to her and leaning in for a lingering kiss.

"You had this whole thing planned."

"And you tried to ruin it."

She grinned. "Of course I did. I wouldn't want you to think I'm easy."

Hooting with laughter, he said, "No worries there, babe."

"So, we're really gonna spoil everything by making it official?"

"We really are." He helped her up and drew her into another long, passionate kiss. "I love you, Samantha."

"I love you, too. So, *so* much."

A big smile lit up his handsome face. "Just think of it this way—at least you can't say I never promised you a rose garden."

Sam laughed, her heart full of joy and anticipation and excitement. "You have a way with words, Senator. You really do."

* * * * *

ACKNOWLEDGMENTS

THANK YOU TO my husband, Dan, and our terrific kids, Emily and Jake, for supporting my writing career every day. To my readers, thank you for being the best part of this crazy ride. To my editor, Jessica Schulte, and the amazing, dynamic team behind Carina Press, thank you for your support and encouragement. It's a pleasure to work with each and every one of you. And finally, to my darling puppy, Brandy, thank you for helping me to build my presence on Facebook. Your mischievous antics have provided entertainment for people neither of us will ever meet but who now call both of us "friend."

*Nick and Sam's story continues...read on
for an excerpt of FATAL CONSEQUENCES
by Marie Force, available from Carina Press.*

ONE

"I'LL BET THERE was less red at the St. Valentine's Day Massacre," Lt. Sam Holland said as she stood in the doorway to the Fraternal Order of Police Hall and surveyed the scene before her.

"Wow." Senator Nick Cappuano took a long look around the big room. *"Wow."*

Sam's sister Tracy joined them. "Oh. My. God. Celia and her friends went freaking *nuts* with the hearts and flowers."

Every square inch of the large room was decorated with red flowers, balloons and streamers.

"I've seen murders that were less bloody than this reception," Sam said.

"It is her first wedding," Nick reminded them. "She has the right to go all out."

Sam wondered if he'd expect his first wedding to be as elaborate. She'd been there, done that and had no desire to do it again. But for him... Well, for him she'd do just about anything. However, she was drawing the line at hearts and flowers. She had a reputation to uphold.

"Holy shit," Sam's sister Angela said when she joined them. "Check out the ice sculpture. Jesus."

"Cupid, not Jesus," Nick said, smiling at the horror on the sisters' faces. "Be nice, you guys. Celia is so excited."

"I had no idea she had this in her." Sam battled her way through the streamers and balloon ribbons to get to the bar. She needed a drink, and she needed it now.

"You'd be well advised to keep her far, *far* away from your wedding," Tracy said.

"No kidding." Sam downed a glass of pinot grigio and gestured for another. "How much of this do you suppose Dad knew about?"

"None of it," Angela said, smirking.

"He's a smart man," Nick said, "so I'm sure he told her to do whatever she wanted."

"Is that what a smart man does?" Sam asked, raising an eyebrow.

"Not *this* smart man. If I did that, we'd end up with beer and peanuts at O'Leary's."

"And that would be bad how exactly?"

Nick bent to kiss her. "We can do better."

Before Sam could tell him she didn't want to do better than O'Leary's, they were interrupted by the arrival of the bride and groom. Sam couldn't deny that her father and his new wife radiated happiness. How could Sam begrudge the woman who had married her paralyzed father the reception of her dreams? Her own wedding, Sam vowed silently, would be as low-key as she could possibly make it. In fact, eloping was starting to look *really* good to her.

DRESSED IN RED satin bridesmaid gowns, Celia's new stepdaughters stood faithfully by her side while she cut the heart-shaped red velvet cake and fed a piece to her groom. They endured the speeches and the toasts and smiled for no fewer than a thousand photographs. The ultimate insult, however, still awaited them.

"She can't make us," Tracy said when the DJ asked the sisters, their husbands and fiancé to come to the dance floor.

"Dad can make us," Angela said. "He still has that *look*. You know the one I mean."

"I've never wanted to be called to a murder scene more than I do right now," Sam said through gritted teeth.

"Ladies," Nick said with that charming smile he'd been using all day to manage them, "it's one dance, and then you're done."

"I know I speak for my sisters when I tell you to shut up and stop defending Valentine's Day Bridezilla," Sam said.

Nick laughed at the dismay on their faces as the first notes of Bette Midler's "The Rose" filled the room.

"I'm going to puke in my shoes," Angela muttered. Three-and-a-half months pregnant with her second child, she'd been green for weeks.

"Those are *my* Jimmy Choos," Sam reminded her, "and if you puke on them, I'll kill you."

Angela scowled at her. "Would you rather I puked on those?" She nodded to the Manolos that Nick had bought Sam to wear the night they got engaged.

Sam glanced down at the precious shoes. "Don't even think about it."

"Mine are from Payless," Tracy said. "Puke away."

Nick took Sam's hand as Angela's husband, Spencer, and Tracy's husband, Mike, did the same with their reluctant wives. The guys made for a dashing trio in the tuxedos they'd worn as Skip's groomsmen.

Across the room, Sam's partner, Detective Freddie Cruz, Detective Tommy "Gonzo" Gonzales and some of her other detectives were sharing a laugh that was—no doubt—at her expense. She'd think of some way to punish them on their next shift. It didn't escape her notice that Freddie had brought his girlfriend, Elin Svendsen, or that Gonzo was there with Nick's chief of staff, Christina Billings. Sam didn't approve of either relationship, but no one had bothered to ask her opinion.

When she realized Nick wasn't going to let her escape the mandatory dance, Sam gave up the fight. Besides, being pressed against his muscular chest was one of her favorite places to be, so she may as well enjoy this obligatory moment.

At six foot four, he was one of the few people in her life who towered over her. Those broad shoulders, the chocolate brown hair that curled at the ends, amazing hazel eyes, smooth olive-toned skin... Sam had never known a sexier guy. And that mouth, *whoa*. Speaking of sexy...

"There," Nick said, apparently sensing her capitulation. "Isn't that better?"

"I'm still mad at you."

"You can punish me later." Bringing his lips in close to her ear, he added, "All night long."

Sam smiled at his softly spoken words. She didn't want to because he was making her dance to the cheesiest, most clichéd song her stepmother could've possibly chosen. But let's face it, she was slow dancing with Nick, and that definitely went a long way toward making things all better.

Nick's lovely chest ruined the moment by vibrating against her cheek.

"Ignore it," he said of the BlackBerry he'd stashed in his chest pocket. "No phones today."

"You won't hear me arguing." They still hadn't managed a full day off together in the nearly two months since they'd reconnected after U.S. Senator John O'Connor's murder just before Christmas. Six years after a memorable one-night stand, they'd picked up right where they'd left off. Nick had since been tapped to complete the last year of John's term in the Senate and was now in the midst of the campaign to win the seat on his own in November.

They'd looked forward to this day off for weeks and had big plans for a romantic early Valentine's Day celebration after the wedding.

Nick's phone buzzed again. "Ignore," he said more forcefully this time.

"What if it's your dad or there's some sort of disaster in Virginia? You can't just ignore it."

"Yes, I can." With all the campaigning he'd been doing lately, she knew he needed the day off even more than she did but if there was one thing Sam couldn't stand, it was a ringing phone.

"Nick."

"Sam."

She worked her hand into his jacket to retrieve the buzzing phone. "Henry Lightfeather," she read off the screen. Even she recognized the name of the senior senator from Arizona.

"Work." Nick tightened his arms around her. "He can wait until Monday."

"He's called twice."

"He can *wait.*"

"There's a voice mail message. Aren't you curious?"

"Okay, it's official—you're an even bigger workaholic than I am."

"Not possible. Hey, he sent a text—'Call me, Nick. 911.'"

Nick stopped dancing and took the phone from her. "Now you've gone and done it," he said with a scowl.

"Done what?"

"If you had ignored it, I never would've seen that text. Now I have no choice but to call him."

She grinned at him. "At least we can escape this nightmare dance before the seed becomes a rose."

Phone pressed to his ear, Nick stalked off the dance

floor. Halfway across the room, he stopped, turned and signaled to Sam.

Curious, she walked over to join him.

"He's actually looking for you, Lieutenant." Nick handed the phone to Sam and went to have a word with Skip and Celia.

"Senator," Sam said. "This is Sam Holland. What can I do for you?"

"I need you to come here," Lightfeather said. He sounded rattled and undone. "Right now. I think she might be dead. I need you. Just you. No other cops."

"Who's dead?"

"Regina." His voice broke. "Beautiful Regina."

"How can you tell she's dead?"

"There's so much blood, and she's cold."

"Where are you, Senator?"

He rattled off an address in Columbia Heights, a culturally diverse neighborhood located in the city's northwestern corner.

"I'm on my way. Don't touch her. Don't touch anything. Do you understand?"

"Yes," he said, his voice breaking. "Hurry."

AFTER A QUICK trip to Nick's house so Sam could exchange the red satin bridesmaid monstrosity for jeans, Nick drove her from Capitol Hill to Columbia Heights. As he dodged the black BMW through traffic, Sam wondered when he'd started driving like a cop and how she'd failed to notice.

"What do you know about him?" she asked.

"He's a friend—one of the first to welcome me to the Senate, the first to tell me what I really needed to know, the first to offer his help."

"And?"

"And what?"

"What else do you know that you're not sure you should tell me in light of current events?"

"There are times when it's terribly annoying that you know me so well."

"Likewise. Now start talking."

He glanced over at her. "I think he might be living in his office."

"Why do you say that?"

"I've seen him there at odd hours in sweats and T-shirts. He showers in the gym, but I've never seen him work out."

"If you're there at odd hours, why can't he be?"

"It doesn't seem like he's actually working, you know? I hadn't really given it all that much thought, to be honest, until right now."

"Why would he be living in his office?"

"A lot of people in Congress struggle to support two places—one in their home state and another here. As we both know, it's not cheap to live around here, and despite what people think, not everyone in politics is independently wealthy."

"Does he have a family?"

"A wife back in Sedona and five children, all adopted, a few of them special-needs."

"That could be why he doesn't have the money for an apartment in Washington."

"Wouldn't surprise me."

"He sounds like a nice guy."

"He is."

"So what's he doing with a dead woman in Columbia Heights?"

"I have no idea."

Covered in blood, Henry waited for them on the landing outside Regina's third-floor apartment. Sam took a quick inventory of the senator: medium build, dark complexion, jet-black hair and eyes. He was younger than he appeared on television—late forties, early fifties at most.

"Hurry," he said when he saw them coming. "This way." Henry grabbed Sam's arm and all but dragged her into a shabby apartment. She let him lead her only because he was Nick's friend. Anyone else would have a broken hand by now. "In the bedroom."

Regina lay naked on the floor in two pools of blood, one by her head, and the other between her legs. Her throat had been slit from ear to ear. She had long dark hair, a slender build, small but firm breasts and smooth skin that was marred only by a few stretch marks on her belly, indication that she'd probably birthed at least one child or lost a tremendous amount of weight. Based on her slender body, Sam was betting on the baby. She judged the victim to be in her mid-thirties and was able to see past all the blood to determine she'd been quite beautiful.

When Nick saw the bloody scene, he gasped but at least he didn't seem faint as he had at previous crime scenes. The more time he spent with her, the more used to such things he seemed to become. Sam wasn't sure if that was a good or bad thing.

Next to Sam, Henry broke down as he stared at the dead woman.

"How do you know her, Senator?" Sam asked Henry.

He was crying so hard he couldn't reply.

"She works for the company that cleans the Capitol," Nick said, his tone flat with shock. Sam had heard that tone far too often after the murders of Nick's friends John O'Connor and Julian Sinclair.

"Did you know her?" Sam asked Nick.

"I've seen her around."

She sensed there was more to it than that, but she decided to wait until they were alone to grill him further. To Henry, she said, "Senator, I need to call this in."

"I have to go," he said, panicked. "I can't be here when the police come."

"I'm afraid you'll have to stay, sir. You're a material witness at the very least." She glanced at his blood-covered dress shirt and then up at his dark eyes.

"At the very least? What does that mean?"

Well aware of the power this man yielded on Capitol Hill, Sam swallowed hard. "I have no way to know whether or not you're responsible for this without investigating further."

Outrage mixed with grief as Henry stared at her. "I called you because I thought you could help me! We have to find the person who did this to her!" He looked imploringly at Nick. "Tell her. You know me, Nick. You know I couldn't have done something like this!"

To his credit, Nick said nothing.

"I can't believe this! *You actually think I could've done this to her?*" He swiped ferociously at the tears cascading down his face.

She fixed her eyes on his bloodstained shirt. "I need to rule you out as a suspect. You can either help or hinder that process, but either way, you're not going anywhere, Senator. Do you understand?"

"Yeah," he said bitterly. "I get it."

"I'd like you both to move to the hallway." After they stepped out of the room, Sam reached for her cell phone. "This is Lieutenant Holland. I need to report a homicide in Columbia Heights."

New York Times Bestselling Author

MARIE FORCE

*Politics can be murder in book three of the **Fatal** series.*

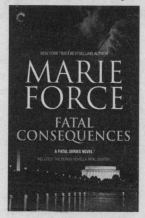

Lieutenant Sam Holland has no sooner accepted
Senator Nick Cappuano's proposal than she's back on the job.
A woman has been found brutally murdered and evidence points to
Henry Lightfeather, a senator and close friend of Nick's. While Sam
investigates, Nick stands by his friend—complicating his own bid for
reelection, and causing tension between the couple.

As Sam's investigation reveals a scandal that rocks the capital, Nick and
Sam discover that the biggest threat to their future might be someone
from her past….

Fatal Consequences

Available April 29, wherever books are sold!

A special *Fatal* series bonus novella, *Fatal Destiny,* is included.

www.CarinaPress.com

Reader Service.com

Manage your account online!

- Review your order history
- Manage your payments
- Update your address

**We've designed
the Harlequin® Reader Service
website just for you.**

Enjoy all the features!

- Reader excerpts from any series
- Respond to mailings and
  special monthly offers
- Discover new series available to you
- Browse the Bonus Bucks catalog
- Share your feedback

Visit us at:

ReaderService.com